THE
BANK VAULT
MYSTERY

BROKERS' END

THE
BANK VAULT
MYSTERY

BROKERS' END

Louis F. Booth

COACHWHIP PUBLICATIONS

Greenville, Ohio

The Bank Vault Mystery / Brokers' End, by Louis F. Booth
© 2016 Coachwhip Publications

The Bank Vault Mystery published 1933.
Brokers' End published 1935.
No claims made on public domain material.

ISBN 1-61646-326-0
ISBN-13 978-1-61646-326-7

Cover: New York City, c. 1931, Library of Congress archive.

CoachwhipBooks.com

CONTENTS

ENGINEERING MURDER
CURTIS EVANS

WHEN AS A NEWSBOY Louis Booth delivered papers on his route in Indianapolis, Indiana, to Booth Tarkington, the Pulitzer Prize-winning author of *The Magnificent Ambersons* (1918), the adolescent never dreamed that he too would become, however briefly, a published novelist, praised by no less a personage than Dorothy L. Sayers. Today comparatively little is known about mystery writer Louis F. Booth, author of a pair of 1930s detective novels, *The Bank Vault Mystery* (1933) and *Brokers' End* (1935). Unlike Booth Tarkington, he never had a bestseller, nor was one of his novels filmed by any cinema impresario, let alone Orson Welles. We know, however, that Louis F. Booth was born in Indianapolis on January 23,1903, the second son of Louis Frederick Booth, originally from New York, and Rosa Lena Koeller, originally from Wisconsin. Besides Louis and his older brother John, the Booth-Koeller union produced two younger girls before ending in divorce not long before 1910. In that year Rosa Koeller Booth and her four young children resided in Indianapolis with Rosa's German-born parents, John and Augusta Koeller. Rosa, who was employed as a stenographer with an insurance company, appears no longer to have lived with her parents and children a decade later, though in fact she was still alive, for in 1930 she resided with Louis' brother John, now an attorney, in Caldwell, New Jersey, not far from where Louis was living with his family in the town of Montclair. However close his relationship with his father and mother may or may not have been, it appears that Louis' more than a decade of life spent with

7

his grandparents exercised a strong influence upon him. His German grandfather was a machinist, a maker of metal parts, and Louis became a civil engineer. Additionally, as we will see, Louis seems to have made nods to both his grandfather and a maternal uncle, Otto Koeller, in his first detective novel, while in the final pages of his second detective novel he included a vignette which appears to have been intended as a sort of homage to his native city.

Having secured a job with the George A. Fuller Company, one of the most prominent construction firms in the United States, Louis married in 1925 and with his wife, May Belle, had one child, a daughter Lois, around 1928. In 1930, the couple and their young daughter lived in Montclair, New Jersey, where their prosperity is evident from the house they owned, which that year was valued at $12,500 (something like $177, 000 today). The next year Louis took an important job for the Fuller Company at Saratoga Springs, New York, helping to supervise the construction at the renowned Spa State Park of two new bathhouses (later named the Roosevelt Baths in honor of former New York governor and United States president Franklin D. Roosevelt, a strong supporter of the project). During his months at Saratoga Springs, Louis was a popular member of the community, winning particular notice for his prowess at the game of bridge.

Unhappily Louis was to feel the sting of the Great Depression the next year, when the Fuller Company, its activities curtailed by the enfeebled state of the economy, terminated his employment. Unable to find work within his trained profession, Louis in 1932 decided to do what it sometimes seems that every other person was doing in the years between the two world wars: write a detective novel. He submitted the novel, *The Bank Vault Mystery*, to Dodd, Mead, one of the premier American mystery publishers, who accepted it within a matter of days. The book was published not only in the United States, where the *New York Times* trumpeted that it was "guaranteed to keep one guessing to the very end," but also in France and England. In the latter country *The Bank Vault Mystery* was praised in the *Sunday Times* by Dorothy L. Sayers, who compared the author favorably with one of her Detection Club colleagues, the prominent Anglo-Irish railway engineer turned crime writer Freeman Wills Crofts.

In her *Sunday Times* review Sayers contrasted what has come to be known as the "hard-boiled," or tough, style of American mystery with the sort of American detective novel which *The Bank Vault Mystery* represented. "There are two kinds of American detective story," Sayers lectured, revealing perhaps more than anything her own personal biases concerning not only English and American mystery fiction but English and American criminal justice:

> The one reads like a Bedlam nightmare; in the other, police inquiries proceed in as orderly and sensible a fashion as in the works of Mr. Freeman Wills Crofts. "The Bank Vault Mystery" is of the second kind, and will appeal to English taste. It is a well-constructed, agreeably written yarn about stolen bank-notes and murder, and the action develops sanely and soberly to a logical and satisfactory conclusion.
>
> There are no gangsters, no graft, no Bowery-flowery language, and no stunts of any kind. Except for a difference of procedure in the case of persons arrested on suspicion and a passing allusion to the third degree, the background might be London instead of New York.

Sayers' likening of Louis F. Booth to Freeman Wills Crofts was perceptive, for Louis indeed composed his detective novels much in the manner of Crofts, soberly and methodically, emphasizing plot over character. "[H]e enjoys writing . . . and . . . goes about it in a systematic way," explained a 1935 newspaper profile on the author. "He believes that his engineering training has been of help in his writing . . . because he approaches his writing unemotionally—with a plan for construction, which he works out carefully and logically, step by step." This sober approach is evident in Louis' two detective novels, though Louis' writing is superior to Crofts' and he has the surer hand at character drawing.

In *The Bank Vault Mystery* Booth's investigative team, Detective Inspector Bryce of the New York police and Maxwell Fenner, a consulting specialist in larceny and confidence cases who is often retained by "the larger insurance companies and bonding houses," are brought into an affair concerning the Consolidated American Bank and Trust Company, which has suffered the theft of $180,000 in currency from its vault. The list of suspects in the audacious crime has been narrowed to a group of men who were present in the vault at a certain time, bank employees as well as several engineers looking over structural damage caused by the nearby construction of the bank's new, sixty-story headquarters. Bryce and Fenner make a solid team, with Fenner being somewhat reminiscent of modern crime writer Emma Lathen's John Putnam Thatcher, the Wall Street banker with a fine nose for scenting both high-toned white collar crime and bloody murder. Bryce and Fenner's theft investigation soon intertwines (or does it?) with what seems to be a case of murder, when old Adolph Knoeckler is discovered dead at the bottom of his cellar steps, his skull fractured. More mayhem follows before Fenner finds the solution to an ingeniously-devised puzzle which in its business detail and technical finesse is reminiscent not only of works of Freeman Wills Crofts but also those of Crofts' contemporary John Street (particularly Street's late "John Rhode" novel *Robbery with Violence*, which also concerns the clever purloining of bank funds). As in the case of Crofts, the Great Depression made a clear impact on Louis' crime writing, in contradiction of the oft-repeated claims of genre historians that classic detective fiction in this era ignored unpleasant contemporary social issues. In both of Louis' detective novels, multiple characters are buffeted by the hard blows of troubled economic times, blows that had more than glanced the author himself.

As Dorothy L. Sayers noted in her review of *The Bank Vault Mystery* in the *Sunday Times*, there are in the novel a couple of bothersome period Americanisms indicative of a cavalier attitude toward defendants' rights. During the course of the investigation a person the police do not believe is actually guilty of the bank theft is arrested for the crime, in order to bamboozle the real thief, and reference is made to another individual, arrested for murder, being third-degreed. Fenner himself proposes the first unethical stratagem, while he is only passingly nonplussed by the thought of violent police treatment of a suspected murderer: "Fenner suppressed a shudder. He had visions of a brutal third degree, and he knew that third degrees are never quite so vicious as when they promise from the outset to be futile. No sympathy, however, was due to [X]. . . ." Readers bothered by these passages are reminded that during the 1930s such attitudes were common not only in the United States, but, Sayers' observations notwithstanding, in much of the world; nor are they necessarily as uncommon today as we might like to believe, as can be seen in comments from the current frontrunner for the GOP presidential nomination.[1]

Also of interest in *The Bank Vault Mystery* are the details that Louis Booth appears to have drawn from his personal life experience. Adolph Knoeckler, the old German instruments maker found dead in his cellar early in the novel, likely was partly inspired by John Koeller, Louis' machinist grandfather. Moreover, in the novel Louis makes passing reference to Adolph Knoeckler's doctor, Otto Kellar, whose name bears a striking resemblance to that of the author's uncle, Otto Koeller, a telephone company wire chief then living in Emporia, Kansas. The character never actually appears in the novel and there was really no need to provide him with a name at all, suggesting that Louis' doing so was intended as a sly shout-out to his uncle. Additionally Louis through Fenner expresses ideas about adultery and divorce that seem rather modern for the conservative mystery genre of his day (one does not glimpse them in the novels of the intensely religious Crofts), reflecting, perhaps, his parents' own irreconcilable differences.

Louis' second and final detective novel, *Brokers' End*, appeared in 1935 and, like *The Bank Vault Mystery*, was published in England and France as well as the United States and generally well-received by critics. Structurally and substantively the novel bears great resemblance to *The Bank Vault Mystery*, having both a prologue and an epilogue (unusual features in crime novels during the Golden Age of detective fiction) and detailing not only murder but malfeasance in a financial institution, this time an investment brokerage named F. W. Strong & Company, which sells real estate mortgage bonds. When the novel opens, the company, wracked by the Depression, has been declared insolvent and placed in receivership for the purpose of liquidation. After the treasurer of the company is found shot dead in his office, Inspector Bryce and Maxwell Fenner are reunited as a sleuthing team, Bryce brought in to investigate this suspicious supposed suicide, Fenner to look into rumored financial irregularities on behalf of Strong's bonding company. As the plot unfolds additional Strong partners die violently, ostensibly at the hands of a self-proclaimed nemesis of fraudulent brokers, who tellingly signs his menacing manifestoes as "Shorn." Are the dead partners really victims of a self-appointed avenger acting on behalf of a heinously cheated small investor class, or is something more devious underfoot?

Like *The Bank Vault Mystery*, *Brokers' End* bears considerable resemblance to novels by Freeman Wills Crofts and John Street, particularly Crofts' *Crime at Guildford* (1935), in the United States published five months after *Brokers' End* under the title *The Crime at Nornes*, and Street's John Rhode novel *Death on the Board* (1937), about the methodical murderous expunging of a company's morally compromised board of directors. Lending unique historical piquancy to *Brokers' End*, however, is the fact that, aside from the murders, the novel is based on a prominent case of financial fraud concerning the real-life firm of S. W. Straus & Co., which made newspaper headlines continually for several years in the 1930s, during the time when Louis composed his crime fiction. S. W. Straus & Co. was formed in the nineteenth century in Chicago (as F. W. Straus & Co.) by enterprising immigrant Frederick William Straus, a Prussian-born Jew. After Simon W. Straus took over for his father in 1886, the firm, now known as S. W. Straus & Co., expanded and hugely prospered. S. W. Straus & Co. is credited with having introduced in 1909 the first real estate mortgage bonds (securities with senior claims on a building), which "were sold to the public at high rates of interest, and in small denominations," luring the burgeoning American investor class and making Straus a "leading financier of skyscrapers." In the 1920s, however, the company relaxed its stringent lending standards, offering in addition to first mortgage bonds seconds and thirds, which Straus salesmen euphemistically dubbed "general mortgages." When, three years after the calamitous occurrence of the October 1929 stock market crash, the brokerage was placed under receivership, a flock of investors holding what they now feared were worthless pieces of paper descended, with their attendant attorneys, upon the firm's rapidly cooling carcass, contending that Straus had misrepresented their junior bonds as first mortgages. With exquisite good timing, Simon W. Straus, the grand old man of the firm, had passed away in 1930, but his successor as president, Nicholas Roberts, was arrested in 1933 and charged with grand larceny. The *New York Times* described the turbulent emotional atmosphere immediately after Roberts' arraignment, as a baying pack of infuriated investors confronted their cornered quarry:

> More than thirty men and women . . . began jeering the defendant as soon as he left the courtroom. "Now you're going to get it," they shouted, or "You've got it coming to you."
> One man in the crowd carried a sheaf of papers. Attendants who picked them up said later that they appeared to be $1000 bonds of some Straus issue. "Here, do you want one," the man shouted, offering the bonds to all comers. No one took them, so he threw them in the general direction of Mr. Roberts.
> A patrolman stopped the crowd at the steps leading from the building, and the defendant was permitted to leave unmolested. . . .[2]

F. W. Strong & Co., the fictional firm in *Brokers' End*, combines the initials from F. W. Straus & Co., the parent of S. W. Straus & Co., with "Strong," a word that may have been suggested to the author by "strife," one of the meanings of "Straus" in the German language. Additionally, Strong's advertising motto, "Forty-five years without loss to any investor," echoes that of Straus, which

OFFICE BUILDING
S. W. STRAUS & CO.
NEW YORK

had been barred in 1927 from continuing to making a similar claim. Was Louis Booth one of Straus' investors, and did writing *Brokers' End* give him a measure of personal consolation? Certainly as a civil engineer Louis was extensively involved in construction projects, likely making the real estate mortgage bond business of special interest to him. In any event, this material, sardonically and entertainingly handled by the author, enhanced contemporary reader interest in the novel and should do so again today, as the United States recovers from a precipitous market crash of much more recent vintage.[3]

In a sign of the times Louis' publisher, Dodd, Mead, pronounced *Brokers' End* a "man's detective story," noting that its background concerned "the inner circle of finance, the complex machinery which can be so easily and unobtrusively manipulated to deviate enormous funds in the desired direction." To be sure, female characters are heavily outnumbered in both *The Bank Vault Mystery* and *Brokers' End*, with just one woman of significance appearing in the former novel and two in the latter; yet these women lend vitality to the stories. (One of the female characters in *Brokers' End*, an intriguingly-presented one, is the Jewish wife of Sigurd Strong, the Jewish president of the brokerage.) It also is worth noting that many of Straus' real-life victims were women, like Anna Kuhlman, who with her sister, she contended at Roberts' trial, had purchased from Straus $10, 000 worth of mischaracterized junior bonds, which were now worthless. In 1933 the vigilant and vengeful Kuhlman had espied Nicholas Roberts leaving an office building and, after hastily apprising a couple of nearby policemen of the facts, she had the satisfaction of seeing the financier hauled off to a local station. Kuhlmann may have been one woman who enjoyed reading *Brokers' End* when the novel appeared two years later.

Two other women who may have enjoyed perusing Louis Booth's novels were, one surmises, the author's wife, to whom he dedicated *The Bank Vault Mystery*, and his daughter, to whom he dedicated *Brokers' End*. Why Louis published no detective novels after *Brokers' End* is currently unknown, but perhaps his plotting inspiration had diminished or his engineering job prospects improved. When Louis passed away in Pinellas County, Florida, in 1996, his fine pair of detective novels had been out-of-print for over six decades. Now, two additional decades later, they are finally back in print again, impressive edifices in the landscape of classic American crime fiction.

Endnotes

[1] However, in his second novel, *Brokers' End*, Louis in my reading expresses only scorn for capital punishment.

[2] James Grant, *Money of the Mind: Borrowing and Lending in America from the Civil War to Michael Milken* (New York: Farrar, Straus and Giroux, 1992), 157-72; "Roberts Is Jeered After Arraignment," *New York Times*, 1 September 1933.

[3] The *New York Times* opened its review of *Brokers' End* as follows: "The exploded realty bond and mortgage racket, sunk by the depression with calamitous results to masses of innocent people, is used for the plot of this timely and interesting mystery novel."

THE BANK VAULT MYSTERY

TO
M.P.B.

FOREWORD

"THAT BANK VAULT CASE," as Maxwell Fenner usually referred to it, was a strange and involved affair, and made no less so for me by the fact that all my ingenuity (and assiduous nagging besides) was required to worm the details a bit at a time from Fenner's reluctant lips. He is ordinarily not close-mouthed with me, but after I had extracted the whole tale I readily understood his reticence. However, by altering names and places and a few of the relationships involved, I have concocted a record which, though it quite closely adheres to the facts, I was able to secure Mr. Fenner's permission to present to the public.

The chronicle includes a brief span of ten days—from a spring Thursday morning to the end of the following week—and the principal actors in the drama were introduced to Fenner from time to time during the early part of that period. To give the reader at the outset the advantage of a background against which, as the story unfolds, the successive events may be seen in their proper perspective, I have preceded the narrative itself with a brief Prologue introducing the more important characters on the morning of that fateful Thursday.

L. F. B.

CHARACTERS

T. Jerome Hanley	*Vice President and General Manager, Consolidated American Bank and Trust Company*
Jeremy Donegan, Sr.	*Vault Custodian*
Jeremy Donegan, Jr.	*Assistant Cashier*
Christopher Dickson	*Chief Engineer, United Construction Co.*
Philip Borden	*Dickson's Assistant*
James Quinn	*Construction Superintendent*
Randolph Morton	*Consulting Engineer*
Stephen Coles	*Morton's Assistant*
Elsa Knoeckler	*Morton's Secretary*
Adolph Knoeckler	*Instrument Shop Proprietor*
Schmidt	*Newsdealer*
Detective Inspector Bryce	*New York Police*
Burke	*Bryce's Staff*
Mcfadden	*Bryce's Staff*
Quade	*Bryce's Staff*
Murphy	*Bryce's Staff*
Dr. Pollard	*Coroner*
Maxwell Fenner	

PROLOGUE

IT IS THE BEGINNING of a day, a Thursday—the last Thursday in March, to be precise—in the Year of our Lord, nineteen hundred and thirty. A chart of the progressing life lines of a number of individuals reveals an interesting tendency to converge. An all-wise graphologist, anticipating this convergence and plotting it in his ledger of fate, would draw, however, no neat intersections, no points of amiable tangency. Rather, his lines would meet in a jumble, a knotty snarl from which some emerge wavering and which some cut straight through, a shambles from which some emerge not at all.

Let us cut a quick cross section through these lines, lay the chart open at a moment on this Thursday morning and for a brief flash examine the lives so exposed:

Detective Inspector Bryce sits before his desk in a dingy, ill-lighted room at Police Headquarters in lower Manhattan. He has pushed his chair a little back and sits straight up; with conscious deliberation he is lighting a heavy black cigar. The eerie glow of the green-shaded desk lamp softens the outline of his face but the quick flare of the match behind his cupped palms catches and brings out an aggressive hardness in the features.

He has just arrived and is assembling his thoughts. He wonders how long he will have to be in court during the morning and whether or not the new Assistant District Attorney, of whom he has no high opinion, will muff the case he has built up against a small-time gambler and racketeer—

Some twenty odd miles north-by-northeast, as the crow flies, Maxwell Fenner is finishing his simple breakfast. As he munches toast
with marmalade and sips his coffee, his glance wanders through
the casement window out over his garden and the adjoining gar-
dens. There is a fresh greenness bursting upon the lawns and the
heavy languor of early spring lies over the whole landscape. Fenner
is thinking that it would be splendid if he could stay away from the
City altogether today and decides, as the next best alternative, to
arrange his day so that at least his afternoon will be free—

Back in Manhattan Mr. T. Jerome Hanley, Vice President and
General Manager of the Consolidated American Bank and Trust
Company, is being whisked to his office in a comfortable limousine. Weary of looking at the back of his chauffeur's head, he turns
to watch the familiar streets flash by. Down Park Avenue, then
down Lafayette Street—the same route he traverses six mornings
out of seven, eleven months out of twelve. He must speak to Oscar
about it. There must be some other way.

He forgets the scenery, for unpleasantly it occurs to him that if
the market has another sinking spell today he will be in a fair way
to be closed out. He will not supply any more collateral—simply
can not; and he has a shrewd suspicion from the display of weakness yesterday that there will be further breaking. If only a temporary rally would set in! He could get out then without a total loss,
and (believe Mr. Hanley!) he'd have brains enough to wait a long
time before he got back in again. Well, the worst they can do is to
close out his account. He will still be V.P. and G.M. of the Consolidated, which isn't half bad at forty-five; and his income from that
source will be undiminished. He sinks back into the cushions, not
sure that it wouldn't be a relief to be sold out and have the uncertainty over with—

On a Subway Express the Jeremy Donegans, Senior and Junior, form
part of a packed mass of swaying humanity being rushed through
the East River Tubes from Brooklyn to the towers of Downtown
New York. Donegan, Sr., is seated half dozing. Donegan, Jr., stands

or, rather, is suspended before him. With one hand he clings to a swinging strap, with the other he holds a skillfully folded newspaper. He reads that the Yankee pitching staff is to be supplemented this season by somebody-or-other formerly with the Cardinals. With three quarters of his mind he is wondering what the girl or woman behind him looks like, whose soft, unwilling body he can feel pressed so tightly against his own—

Somewhere between Hanover Square and Canal Street a jolting, rattling Second Avenue Elevated train snakes its tortuous way downtown, "—less crowded and it gets you there quickly, too," as their advertising points out. In the third car, carefully separated by a few inches from an Italian laborer on one side and a homeward-bound charwoman on the other, sits Randolph Morton. His ankles are crossed; a brown leather briefcase rests upon his knees; in one hand he holds a pair of immaculate tan pigskin gloves with which from time to time he absently flicks imaginary specks of dust from the portfolio.

Business has been rotten. In the last six months he hasn't made expenses. At Chatham Square he is thinking, gratefully, that his commission for designing and supervising the foundations for the new Consolidated American Building will pull him out of the hole. That job is certainly proving a life saver. Still—it is almost completed. If nothing new comes in, he might yet have to dispense with Steve Coles, his only remaining assistant. The firm has surely fallen upon evil times! He glances about. At Fulton Street he is pondering his home life, or lack of it. He is marveling that a woman could change in a few years to the extent that his wife has changed. He thinks of his children away at school, but suddenly it is Hanover Square and he has to get off—

In lower Fulton Street old Adolph Knoeckler steps out of his shop and glances up and down the street. The morning sun, burning away the faint haze, falls kindly upon his bald skull. He hobbles several doors up the street and into the stationery shop of his friend and countryman, Schmidt, for his morning paper. He is puzzling over an unwonted abstraction which he fancies he has observed in his daughter of late. He folds the paper across, scarce seeing it at all, caught in a sudden nostalgic surge of recollection.

Back in Germany in his youth Knoeckler had been a fine lens maker. He had met reverses and had come to New York, almost a middle-aged man, and had married and set up an instrument repair business in lower Fulton Street. His wife had died when Elsa was born. Adolph sometimes wonders if things might not have been different with his daughter if her mother had lived. Adolph had been both father and mother to Elsa during her childhood. He remembers her dandled on his knee listening to stories in his broken dialect; he remembers how he used to take her places on Sundays, to see the animals at the zoo, to the harbor to watch the ships; how he used to buy her pretty little frilly dresses; how he himself braided up her pigtails. The recollection saddens him. As she had grown up they had grown apart; as she had found outside friends and amusements Adolph had quietly withdrawn into himself. There had been steadily less in common, less to talk of, until now she has almost slipped from him completely—

At this moment it is not alone Adolph Knoeckler who is worrying over Elsa. On that same Subway Express which brings the Donegans to work, and not half a car's length removed from them, we find Stephen Coles. Coles and the Donegans have never met and will never come face to face, yet their lives from this morning forward are inextricably woven into a single confused pattern.

Coles' usually stolid face reflects quiet concern. He is worried about his job with Randolph Morton. The foundations for the new Consolidated are nearing completion and Morton has nothing else in prospect. But it is not the possible loss of the job as such which troubles Coles this morning, though in times like these leaving any job is not an enviable necessity. It is that he would also be leaving Elsa Knoeckler. No longer, then, would he be able to glance up and watch her at her desk, to absorb covertly for minutes on end the sweet, half-turned profile, to memorize the soft line of cheek and chin. It is true that Elsa has never encouraged him, though she has occasionally gone out with him upon repeated urging. It is true, in fact, that she has always done her best to discourage his attention, but Coles is not quite able to abandon hope altogether. He wonders why her father has formed such an odd dislike for him. If it weren't for that perhaps—

A half dozen blocks southwest of Knoeckler's shop, or three blocks due west of the Consolidated Bank, at a few minutes after nine o'clock—she had heard the Trinity chimes around the corner booming the hour as she entered the building—Elsa Knoeckler unlocks the offices of Marten, Morton and Purcell, Consulting Engineers. She finds the place dusty and hot with the stuffy quiet that offices acquire simply by staying shut up over night. The sun streaming beneath the half drawn shades pours in two oblique shafts of light and draws into emphatic relief the same thin film of dust Elsa has carefully removed from Mr. Morton's desk morning after morning for the past ten months.

A little wearily she crosses the office to raise the shades and throw the windows open. She stands before one, slowly peeling off her gloves, and looks out. There is stolid resignation in the almost imperceptible droop of her lips, scarce belied by the frown gathering between her eyes. Across the narrow canyon she can see in another building tier on crowded tier of offices with different names and varying occupants but somehow of an essential sameness. Mechanically she notes faint stirrings here and there signaling the beginning of another bustling day. Elsa is weary of bustling days. Though of late there hasn't been so much work, there is always the deadening pressure of office routine, and in her life generally a poisoning monotony of hopeless and pointless repetition. Several times—long ago they seem to her now—she had fancied she saw avenues of escape but always they had failed to materialize. There was Henry, first, whom she had "gone with" for more than a year, but somehow he had drifted away; that was four years ago—then Lawrence with whom she could not have gotten along anyway—then Marty with whom she had fallen madly in love only to discover that he had a wife and three small children out in

Flatbush. For a while after that Elsa had wanted only to die, but somehow it had been simpler to go on living, swallowing her misery, penning up her despair so effectually that even her father never quite suspected the depth of her bitterness. For a while she had drifted, changing positions frequently, until she had happened to become Randolph Morton's secretary.

Thinking back, Elsa sighs a little relief at this stage. It has been nicer here than in any of the other places she has worked. She has become gradually resigned to the groove into which her life has been arbitrarily fitted, but she is not able to avoid a depressing consciousness of the passage of time and a haunting, recurrent bitterness that life is passing her by. Elsa is twenty-seven; her mirror shows her tiny crow's-feet outside the corners of her eyes; a vague growing weariness warns her that youth is but a transient stage. Elsa is not hard to look upon, clear-eyed, comely in a wholesome way, with brown hair she has never cut and usually manages to keep in soft waves. Her frown deepens. She ponders a decision she has been making over night. She had thought her mind made up but there are so many things to consider. Her father will be heartbroken— Footsteps in the corridor outside remind her of the time, so she puts away her hat and coat and starts to arrange her employer's disordered desk—

A mile and a half southwest of the tip of Manhattan in the smoking cabin of a Staten Island Ferry, New York bound, Christopher Dickson sucks upon a consoling pipe. He is late, for him an unusual circumstance. By now he should be at his office far uptown. It had been necessary to wait at St. George for his bank to open so that he could procure from his safe deposit box a number of Liberty Bonds. Nervously his hand touches his breast. Yes; the bonds are still there, reposing in a long fat envelope in an inner coat pocket. Reluctantly he will post the bonds at his brokers to protect his dwindling margins. Three months ago the wiseacres and quidnuncs had proclaimed, "The bottom has been reached!" Three months ago he had read in reputable journals, "Now is the time to lay the foundations of a fortune!" The wiseacres had been wrong; so had the quidnuncs.

Dickson is thinking: "If Myra ever finds out about the bonds— Still, there is no reason why she should, and what women don't know won't hurt them." Irritably he raps his pipe out against the edge of the bench and walks out to the front deck—

In an ultra-modern office building uptown Philip Borden is being raised from the first to the twenty-eighth floor in a high-speed, micro-drive elevator. The uniformed operator says, "Mornin', sir."

The lone passenger replies, "Morning, Doc. Take the boss up yet?"

"Nope; Mistah Dickson ain't been in yet."

The reply barely registers. Borden is thinking that his mother ought to see a doctor about that peculiar pain between her shoulder blades. It might be something serious which shouldn't be neglected. He'll have to be more insistent—

"Twenty-eight, sir."

The car stops—

But now we have seen enough. Let us close up the chart and get on with our story.

1
THURSDAY
MARCH 31ST

1

THE JEREMY DONEGANS, father and son, halted at the entrance of the Consolidated American Bank and Trust Company Building. Old Jeremy had worked for the "Consolidated" for thirty years, his son for five. Without thinking much about it, both felt that they had become parts of the huge banking institution.

It was a rare morning, even for the sunny end of March; much too fine a morning for old Jeremy or young Jerry to go inside until the last possible moment. Jeremy glanced up the street to where Trinity Church loomed at the end of it, purpling in the morning sun. The golden hands on the tower indicated a quarter before nine o'clock.

"Let's take a look at the new building job. We've got ten minutes yet," he suggested. Across the street the Consolidated American Company was starting the erection of its new sixty-story home.

Young Jerry nodded and they sauntered across and leaned against the railing of a truck-loading platform overlooking the building site. Through the spaces in the cross-lot bracing they could see away down beneath them in the bottom of the excavation swarms of laborers, their figures from that height foreshortened grotesquely, picking away and shoveling, loading up dirt buckets and stone skips. Periodically the heaped buckets were hoisted by derrick out of the hole and, with a great creaking of booms and rattle of cable, swung in a swift, high, wide arc to trucks waiting in the street where they were noisily dumped, then sent back for more.

"Some job, huh!" Young Jerry's eyes sparkled appreciatively. "Some hole in the ground!"

The new building would occupy most of the block and was to have four basement levels below the street floor. The excavation had been carried fifty feet below the street and was progressing in solid rock.

"Yeah, some job! Some different from the old days. Puts me in mind of when they built this." With his thumb Old Jeremy indicated the Consolidated Building in which they then worked. "I was a brickie then; three dollars a day was big money. Everything was donkey engines and horses; none of these electric hoists and trucks. Took us three years to finish it. They say this'll be done in a year and it's five times as high." He stroked his chin thoughtfully. "That was—let's see—thirty years ago."

"Look," Jerry interrupted. "They're going to shoot." He pointed to one side of the hole where a large mat of woven cable and logs was being let into place to cover the blast.

One of the foremen scrambled up on the bottom layer of bracing and bellowed a warning to the men working near by. Dropping their tools they scurried from the spot in all directions, seeking shelter behind the bracing posts and wherever refuge offered. A moment after the warning cry the foreman was the only man Jerry could see completely, though there were enough heads peering cautiously and knees and shoulders projecting from behind every timber to account for most of the swarm that had so quickly dissolved.

The foreman straightened up for a last glance around, then stepped into the lee of a pile of blasted rock, bent over and gave his dynamo handle a quick plunge. There was a deep, dull thud trailing off in a muffled roar. The platform upon which the Donegans stood jumped beneath their feet, then after a second of diminishing vibration resumed its dead stability. A sudden cloud of dust hovered over the entire ramp surface, then slowly settled back in place.

In the bottom of the excavation Jerry saw the heavy blasting mat leap into the air, hang suspended, and fall heavily back to almost exactly where it had been before. A thin cloud of gray smoke and rock dust filtered from between the logs and drifted lazily upward and out over the street. As the roar of the explosion ended they heard a brief staccato, like distant musketry, swelling and dying as a quick shower of small stones and fragments which had escaped the smothering mat, rained on the job and rattled down through the bracing. No sooner had the hail of pebbles stopped than the men swarmed out of hiding and converged, like an army of beavers, on the blast location. In a twinkling the heavy mat was hoisted clear and the gangs set to work, by hand and with pick and shovel, loading the newly shattered rock into buckets and skips to take it away.

"Gosh! That was some blast, wasn't it?" Jerry exclaimed. "You could feel this platform tremble, all right."

"That was a damn' good shot," Old Jeremy explained. "You see, those deep shots that you feel but don't hear so much are the ones that do the work. When you get one of those roarin' kind that you hear all over town you generally won't feel 'em at all; an' you can be pretty sure most of the force went out the drill holes."

"Yeah? Well, you could feel that one all right. I'll bet they felt it in the bank, too. Did you know a lot of plaster fell down up on the fifth floor yesterday? And right up over my desk a couple of big cracks are opening up in the wall. Maybe the building'll fall down. Only if it's going to I hope it waits until the new one's built."

"Don't worry about that old building ever falling down," Jeremy answered. "It's wall-bearing, but it's solid and'll be there till they tear it down. I guess it's settling, though, or shifting a little. The last couple of days I can hardly get my vault door open or shut, it binds so—"

He was interrupted by the sudden notes from Trinity starting its mellow preamble to the stroke of nine.

"Come on. We'd better get over to work," he urged. Reluctantly Jerry assented and they went into the building.

Old Jeremy was Custodian of the Central Vault. He had entered the employ of the Consolidated American Bank as a guard thirty years before when they moved into their then new building.

Jeremy had been a bricklayer during its construction but he had gladly exchanged the uncertainties and vagaries of building work for the steadiness and security of a job with the "Big Bank." Within a few years he had become captain of the guards, and, as the bank grew and the force expanded, he had developed and disciplined his little army until it had become an example for the rest of the financial district. As he had grown older his health had failed until finally he had retired, but after a short time he had found the retirement so irksome that he had returned and taken a post as Custodian of the Central Vault.

Young Jeremy—Jerry, they called him—had started in the bank as a clerk and had gradually moved along until after five years he had become an assistant cashier—one of many. Most of the time Jerry liked the bank and was contented working there. He lived with his father but expected, as soon as he had saved enough money, to marry a girl to whom he had been engaged for a little more than a year. His future lay before him, well defined: a small raise each year, a house in the suburbs, a mortgage, babies at (he hoped) infrequent intervals. If he was lucky and tended to business he might get a larger raise some years; if he was unusually lucky he might some day even become an officer in the bank, but the chances in that direction were distinctly limited.

Sometimes when Jerry was moody and looked ahead he pictured his life as a smooth groove stretching away down into the future without turn or deviation as far as the eye could see, and himself in it sliding solemnly along, glancing furtively to right and to left. There were other parallel grooves in which slid his friends and the people he worked with, but all of the grooves converged in a point on the horizon.

Sometimes, especially in the spring, the metal lattice of the cage in which he worked seemed to shrink and close in about him until it left an impress in his flesh, and he could hardly wait until the end of the day brought liberation. But these moods were infrequent, usually accompanying slack spells and passing when he became busy again. Most of the time Jerry was quite content with his lot.

On this particular late March morning Jerry's duties were pretty
well caught up. He went to his desk complacent in the knowledge
that he had plenty of time. As he sat down he noticed with a start
that the small irregular crack in the plaster that he had from day
to day watched extend itself from the floor up through the wall to
the ceiling cornice, had overnight opened up to a jagged, yawning
crevice wide enough to thrust a pencil into and extending out over
the ceiling half way across the room.

Even as he sat there, astonished, he felt a quick tremor and
heard the dull boom of another blast across the street. A thin
sprinkle of plaster dust filtered out of the crack and settled swiftly
to the floor. The luster of the mahogany desk top was dimmed with
an even gray film; the papers on the desk were gritty with it.

For a minute Jerry was alarmed in spite of his father's opinion
of a few moments before. Perhaps the building was "solid and'll be
there till they tear it down," but just the same the plaster over his
head looked suspiciously loose to Jerry. He telephoned the vault
and told Old Jeremy about it.

"Oh, well; a little plaster shaken down won't do anyone no
harm," came the reassuring answer. "When they get through shooting they'll patch it all up. But my door here is worse than ever this
morning. I've got to have T. J. see about it and I'll tell him about
the cracks too." "T. J." (T. Jerome) Hanley was the bank's manager. A short time later he came into Jerry's cage. He looked at the
cracked wall thoughtfully.

"It's gotten quite a little worse over night, hasn't it, Donegan?"
he asked.

"Yes, sir; I believe it has. Yesterday the crack was much narrower and didn't run into the ceiling at all."

"Hmm— There are some new ones upstairs, too. Well, the
engineers are coming over this morning to have a look at the vault
doors. We'll get them to examine this at the same time. Some sort
of settlement, I presume; or maybe it's on account of the vibration
from their blasting. I'm told they're almost through with that work
now, so it won't get much worse. I suppose there's nothing to worry

about, anyway." With this dubious reassurance Hanley left and Jerry turned to his work.

First there was a cash shipment for an uptown branch to be prepared, an unusual sum and in large denominations. Jerry assembled the amounts and packed the currency into one of the small canvas sacks the bank used for this purpose. He filled out and initialed the metal-rimmed fiber tag with the destination, amount, time, etc., and attached it to the sack. After packing up a number of smaller consignments, he rang for a boy to remove the sacks to the vault to await the afternoon armored-car pickup. Presently a boy trundled to a stop at Jerry's cage a low platform truck similar to those used in freight stations and warehouses, except that it was smaller, neater, and rolled quietly on pneumatic tires. It was stacked three feet high with canvas bags similar to those Jerry had just packed, some containing securities, others currency. Jerry stacked his consignments on one end of the truck and handed the boy a copy of his check list. The boy glanced at it absently, slipped it into a clamp with a sheaf of others, and trundled his load away toward the vault.

Jerry watched the truck roll to the door, idly musing.

"Probably three or four million dollars' worth of bonds and stocks and cold cash in the bags," he reflected, "yet they cart them about like so many sacks of potatoes, or bolts and nuts, and think nothing of it. Of course it was all checked and tallied at every corner and turn, but even so— It was more money than most people ever saw in a lifetime. Why, probably any one of the bags contained enough to enable a man to live comfortably for years—and not in cages, either."

His speculations were cut short when the truck rounding the door corner bowled into a party of men entering the room. Mr. Hanley, leading the group, stepped nimbly aside but the three men following were not so quick and the truck collided with one of them none too gently.

"Take it easy, son," Hanley admonished curtly. "You'll get there sooner if you're more careful."

The boy stammered an apology and backed the truck out of the way to allow the group to pass. The three men came in behind Hanley. All examined the cracks in the wall and ceiling, discussed

them from various angles, and asked Donegan questions as to when
he had first noticed them and how fast they had developed. Then
they launched into a technical discussion as to whether the cracks
were the result of vibration or settlement and were still debating
the point when they departed to go down, Jerry gathered from their
talk, and inspect the vault door.

2

The doorman at the entrance to the Central Vault swung open the
barred grille so the truck could roll in unimpeded.

"Here's some business for ye, Jeremy," he called to the old man
within.

"Bring 'er on, Pat. The more, the merrier!" Old Jeremy replied.
He turned to the boy who had brought in the truck. "Take this
empty out of my way, sonny," he said, indicating a truck he had
unloaded a short time before.

With a cheerful "O.K., Pop!" the boy handed the check lists to
Jeremy and maneuvered the empty truck out of the vault. Jeremy
glanced over the lists quickly and noted with mild satisfaction that
most of the bags were for the afternoon delivery and could be
simply checked off the lists and left on the truck until the various
armored-car crews picked up their consignments after lunch. A few
bags were for temporary storage and would have to be racked. The
bank had very much outgrown its vault space and Jeremy welcomed
no additional crowding. He had started picking out the packets
which were to remain in the vault when he was interrupted by the
doorman's buzzer.

"Mr. Hanley and some gentlemen," the man announced.

Jeremy pushed the truck into a corner out of the way and went
to the grille.

"These gentlemen have come about the door, Jeremy," Hanley
said. Jeremy admitted the group. The manager turned toward the
men behind him. "This is our vault superintendent, Mr. Donegan,
gentlemen," he said, and to Jeremy, "Mr. Morton, Mr. Dickson,
and Mr.—uh—"

"Borden, sir." The last of the group, a younger man, supplied the forgotten name. Jeremy acknowledged the introductions and the men glanced around briefly. Borden placed on the floor a rectangular mahogany box and leaned a heavy tripod against the wall.

Mr. Morton was the consulting engineer for the foundation work in connection with the bank's new building; Mr. Dickson was chief engineer of the construction firm erecting it, and Borden was his assistant. They had come at Hanley's request to examine the vault and determine the cause for the difficulty of operating the door, which had been troubling Jeremy, and to discuss means of preventing further settlement or damage.

"Let's try the door, Donegan," Hanley suggested. "Then we can all see how bad the thing really is."

Jeremy and the doorman removed the small approach platform which sloped up from the outside to the higher vault floor level. They grasped the massive door and with very obvious effort started it slowly swinging. Once past the midpoint of its swing it required just as much effort to prevent it from slamming.

"You see; she's not balanced," Jeremy explained, panting a little. "She ought to stand still in any position and be as easy to swing one way as the other."

"It looks as if the frame, or maybe the whole vault, has tilted back, doesn't it?" Morton suggested. "Is there any way of checking up on that?"

"We could try the floor for level," Dickson replied. "That would tell us if the whole vault had moved—assuming, of course, that it was level before." He turned to his assistant. "Set up your level. We'll try the four corners of the floor," he instructed.

Borden kneeled down and, opening the wooden box, carefully lifted out the parts of his level; a small telescope and a bracket arrangement to support it. He assembled the instrument and screwed it to the tripod, then set it up in the corner of the vault farthest removed from the door.

"This instrument won't focus at very short range," he remarked, "but I guess I can make it from here." He rolled the dispatch truck a little to one side so that he could get behind his level.

"That truck in your way?" Jeremy asked, starting over to move it.

"Not at all, now," Borden replied. "I just needed room to get back here."

He leveled up his machine and read a rule held by Dickson at each of the four corners. The results indicated that the floor was lower at the back by a half inch or so.

"Well; that's that! Small wonder that your door won't swing," Dickson exclaimed to Hanley.

"Odd that the back part of the vault should have settled when the enormous weight of the door and its frame is all concentrated at the front," interjected Morton dryly. "How do you account for that?"

Dickson hesitated, puzzled for a moment. "I don't know, of course; but I rather imagine that when they built this building they figured on that vault door and put a good heavy foundation under it, but probably less under the rest of the vault. Now with the vibration from the blasting the less-supported part goes down a little and the vault tips back. If I'm not mistaken, that cracking and settlement we noticed upstairs is just about over the rear portion of this vault."

"That's possible—quite possible," Morton agreed.

"Assuming you're right," Hanley broke in, "the question is: What are we going to do about it? Aside from being hard to swing, the door binds a little when it's closed. If the condition gets much worse it might not shut at all. Then there'd be hell to pay!"

"It won't be a difficult thing to correct," Dickson assured him. "We can go under the back edge of the vault from the outside—dig out a small section at a time—and jack cylinders down to rock; then jack the vault up until it's level again."

Hanley nodded understandingly.

"How long would that take?" he asked.

"Two or three weeks at the outside," Dickson replied.

Morton cut in: "I certainly wouldn't recommend attempting any shoring here while that shooting is going on. If you lost a little ground under the vault it would get worse with every blast."

"Oh, no; of course not," Dickson agreed, "but the blasting will be all finished in a few days." He turned to his assistant. "Borden, how much rock is left to come out of that cellar?"

Borden was back in the corner tugging at his instrument bracket in an effort to disengage it from the tripod. He looked up, then thought for a moment.

"I should say about four feet, on the average, over the lot, sir."

"That'll take four or five days," Dickson estimated. "We've been shooting there for two months; another week isn't likely to make things much worse."

"I suppose not," Hanley agreed a little doubtfully. "I hope not, anyway."

With the aid of pocket flashlights Morton and Dickson now began minutely inspecting the vault walls for cracks or other evidences of settlement. Borden had finally succeeded in getting his instrument dismantled and was packing it in the mahogany case.

"I hope Mr. Dickson's right about that," Old Jeremy whispered in an anxious aside to Hanley. "It's funny, though, that it should have got so much worse the last couple of days."

"Well, I guess they know what they're talking about, Jeremy."

Morton, who had been examining the lower part of the wall over in the far corner by Borden, straightened up and called to Dickson.

"There are quite a few cracks along here that appear to be new. Take a look at them, will you?"

Dickson and Hanley went over to look and Jeremy stepped quickly across and rolled the truck out of their way. While they were thus engaged there came a sudden, well-defined tremor and then the deep, dull roar of a blast going off.

"I'm glad they fired a charge while you were all here," Hanley said. "Now you can feel for yourselves the shaking up this place is getting."

"Oh, I admit it's getting a little shaking," Dickson agreed; "but I don't see how we can be expected to excavate four stories of solid rock without jarring things a trifle—and the damage so far is slight and easily repaired."

Thus the discussion went on—about the cracks and the settlement, the feasibility of cutting down the strength of the charges, the method of underpinning the vault, and so forth until Morton, glancing at his wrist, discovered that it was almost noon. He called attention to the time.

"We've done about all that can be done now," he suggested. "I suppose we all agree that the best course is to let well enough alone until the blasting is finished." He looked around the group and, finding no dissent, continued: "I'm going to leave now. I've got to get my lunch and make a one o'clock train from Grand Central. Have to go to Detroit until Monday." He added the last almost apologetically.

The party filed out of the vault and through the basement to an employees' exit where they paused. Borden stopped to collapse the telescopic legs of his tripod so that it would be less cumbersome to carry through the crowded streets. He said to Dickson: "The threads on this tripod head are so badly stripped it's almost impossible to get the level apart or together. I think I'll take it around to Knoeckler's and get it put in shape."

"Good idea," Dickson agreed.

Morton glanced up.

"Knoeckler's? Is that in Fulton Street?" he asked.

"Yes; east of William Street."

"Oh—I guess I've seen the sign. We need some work of that sort done once in a while. What sort of a fellow is this Knoeckler?"

"He does good work, if that's what you mean," Borden replied. "He's a queer duck, though."

"In what way?"

"Oh, not in any particular way. He's one of those old-school instrument men,—an old German. I don't see how he pays his rent with the little business he gets, but somehow he seems to."

"He does, huh?" Morton led on.

"Yes. But he's an awfully stubborn old coot. Refuses to believe that anything's different from what it was twenty years ago—sort of always resisting the changes of time. He's far from dumb, though. I like to get him started talking once in a while when I'm in there—"

They were interrupted at this point as Hanley and Dickson shook hands, the latter preparing to leave.

"We'll do nothing, then, until the blasting's finished," he was saying to Hanley; "and if any material change occurs in the condition of the vault, you can get in touch with me."

Hanley agreed. Morton also shook hands with him and, together with Dickson and Borden, went out. Outside, he declined Dickson's invitation to lunch and the group broke up.

3

In silence Jeremy had watched the party file out of his vault. With a hollow clang the barred grille had swung closed in their wake. For some time he sat quite still, staring at it, lost in thought. Then he remembered he was hungry and phoned for his lunch. It was his custom to have a tray sent in each noon from the employees' restaurant upstairs.

He glanced at the money truck speculatively. After lunch there would be time enough to take care of it, he decided, and relaxed to wait for his meal. Soon it arrived, a savory tray. The doorman swung open the gate so the porter could bring the tray directly to Jeremy's desk. Sometimes Jeremy asked Pat to step in and pass the time of day with him while he ate. On this particular noon, however, he did not. When he had finished his meal he ran through the morning paper for a few minutes. The waiter found him so engaged when he returned for the tray and soiled dishes.

It was a little after one o'clock when Jeremy resumed his work upon the money truck, first racking up the packets to be stored, then checking off the sacks for the afternoon delivery. He checked them twice; then a third time, very carefully. Then he went over the bags he had racked up for storage. A little nervously he telephoned his son.

"Are ye preety sure of the list ye sent in this marnin', lad?"

"Sure? Why, sure I'm sure," Jerry replied cheerily.

"Well, check it over again; then come down here, will ye."

Jerry was instantly alarmed. His father's voice had sounded somewhat unsteady over the phone; but, more significant, he had dropped into the old vernacular, a certain sign of some sort of mental stress.

Jerry picked out his carbons of the lists covering the consignments of the morning, glanced hastily about, locked his cage and went to the vault. His father was awaiting him, seated at his desk. He shoved toward Jerry a list with checks and double checks after all of the items except one. It stood out in the column like a soldier out of step.

"There's nothing like this on the wagon, Jerry," said Old Jeremy gravely. He indicated with a pudgy forefinger the unchecked item in the column.

One look at the list told Jerry that the item in question was the unusually large consignment he had packed that morning.

"Why, it must be there! Good Lord! I spent a third of the morning getting it together. Are you sure? Have you gone over it again?"

"I'm sure, all right, Jerry. I went over everything three times— and what's more, not a shipment has left this vault since that truck came in. There can't be any mistake that way."

"Something must be wrong," Jerry said weakly. "Anyway, it went on the truck. I put it on with my own hands."

"That's all I wanted to be sure of," Old Jeremy replied enigmatically. He picked up the telephone and asked for Mr. Hanley. His voice was firmer now.

"Can you step down a minute, sir? Right away? It's important."

In a moment Hanley appeared. He glanced from Jeremy to Jerry inquisitively.

"There's something wrong, sir," Jeremy said nervously. He handed Hanley the list. "There's a bag missing."

Hanley's eye running swiftly down the column stopped short at the unchecked item. "A hundred and eighty thousand!" He whistled his dismay. From the initialing he noted that the consignment had come from Jerry, and looked toward the younger man, though without suspicion or accusation. There was only bewilderment written on Jerry's open countenance.

"It went on the truck, sir. That's all I can say. I loaded it with my own hands." He looked up and added quickly, "In fact, it was the very truck that almost bumped you when you came in with those men this morning."

Hanley nodded. "I believe you, Jerry," he said simply. "Why wasn't the truck checked as soon as it came in, Jeremy?" he asked the older man sharply.

"I had just started on it when you brought the engineers about the door, sir."

"Oh; it was that truck you shoved over into the corner, eh?" Hanley recalled. A sudden quick suspicion seemed to form in his mind. The same thought apparently occurred to Old Jeremy.

Hanley reached for the telephone.

"You're both absolutely sure there's no mistake?" he urged. "We don't want to make fools of ourselves over this."

In unison Jerry and Jeremy desperately assured him that there could be no mistake. Hanley called a number and asked for Mr. Fenner. In a low voice he asked him to come to the bank immediately, giving no details but only urging haste. "You had better bring along a police detective, too. We shall possibly need the police. Of course it's all strictly on the quiet until we find out more about it."

He hung up the receiver and turned to the Donegans.

"You boys had better wait right here," he said. "I'll be down again when Mr. Fenner gets over." Father and son simply stared at each other.

4

Maxwell Fenner met Inspector Bryce at the entrance to the bank. They shook hands warmly. Bryce and Fenner had been associated with each other on a number of important cases and together had shared a gratifying average of successes. Of late they had not been thrown into contact, so each welcomed the sight of the other.

Bryce and Fenner were as different in temperament and method as two individuals following the same calling could very well be, but this fact never hampered them when they were engaged together on cases; rather, the methods and tactics of each supplemented those of the other to perfection. Bryce was a detective inspector with a long record of police service, thoroughly steeped in the police method and imbued with the police point of view.

"Action!" was his motto; and, given something to start from, he pursued his course with a relentlessness and vigor that left no stone unturned until he either arrived at an answer or reached an impasse that balked further inquiry. More often the former was the case.

Fenner, on the other hand, had a languid, easygoing way about him, sometimes partly assumed but more often genuine, which, though it irritated Bryce, usually deceived their quarry and was almost invariably effective. "Give them time," he sometimes said, "and they all make the breaks that hang them. The odds are so overwhelmingly on our side it shouldn't be necessary to do more than to be sure that we miss no tricks." His idea was to sit back with his finger tips alertly on all the aspects of a case, to prod gently here and there when things became too quiet, and to wait for the opening that experience had convinced him would inevitably occur.

Aside from possessing a trained, reasoning brain in a strictly intellectual sense, Fenner was blessed with a deep insight into the mental and psychological processes of his fellow men, and it was more often by the application of this insight to specific situations than by any marvels of deductive reasoning that he produced the remarkable solutions for which he was known.

Fenner had served his apprenticeship with the New York City Police years before, but the driving pressure one moment alternating with political hampering the next had irked him until he had resigned to initiate a practice of his own. His success and reputation (among a limited circle permitted to know of his exploits) had grown slowly and steadily until, after twenty leisurely years, he was regarded by some as a leader in his particular field. Fenner specialized in larceny work and confidence cases, and was retained by several of the larger insurance companies and bonding houses. In his experience, however, he had also been called upon from time to time to investigate murders and other crimes of violence, and was an ardent student of criminology in all its phases.

Fenner was acquainted with the manager of the Consolidated American Bank though he did not know Hanley intimately. The

Consolidated was so managed that services of the type he offered were not often in demand.

After a quick exchange of greetings Fenner and Bryce turned into the bank. Bryce compared his watch with the clock in the lobby. It was half past two when they entered the elevator.

"What's the story?" he asked with his customary impatience.

"I only know what I told you on the phone. Hanley wants us posthaste," Fenner replied. He pictured Bryce as a great, penned stallion, chafing at his bit, pawing the turf, anxious to charge ahead.

Bryce's appearance lent itself well to this characterization. He was a powerful man, heavily featured, his head set aggressively forward on a thick bull neck, his black eyes peering keenly—fiercely when it was expedient—from beneath bushy, overhanging brows. In a word, he looked steely hard and this aspect of his appearance so overshadowed all else that one hardly suspected the astuteness that lay beneath.

They found Hanley pacing the floor of his office, awaiting them. Another man, who from Hanley's deference they inferred was one of the higher officers of the bank, sat in an easy chair at one end of the desk, quietly smoking. He was introduced simply as Mr. Mortimer.

"I'll give you the facts quickly," Hanley began, barely acknowledging Fenner's introduction of Bryce. "When you've heard them I think you'll agree with me that speed is the essential thing at this stage if we're to get anywhere."

"True of all cases all of the time," remarked Bryce. Fenner smiled and crossed his knees in a leisurely fashion.

"This morning about ten-thirty," Hanley continued, ignoring the interruption, "one of our cashiers—assistant cashier, to be literal—packed a consignment of one hundred and eighty thousand dollars in currency for one of our uptown branches. He sent it, together with half a dozen other consignments, by hand truck in our usual way to the vault to await the afternoon delivery. A few minutes after the truck reached the vault, and before the custodian had been able to check up the load, a party of three engineers conducted by myself went in to look at the vault and stayed there until about noon. They're blasting across the street and the vault has been settling. The vault custodian, who, by the way, is the father of the cashier who packed the shipment, delayed checking up the truck until he'd eaten his lunch. He discovered the sack missing and called his son. Then they called me."

Bryce started to say something but changed his mind and looked toward Fenner for his cue. The latter extracted from his pocket a small gold pencil which he twirled idly between his thumb and forefinger for a moment.

"Inside job?" he asked rather than suggested, quite casually.

Hanley shook his head slowly.

"Of course anything is possible," he admitted, "but if you mean the Donegans—that is, the custodian or the boy—I'm inclined to feel they're both above suspicion."

"Who were the men you took into the vault with you?" Fenner asked.

"There were Mr. Morton, Mr. Dickson, and a helper of his—I forget the name. I suppose they would seem above suspicion—at least the first two. Morton is consulting engineer for the foundation work across the street; quite an eminent man. Dickson is chief engineer of the construction company doing the building, and also pretty well known. Of course the other fellow I know nothing about."

"Let's get them down here—the quicker, the better," Bryce suggested, fidgeting in his chair.

"Where are your Donegans now?" Fenner asked.

"They're in the vault waiting for us," Hanley answered. "We'll go down and you can get the whole layout direct."

"But let's round up the others first," Bryce insisted. "These fellows of yours will keep."

Fenner nodded agreement. Hanley turned to the telephone.

"I'm afraid we might not get Mr. Morton," he said as he jiggled the receiver rest. "He was in a hurry to leave this noon. I believe he said he was catching a train for Detroit. I'll try his office, though."

At first he was informed by Morton's assistant there that Mr. Morton was out of the City and would be back Monday.

"This is Mr. Hanley at the Consolidated Bank. It's very important that I get in touch with Mr. Morton immediately. Do you have
any Detroit address where he usually stays. There must be a way
of getting hold of him. What train did he take? Who is this speaking?" Hanley rattled off the questions impatiently.

Presently he hung up and said to Fenner and Bryce: "Chap
named Coles there; has no idea where Morton would stop—he
doesn't go there often. Coles says he spoke of a one o'clock train
from Grand Central that he intended making."

"A one o'clock train, eh?" Bryce repeated, biting off his words. "Tell
me what he looks like and, if you can, what he wore. We'll get him!"

"But you can't arrest a man of his position simply on suspicion," Hanley protested.

"Of course not; but this is only Thursday. We can pick him up
and tail him between now and Monday," Bryce explained impatiently. He went on: "Let me tell you one thing: In a case of this
kind no one is above suspicion. Everybody has got his price and
damn' few of them are above a hundred and eighty grand. You've
got to assume that right from the start. Now what's he look like?"

Hanley gave him a brief description of Morton. Bryce jotted
down notes on a slip of paper which he tucked into his vest pocket.
"Now, how about the other two?"

Without replying Hanley again picked up the telephone, this
time calling the construction company's offices. When he asked
for Dickson, Borden replied. The latter was unable to say where
Dickson could be located. When he, Borden, had come into the
office early in the afternoon he had found a note saying that
Dickson would be back late in the day. Borden had no idea where
his chief had gone but if it was important Borden would be glad to
canvass the Company's various building operations by telephone
and endeavor to locate him.

Hanley told him to do that and to have Dickson come to the
bank and then to come down himself as quickly as possible. Then
he settled back into his chair with a sigh.

"Have you got a phone not connected through the switchboard?"
Bryce asked when Hanley had finished.

The bank manager indicated a second instrument on the desk but, observing a slight hesitation on the inspector's part, told him that there was also another in the adjoining room. Bryce excused himself and closed the door behind him, and in a moment they heard the steady rapid rumble of his voice as he issued instructions over the wire. Hanley looked curiously at Fenner, as did also Mr. Mortimer from his chair at the end of the desk.

"He's just setting a few of the wheels in motion," Fenner explained at the unasked question in their look.

After a short wait Bryce returned, pausing to light a cigar as he joined the group. There was a certain grim satisfaction in his manner.

Hanley got to his feet, suggesting: "Shall we go downstairs now?"

Fenner rose but the elderly bank executive remained in his chair. He had not uttered a syllable except when Fenner and Bryce had been introduced. Now he said shortly: "I'll not go down. Keep me posted, Hanley."

5

When they got to the vault they found Jeremy Donegan seated at his little desk staring silently into space. His son, half sitting on a corner of the desk, smoked nervously. He straightened up when Hanley brought in Fenner and Bryce, and dropped a cigarette butt to the floor, grinding it out with his sole. A half dozen others littered about the usually spotless linoleum, each in its tiny whorl of ash dust and carbon, bore mute testimony to Jerry's disturbed state of mind. His father seemed serene by contrast.

Hanley spoke first, presenting Fenner and Bryce, and concluding with: "They're going to help us. First we want to get your stories direct."

Bryce rolled his cigar around in his mouth, blew a thin cloud of smoke up toward the ceiling and watched it, caught by the suction, swirl into the ventilation register. He dropped his eyes now and again to Jerry and Jeremy with a hint of glare they could not fail to observe.

Jerry made as if to speak but Fenner stopped him, saying kindly: "What we want you to do is to think carefully and tell us just what happened today. Try to remember every little detail. Something that may not appear important to you may be very significant when taken with everything else."

In appearance as in method Fenner differed radically from Bryce. He was tall and rather spare of figure, invariably immaculately turned out, and carried his fifty odd years lightly enough. There was a certain aquiline keenness about his features but his ruddy complexion and his shock of prematurely snow-white hair softened this. His eyes, gently blue, genial, invited confidence.

"We had better have your story here," he went on, nodding toward Jeremy. "We'll have yours later in your own office." The last to Jerry.

Jeremy thought for a moment, then launched into as complete a description of the events of the morning as he could remember. He had started checking up the truck immediately upon its arrival but had scarcely commenced when Mr. Hanley had brought in the engineers about the door. He had shoved the truck into the corner and had attended their questions. He'd showed them how the door was binding and they'd talked about it a while. Then they'd tried the level of the floor with a machine and then had talked some more. Then they'd looked over the walls for cracks. They had all gone out about noon—maybe a few minutes before. He'd decided to eat before unloading the truck, and had ordered his lunch. Then he'd read a newspaper till one o'clock. Soon after he had resumed work he'd found that one bag on the check list was not on the truck, and had called his son down to the vault. They'd checked it all over and had then reported to Mr. Hanley. That was all.

Hanley nodded from time to time, corroboratively. Fenner watched Jeremy while he talked, pigeon-holing the facts in his orderly mind. Bryce jotted down notes in a small pocket notebook. They examined the truck which still stood where Jeremy had unloaded it.

"You say they had to shift the truck a little in order to set up this instrument?" Fenner asked when Jeremy had finished.

"Yeah; they moved it out a little to get into the corner behind it."

"Was that after you and the doorman had stepped out to try the door?"

"Yes; we had tried it and had come back inside."

"They found the door unbalanced and that's what led them to want to try the level of the floor," Hanley explained.

"Then later Morton found the cracks over there and they all crowded over to look at them. Is that right?"

Jeremy and Hanley nodded.

"Can you show us the cracks and put the truck about where it was at that time?"

Hanley pointed out several small, irregular cracks in the rear wall of the vault near the floor. They were very fine and only noticeable from fairly close by. Jeremy studied a minute, then shifted the truck to a point a yard or so from the corner and looked to Hanley for confirmation.

"That's about right," the manager agreed.

"Say, how big was this sack?" Bryce asked abruptly.

No one answered until Hanley turned to Jerry.

"Why, it was about eight inches long and four inches wide and six or seven inches deep," the latter said after a second of hesitation, indicating the size with a spread of his hands. "It was large denominations, sir." The last explanation was directed to Hanley.

"How were all of these men dressed?" Fenner next asked.

Hanley volunteered the answer to that question.

"Let's see; Morton had on a topcoat and Dickson carried one over his arm, or a light overcoat. The other fellow had no overcoat at all; just a suit coat." He finished: "Now that I think of it, Mr. Morton carried a briefcase—pretty sizable one, too."

Bryce audibly grunted.

Hanley said: "We may get more from the entrance checker. I've questioned him already and he noticed nothing suspicious; but the party entered and left by the employees' door which he watches. We'll see him directly."

"By the way," Fenner asked Jeremy, "you say you had your lunch here? Then you really haven't left the vault at all since this happened?"

"Haven't had my foot out of the door since ten o'clock this morning."

"Always have your lunch here?"

"Almost always."

"Usually alone?"

"Sometimes Pat comes in." He indicated the doorman on duty outside the barred grille.

"But today?"

"Nope; alone today."

There were a few minutes more of discussion and repetition; then the party, without Jeremy, went up to Jerry's cage. The tellers and clerks looked curiously at the group when they came in, but at a general glance from Hanley went on with their work.

Jerry told his story a little nervously, beginning at the point where Hanley had come in to look at the crack in the wall. He spread out his check lists on the desk, though none of the party bothered to examine them closely.

Fenner was interested in the method of packing and handling the currency. He asked to see one of the dispatch bags. Jerry showed him one and also explained how the packets were identified with metal-rimmed fiber tags wired through eyelets in the top of the bag. Fenner pocketed a blank tag.

Next they called the truck boy who had taken the load to the vault. He came in, obviously badly frightened. Fenner quickly reassured him and plied him with questions about the particular trip. Apparently nothing unusual had occurred except for the slight near-collision at the door. The stop at Jerry's cage had been the last one on that round and the truck had gone, from there directly to the vault.

Hanley enlarged a little on the incident at the door. He had side-stepped the truck but it had gently bumped at least two of the men following him, he explained.

Bryce grunted with disgust: "You could have hauled that bag through Wall Street at noon time on a kiddie car and not have had it much more exposed, all in all, than it was."

Fenner said nothing, nor had Hanley any reply.

As they were about to leave Fenner inquired casually of Jerry: "Do you have lunch in the building like your dad?"

"Sometimes I eat at the employees' restaurant, but more often I go outside," Jerry answered.

"Would you mind telling us what time you went out this noon and where you went."

Jerry hesitated perceptibly, flushing a little.

"I went out a few minutes one way or the other of noon," he said. "I had lunch at the new Automat around the corner in Pearl Street. Then I walked down around the Battery for a while. When I got back it was quarter after one. I had only been back a few minutes when Pop called up."

"I see. Ah—thank you." Fenner seemed satisfied.

Having exhausted the possibilities of this location, Hanley took Fenner and Bryce to interview the entrance guard. Jerry went back to his work.

In the employees' entrance lobby of the bank there was a counter beside the door. Behind a glass screen sat two men. All day they watched the employees and messengers come and go. Every employee was known by sight to one or the other of these two men, as were also most of the messengers and runners who came regularly to the bank. Anyone coming or going whom they failed to recognize was required to explain his errand. If the slightest suspicion arose in their minds the explanation was checked by telephone. It had proved, Hanley told Fenner and Bryce, as nearly an airtight system as they could devise without hampering the operation of the bank.

Hanley explained to the man who had been on duty in the morning that they wanted to know what each of the party of engineers had worn or carried.

"Well, seeing that they were, with you I didn't give them much attention," the guard said. "The big fellow had on a tan topcoat, a light brown hat, a brown suit, I think, and carried a brown leather briefcase—looked fairly well crammed."

"That's Morton," Hanley put in.

"The one with the glasses had on a light gray overcoat and a gray hat. His partner had on a blue suit and no overcoat. He was carrying a reddish wooden box with a leather strap handle, and he had a sort of collapsible stand under his arm."

"That's Dickson and Borden."

"When they went out," the man continued, "the big fellow looked just the same to me. He changed his bag from one hand to the other when he shook hands with Mr. Hanley. It looked heavy but no more so than before. The man with the glasses had his topcoat over his arm instead of wearing it. The other one was just the same."

Fenner nodded approvingly. "There's the kind of a person I like to ask a question of. Shows what a trained observer will take in." To Bryce in an aside he commented: "—and he admits he didn't pay 'special attention'!"

"Do you know the Donegans?" Fenner asked the checker.

The latter nodded that he did.

"Can you tell me if either of them went out this noon, and when?"

"Not Old Jeremy. He never goes out at noon. Jerry was out to lunch, though. Let's see—I don't remember him going out but I remember him coming back a little after one, picking his teeth. We talked for a minute."

"Can you recall what he said?"

"Nothing much. Just a remark or two about getting spring fever."

Hanley wondered mildly at Fenner's odd line of questioning but said nothing. It was a little after three o'clock when they adjourned to his office.

6

Hanley drew up chairs for Bryce and Fenner and then sat down himself. He waited for one of the others to speak.

"Not much to get hold of so far. I want to browse around a bit between your working floor and the vault," Fenner began.

"Have you really an idea this is an inside job?" Hanley asked.

"I haven't any ideas at all at present. I refuse to formulate any theories or conclusions until we've talked to Morton and Dickson and Borden."

"You don't expect their versions of what happened in the bank to differ much from what we've been told, do you?" Bryce asked.

"Certainly not; but there were five people there and we've heard only two." Fenner inclined his head toward the bank manager. "Without any reflection at all on Mr. Hanley here, or Donegan either, for that matter, I have no doubt that there are details which they have failed to notice but which might be remembered by one of the others. Possibly nothing of any significance, but that remains to be seen."

"If this should be an inside job—though I can't refrain from expressing my firm conviction that it's not—would you be inclined to suspect Jeremy or young Jerry or both?" Hanley persisted in his line of inquiry.

"It's hard to say," Fenner answered shortly, "but until it's all cleared up every move either of them makes, in the bank or out of it, ought to be observed." He glanced at Bryce and continued: "If either of them or the pair together have anything to do with this they'll soon give themselves away. If it was the vault custodian alone, the stuff's not out of the bank yet. If it was he and the boy, or the young man alone, he probably cached it somewhere this noon and will have to go back for it soon." He paused. "Then, too," he went on, "don't forget that you're not limited to the vault. The bag was loaded on the truck about ten-thirty in Donegan's cage—that is, presumably it was. Its loss was discovered after one o'clock in the vault. The truck had to travel from the cage to the vault."

"Yes, but Jerry's cage was the last stop. The truck went straight to the vault. That lad's pretty dependable, and the way is all guarded, anyway. No office space to go through or anything of that sort—just the corridor behind the cages and the elevator to the vault anteroom. No loopholes en route, I can pretty well assure you."

Fenner only raised his eyebrows.

The discussion was interrupted by the jangling of the phone. Hanley answered it and, with a "For you," handed it to Bryce. The

latter acknowledged himself and listened. Fenner and Hanley waiting curiously watched a slow frown darken his face. Presently he
hung up and said to them: "There's no Detroit train leaving any
New York station within forty-five minutes, one way or the other, of
one o'clock. Mr. Randolph Morton hasn't been at his apartment since
morning, nor at his club all day, nor at his office since he came here
this morning. Looks bad. I'd like to bet that when we find him we'll
be pretty near to the bottom of this. We'll find him, too. There's a
lot of good men out looking for him right at this minute."

"Let's not jump too quickly to conclusions," Fenner cautioned,
and at an impatient gesture from Bryce amended amiably: "I mean
by that, let's not forget the others."

"Don't worry! We're forgetting no one!" He paused but continued: "Wouldn't it help now to give something to the newspapers?"

Hanley looked uncertainly at Fenner and said: "I know that they
would prefer upstairs—the Board Room—to do without the publicity, but if it will help at all, why, of course we can't yield to their
feelings."

"I think a little well worded publicity might be of service,"
Fenner said thoughtfully. "It is entirely possible that Mr. Morton
has absented himself for perfectly legitimate reasons of his own.
In that case he would immediately come forward; and if, as you
seem to feel, it's not an inside job, why the story's got to come out
sooner or later anyway."

Hanley had no answer. Bryce shrugged his shoulders, and said:
"We'll see, anyway. Let me give out this story and I'll mention no
names. I have a few reporters who are a real help sometimes and I
like to pay them back with these little scoops. Back in a moment."
He went into the adjoining room to use the outside telephone.

While he was gone an office boy glided in and spoke to Hanley
in a low tone. The banker straightened up in his chair.

"Bring him right in here," he told the boy, and to Fenner explained: "It's Borden."

A moment later Philip Borden was ushered in. He was a clean-
cut, youngish looking man with an almost military erectness of
carriage, whom Fenner judged to be in his late twenties. He came

directly to the desk, looking from one to the other with politely restrained curiosity, and nodded to Hanley whom alone he knew.

"Sit down a moment," the bank manager said. "We've a few questions to ask you when the inspector gets back. Oh, by the way, did you find Mr. Dickson?"

"No; I'm sorry but I couldn't locate him. I left a note for him, though. I have no doubt he'll be back at the office in time to stop down here."

"I hope so. Uh, this is Mr. Fenner."

Fenner pushed a chair toward Borden as Bryce returned from the other room. Hanley opened the inquiry.

"There has been discovered since this forenoon a shortage in our central vault. You understand, of course, that you are being in no way accused." He looked at Fenner who smiled reassuringly at Borden and took up the talk.

"We would like you to tell us in as much detail as you can just exactly what happened during the time you were in the bank this morning. There may be something that happened or that you noticed which may afford us a clew."

Borden told his story, a little haltingly at first but more fluently as he warmed up. It differed in no important detail from the stories told by Jeremy and Hanley. Fenner prompted him now and then and tried to draw him out with leading questions, but no information as to the visits to Jerry's cage or the vault was elicited which they did not already possess. When he had concluded Fenner asked: "What time did you leave the bank?"

"Somewhere close to noon," Borden replied.

"Alone?"

"Yes; that is, practically. Mr. Morton walked down to the corner with me, or, rather, as far as the Mercantile Bank."

"He left you there?"

"Yes."

"Did he go into the Mercantile Bank?"

"Yes; I believe so."

Bryce appeared about to speak but Fenner prevented him with a motion of his hand. "Where did you go from there?"

Borden thought a moment. "I went to a little instrument repair shop in Fulton Street; Adolph Knoeckler's. Our level needed some repairs and I left it there."

"And from there?"

"I went to lunch and then to the office."

"Where do you usually take your lunch?"

"When I'm in this neighborhood I usually go to a place in Pearl Street called Billy's, but today I went to an Exchange Buffet up in the Hudson Terminal."

"You must have gotten back to your office shortly after one o'clock. I suppose Mr. Dickson had been there and left in the meantime?"

Borden hesitated and then said: "No; it was half past one or after. It took a little while at Knoeckler's and I ate a sizable lunch. However, I couldn't have missed Mr. Dickson by much, because he usually takes at least an hour for lunch himself. He must have gone out only a few minutes before I got back."

Fenner turned to Bryce and Hanley. "Do either of you think of anything?" Apparently neither did. As an afterthought Fenner asked: "How do you go uptown to your office?"

"I took the B. M. T. from Cortlandt Street."

Fenner thanked Borden and with a little gesture of dismissal indicated that the interview was over. Borden got up to go.

"It would be better if you mentioned this affair to no one," Hanley cautioned him.

"All right, sir; and if I can be of any more use please let me know. I'm sure those are the boss's sentiments too—Mr. Dickson's, I mean." He looked at his watch and found that it was a quarter before four. "I've time for a little work at the office if I get on back," he apologized, and left.

Fenner waited until the door had clicked behind him and looked quickly at the inspector.

"Don't worry." The latter read his question. "He's had company since he left his office and they'll stay right with him."

Fenner picked up his hat from the desk.

"Say," Bryce said abruptly, "did you get that about Morton and the Mercantile Bank?"

"I understood Borden to say that Mr. Morton went there. I don't know that I 'get' anything from it," Fenner answered, quite unexcited. "However, I'm going to stop by there right now. I'm going to pop in on Mr. Adolph Knoeckler, too, but I should be back in half an hour or thereabouts. If Mr. Dickson turns up, would you mind amusing him until I get back?"

Hanley was somewhat taken aback but Bryce only nodded and smiled wryly.

"It just means he's got a little brain wave when he gets sarcastic like that," he told Hanley.

Fenner had been gone only a few minutes when Christopher Dickson was ushered in, a little flustered but apparently enormously curious. He was a pudgy little man with a full, round face and a sort of foxy-grandpa air about him at first impression. He peered at them through thick-lensed, gold-rimmed spectacles.

Hanley, apologizing first, told him in a few words what had happened and introduced Bryce. Dickson thought a moment and then started to tell his story but Bryce stopped him.

"Might as well save yourself going over it twice," he said. "Mr. Fenner will want it first hand, so we'd better wait a few minutes until he gets back."

Dickson with a shrug of indifference settled back into his chair, though a momentary shadow of impatience crossed his face when he drew out his watch and perceived that it was well after four o'clock. Bryce went over to the window, seated himself on the sill, relit his cigar, and looked thoughtfully out. Dickson and Hanley fell into a desultory discussion of the new building which they carried on until Fenner returned.

The latter did not come in until shortly before five. He spread several afternoon papers out on Hanley's desk and said to Bryce: "Your boys work fast, don't they? Have a look at these."

Across the top of one of the papers, a pictorial tabloid, there was spread the glaring legend: "$200,000 CONSOLIDATED AMERICAN BANK THEFT" and, in smaller letters, "Story on Page 3." Inside there was a brief quarter column to the effect that a shortage of $180,000 had been discovered at the Consolidated

American Bank, that the police and bonding company detectives had formulated no theory as to the theft, that certain employees of the bank were being detained, and that members of a party of engineers who had visited the vault during the morning were "being questioned or sought for that purpose."

"That ought to fetch Mr. Morton if he's on the level," Bryce remarked cryptically.

"If he sees it, you mean," Fenner corrected.

"Of course. But if we don't hear from him by morning I'll get the boys to play it up more tomorrow. Looks to me offhand, though, as if he's flew the coop—"

"Well, we'll see."

Dickson looked from one to the other. Fenner folded up the newspaper and sat down and Bryce returned to his place by the window.

"I've told Mr. Dickson why we asked him down," Hanley informed Fenner. "We thought it better to wait for you before hearing what he has to say."

"Ah, thanks." Fenner seemed very gracious and quickly put Dickson at ease. "It's the details we want, sir. We've no idea whether this is an inside job or what, but it's just possible that something you may have seen or noticed will help us in some way."

Dickson described at some length what had happened during the morning, but could add nothing material to the facts they had already accumulated. When he had finished Fenner asked: "Mr. Morton didn't by any chance leave with you, did he?"

"Why, no; that is, we left about the same time but not together. It seems to me I remember him starting up William Street with Borden. He was in a bit of a hurry—had to make a train for Detroit, I believe he said."

"Ah; well, then of course you'd have no idea as to where he could be found now?"

Dickson shrugged his shoulders. "I'm afraid not." He looked up suddenly. "Certainly you haven't an idea he's connected in any way with this!" he exclaimed, incredulous.

"Not necessarily," Fenner was quick to reply.

"Nonsense! It's absurd! The whole business is ridiculous. Now all you've told me is that a shortage in the vault was discovered today, but I should think that in a bank the size of this, with all the people and red tape you have here, there must be plenty of more likely explanations of a shortage than to assume that your money was hauled out in broad daylight by a reputable engineer. Bah! It's preposterous!"

"Not too fast, Mr. Dickson," Fenner interrupted placatingly. "In all fairness I confess a little more explanation is due you. This money, packed tightly in a small canvas sack, was removed from a hand truck in the vault some time between ten-thirty this morning and one P.M. Your inspection of the vault consumed a sizable portion of the two and a half hours elapsed. Now you must admit that everyone who went into that vault during that time is naturally tied into this inquiry by what you might call pure coincidence, if by nothing else."

Dickson thought this over for a minute. "That of course includes me," he said somewhat testily, "though I wish you had been a little more explicit to begin with. I remember the hand truck you speak of. It ploughed into me, hell bent, at the door of that office we looked at first. I've got two Charley horses yet." He rubbed his thighs. "However, that's neither here nor there. Well, fire away. If there's any more I can tell you I'll be glad to do it." He made his air of resignation very obvious.

"Do you mind telling us where you went from here this noon?"

"I went around to the India House for a bite to eat. After that I went to the office and looked over a few papers."

"What time did you get to your office?"

"A few minutes after one, I think."

"And then?"

"I went to my brokers, Halstead and Rice, and stayed there until the market closed. Then I went back to the office. When I found Borden's note of course I came down here."

"Oh; I say, how was the market today?" Fenner asked the question with such bright irrelevance that a tiny bond of common understanding was instantly established.

"Pretty rotten! Everything was off badly—a flock of new lows for the year."

"Ah, well; it's got to end somewhere, and it certainly ought to be soon," Fenner consoled.

"I hope you're right," Dickson said fervently.

Fenner got up and extended his hand, terminating the interview. "Sorry to have put you to so much trouble. I'm sure we're grateful for the time you've given us. If anything turns up I presume we can get in touch with you at your office?"

"Certainly; and don't hesitate to do so if I can be of any further help."

"Thanks. Oh, now; one more thing. How long have you known Borden?"

"About five years, I guess. He's worked for me three years and I knew him for two years before that."

"I see. Always quite satisfactory?"

"Oh, yes, indeed; a fine lad in every way. Thorough. Dependable—" Again Dickson looked incredulous. "Why, he's no more connected with this business than I am," he assured Fenner when he realized the implications of the question.

"Probably not," Fenner agreed.

When Dickson had gone Bryce grunted, "Not much help from that fellow! Morton's the only one left now, and that makes it begin to look just too bad for him. What'd you find out?" The last was to Fenner.

"I saw the manager of the Mercantile Bank. Morton drew a substantial portion of his checking balance this noon. Also he visited his safe deposit box. He took it to a booth, so they have no idea whether he had removed or added anything. I also went around to Fulton Street and saw Mr. Adolph Knoeckler. He bears out Borden's story in every detail." He waited a moment, then suggested: "We seem to have reached somewhat of an impasse until Mr. Morton turns up—or is turned up. Any ideas before we adjourn for the day?"

Hanley replied first. "Our auditors and Department heads are going over everything with fine-toothed combs. By midnight I think

I'll have a pretty definite idea as to the possibility of this being an inside job involving anyone but young Donegan; though I may as well say that I don't expect to find anything. As for Jerry, I simply can't reconcile his character or conduct since the loss with the idea of his being involved."

Fenner made no comment but looked toward Bryce.

"If Mr. Hanley doesn't uncover anything, my hunch would be to concentrate on Morton," he said tersely. "But, in any case, Borden and Dickson and old man Donegan and the boy won't be lost sight of for a split second until this thing is cleared up, if it takes six months. Same way with Morton, as soon as we do get hold of him."

"That's right," Fenner said, "but I hope your boys tread softly. The whole purpose is defeated the moment they even suspect they are being watched." He paused. "Perhaps we'll know more tomorrow. I shouldn't be surprised if Morton turned up."

All three got to their feet.

"We'll meet here in the morning to compare notes," Bryce suggested.

"I'll be able to tell you more then, as far as the bank's concerned," Hanley promised.

Fenner and the inspector went out. It was late March but the warm sun declining in a faint haze indicated the end of one of those premature May days that are sometimes sprinkled among the last days of the calendar winter and the first days of spring.

Fenner sniffed the air. "Glorious weather!"

"Weather be damned!" Bryce countered. "What do you make of this case?"

"Ah, yes." Fenner reluctantly brought himself back. "We have to watch our step. As things now point it would be easy to go off half-cocked."

"As things now point?"

"Of course. Young Donegan, you know. He told us he ate his lunch right after twelve o'clock and wandered around the Battery for an hour. According to that super-observant doorman he came in 'picking his teeth' at quarter after one. And then there's that gloomy, stuffy place he's cooped up in for eight hours a day in weather like this. Motive, what? Put yourself in his shoes, man!"

Bryce thought over this angle. "But this fellow, Morton, who seems to have disappeared?"

"That's why I say we have to go carefully. For that matter, Mr. Dickson, too, was using his words to conceal his thoughts this afternoon. Does it strike you as odd that he should have at once recognized that the truck we spoke of as in the vault was the same one which bumped him at the door of Jerry's cage? Not only that, but consider the testimony of that same efficient doorman to the effect that Mr. Dickson went into the bank wearing his topcoat, but came out with it draped over his arm. Nothing criminal in that, yet—"

Bryce was in a brown study.

Fenner went on: "Well, you've got them all under your eye now—all but Morton. We'll mull things over and watch these fellows and see what turns up. Whoever turned this trick must give himself away sooner or later. We'll simply have to be there when it happens. I only hope he doesn't keep us waiting too damned long!"

2

FRIDAY
APRIL 1ST

1

BRIGHT AND EARLY the next morning Bryce waited for Fenner opposite the employees' entrance to the bank building in almost the identical spot where Old Jeremy and his son had stood the day before.

The creaking of derricks, the rattle of buckets and cable, the hammering and shouting of the men below in the excavation for the new Consolidated Building, all fell on deaf ears as far as Bryce was concerned. The morning crowds were streaming to work; fresh, eager faces; worn, tired ones—something written on all of them; youth, age, fear, hope. To Bryce on this Friday morning they were just people.

His glance fell upon the Donegans rounding the corner and he faced about and gazed into the excavation; turning around only after out of the corner of his eye he had seen them disappear into the entrance of the bank. With grim satisfaction he watched a workman who had come along a half block behind them but had increased his pace to close up the distance. The man glanced into the entrance after the Donegans, then sauntered over to where Bryce stood. He asked for a match and, receiving a pack, lit a cigarette, mumbling the while, "Nothing special, chief. It's all written out." He handed back the matches and a small folded slip of paper. Bryce thrust both into his pocket as the man went on.

Presently Maxwell Fenner came along, gay, debonair, immaculate even to pearl gray spats, a prim carnation and a walking stick.

"Well, old man, what's new?" he greeted Bryce.

"Nothing startling. No sign of Morton. Shall we go inside?"

"Might as well," Fenner agreed cheerily. "Maybe Hanley's got everything worked out and we can go play golf today."

Bryce only grunted. Golf was not one of his accomplishments.

They found Hanley at his desk, his face careworn, his eyes bloodshot, his whole bearing reflecting dejection. He looked up at them a little hopefully. From his dispirited air and drawn appearance they gathered that he had been there all night. When they had sat down Fenner looked at him curiously and said: "You found nothing; right? But you didn't expect to, so I don't know why you should be so forlorn."

Hanley looked up quickly. "Oh, yes; we found something. We found everything in gratifying order. To anybody bred in a bank that's immensely satisfying." There was no mistaking a certain pride in his voice. He went on: "I am satisfied of one thing: that the money, bag and all, is no longer within this bank. I'm quite convinced of another: that old Jeremy Donegan had no hand in this; and I'm almost as sure of his boy."

Fenner and Bryce exchanged glances. "If what you say were true, though I don't necessarily subscribe to it," the former remarked, "our field would be limited to three people. I had hoped Morton would turn up, but if he is going to I suppose we should have heard from him by this time." He looked at his watch and then at Bryce. "I've some people to see and also some looking around to do here," he remarked suggestively.

Bryce flipped open the small notebook. "All right; I'll make it snappy." He settled into his seat and started: "Plenty of details but no nourishment in any of them. First, Morton: No sign of him nor word from him at his office, his apartment, or his club. His wife, from whom he is separated, has not heard from him for two weeks but is not disturbed because she says that she sometimes does not hear from him for a month at a time. In other words he dropped out of sight yesterday at noon."

"Or rather, yesterday at half past twelve," Fenner supplied. "Don't forget his stop at the Mercantile."

"Twelve-thirty, then," corrected Bryce, and went on: "Now Dickson: Went home from here—Staten Island by ferry, then by train—lives near Stapleton. Had dinner home; not out of the house all evening. About eight-thirty his next-door neighbor came in; left at ten-thirty. Lights out shortly before eleven. No telephone calls either way. Left house about seven-forty-five this morning and went to his office.

"Now Borden: Went to his office from here late yesterday afternoon. Received several phone calls, all business. Got a call about four-thirty and from what tapper could gather went out early in response to it and stopped at Knoeckler's shop in Fulton Street. Stayed there from five to five-fifteen; from there went home. Lives out in Bloomfield, N. J., with his mother. Had dinner at home. Made no phone calls and received one—from the local Y.M.C.A. Went out with his mother at eight-forty-five to the Strand Theater; home at eleven. Left his house this morning before seven; went direct to office but stayed only a few minutes and then came down to the job across the street."

Bryce shut up the book and pulled a folded piece of paper from his pocket.

"Now, the Donegans: Left here together late last night—about ten-forty-five—"

"That's right," Hanley confirmed.

"Went home together. Lights out at midnight. Left house—Brooklyn, by the way—about eight o'clock this morning and came straight to the bank." When he had finished Bryce looked around.

"Certainly nothing overt in any of that," Fenner said dryly.

Hanley looked from one to the other and commented: "You fellows certainly are thorough. I should hate to have you turned loose on me." Bryce looked up at him queerly but made no answer.

Fenner and Bryce went out together, the latter to go to headquarters, the former to utilize certain sources accessible to him for obtaining information about the financial affairs of the men he was investigating. They agreed to meet for lunch.

Fenner reached the appointed place a little early. He secured a table and sat down to wait, turning over in his mind the various aspects of the case. It was all very baffling. He could not recall a larceny case in his experience in which so many and such a variety of people were in a position to have accomplished the theft. To make matters worse, his morning's investigations had yielded the fact that any one of them might be considered to possess sufficient financial motive.

If it was an inside job, he meditated, the perpetrator had received the screening benefit of an almost unbelievable chain of outside circumstances. Certainly neither Jeremy nor Jerry Donegan knew until the event that the vault was to be visited by the party of engineers. Fenner was almost persuaded that such a theory put too great a strain upon the possibility of coincidence, but he tried to keep his mind open on the subject.

And yet if the inside job theory were rejected it meant that the theft had been accomplished on the spur of the moment and without preparation of any sort, for neither Morton nor Dickson nor Borden had known a half hour before they went to the bank that they were going to be called there at all. The job required a "cool customer" and an opportunist to a high degree. Could Dickson or Borden answer to that description? Fenner had his doubts.

As to Morton, from what he had been able to learn of him and from what he knew of him by reputation, he intuitively found it difficult to reconcile him with thievery, even to the tune of $180,000, though of course there was no denying that his ill-timed disappearance justified Bryce's suspicions, and then some

His reflections were interrupted by the arrival of Bryce for lunch. Fenner instantly perceived that his colleague had something to report. When the waiter had taken their order and moved out of hearing Bryce said: "We got a line on Morton's car. Didn't find it but we found the garage where he keeps it. Packard sedan. Morton left word on Wednesday to have it completely serviced, gassed up and oiled. He came for it around one-forty-five yesterday afternoon and hasn't been back since. What do you think of that?"

"You say he left word on Wednesday to have it serviced? Do you know whether he indicated that he contemplated a trip?"

"That's exactly the question I asked the garage man. He couldn't recall that Morton said that he was going anywhere, but the fellow says that somehow he got that impression."

"Well, it looks as if Morton's away on the quiet, all right. But it must be for some reason of his own not connected with this business at all. You see, in the first place, he had no way of knowing there'd be any loose money lying around that vault, and, in the second, he didn't know until he reached his office on Thursday morning that he'd be going there at all. Another thing: I talked to his assistant this morning,—a fellow named Coles. Morton told him before he left on Thursday morning that he was going to Detroit and had even mentioned the possibility on Wednesday."

Bryce's jaw dropped a little as he digested these facts but he countered: "Still, if it wasn't an inside job it's more likely to have been Morton than either of the other two. He was carrying the briefcase, which would make it easier for him, and if he intended going away for some other reason, why, he wouldn't have to worry about a getaway. He was all set!"

Fenner was silent for a long moment, then mused: "I never met the fellow in my life, but by reputation in engineering and building circles he's highly conservative. For instance, if soil is good for five tons per square foot he designs his foundations so that the load is only four; if an eight-inch brace is apparently required he specifies a ten or twelve. He's not a type that takes chances; he always wants to be sure. Now this theft, if it's not an inside job, was born of a quick impulse. It's not the sort of a thing a fellow like Morton would be apt to tackle."

Bryce was not quite convinced but he knew from experience that Fenner's intuition in these matters seldom led him astray, so he changed the subject.

"By the way," he said, "I worked one of my men into the job-office at the new building. A clever chap by the name of Quade. Got him put on as an assistant timekeeper. He'll keep an eye on Dickson and Morton and Borden on the job for us. Drop in on him sometime and then let me know what you think of him. He's been doing vice squad work but wanted to get out of it."

Fenner promised to do as Bryce asked. They ate the rest of their meal in silence broken only by occasional comment on the food and service. At its conclusion Bryce lit his cigar and Fenner's cigarette and settled back comfortably. He glanced from the end of his cigar to his companion.

"Max," he presently ruminated, "what about our friend, Mr. Hanley?"

Fenner returned his look without surprise and said: "I expected that question sooner or later. One canvasses all of the possibilities. Hanley has been badly burned in the market. He had a lot of stuff on margin at the first break and has been covering all the way down. However, that fact alone doesn't mean a thing! I found out that about half of the officers of the bank are in the same boat. I believe that has something to do with the anxiety to have this conclusively proved to be an outside job. There are so many people in the bank with what you might call 'known motive' that if the thing isn't cleared up fairly speedily the situation there will be very uncomfortable."

"Well, if one of these other birds doesn't make a misstep soon I'll begin to believe myself that it was an inside job," Bryce said. He dragged heavily on the cigar and went on thoughtfully: "You know more about the bank end of it than I do. Tell me something: Hanley was pretty positive this morning when he said they'd found everything in such apple-pie order. Now with all the red tape and rigmarole they have in a place like that, how can he be so sure so quickly? There are a lot of employees besides the Donegans. How about some of those guards, or almost anyone on the inside?"

"As a matter of fact, he can't be. They have a pretty thorough system of checking up from minute to minute but of course it isn't one hundred percent foolproof. I think Hanley is to a certain extent guided by his instincts in the matter; but on the other hand, the instincts of a fellow with his experience and position are likely to be pretty accurate."

"Maybe his wishes are father to his instincts," Bryce suggested.

"Anything is possible." This was Fenner's stock reply in lieu of no answer at all.

"Who was that other bird with him at first yesterday? Mortimer?"

"'That other bird' as you call him, Mortimer, is the power behind the throne in the Consolidated American Company, and also in a lot of other outfits around here. I've heard of him often but never encountered him face to face before."

"Didn't have much to say, did he?"

"He never does. I think that's half his secret. It builds up an aura of mystery about him that awes people who don't understand the psychology of it. I guess he's got something on the ball, though, and money no end!"

"Funny that I should never have heard of him."

"Not at all. Few people have. He keeps off directorates and out of the papers. That's more of his secret."

They smoked for a few moments in silence. "Morton's a little crowded, too, financially," Fenner resumed. "The foundations for the new Consolidated Building are about all he has on his drawing boards right now. He was caught in the market, too, but not quite so drastically. Strangest of all, though, is Dickson. I suppose you gathered from his talk yesterday afternoon that he is anxious? Well, he's in to his ears, with the margin clerks pestering him from dawn to sunset. Rather surprising, too, because until a year ago he wouldn't touch the market with a ten-foot pole. Had all of his investments in high grade bonds and real estate."

"In other words," the inspector concluded for Fenner, "they all needed the dough!"

"Exactly."

The talk lagged until Bryce pushed back his chair and said: "I'll go back to headquarters now. I have hopes of that car of Morton's being turned up somewhere pretty quick."

"Good. Well, I'll be at the bank in case you want to get hold of me."

Fenner sat for a few moments after Bryce left. He was pondering, not for the first time, Mr. Hanley. That gentleman, he reflected, had motive enough and as much opportunity as any of the others to commit the theft and, furthermore, he was the only one on the inside who could have anticipated the vault inspection by the engineers and arranged to take advantage of it. Yet with a little shrug Fenner dismissed Hanley from his list of possibilities, or, perhaps better, relegated him to his list of "improbables." His reason for this was one he would have been too modest to explain to Bryce, namely: that though he had solved only several simple cases for the Consolidated Bank it was common knowledge in inner bonding and banking circles that he had brought to successful conclusions a number of involved and difficult ones which had bid fair to defy solution; and Fenner did not believe Hanley would have had the temerity to call him in had the bank manager himself been involved.

After several minutes of musing along these lines Fenner, too, left the restaurant and went back to the bank.

2

Fenner found Hanley about to leave. His face had a gray pallor, his eyes a heaviness that bespoke complete exhaustion.

"I feel I could go home and sleep for a solid week," the manager mourned. "Anything new?"

"Nothing much. Bryce has got a line on Morton's car they're working on. It might net something."

"Yesterday I would have sworn that would be the last direction in which to look. Today it seems to be about the only hope we have left," Hanley sighed.

Covertly Fenner searched Hanley's face but could detect no trace of purposiveness behind the remark.

"Not at all," he replied. "Quite frankly, I'm not especially hopeful on that score. To watch and to wait—that's our program now. Eventually it'll bear fruit."

"I wish I could share your optimism," was Hanley's gloomy rejoinder.

Before the manager went out Fenner arranged to go over certain of young Donegan's books and also the vault records. Without any specific objective he wanted a plausible opportunity for being in the bank and for conversing with Jerry and old Jeremy. He had just gotten down to the former's cage when one of the bank's office boys tapped his shoulder.

"Mr. Fenner, sir? There's a call for you on Mr. Hanley's phone. Will you take it here?"

"Yes, thanks." He picked up Jerry's phone and in a minute heard Bryce's voice at the other end.

"Will you step around to Adolph Knoeckler's shop?" Bryce requested. "There's been an accident. It may be just that but to me it looks kind of queer."

Without waiting for details Fenner hung up and hurried out of the bank. It was less than a ten-minute walk around to Knoeckler's shop. When Fenner got there he saw the familiar blue Police Department roadster parked in front of the place and Bryce waiting in the door.

"When I got back to the station," the inspector explained, "I was just in time to hear the desk sergeant get this call from the officer on the beat. Old Knoeckler was found dead at the foot of his cellar steps. It seemed odd that such a thing should happen just now to this fellow indirectly connected with our case, so I hopped over."

"By all means."

"The coroner will be here directly," Bryce went on, "and the photographer and a finger-print man. In the meantime we can look around."

They turned into the shop, Bryce repeating: "As I say, I'm not sure this isn't a pure accident. There's nothing offhand to indicate anything different, but I just had a hunch—"

Inside the shop Fenner saw a policeman in uniform, a man very patently a plain-clothes detective, and a third, older man, the last distraught and nervous, leaning on and clinging to the counter.

"That's the man who found him," Bryce explained, inclining his head toward the last of the trio. "We'll take a look downstairs and then come up and talk to him."

"As you say."

The entrance to the cellar was in the extreme rear of the shop. Bryce opened the door at the head of the stairs and snapped on the light. It was a poor light but by its feeble glow Fenner could see a dim form sprawled on the cement floor at the foot of the stairs. Bryce preceded him down the stairs and they stepped gingerly around the body.

Fenner glanced around and saw in the far end a heating plant and a small pile of coal. Other than to house these, the cellar apparently served only as a repository for the accumulation of a miscellany of junk. He walked to the furnace and opened the door. The firebed was black and quite extinct, but it radiated a faint residual warmth that indicated it had been out for only a few hours.

He came back and looked at the body thoughtfully. He had talked to Adolph Knoeckler less than twenty-four hours before. Now the man lay on his face, quite lifeless; his arms stretched out before him, his face smudged in a small dark pool of his own congealed blood.

Fenner bent down and felt the dead man's cheek; it was quite cold. He lifted a frail forearm and found it rigid.

"Last night some time," he said briefly.

"Yeah."

"Let's go up."

Even to Bryce, a hardened veteran in matters of crime and violence and death, it was a relief to get up out of the dank cellar into the fresh daylight of the shop.

"You had better tell Mr. Fenner what you told the officer and me, Schmidt," Bryce said to the old man.

"Yah—yess," the man agreed nervously. He was a German of about Knoeckler's age and conducted a newsstand and stationery store two doors from Knoeckler's shop. He went ahead with his story, using good English except when he became excited, at which time he dropped into the German accent. He had known Adolph for ten years, he told them—ever since he had opened his little magazine shop. Of late he had been taking his dinner with him quite often at a German restaurant a few blocks away. The old man's daughter was out a great deal of the time lately. Last night he'd sort of expected the old man but when he hadn't showed up Schmidt

had thought nothing about it because they had no definite arrangement. "Then this morning he didn't come in for his paper—first
time in months except when he was away—so I got to wondering
and kept my eye on his shop. There didn't seem to be anyone
around so when I come back from my lunch I tried the door. I found
it open and went in. Adolph wasn't downstairs. I called and nobody answered. I looked upstairs in the sittin' room and in the
bedrooms and nobody was there. I thought he'd probably gone off
somewheres and forgot to snap the lock on his door, so I thought
I'd lock it for him. Then I thought I'd peek in the cellar first and—
ach ven I turned on de light dere he vas!" The old German shuddered at the recollection.

Schmidt had scarcely finished when the coroner, a Dr. Pollard,
and two other men from Headquarters arrived. Bryce introduced
Fenner and the three went downstairs to the cellar.

The coroner leaned over the body for a brief examination.

"Dead from eighteen to twenty-four hours," he said as he stood
up. "Fractured skull—frontal." He looked up to the head of the cellar steps, then down at the body meditatively. "He must have just
about pitched all of the way down, though, and landed head first
on the stone floor, too, to get a nasty fracture like that. However,
we can tell more from an autopsy. It's too dark here." He turned to
Bryce. "Do you want any pictures before we move the body?"

Bryce in turn looked at Fenner.

"Better take them," the latter advised, and to the coroner he
said: "In your opinion, then, Doctor, he's been dead between eighteen and twenty-four hours. Which would you say was nearer?"

The coroner stooped over the body again. "It's hard to be sure—
Hmm—rigor-mortis pretty well advanced—muscles pretty well con-
tracted. Probably twenty-one hours is closer than either, though it
might have been as little as eighteen."

"That would put it around five-thirty yesterday afternoon but
possibly as late as eight-thirty in the evening—say, between five
and nine?"

"That's a safe assumption, all right," Dr. Pollard agreed.

"I know he couldn't have taken his tumble much before then, because I was in here talking to him a little after four. He wasn't exactly a healthy looking specimen but he certainly didn't look ready to keel over, either. Well, let's see—" Fenner bent down and picked up each of Knoeckler's hands, turning them palms up to examine them. "Anything strike you as odd about them?"

Bryce and the coroner looked at them. Bryce leaned down and drew his palm across the cement floor, then looked at it, grayed with dirt and ashes. He looked again at Knoeckler's upturned palms. "Pretty clean, ain't they—for a man that's fallen forward from the top of those stairs?"

Fenner did not reply.

Bryce called his photographer down and instructed him to take the customary pictures. Then they went upstairs to get Schmidt's testimony for the coroner's records.

The newsdealer repeated his story substantially as he had told it first to Bryce and later to Fenner.

When he had finished Fenner asked: "Knoeckler lived in the rooms upstairs, did he?"

"Yes." Schmidt nodded.

"Anybody else?"

"Oh, yes; Elsa, his daughter. She sort of keeps house for him."

"Where is she; do you know?"

"She works somewhere near here in an office. She's a secretary." He made the announcement with a certain deference. He shook his head a little sadly and went on: "She's gone now, though. She went away last night."

"Yes? Where to?"

Schmidt shrugged his shoulders. "I don't know. She's hard to keep up to, lately. She went away with a man in a car. She had a suitcase."

"When?" Fenner smothered his impatience.

"Last night. I just came back from supper a little before. It must have been seven o'clock."

"Tell us more about it. How did you happen to notice it?" Fenner urged.

"From about four o'clock on I stay out by my stand—the afternoon papers—people going home then," Schmidt explained. "Usually I stay out about a half an hour after supper. People buy magazines then. Not long after I came back from supper a car pulled up and stopped about halfway between my place and here. I saw Elsa get out and run inside. It struck me kind of funny they hadn't pulled right up to Adolph's instead of stopping almost next door. There was a man driving the car. As soon as Elsa went inside he got out and walked around the car, kicking the tires and sort of looking it over. Then he went inside too. In about fifteen minutes they both came out. Maybe it was a little longer—twenty minutes or so. I'd gone in my shop a couple of times, it seems to me, to wait on customers. He had her suitcase. They got in and drove off. Pretty soon after that I shut up for the night."

"What kind of a car was it?"

"Why, it was a big expensive looking, closed car."

"Would you know it again if you saw it?" Bryce put in.

Schmidt scratched his head. "I'm not sure if I would or not."

"Would you know the man?"

"Maybe; but it was pretty dark then."

"Where'd you say the girl worked?"

"I don't know; except it's around here somewhere. She walked back and forth and sometimes came home at noon."

"When did you last see Knoeckler alive?" Fenner cut in abruptly.

Schmidt thought a minute, then replied: "He came in about four o'clock yesterday afternoon. I gave him a late paper and we talked a few minutes. Then he went on back. It wasn't long after that when you were here." Schmidt addressed the last remark to Fenner alone.

Fenner was somewhat startled but concealed his surprise. "Yes; I didn't get here until about four-fifteen." He paused. "You're observant, aren't you?" The comment was in a cutting tone but he took the edge off by adding: "It's always a pleasure and usually a help to have someone around who sees things. Now maybe you can tell us if there were any other visitors or customers in the afternoon or evening—say, after I left?"

Again old Schmidt stopped to think. "There was two I know of," he started slowly. "There was one fellow, a young fellow. He came a little after five and stayed for ten or fifteen minutes. Seemed to know Adolph. When he came out he was laughing and yelled something back through the door to him. He stopped and bought a paper off me and then went on up toward William Street." Schmidt stopped and shook his head a little wearily as if the effort of recollecting these events strained his mind.

Fenner looked quickly at Bryce, inquiringly. The latter pulled out his notebook. "That must've been Borden, all right. Five-ten to five-twenty-five. Shall we get hold of him? I think he's at the bank job right now."

"I think we'd better—and also that man you've got on him; Murphy, isn't it?" Fenner replied.

"We'll get Borden. Murphy'll come along. Don't worry about that," Bryce assured him. He picked up Knoeckler's telephone and called the job office. Borden, it seemed, was somewhere down in the excavation and Bryce had to wait ten minutes while he was found and summoned to the telephone. When Bryce asked him to come around to Knoeckler's, he seemed surprised and curious but promised to come at once.

Fenner turned back to Schmidt. "You said there were two. Now what about the other fellow?"

"That was later on—not long before Elsa went away. It was a young fellow, too. He was hangin' around in front when I came back from supper. I saw him go inside but I never saw him leave. He must've gone out while I was in my store."

"Do you know him or anything about him?"

"No; only I think maybe I've seen him there before."

"You'd know him again, then?"

"Oh, yes."

Bryce was jotting down notes industriously.

"How was Mr. Knoeckler's health?" Dr. Pollard put this question.

"He's been feelin' his age a little, lately," the old German answered cautiously. "His stomach's been bothering him now and then, and he's had a sort of weakness in his left side. His left arm trembled a lot. He's been afraid of a stroke and was up to see Dr. Kellar only last week."

"Dr. Kellar? Where?"

"Up in Park Row, I think."

The coroner wrote down the name and picked up the telephone directory. "Is it Doctor Otto Kellar?" he asked.

"Yah—yess; that's right."

"I'll see him."

Fenner and Bryce started looking about the shop.

"You need me any more?" Schmidt asked apologetically. "My store—"

"You'll be in your store if we do?" Bryce wanted to know.

"Yah." Schmidt nodded vigorously.

"Just a minute," Fenner broke in. "There's a chap on his way over here—be here in a minute. I want you to tell me if he's the first young fellow you just told us about—the one who bought the paper from you. Then you can go."

Only a few minutes later Borden came in. He hesitated in the entrance, glanced around, then came over to the group. When Schmidt saw him he looked at Fenner and nodded affirmatively. Fenner dismissed him with a wave and a curt "Thanks," and turned to Borden.

"I understand you knew Mr. Knoeckler?" he began.

At the use of the past tense Borden looked up sharply. "Why, casually, I do. We usually have him repair our instruments when they get out of shape."

"When did you last see him?"

"I saw him yesterday afternoon around five o'clock—maybe a few minutes after," Borden replied. Nobody spoke, so he enlarged upon his answer. "We have a level here for repairs. I thought it wasn't much of a job but Knoeckler called up yesterday afternoon and said he'd either have to send it back to the factory or substitute some old parts he had around. I left the office a little early and stopped here to go over the thing with him."

"Did he seem ill or in any way act unusual when you were here?"

"Why, no; at least, not that I could notice." He hesitated. "We had a good-natured argument about the price he wanted to charge for a second-hand tripod head. Not serious, of course—the bank's paying for it anyway. No—he seemed all right to me. When I went out I called him a robber and he laughed at me." Borden glanced around the semicircle of faces. "Why? What's happened to him?"

"He's either had an accident or been murdered—we hope the former," Fenner replied.

Borden winced at the word but recovered quickly. He drew in his breath sharply, stammering in astonishment: "But—but what—but who—who would want to kill old Adolph?"

"That's precisely what we're most interested in finding out." There was a steely hardness beneath Fenner's tone and in the sharp way his words were clipped off. If Borden noticed he did not give any sign but simply waited for Fenner or Bryce to say more.

"Do you know anything about the man—his private life or anything of that sort?"

"I never saw Mr. Knoeckler except in this store and then only when business brought me here," Borden replied. He had quite regained his composure.

At this point Bryce excused himself, remarking that he would return within a few minutes. Borden looked at his watch and fidgeted impatiently. "Is there anything else you'd like to ask me, sir? If not, I'd better get back to the job."

"Better wait just a minute. Bryce might have something in his mind," Fenner suggested amiably.

Borden waited, glancing around the shop.

"There's our level," he said, pointing to an instrument on Knoeckler's work bench in a rear corner of the shop. Beside it stood the open mahogany case; around it lay a miscellaneous assortment of tools. Borden went over to look at the machine. He looked around the bench, then at the old-fashioned roll-top desk which stood beside it.

"Don't touch anything," Fenner admonished sharply. "Finger prints, you know," he explained more coolly.

Borden stepped back quickly. "Oh, of course. I didn't think," he apologized. Just then Bryce returned.

"Anything you want to ask Mr. Borden?" Fenner inquired.

Bryce shook his head. "No— Nope. I guess not."

Borden picked up his hat from the counter. "I'll be going along, then?" he asked rather than stated, and at Fenner's permission he hurried out.

When he had gone Bryce said a little disappointedly: "I was outside talking to Murphy. He confirms what Borden and Schmidt told us to a 'T.' All the details about the time and about Borden calling back and about him buying the paper, he confirms exactly." Murphy was the aide of Bryce's who had been shadowing Borden on the previous afternoon.

The coroner had been standing by in growing mystification. At his obvious curiosity Bryce explained, "There are some angles to this that we'll have to go over with you afterward, Dr. Pollard. We'd better look around here now and see what we can turn up."

There was little semblance of order about Knoeckler's establishment. The counters and showcases were scantily stocked with a varied assortment of tapes, rods, drawing instruments, and other surveying and drafting paraphernalia. The rear portion, which had apparently served for his repair work, contained several work benches and in one corner the old roll-top desk. The benches were littered with tools, parts and odds and ends of instruments, and several instruments in process of repair.

The desk was covered with a jumble of papers, mostly bills and receipts. There were a few letters, a German newspaper, and on top of the pile—staring Fenner and Bryce in the face—a day-old copy of the tabloid newspaper opened to the article on the Consolidated American Bank theft.

Fenner and Bryce stared at the paper for a long time. "Must be the paper Schmidt gave him yesterday afternoon," Bryce finally suggested.

Fenner agreed absently; he seemed suddenly lost in thought. "Bryce," he announced abruptly, "that paper was spread out just like that, open to just that article, when I came in yesterday afternoon to question Knoeckler about Borden—only then it was over on the counter. Knoeckler was so absorbed reading it that he didn't even hear me until I was almost on top of him. I wonder—" He stopped as abruptly as he had started. For a moment more he was thoughtful, glancing around and resolving the arrangement of things in his mind. Then he was off on a new tack. "The next thing is to locate the girl. Let's see what we can find upstairs."

They went up, Fenner leading the way. In the small sitting-room they found nothing of interest or significance; nor in the kitchen-dining room combination at the rear. Elsa's bedroom they found mildly disordered. "She packed in a hurry," Fenner commented. The bed had not been slept in but on the counterpane they could see the rectangular imprint left by her small suitcase where she had placed it on the bed to pack it. One of the dresser drawers was partly pulled out and the closet door stood open. Several dresses and an empty hanger had been tossed at the foot of the bed.

Bryce rummaged hurriedly but skillfully through the dresser drawers. "Not a thing," he grumbled; "not so much as a single scrap of paper of any kind. Funny damned thing, when you think of it—"

Last they went into Adolph's room. They found it neat and clean and in surprising order, considering the habits of carelessness which the disordered condition of the shop would have indicated Adolph Knoeckler had possessed. On the dresser, weighted down with a hairbrush, they found a hastily scribbled note. Fenner scanned it rapidly, glanced at the reverse side and handed it to Bryce. The note was written in lead pencil on plain paper and read:

Father—
I had a chance to go up to the country over the week-end so I got off from work and am going. I expect to be back Sunday night or Monday morning.
    I brought some things in. You will find them in the ice-box.
                              Elsa.

Bryce read it slowly and looked up at Fenner. "Do you make anything of it?" he asked.

"There are a lot of things you can make of it. For one thing, it looks as if Miss Knoeckler had purposely avoided meeting her father. They parked the car next door instead of out front. She came for her things at a time when she must have known he would be likely to be out for dinner. That may have been just a coincidence, of course. Her obvious haste in packing may have arisen from a desire to get away before he returned, though she might have been in a hurry for some other reason. The note indicates that she certainly expects to be back by Monday morning." Fenner rubbed his chin meditatively and went on slowly, thinking aloud, "It's going to be interesting to talk to the chap she went off with—if we ever see him. I suppose there's no way of getting a line on him until we find Miss Knoeckler."

"Pretty hard," the inspector agreed.

"I wonder why they stopped the car next door. I wonder why she went in alone first. There may be perfectly simple explanations for these and a lot of other things, but I'm very much afraid we're going to have to wait until Monday to learn what they are. As for the old gentleman—"

"The autopsy might show something," Bryce reminded.

"It might." But Fenner was obviously skeptical. After a further cursory, and quite fruitless, search of Adolph's room, they went back downstairs. The morgue wagon had arrived and the coroner was awaiting word from Bryce before removing the body.

"Find anything?" he inquired.

"Not to speak of," Bryce replied. "The girl's gone away for the week-end." He handed him Elsa's note.

The coroner perused it, quickly. "Your men through in the cellar?"

"We're all done, Chief." The photographer spoke up without waiting for Bryce to inquire.

"You don't think of anything?" Bryce asked Fenner, and at the latter's negative reply he said to Pollard: "You may as well get ahead with it, then. Let me know the results of your autopsy as soon as you can, will you? Also what you find out from Dr.—Kellar, wasn't it?"

The coroner agreed to hasten things as much as he could and, summoning the ambulance attendants, directed the removal of Knoeckler's body. Bryce posted a detective in the shop and with Fenner went back to the bank, from there to his own headquarters at the police station.

3

Fenner resumed his browsing in Donegan's records just where he had been interrupted scarce two hours earlier. Before he left the bank late in the afternoon he telephoned the inspector. He learned that no trace of Morton's car had yet been found. He learned also that a preliminary examination of Knoeckler's body indicated without question that he had died of a fractured skull. The coroner had reported, according to Bryce, that the fracture could have been caused by a fall from the first floor to the basement where the body was found. Last, Dr. Pollard reported that he had been in communication with Dr. Kellar who had informed him that old Knoeckler's ailment was such that a sudden seizure was not at all unlikely, and that, furthermore, in the event of such a seizure the man might have lost consciousness so abruptly as to have been incapable of breaking his fall with his hands. A more complete report would be forthcoming within a day or two, Bryce told Fenner.

Fenner grunted. "I suppose, it's barely possible that Adolph Knoeckler's demise was accidental," he said when Bryce had finished, but his tone lacked conviction. He made a mental note to interview Dr. Kellar himself. "It looks, though, as if events were conspiring to compel me to play golf tomorrow and Sunday. We seem to be at somewhat of a standstill until Monday, or at least until Morton shows up."

"Assuming that nobody else makes a break," Bryce supplemented.

"Of course; but I think it's a little early yet for that. Don't you? But I suppose we had better go over things again in the morning, anyway."

Bryce assented and Fenner disconnected, anxious to go home for the day. His appearance and manner of a dilettante bachelor to the contrary, Fenner was a family man; more than that, he was a man who consciously enjoyed his family. When he left his office, or wherever his cases happened to take him, he tried to forget his work as completely as he could. On most of his ordinary cases he was able to do this with slight effort, but when he was dealing with the more puzzling ones he found it harder to clear his brain. Various aspects of the questions confronting him had a way of suddenly poking their heads up into his consciousness, regardless of where he was or what he was doing. Fenner usually revolved the ideas for a moment, examining them from different sides, then thrust them down again for more processing by his subconscious mind.

On his way home on this Friday afternoon the picture that kept recurring to him was that of old Knoeckler as he had found him on the previous day when he had gone there to check up Borden's story of his stop to leave the level. Adolph Knoeckler had been leaning on the counter, absorbed in the perusal of the tabloid spread before him. He had seemed almost reluctant to tear himself away from the paper and had been barely civil. When Fenner had told him the purpose of his call, the old man had seemed to unbend a little. At the same time Fenner fancied he had detected a masked keenness in the man which belied the initial vagueness of his answers.

He had generally confirmed Borden's story, however, so Fenner had dismissed the incident from his mind. But today when he had recognized the paper spread on Knoeckler's desk and had realized the subject of the article in which the old man had been so absorbed the day before, the incident had lost its insignificance. What new significance it would take on Fenner was at loss to predict. So far, it was just another thing to puzzle over, but that it was an aspect not to be dismissed he had no question. That its true significance would sometime be revealed he was less sure than hopeful of.

3

SATURDAY
APRIL 2ND

1

ON SATURDAY MORNING Fenner and Bryce and Hanley were again gathered in the bank manager's office. Hanley looked distinctly better than when the others had left him the day before. He was refreshed with sleep and clean shaven, but he wore a sober air that bespoke discouragement at the progress they had made toward the solution of the theft.

Fenner was attired in knickers and wore a gay sweater beneath his jacket. Obviously he intended holding to his threat or promise to get in a weekend of golf. Bryce leaned forward with his elbows and forearms on the desk, mouthing an unlit cigar, his appearance quite unchanged; a good night's rest or a sleepless vigil—either affected him not in the least. He was always the same—stolid, grim, relentless.

Hanley looked from one to the other. "Anything happen?" He asked the question glumly as if a negative answer was a foregone conclusion.

"Not much, I'm afraid," Fenner replied. "Bryce has the chronicle."

The detective thumbed through his little, black book and read off concise but complete accounts of the actions of Jeremy Donegan, his son, Mr. Dickson, and Borden since the previous morning. There was not an unusual or suspicious act or event in the entire account. Nor was there any word of Randolph Morton or any trace of his car.

"You say Borden went to Knoeckler's yesterday afternoon at your summons? What was that for?" Hanley inquired when the inspector had concluded.

"Knoeckler fell downstairs Thursday evening and killed himself. Borden had been there during the afternoon. We thought he might possibly be able to shed some light on it."

"Killed, eh? You don't say! And you suspect it may not have been accidental?" Hanley ventured shrewdly.

"Well, we're not at all sure of anything; we're just trying to find out," Bryce evaded. He described without detail the discovery of Knoeckler's body.

Hanley listened attentively. "You don't suppose there's any connection between the—er—accident and our affair here, do you?" he asked when Bryce had finished.

"There's no evidence that Knoeckler's death was anything but accidental," Fenner put in quickly. "The coroner will have out his final report tomorrow. I rather imagine he'll ascribe the man's death to a fall from the first floor to the cellar, possibly preceded by a stroke of some sort and presumably quite accidental. As a matter of fact, I made it my business last evening to telephone Dr. Kellar, who has been attending Mr. Knoeckler. From what he told me, Knoeckler had been in pretty rotten shape for some time. He'd had some sort of a partial stroke several weeks ago, though of course Dr. Kellar didn't let the old man know that, and was in precarious condition any way you look at it."

"That's good," Hanley replied. "Things are bad enough the way they are without getting a murder messed up with them. It would be spread over every scandal sheet in the country."

"Quite," Fenner agreed.

"Nothing more on the inside job theory, I presume," Hanley presently suggested.

"No; I think not," Fenner reassured him. "Young Donegan's records are in first-class order. He seems to be a careful, methodical, thoroughgoing sort of a fellow. Jeremy Donegan the same."

Hanley only grunted. It was too soon to say: "I told you so."

After only a few minutes of futile discussion the talk ended and Fenner and the inspector went out together. They were silent until they reached the street, when Bryce said reproachfully: "I suppose you have your own reasons for not wanting Hanley to connect Knoeckler's death with the theft down here."

"No special reason," Fenner countered. "Just general policy. The fewer people there are who know what you're thinking about or working toward, the less likely you are to be checked."

"That's right, but you might have said something to me. Suppose I had spilled the beans?"

Fenner looked at him and smiled. "I knew it wasn't necessary. Unless I'm much mistaken, you've got space for Mr. T. Jerome Hanley in your little book right now."

Bryce was not surprised. "As a matter of fact, I have," he confessed, "though I have to admit that he's been quite above reproach during the short time we've been keeping an eye on him. I am going on nothing but a hunch—not an awfully strong hunch, either. In some way he just doesn't seem quite all out in the open."

"I'm afraid he hasn't been, but I think it's more from habit than from intent. I had a talk with their personnel director when I went back to the bank yesterday. I learned quite by chance that the boy who handled that money truck is a nephew of Hanley's. A minor, irrelevant matter, yet when we talked to the boy on Thursday Hanley didn't mention the relationship. Probably an oversight on his part, yet it instantly raises suspicion. However, all good bankers are notoriously close-mouthed."

They had crossed the narrow street to the truck-loading platform which overlooked the excavation for the foundations of the new building. Suddenly Fenner grasped Bryce's arm. "Look! There are two of your customers now."

Below them and out toward the center of the lot Bryce saw Dickson and Borden. They were standing on the top layer of cross-lot bracing about halfway down from the street level to the bottom of the pit. Borden had a blueprint, half unrolled, from which he seemed to be explaining something to Dickson. Occasionally he stopped talking and pointed around the lot. Dickson took the print from him to study it more closely.

Suddenly overhead, even as Fenner and Bryce watched, there was a dull metallic clang and a slow rumble. A stone skip which had been hoisted high and started on its swing toward the hopper rocked crazily. One of the four chains which suspended it from each corner had snapped, and with each lurch the skip spilled out a half dozen bowlders and a slither of rock fragments.

From where they stood it looked to Fenner and Bryce as if Dickson and Borden were directly beneath the arc through which the pan would swing to reach the truck hopper. Apparently Dickson thought so, too. With one glance at the skip swinging high and toward them, he dropped the blueprint and started running along the bracing, but after a few steps he stopped, hesitated, stepped back, clutched at Borden for a frightened moment, then ran the other way, hunched over like a scared rabbit.

When Borden heard the warning snap and looked up and perceived their peril, he seemed scarcely moved. He leaned over the rail to shout a quick, shrill "Heads up!" to the men in the hole below, then turned and watched the huge metal pan swaying toward him, the broken chain dangling and yanking, large and small stones and fragments spewing down with each lurch of the skip. He watched it for a long moment, gauging its speed and swing; then, when it was almost above him, he coolly sidestepped the descending slither of muck and bowlders. The skip had no more than passed him when he recovered the blueprint from where Dickson had dropped it and waited, undisturbed, for the latter to return and resume their work.

Fenner and Bryce watched the enactment of the near-tragedy with bated breaths. "Phew! Close call!" Bryce exclaimed when the danger was over.

Fenner did not reply at once. With his fingers he tapped the handrail upon which they leaned, drumming out a gentle tattoo. He watched the two men below with thoughtful interest.

Bryce, puzzled at his absorption, hesitated before speaking again.

"Dickson sort of lost his head, didn't he?" he ventured presently.

"Quite," Fenner agreed; "but not the other fellow. He didn't worry much at all."

"No. I guess he's around this kind of work so much that he gets used to it."

"Thoughtful of him to warn the men down in the bottom, wasn't it?"

They looked into the lot a short time more. Then Fenner suddenly straightened up, clapped his companion on the shoulder and exclaimed: "I'm going to be off. Where can I call you this evening?"

Bryce gave him a telephone number and added a little enviously: "You're a lucky devil! I wish I could shed my cares the way you do."

"I don't always shed them—that's one of my troubles. They go right along with me. But I am getting better at it," Fenner added hopefully. His tone became serious. "I hope you have some word on Mr. Morton, but I'll be surprised if you do. On the other hand, I'll be a hell of a lot more surprised if he doesn't show back Monday. I have an idea for bringing things to a head that we'll go over Monday, after we've seen Morton or if he doesn't return. I'll telephone you tonight from the house."

They parted, Bryce heading for the station, Fenner for the country. The latter told himself ruefully that if his golf game was anything but pretty rotten on this Saturday afternoon, it would certainly be pure luck. He knew there would be no such thing as concentration.

2

The rest of Saturday passed without incident. In the evening Fenner telephoned Bryce, finally locating him, despite the hour, still at his desk at headquarters. There had been no developments of consequence. Knoeckler's daughter was still away. They had been able to discover nothing as to the identity or whereabouts of her or her companion, or that other visitor to Knoeckler's shop on that eventful Thursday evening. Hanley, the Donegans, Dickson, Borden—

all were going about their business. As Fenner had predicted, no word had come from Morton. Nor had a quiet but thorough search yet uncovered any trace of his car.

However, Fenner was not discouraged on that score. He was confident that Morton would put in his appearance in his own good time and with a plausible explanation of his absence. Fenner tried to keep an open mind as to Morton's probable guilt or innocence as far as the. Consolidated Bank theft was concerned. What he had learned of the man by diligent inquiry had convinced him that, while Morton might have had ample financial motive for attempting such a coup at this time, and while he might have been without scruples as to means or methods for accomplishing that end, yet he was not a man apt to act quickly or except upon a carefully conceived plan. Last of all, he was not a man who would plan a flight. To a man with his professional and business connections it would not be worth while. Fenner repeated to Bryce that as far as Morton was concerned he was quite content to await his return.

Sunday was equally uneventful. Fenner spent the morning again on the golf course. His game, seldom better than fair, was not much worse than usual. A little absently he trod the course, a little indifferently he played his shots, a little half-heartedly he entered into the repartee of the other members of the threesome. He drove slowly home from his club along winding back roads, avoiding the throngs of Sunday motorists.

His wife observed his preoccupation and wisely left him to his own devices. In the afternoon he lounged about the garden, now picking up a current magazine to read a few paragraphs without sensing their meaning and tossing it aside in disgust, now getting up to putter in the flower beds, now going into the kitchen to mix himself a drink. Finally he settled into a comfortable deck chair and fell into a light sleep, though Sunday afternoon siestas were decidedly not one of his habits.

When he awoke it was close to five o'clock and the sun had dropped behind the trees, leaving him in the shade and chilly. He glanced about the garden a moment, blinking; then brought his mind back to the time and the place. He felt greatly refreshed.

Suddenly he realized that the disorderly maze of questions, ideas, suspicions, which had cluttered up his mind when he dropped to sleep had magically resolved themselves into a neat series of workable hypotheses, even arranged for him in order of probability. It was true, of course, that numerous open links and unanswered questions marred the completeness and symmetry of each pattern, but Fenner had a quick gratifying conviction that time would inevitably if slowly weave in these bare spots and make the design whole.

It was also true that what Morton might reveal or do when he reappeared—or Knoeckler's daughter either, for that matter—might completely alter the complexion of everything. Fenner did not dispute with himself these possibilities, but he could not help discounting their likelihood.

He went into the house to telephone Bryce. The inspector had nothing new to report. Both the Donegans, it seemed, and Dickson and Borden and Hanley were behaving with disgusting normality. Fenner smiled at Bryce's persistent inclusion of Hanley but said nothing. There had been no word from Morton, nor from Knoeckler's daughter or her companion. Bryce made no effort to disguise his growing impatience. It seemed inconceivable, he told Fenner, that a man like Morton and a Packard sedan could both drop so completely out of sight and for three days elude such a search as he was having conducted.

"He probably isn't consciously eluding you, old man," Fenner consoled, "and that's what makes him so deuced hard to turn up. If he were really hiding you'd probably have him by now. Wait till tomorrow; I venture he'll come sidling in like a truant schoolboy."

"Maybe you're right. I hope he does. But, even so, he's going to have plenty to explain."

Agreeing to meet in the morning—not too early, Fenner stipulated—they disconnected. Now Fenner found himself able to forget the case and to turn himself to lighter occupations.

4
MONDAY
APRIL 4TH

1

ON MONDAY MORNING, the first Monday of April, in spite of himself Maxwell Fenner came downtown early. He felt rather than reasoned that some sort of a break was due; and then, of course, there was the scheduled return of Randolph Morton to be anticipated. Fenner would have staked considerable upon Mr. Morton's appearance some time during the day. At the same time he recognized the day's end as the limit of grace. If Morton had not materialized by then, Fenner would regard his calculations as upset and rebuild from a new base.

And, too, Knoeckler's daughter and her mysterious companion should be coming back this morning. From her they would probably be able to find out something of that other Thursday evening visitor to Knoeckler's shop whom they had so far not been able even to identify. Since his talk with Dr. Kellar, Fenner had been less certain about the Knoeckler affair. At first he had regarded the accident theory as absolutely untenable, but now he was not so sure. From what Kellar had told him of the old man's condition, the idea appeared well within the realms of possibility; for he'd learned that, aside from the purely physical aspects, any severe mental agitation would have been just the stimulus required to send the old gentleman off.

He was revolving these things in his mind when he reached his office, and if he believed the day would bring forth developments, his expectations were to be promptly fulfilled, for before he'd had time even to remove his hat the telephone bell jangled. It was Bryce calling to inform him that Miss Elsa Knoeckler was en route to Police Headquarters. Without waiting for details Fenner hastened out.

At the station he found the inspector alone at his desk. Upon receiving the news of her father's death from Bryce, the girl had fainted. She had revived shortly and was in the care of a matron. Bryce had refrained from questioning her pending Fenner's arrival. Together they went into the small anteroom where she was detained. They found the girl sobbing quietly.

"You've had a most distressing shock, Miss Knoeckler," Bryce opened in, for him, a kindly tone. For once the cigar was not in evidence. "It's our painful duty to ask you a few questions, but we'll be as brief as we can and get it over for you as quickly as possible."

The girl looked up, choked her sobs, and nodded miserably. Fenner drew his chair closer but said nothing.

"First off; when did you see your father last?" Bryce began.

Elsa took a moment to collect her thoughts. "It was last Thursday late in the morning." She stopped and waited.

"Tell us more about it."

"I'd not been feeling well and came home from the office. Father was in the back of the shop working. I only said a few words and went upstairs. I worked a little while, dusting and straightening things up. I'd decided to go away for a few days with a friend, so I went out to get in some groceries and things. Father once in a while got himself—got his own meals if he was alone and didn't feel like going out. When I got back Father wasn't there. I guess he was out for his lunch, because the shop was locked. I had a date and was in a hurry, so I only stayed to change my clothes and then went uptown." Again she stopped.

"Go ahead," Fenner put in gently.

"That's all. I didn't see him at all after that. I was only home again for a few minutes around dinner time—long enough to throw a few clothes in a bag. Father hadn't come back yet when I had to go, so I left a note for him. I went away and came back this morning."

"Do you have any idea where your father could have been at that time?"

"I guess he was at dinner. It was around his meal time."

"I see." Bryce paused, looking to Fenner.

Both were impressed by the girl's sober frankness as she outlined these facts. However, when Bryce began to question her about
herself, Elsa became a more reluctant witness. It was necessary
almost to drag the bare facts from her. She had lived alone with
her father all her life. They had few acquaintances or friends. She
and her father had disagreed mildly about some of them. At present
she was in the employ of Marten, Morton & Purcell, a firm of engineers—"

At the mention of Morton's name Fenner instantly perceived
the whole situation. "Where is Mr. Morton now?" he quickly asked.

"At the office," she innocently answered.

"You're sure?"

"Why, yes; I—" She flushed uncomfortably. "That is, I suppose
he is."

"When did you see him last?"

Elsa thought a long time over that, Fenner observed. She
finally stammered, "Why—why do you want to know that?"

Fenner answered with a friendly smile and in as kindly a tone
as he could muster: "My dear girl, your father is dead. Nothing
we can do now will alter that fact. But circumstances indicate that
he may not have died naturally, or even accidentally. Murder is a
serious thing. We are not particularly interested in where you have
been since Thursday; we want to spare your feelings in every way
we can. But you must understand that considerations of that sort
can not be permitted to interfere with our efforts to get to the bottom of the thing. There are one or two more questions I must ask
you now; we can talk things over at greater length when you've
had a chance to rest and compose yourself."

Elsa started weeping anew but soon dried her tears and awaited
his further questions.

"When you went to your home Thursday evening for your things
was the door locked?"

"No; it was unlocked. Father only goes a few steps around the
corner and sometimes leaves it unlocked."

"When you went out did you lock it?"

"I don't remember. I don't suppose so. I was in a hurry and thought Father would be right back."

"Oh. Now one other thing. When you came downstairs after packing, you found your friend—Mr. Morton—in the store. Is that right?"

"Yes."

"Did you expect to find him there?"

Elsa hesitated. "Not exactly," she admitted. "I came in the store alone."

"Why do you suppose he decided to follow you in?"

Elsa scarce found her voice to reply: "He wanted to see my father—about me. He wanted to talk to him. He thought perhaps Father'd come back before we left."

"But he didn't?"

"No." Again Elsa broke into tears.

"What was Mr. Morton doing when you came downstairs?"

"He was just standing there—by the desk; just standing there; that's all."

At this point an officer interrupted them with word that Mr. Hanley was on the telephone. Bryce took the call and Hanley very excitedly informed him that Randolph Morton had returned and was on his way to the bank. The inspector grunted an acknowledgment and promised to be on hand. He motioned Fenner a few steps to one side and told him of Hanley's message. "Miss Knoeckler can stay here and we'll finish our talk when we get back."

"By all means."

So Elsa was left to the tender mercies of a police matron while Fenner and the inspector hied themselves to the Consolidated Bank to participate in the reception of Randolph Morton.

2

On that same Monday morning a very unhappy Mr. Stephen Coles, slightly to his surprise and considerably to his annoyance, found that it was necessary for him to unlock the offices of Marten,

Morton & Purcell. Usually Miss Knoeckler arrived ahead of him—
sufficiently ahead of him to have the place unlocked and aired out
by the time he got there. Not so, however, this morning.

Coles tried bravely to pretend to himself that the annoyance
arose from the necessity for fingering through his keys to unlock
the office door, and for raising four shades and opening four windows. This harmless deception occupied his mind but fooled him
not at all. The real source of his trouble—it was rapidly becoming
too acute to be termed merely annoyance—or rather, the source of
the particular accession of it on this Monday morning, was that
Miss Knoeckler's casual tardiness afforded the last tiny increment
to a ghastly, torturing suspicion which had been forming in his
mind since last Thursday forenoon. Elsa and old Morton! The idea,
when he permitted himself actually to formulate it, drove him almost mad; and the recurring waves of increasing, jealous suspicion had intermittently flooded his mind for the past three days.

During saner moments between times, he rejected his suspicions angrily. During one or two rare moments of exceptional
lucidity, he even admitted that it was none of his business. But the
rational moments were all too few and brief. That Elsa had from
the beginning firmly rejected his own attentions, Coles could not
deny; it had been a bitter and disappointing pill to assimilate. But
that she should then lavish herself on Randolph Morton, a married man old enough to be her father, was infinitely harder for Coles
to bear. That she had, Coles could not be sure, but each mounting
surge of envy left him less doubtful.

When he had opened the windows he flopped discouragedly into
his chair, buried his face in his hands, and for the first time gave
way to his despair. If only he could forget her—put her out of his
mind and heart! Then there would be emptiness but peace. But
there could be no forgetting while her distracting person worked
diagonally across a small room from him the better part of six days
each week. He would have it out with her today; then he would quit.

But perhaps he was mistaken. He laughed bitterly at the
thought. He'd been simply blind for months. A score of little inci-
dents, unnoticed at the time, returned to torture him with new

significance. Morton leaning over Elsa to amend a letter yet in her typewriter—Elsa and Morton repeatedly happening to work late the same evenings—Elsa and Morton laughing together, an alien, exclusive laughter that somehow died when Coles came into the room.

On only Thursday last he'd thought nothing of it that Morton had told Elsa to take the few days off while he was to be away. She'd not been looking well and needed a rest. At the time he'd wondered why the boss could not have told him also to take at least the Saturday off. Then the queer business at the Consolidated Bank had come up. When it developed that Morton's supposed business trip to Detroit was a blind to cover an absence of another sort, Coles had not been slow to suspect its nature. The torturing truth had been mercilessly quick to dawn upon him. Then Thursday evening he hadn't found her at home.

The ardent and repeated efforts of Mr. Hanley and a number of men who seemed suspiciously like police to locate Mr. Morton had proved an inadequate distraction to Coles' tormented soul. He had read with what interest he could muster the few accounts of the Consolidated Bank theft he found in the newspapers, but there was little real information in any of them. He hoped, maliciously, that Morton's return would be marked by a warm reception. It had not occurred to him actually to connect his employer with the theft, though on account of the disturbed state of his emotions he hadn't given that aspect much thought. He suddenly wondered if Morton had chanced upon a paper or had in any way heard of the affair, but suspected not.

Coles straightened up in his chair and made an effort to pull himself together. There was work to be done—detail, detail, detail! The detail mostly fell upon Stephen Coles, for Marten, Morton & Purcell consisted only of Randolph Morton. Marten had retired several years before and Purcell was as many years dead. Coles thought of the days when he had first been hired. There had been a staff of half a dozen draftsmen, designers and several typists. Times had changed; the bottom had fallen out of the market; all industry was in the throes of depression; in men's minds hope had been displaced by fear. Little building or construction was being planned, and the business of Marten, Morton & Purcell had dwindled to an insignificant proportion of its former volume. The office force had dwindled with it until now it consisted of Morton himself, Coles, and Elsa Knoeckler. Even the field inspectors had been let go, and Morton went out on the job, or sent Coles.

Today, Coles suddenly remembered, there would be plenty to do over at the Consolidated foundations. He'd better get caught up and ready. He stepped to the washbasin in the corner, splashed cold water over his face and wrists, slicked back his hair and instantly felt better. One way to forget Elsa was to keep thoroughly busy.

He had barely finished slitting open the mail and putting Morton's jumbled desk in order when that gentleman walked in fully a half hour ahead of his customary time. He gave Coles a cheery "Good morning!" and crossed over to his desk, leaning over it without sitting down and shuffling rapidly through the small pile of papers. "Anything new?" he asked absently.

"Nothing, sir, except that Mr. Hanley is anxious to get in touch with you. He's phoned a half dozen times since you left Thursday." Coles watched for his employer's reaction but was disappointed; Morton did not even look up.

"What's he want?"

"He hasn't said, though I'm pretty sure I know what it is." Coles volunteered the last with an air of hesitancy.

"Yes? What's that?"

Instead of replying Coles handed Morton a newspaper with an article circled in red. "I was afraid you might not run across this so I saved it."

Morton read the article through carefully and then glanced up at the date of the paper. Coles could see a slow flush creep up the back of his neck.

"Well, I'm damned!" he exclaimed in a moment.

"There have been several other men to see you, but none would leave any names or messages. I presume they were here in connection with the same business."

"Get Hanley on the phone for me, will you," Morton ordered abruptly.

The bank manager, it developed, had not yet arrived. Coles left word for him to call Mr. Morton. Morton peeled off his gloves and sat down at his desk. He attacked the pile of papers, penciling notes on the margins of some and placing them to one side, crunching others into small wads which he tossed into the waste basket. He had almost reached the bottom when the telephone rang. Morton took the call himself and heard Hanley at the other end of the wire.

"I understand you're looking for me?"

Hanley started a reply which would have been a cross between an explanation and an apology but Morton cut him short.

"I know. Coles showed me a clipping. I'm sorry I didn't happen to see it sooner; I'd have certainly gotten in touch with you. I'll run over now, anyway."

He clapped on his hat and hurried out without so much as a word to Coles. The assistant concealed a smile until Morton had left the office, when he broke into a broad grin. But in a moment the grin gave way to perplexity, then to quick rage, for it occurred to Coles that Morton had not commented at all on the absence of Elsa Knoeckler, apparently had not expected her. For the first time in a hitherto simple and orderly life Stephen Coles knew the meaning of cold, deadly, growing hate!

3

When Morton was ushered into Hanley's office he found, in addition to the bank manager, Inspector Bryce and Maxwell Fenner. He acknowledged Hanley's introduction of the two with cold civility. Hanley opened the interview by reciting briefly the details of the discovery of the vault shortage immediately after the inspection trip of the previous Thursday. Morton listened attentively. Hanley concluded by asking, somewhat awkwardly, if Morton could tell them anything that would shed any light on the matter.

Morton perceptibly bristled. "You're not by any chance accusing me of being connected with your shortage?" he demanded indignantly. "Why, I never heard of such—"

Fenner broke in placatingly: "Not at all, Mr. Morton; not at all. But upon reflection I think you can see for yourself that under the circumstances we are justified in questioning the members of that inspection party. However, we don't pretend to stand upon any of our particular rights in this matter. We're simply trying to get, in as much detail as we can, exactly what happened in the vault on Thursday morning. There were five men in the vault—including Mr. Hanley and the custodian, Donegan. Of the five, each might have observed some little detail that escaped the notice of the others. Some little detail you may have observed might prove very helpful taken in connection with everything else." He hesitated. "I'm sorry we weren't able to go over this with you earlier while the thing was fresh in your memory." Fenner watched Morton's face closely as he made the last remark.

Morton looked away a moment, then said more agreeably: "I'll tell you everything I can. I don't know how much it'll help you. We went to the vault—that is, Hanley and Dickson and young Borden and myself—some time around half past ten, it must have been. We tried the door a couple of times and looked at a few cracks in the wall and talked, mostly talked. Oh, yes, and Borden took some level shots on the floor in the four corners. We found the vault structure had tipped back bodily and discussed shoring it up. That's about all I remember." He shrugged his shoulders and looked at them as if to say: "I don't see how it will help you much."

"Do you remember a hand truck full of money being in the vault at the time?" Fenner asked.

Morton thought for a moment. "Yes; there was one—that is, a truck full of little sacks and bundles. I suppose it was money."

"Do you recall the position of the truck in the vault?"

"I can't say that I do. I just remember seeing it there. I believe we moved it or something."

"That's right; you did."

"Not me. I didn't touch it." Morton was emphatic.

"Do you remember who did?"

"I'm not sure. It seems to me the guard moved it—or maybe it was Borden when he set up his level."

"You see, your memory's better than you realized. Your recollection agrees in almost every particular with the stories of the others the same day it happened."

Morton looked somewhat relieved and considerably less ruffled.

"Do you remember what time you left the bank?" Fenner pursued the inquiry.

"About noon, I think."

"Where did you go from there?"

"I went— Look here! What has that got to do with your shortage? I'll tell you this: I was tending strictly to my own business." Again Morton was becoming indignant.

"I'll tell you where you went," Bryce broke in, chewing his unlit cigar savagely. "You went to the Mercantile Bank and visited your safe deposit box, and from there you—"

"Wait a minute," Fenner stopped Bryce soothingly and turned to Morton. "We want to be fair with you, Mr. Morton. There are a lot of angles to this affair of which you're not yet aware. I think you have unwittingly placed yourself in a very unfortunate position. Now I am going to tell you one or two things frankly, and in return I expect complete candor from you. Nothing you say need pass the four walls of this room. Indeed, as far as that's concerned, I think Mr. Hanley would excuse us."

Hanley had been sitting by observing with growing astonishment and no little curiosity the turn which the inquiry was taking. With ill-concealed reluctance he got to his feet. "Why, if you gentlemen think you'll be able to talk more freely without me I'll certainly be glad to withdraw."

It was Morton's turn to interrupt. "Not so fast," he said quickly. "What is all this about, anyway? Sit down, Hanley. I've known you quite a while; I don't know either of these other chaps from Adam. Now, Mr. Fenner, go on with what you were saying."

Fenner looked at Bryce, then replied: "Well, the first thing is that I talked to your er—secretary a little while ago." He stopped and waited.

Morton was silent for a long moment. He looked at the faces of his interrogators, then away out of the window. They waited for him to speak and saw his face slowly tauten. Presently his clenched fist came down on the table, startling them.

"So that's the way it is," he muttered. "All right; I'll tell you this: I've done nothing of which I'm ashamed." His tone was low but it was even and carried conviction. "If you've talked to her, though, I don't see why it's necessary to question me; and, furthermore, I don't see what it's got to do with—"

"Possibly nothing at all, but before we get through you will quite well understand the reasons for this interrogation," Fenner assured him. "Now will you be good enough to go ahead from where you left off? You needn't mention any names."

Morton hesitated and looked toward Hanley. Obviously he regretted his impulse of the moment before. However, he shrugged his shoulders and began to talk: "As you remarked"—there was the faintest suspicion of sarcasm in his nod toward Bryce—"I went to the Mercantile Bank where I visited my box and deposited some stock certificates I had recently acquired." He reached into his pocket for a keyring from which he detached a key and placed it on Hanley's desk. "You're welcome to examine the box all you please. I also cashed a sizable check as my pocket money was running low and I had reason to believe I might need some over the week-end.

"From the bank I went to the Grand Central Station where I had an engagement. I met a very dear friend of mine there and have been in her company ever since. Now, there you have it. Surely there isn't anything more you can want to know." He smiled a little wanly.

"I'm sorry, but there is," Fenner replied. "What did you do after you left the Grand Central Terminal?"

"We had lunch—my friend and I—at the Biltmore. We made some plans and I left her there to wait for me while I went to a garage in East 44th Street for my car. I called back for her and we drove up into the country—up Westchester way— for most of the afternoon. We came back in time for an early dinner. Then we went to my friend's home—she needed some clothing and things. After that we drove out to a small summer cabin in Jersey—on a little lake near Morristown. We drove back to town this morning," Morton finished simply.

"When you stopped for your friend's things on Thursday, did you go inside or did you wait in your car?" Fenner asked thoughtfully.

Morton hesitated, apparently puzzled at the nature of the question. "Well, I was going to wait outside. We had decided it would be better not to meet anybody there. But after Miss—that is, after my friend had gone in, I began to think things over and concluded it would be as well to go on in and perhaps get a lot of unpleasant arranging over with—clean slate to begin with, you know—so I went inside. I stood around in the store—that is, downstairs—until my friend came down with her bag. I carried it out to the car and we left."

"Did you see anyone while you were waiting downstairs?" Fenner asked.

"No; not a soul."

"Now, think carefully, did you leave the front door unlocked when you left?"

"I'm afraid I can't answer that. We just went out and let the door slam. I don't know whether it was locked or not. But what the devil has this got to do with—?"

"I'll tell you what," Fenner cut him off quickly. "Mr. Adolph Knoeckler was killed in his store, accidentally or otherwise, late Thursday afternoon or early Thursday evening." Fenner watched the engineer as he hurled this information at him. The latter started up, then sank into his chair, his face ashen; he could not find his voice. The man was either genuinely surprised, Fenner decided, or an unconscionably clever actor. Fenner turned in time to see that Hanley, whose countenance to now had been a picture of bewilderment, was also watching Morton intently.

When Morton found his voice he gasped: "Poor Elsa! This is terrible!" The thought evidently set his faculties working again, for he asked quickly: "Where is she? What have you done with her?"

"She's all right," Fenner assured him. "All things considered, she's bearing up remarkably well. She's being temporarily detained at the station house, but you need not be concerned about her. She's in excellent hands."

"I must see her! I must see her at once!" Morton started to rise. "Tell me more about it, please, and then you'll have to excuse me."

"There isn't much to tell," Fenner answered. "Mr. Knoeckler was found early Friday afternoon stretched out at the foot of the cellar steps, dead of a fractured skull. The coroner puts the time of his death at between five and nine o'clock Thursday evening. He believes that the injury could have been caused by a fall from the first floor, but he hasn't yet officially reported. We have also ascertained from Knoeckler's physician that his health was in a precarious state and that he was likely at any time to suffer a stroke that might carry him off or leave him paralyzed. Mr. Knoeckler's death may be purely accidental; I hope it was. But there have been just enough odd little inexplicable factors to arouse suspicion. That's about all I can tell you now."

Morton got up to leave. "Well, what's the next step?"

"I believe the coroner will report an accidental death," Fenner answered, "but if he decides that circumstances warrant it he will turn over what facts he has to the District Attorney's Office. That will mean further investigation, possibly more difficult to 'gag.' That's what I meant before when I said you had put yourself into an unfortunate position. Perhaps I am prematurely alarming you; it may come to nothing. For your sake and Miss Knoeckler's, I hope so." Fenner, too, got up, indicating that so far as he was concerned the interview was over.

Bryce sat silent. All the questions he had entertained concerning Morton had been summarily disposed of. Most disarming had been the casual offer of his deposit box key by Morton. However, the inspector had so confidently built in his mind upon the apparent mass of facts pointing toward Morton that he was reluctant to see his case crumble. He clutched at one last straw. "Would you mind telling me," he asked, "where the briefcase now is which you carried on Thursday?"

Morton answered readily enough: "It's in the back of my car, or was an hour ago, in a parking space under the Elevated station at Hanover Square. I intended taking it back to the office this morning but forgot to." He turned wearily to Fenner. "Now, if you don't mind, I should like to be taken to Miss Knoeckler. She must be frightfully upset."

Bryce stepped to the door and called in a man who had been stationed outside. "Show Mr. Morton to the station. I'll call the captain while you're going over," he explained to Morton.

He closed the door after them and returned to the desk where Fenner and Hanley were still seated. The latter seemed frankly dejected but Fenner appeared composed and not unsatisfied.

"We're just about back where we started from, it seems to me," the manager complained.

"Not quite so bad as that," Fenner denied. "The facts are filling in. Now the next step is to arrest young Donegan."

Both Hanley and Bryce showed their surprise.

"But you haven't a ghost of a case against him," the former protested.

"That's all the more reason why it'll do him no permanent harm, and I believe it will stir things up a little. At least, we can try it."

"O.K. with me." Bryce with his own pet theory just demolished was in no frame of mind for questioning his colleague.

Hanley was not so easily convinced. "It's sort of rough on the boy, isn't it?" he argued.

"Rough for a few days, perhaps, but if he's publicly cleared in the end there'll be no permanent damage; and it may make all the difference between clearing this up in a week and taking six months, or even a year."

"I suppose you know what you're about," Hanley conceded, "though I don't mind admitting I'd like to see the thing avoided. When do you want to tend to it?"

"Not me; you and Bryce—right now," Fenner replied, grinning. He instantly sobered. "You must be sure to make it seem genuine. I can see right now"—he was addressing Hanley—"your inclination will be to drop him a hint that the arrest is with an ulterior motive and in that way to spare his feelings. You must be very careful to do nothing of the sort." Fenner was very emphatic on the point.

Hanley and Bryce exchanged glances.

"The sooner, the better," Fenner hinted.

Hanley looked sheepish, Bryce grim, as they left upon their unpleasant errand.

Fenner settled into an easy chair in Hanley's office, lit a cigarette and allowed his gaze to wander idly out of the window. His mind kept harking back to Elsa Knoeckler. She was a comely creature, he reflected, somewhat inarticulate but a restful person and fascinating in an indefinable way. He pitied Elsa; for Morton he felt a dim envy.

His thoughts traveled back to his talk with her that morning. Morton had let her out of his car a half block from the shop at the corner and she had walked from there home, he had learned. The poor girl must have been frightened and surprised when she entered the store and found the plainclothes officer lounging against the counter instead of her father. She had been brought to the station house where Bryce and a matron had informed her of her father's death. The news had certainly completely overcome her. Fenner was glad he had been able to get over to headquarters before she was questioned. First impressions were always important.

As a matter of fact Elsa had been able to add very little to what they already knew, except, of course, the fact of her relations with Morton. Her father, she was sure, had had no enemies. He had had few friends, either, or acquaintances of any kind. He had been a poor man barely able to eke a meager subsistence out of his dwindling business. She could think of no reason why anyone should wish him harm.

Fenner mulled over the details of their conversation as he could remember them. The girl had certainly done her best to give Morton a clean bill of health. He wondered if Morton appreciated her loyalty. According to Elsa, Morton had gone into the shop on the off chance of seeing old Knoeckler about her. According to Morton's own words he'd gone "to get a lot of unpleasant arranging over with!" Precisely what the devil did he mean by that? Odd way to put it, at best. Well, the necessity for that sort of unpleasant arranging was for good and all obviated now. Fenner wondered what, exactly, Morton's feelings for the girl amounted to. From his reception of the news of her father's death it would appear that his affection was deeply enough rooted. But you never could tell—

From pondering on Morton and Elsa, Fenner's thoughts veered round, and with no little chagrin, to an aspect of the case which had annoyed him in the few free moments he had had since learning of the relationship of Morton and Elsa Knoeckler. It was that he could have been so stupid as to have omitted asking Coles about the other employees in Morton's office. The mere mention of Miss Knoeckler's name, her address, the fact that she also had been away from Thursday on, must have inevitably put them on the right track. It would have saved Bryce a great deal of mental strain, Fenner thought, smiling, if he had been aware earlier of the real motive for Morton's absence. Fenner's musing was cut short by the return of Bryce and Hanley to the bank manager's office.

"Well?" Fenner asked.

"The dirty work's all done," Bryce informed him.

"Took it like a man, too," Hanley supplemented.

"He'll get over it," Fenner said. "Let's only hope it bears fruit quickly."

Fenner and the inspector left to return to the station house to finish their talk with Elsa Knoeckler. "Their stories tallied pretty well, didn't they?" Fenner said when they got outside.

"Morton's and the girl's, you mean? Yeah; they did."

"Too well, maybe."

"What do you mean? They didn't have any chance to compare notes," Bryce argued.

"No; except all week-end."

Bryce looked at Fenner incredulously. "You mean they agreed on a story? They knew about the old man? Impossible!"

"Oh, I agree with you; though I can't refrain from moralizing that nothing's impossible in this racket. I only wanted to be sure our reactions tallied. You're satisfied the girl was surprised this morning?"

"Yeah; sure."

"Well, I'm quite satisfied it was news to Morton when we sprung it on him a while ago. If it wasn't, the man has certainly missed his calling. He belongs on the stage."

4

Sharing the limited view from the high, barred window, Randolph Morton and Elsa Knoeckler hovered close together in the cheerless anteroom of the police station. Morton was talking to her in a low tone, earnestly, while Elsa stared vacantly out into the gray courtyard. Morton became silent and they drew quickly apart when Fenner and Bryce entered the room. The engineer greeted the two coldly and waited for them to open any conversation.

"We should like to ask Miss Knoeckler a few more questions about her father, if you will be good enough to excuse us," Fenner said to Morton.

"Certainly—of course." Morton drew out his watch and added: "I've got to be getting back to my office anyway." He looked at Elsa. "You will come over?" It was more a suggestion than a question.

Elsa nodded without speaking and Morton left. Fenner knew not what Morton had told Elsa but he decided that, whatever it was, it had certainly produced a remarkable change in her. She was serious—sad, still—but not in the forlorn abandoned way in which he had found her earlier in the day. When he talked with her he found her quite composed. He drew up a chair for her and another for himself and sat down with his back to the window. Bryce, too, sat down, but somewhat in the background.

"I'm glad to see you feeling better. You've had a terrible shock," he opened sympathetically. "I regret disturbing you with questions at a time like this, but we're compelled to do our utmost to get to the root of these matters. Tell me, did your father have any money over and above the returns from his business there?"

"Not that I know of. He was pretty hard up—especially the last year or so. I helped him with the rent and food as much as I could."

"Was he ever engaged in any other ventures except the store and shop in Fulton Street?"

"No; I'm pretty sure he wasn't. You see, he didn't mix with people very much. He always preferred to stay to himself."

"Do you know the newsdealer, Schmidt?" Fenner next asked.

"Why, yes; I know him. Not well, though; not nearly so well as Father did."

"He and your father were very friendly?"

"Oh, yes. They argued about a lot of things; oh, you know, German politics and things like that, but never seriously. Father used to eat with him when I was out."

"What do you know of your father's health?"

"It hadn't been very good. He'd been complaining a lot and finally I made him go to a doctor. He had a sort of weakness in his left side. It had become a lot worse the last few months."

Fenner nodded understandingly. He thought a moment, then launched a different line of questioning. "How long have you been in the employ of Mr. Morton?"

Elsa fidgeted uncomfortably at this turn of the inquiry. "About a year; perhaps a little longer," she replied.

"Did Mr. Morton in that time ever have occasion to meet your father?"

"No."

"Did he ever meet him in a business way?"

"No. At least, I'm pretty sure he didn't."

"Did your father know of your friendship with Mr. Morton?"

"I don't believe so. Mr. Morton had never been to my home."

"Until last Thursday evening, you mean?"

"Yes."

"This morning you said Mr. Morton came into the store because he wanted to see your father about you. Is that right?"

"Yes." Elsa's eyes were cast toward the floor.

"Did he see him?"

"No; Father hadn't come back from supper when we left."

"How do you know?"

Elsa looked up sharply at the last question. She caught her breath when she realized its implications but refused to recognize them and answered evenly: "Mr. Morton or I would have seen him."

"When you came down with your bag Mr. Morton was standing by the desk, you told me this morning?"

Elsa nodded.

"According to old Schmidt," Fenner went on, "Mr. Morton was in the store ten or fifteen minutes before you both came out. Could your father not have come in during the time you were upstairs packing, without your hearing him?"

"No; he couldn't have."

Fenner started to speak but Elsa broke out wearily: "Oh, I see what you're driving at! I don't know how you can think such a thing."

"We have to think of everything."

"I tell you," Elsa gasped, "I never saw my father after Thursday morning; and Ran— Mr. Morton never saw him at all." The girl started weeping quietly, twisting and untwisting her handkerchief, biting her lips, and controlling herself as best she could.

Fenner waited a moment, then said: "Now, just one more matter; then you may leave. The fellow, Schmidt, tells us that only a short time before you stopped for your things on Thursday evening a man loitered about and finally went into the store. He describes him as a fairly young man and says he has a faint recollection of having seen him there before. Can you tell me who that's most likely to have been?"

Elsa raised her head wearily, stared vacantly about while she racked her brain. Finally she said: "I can't think of anyone. You see, my friends never came to the store. Father didn't like me to go out with men."

Though its content disappointed Fenner, the simplicity of the reply touched his heart. The few words and their tone spoke volumes and gave him a complete and vivid picture of a lonely girl, growing into starved womanhood, denied the normal friendships and companionships of youth, living her whole life under the roof that had sheltered her birth and, withal, homeless!

He looked away, then turned back. "Think carefully. Didn't you know any of your father's friends?"

Elsa waited a long moment. "No; I'm afraid not. He did business with a lot of youngish men, though—selling them instruments and making repairs. You could look at his books and get a lot of names."

"We thought of that but hoped you might save us the necessity." After a moment Fenner got to his feet and Bryce did likewise.

"You're at liberty to go where you please," he said gently to Elsa—looking at Bryce for confirmation—"but I think it would be best if you kept Inspector Bryce posted as to your whereabouts. We shall soon have the coroner's report—perhaps yet today. If I can then be of any help in connection with the funeral arrangements or anything of that sort I shall certainly be at your service."

Elsa thanked him and told them that she would go home first and then to Morton's office. She went out.

It was noon. Fenner said to Bryce: "Come on— I'll buy you a lunch. We can talk."

"O.K., but let's see Dr. Pollard on our way out. Maybe he'll have something new for us." They stopped at the coroner's office. They did not expect much, so were not disappointed. He had completed his work, but the only thing he could tell them which they did not already know was that Adolph had eaten nothing after the noon of the day of his death.

5

At lunch they went over the morning's yield. Fenner was optimistic.

"Things seem to be opening up a little," he said.

Bryce was not so sure. "They may be, but I'm damned if I can see any light yet." He had attached a great deal of importance to Morton's abnormal conduct and suspicious disappearance, and when that gentleman reappeared according to schedule and disarmed these suspicions with a plausible account of his actions, and with decidedly human if not strictly moral motives, Bryce was confronted with the necessity of starting all over again from scratch.

Similarly, he had pinned considerable hope on what Knoeckler's daughter and her companion could reveal when they were apprehended, and now it appeared that they could reveal nothing whatever.

"It looks as if Knoeckler didn't go out to supper after all," Fenner continued, ignoring Bryce's last remark; "or at least if he did, he didn't eat anything."

Bryce halted, a forkful of food poised halfway to his mouth. "You mean he was dead before Morton and the girl got there?"

"Not necessarily, but he was a man of regular habits. I think Miss Knoeckler counted on that when she went for her things at the time she did. It is not likely he would have delayed his supper much past his usual hour. It's not likely, either, that he could have gone out and come back without Schmidt seeing him, even though Schmidt says he was not out in front of his stationery shop continuously. The probability, then, is that he didn't go out at all."

"I suppose there's no question about Schmidt, eh?" Bryce suggested.

"There's no reason for doubting him. We've found nothing to connect him with the affair at all."

"Except that he found the body and seems to know so confounded much about what went on Thursday evening. Sometimes when a bird sees too much and knows too much it's not accidental." Bryce was born a skeptic.

"It isn't impossible; but somehow Schmidt doesn't fit into the picture. He'd no motive, in the first place; and would probably have let someone else discover Knoeckler and call the police if he had been himself involved."

"Maybe so," Bryce admitted.

"The last we really know of Knoeckler is that Borden left him in the shop a little after five," Fenner went on. "He had a caller; or at least Schmidt saw someone, whom he vaguely recalls having seen there before, go into the store a little before seven. A little after seven Morton and Elsa Knoeckler were there for a quarter of an hour and say they saw nothing of him. That's the layout. What happened between five and seven and who was the caller? That may be the key. I'd hoped the girl could help us there, but now I'm afraid not. We'll have to go through his desk and see if we can pick up a few leads. We'd better get after Schmidt again, too." He paused ruminatively.

"Here's another thing," Bryce cut in. "How do you suppose a fellow like Morton could've gone from Thursday noon to Monday morning without seeing a newspaper? Seems damned odd to me!"

Fenner shrugged his shoulders. "I think he could have, all right. His mind hasn't been bothered with current events the past few

days. But all the same, Morton's in a spot any way you look at it—
perhaps not a dangerous one, but with possibilities for enormous
embarrassment. Suppose Dr. Pollard turned in a report which cast
any doubt on Knoeckler's tumble and then we told what we know
of Thursday evening. I believe the district attorney would hold the
pair, or at least Morton, on suspicion. Adolph Knoeckler could have
come in while Morton was waiting downstairs. He'd probably be
pretty mad at a man who was endeavoring to take his daughter
away; especially a married man in Morton's circumstances. He
wasn't dumb, and it wouldn't be surprising if he was more aware
of what was in the wind than Miss Knoeckler thought. They might
have had an argument that led to blows. If Morton had killed him,
even accidentally, he'd have had time to carry him to the foot of
the stairs. He might have simply opened the door and shoved him
through. The cellar light was off; remember that.

"It could all have happened without the girl having heard anything
if her bedroom door had been shut. I don't say it did; it's just a physical possibility. I wager the district attorney would figure it enough
to hold them on. A good stiff grilling might bring out something,
too, that we don't know, though I'm not very sanguine about that."

Bryce shook his head. "I wouldn't be, either. I'd swear that girl
doesn't know anything. She was genuinely surprised this morning
and nothing'll make me believe she wasn't; and if Morton had anything to do with it, it's a cinch she doesn't suspect it."

"If Morton had anything to do with it," Fenner rejoined, "he's
such a consummately clever actor that Miss Knoeckler might not
suspect it, and that in spite of having spent the intervening time
with him." He fell to thinking.

Bryce broke into his speculations. "We mustn't forget that
maybe Knoeckler did have a stroke and fall down on his head. In
fact, I'd be willing to concede that and forget that angle of the business if somebody would give me a new track on the bank robbery."

"A new track! We've got plenty of tracks now, only they don't
lead anywhere. If only they'd round some curves or do something
interesting! Which reminds me— How about all of our clients?
Anything develop the last twenty-four hours?"

"Nothing much. Hanley gave us the run around for a while last night, but I guess he didn't mean anything. I meant to tell you earlier this morning, but this Knoeckler business drove it out of my head. Hanley started out about six-thirty last evening in his car, chauffeur driving, of course. They went through the Holland Tunnel and later turned off down the Belleville Turnpike. They were looping right along, and, with the homeward bound Sunday traffic to contend with, the boys had quite a job keeping them in sight, but they managed all right until they got a bad break at the Passaic River draw. The bridge opened between them, and that ended it. They picked him up at this end of the tunnel coming back about eleven-thirty, and he went straight home. You can pump Hanley about it when you see him this afternoon."

Fenner had listened attentively. "Six-thirty to eleven-thirty. Five hours' running time. They could cover quite a little ground in that time. Well, we'll see. Anything more? Anything on the others?"

"Not a blessed thing!" Bryce reached into his pocket for the little book but Fenner stopped him.

"Never mind. I'll take your word for it. I suppose now you've started a page for Randolph Morton, too?"

Bryce admitted he had.

"And Elsa Knoeckler?"

"Yeah; sure."

Fenner smiled. "I should think one page would pretty well do for the two of them."

"I suppose they'll be sticking pretty close, at that." The inspector grumbled on, "We seem to be tied up again waiting for something else to break. Young Donegan's pinched and we haven't got a shadow of a case against him and don't even really suspect him. Progress! What!" His own summation seemed to make Bryce more disgusted and dejected than he had been before.

Fenner was exasperatingly cheerful. "We're just temporarily delayed, that's all. We have to be content with waiting. We're all set up with our fingers on all the strings. The other fellow is bound to make a break. I've seen a lot of cases where everything seemed at an impasse, and just when they seemed quietest something popped and it was all over but the shouting."

Bryce smiled doubtfully, a little encouraged by Fenner's optimism but far from convinced. "I only hope you're right."

6

When Fenner got to the bank he found that Hanley was engaged in a meeting that might last for some time. He settled into an easy chair in the manager's office, welcoming the opportunity for undisturbed reflection. The rattle and clank of derricks, the chugging of dirt trucks across the street, the whir of electric hoists, all mingled with the screeching of brakes, taxi sirens, police whistles, and the other street noises of downtown New York, combined to form a subdued, throbbing roar that attacked his mind the moment he started to relax.

Spring was in the air; Fenner had lunched heartily; he felt an increasing lassitude but he forced his problem before his mind, examining it, revolving it, ever probing. The cacophonous din floating up through the open windows seemed to fall away; Fenner's drowsiness gradually fled. From the pigeonholes of his brain he drew forth the characters of his play, ticking off on his finger tips the salient facts he'd learned about each of them. Jeremy, Young Jerry, Dickson, Borden, Morton—all paraded across the stage of his consciousness, even Hanley and Elsa Knoeckler bringing up the rear.

He reviewed the scenes as he had learned of them from others, as he had seen them with his own eyes: The party examining the vault, talking, measuring, swarming about its tiny confines and around a hand truck laden with a dozen fortunes. The discovery of the theft, father and son eying each other askance, awaiting the arrival of the law to wreak punishment upon whom they knew not, or feared to suspect. The inquisitions of Jerry, the old man, Borden, Dickson, and then today of Morton and Elsa Knoeckler. In his mind's eye he saw Morton and Elsa driving into the Jersey countryside in the cool of the evening while old Adolph sprawled lifeless in the inky cellar, his bald skull flattened against the concrete, a clammy, ghastly center to a slowly widening dark pool. He saw old Schmidt seated before his store watching with unrealizing eyes the disjointed steps of a drama enacted before him. He saw Dickson, haunted by margin clerks, fleeing swinging stone skips; Borden, laughing, calling old Knoeckler a robber; Hanley, disheveled, sleepless on Friday morning and neat and businesslike today. He saw Morton, indignant, clapping a deposit box key on Hanley's desk, Morton defiant, a slow flush creeping over him at the expose of his affair with Elsa.

Carefully, thoughtfully, Fenner assembled the various components—assorting, rearranging, shifting, sifting, searching for the thread of purpose which must pervade the whole; and, as he pondered, his brain clarified. Illogicalities stood out; he lopped them off. Then in an illuminated moment he suddenly found one answer—a possible answer. He tested it from various angles and found it at least within the limits of physical possibility. Details hitherto meaningless assumed a new significance. But there were gaps and loopholes galore. Still—it was simply up to him to fill them in, to order subsequent events that would fill them in. He rose from the chair and for a moment paced the room in suppressed excitement, then crossed to the window and stood looking into the excavation below. Hanley found him thus, absorbed in thought, when he returned to his office about midafternoon.

"Anything new?" the bank manager asked.

"Not especially, but we're getting along," Fenner replied cautiously. "How is your vault standing up—the one that started all this trouble?"

"All right, I guess. Jeremy says the door works about the same, and there are no new cracks. The bulk of the blasting will be finished today so I guess we won't have to worry about any more settlement."

"Is that so? Good! That fits in with an idea of mine better than I could have hoped. I'll tell you what I'd like to do, Hanley, or rather, to have you do. I'd like to have you call up Morton and Dickson and tell them that, inasmuch as the blasting is about done, you'd like to have them come over and make another examination of the vault to see if it has gotten any worse or settled any more since last Thursday. Get the same crowd in here as before, at the same time in the morning. Can you do that?"

"Oh, I see; the old game of reenacting the crime, eh?" Hanley smiled.

"Not exactly, but somewhat along those lines. There are some things puzzling me that I might get a line on in that way."

"But there won't be any startling *dénouements?*"

"I'd like to be able to promise something like that but I'm afraid I can't. In fact, I can guarantee against it."

"They'll all be disappointed," Hanley chided.

Fenner ignored the vein of levity. "Another thing I want you to do is to let them know about young Donegan. Don't make a point of it, of course, but just casually mention that you believe the theft has been solved, or something of the sort. You can say we've found enough evidence to satisfy us as to his guilt but haven't assembled our case yet. Be sure to tell them he's under arrest, though."

"All right; I'll see what I can do," Hanley agreed cheerfully. He telephoned Morton and asked him to come to the bank in the morning, explaining that he thought it advisable to have the vault looked over again. Morton fell in with the plan, not only agreeing that it would be well to examine the vault but suggesting also that it would now be apropos to discuss ways and means of restoring it to its original level. Hanley had some difficulty in locating Dickson but when he did and extended the same invitation, Dickson, too, thought the idea a good one and promised to be on hand with Borden the next morning.

Observing that the arrangements were completed, Fenner got up, well satisfied with what he hoped would turn out to be the beginning of the end. He was about to leave when, after a gentle tap, the door was pushed open and Jeremy Donegan stepped in.

The old man was still in his uniform, though it was late enough for him to have changed to his street clothing. He looked at Hanley bitterly, unable to keep tears back from his eyes.

"I understand ye've arrested the boy, Mr. Hanley," he choked, and at the manager's mute nod went on: "You're all wrong. God knows how wrong you are! I'll swear my boy had nothing to do with that shortage. Why, man! Ye know it as well as I."

"I don't know anything of the sort." It was with an effort that Hanley was able to instill the coolness in his retort.

"Ye've known the boy—years. He's as honest as they make 'em. Ye've got nothing on him and arrest him just the same—like a common crook—just to arrest somebody!"

Fenner cut in: "You're at liberty to see your son. Tell him this: that when he tells me the truth about what he did during his lunch hour last Thursday, and also tells me why he lied about it in the first place, I'll be more inclined to believe whatever else he tells me."

Old Jeremy blanched as if struck an unexpected blow. Hanley, pitying him, said gently: "Jeremy, the truth will come out. If Jerry's in this, God help him! If he's not, he'll be cleared and no harm'll come of it. I'll see that he gets an even show, you know you can depend on that." He turned back to his desk.

Jeremy nodded dumbly, accepting the dismissal, and shuffled dazedly out. Fenner watched him go.

"Tougher on him than on the boy," he commented.

"Yes; Jerry has simply shut up like a clam. He's not excited and not alarmed, though his feelings are damned well hurt."

"So Bryce was telling me. Well, it'll all come out in the wash!" With this trite comment Fenner left Hanley and returned to his own office to finish his day's work.

That operation consisted of participating in three very brief, cryptically worded, telephone conversations. One was with Bryce from whom he learned that Elsa Knoeckler had been established with a spinster sister of Randolph Morton's in an apartment in the Columbus Circle section of the city, also that Jerry Donegan was so far thriving upon prison fare. The second was with a semi-agent of his own who informed him that Mr. Christopher Dickson had posted no further collateral against his brokerage loans since the deposit of certain Liberty Bonds on Thursday last. And the third was with another agent who told him, among other things, that during the course of the day Mr. T. Jerome Hanley had arranged for the deposit of $30,000 in cash to bolster his by then practically extinct margins.

The last bit of information bid fair to leave Maxwell Fenner completely flabbergasted. It set him off upon a tack he had once already abandoned. If Hanley was involved in the shortage, Fenner had once concluded, the bank manager would not have called him into the case. But perhaps Hanley was thinking one step ahead and expected Fenner to follow just that reasoning. He would then have deliberately invited him into the case. But if Hanley's mind worked in that direction, would he stop there? Would he not reason ahead another step and realize that Fenner would perceive his, Hanley's, method of figuring, and therefore not have invited him into the case? Or still another step— It could go on forever. Whether you came out right or wrong depended upon which step you stopped at. Like the old Chinese odd-and-even finger game, Fenner thought to himself with disgust, except that in China the host was bound to do his utmost to permit his guest to guess correctly. Jerome Hanley, Fenner concluded, would make anything but a proficient Chinese host.

5

TUESDAY
APRIL 5TH

1

MORTON CAME IN a few minutes ahead of the others the next morning. Hanley was busy at his desk but he stopped long enough to indicate a chair for the engineer, then excused himself and turned back to his papers. If Morton thought it unusual, there was nothing he could say, so he simply sat figuratively twirling his thumbs and gazing around the office. Soon, however, to his relief, Dickson and Borden were ushered in. Hanley glanced at his watch, shoved his work aside and got to his feet.

"I don't want to take too much of your time, gentlemen," he began. "I asked you in this morning to look over our vault again and see if it's any worse than last week. Then we'll try to decide on something in the way of fixing it up. I understand that the bulk of the blasting across the street is over now." He looked toward Dickson and Borden.

"That's right," Dickson said. "Of course there will be smaller shots for a week or two yet, while the column footings are being excavated; but they won't compare in strength or frequency with the charges required for the general rock removal."

"Would they affect anything we might try in the way of shoring up the vault?"

Dickson seemed uncertain. "It's hard to say. They might possibly, but I rather think not."

Morton broke in: "Shoring that vault is going to be a ticklish operation at best. In my opinion it would be very inadvisable to

121

monkey with it before the blasting is completely done and over with. It's true that nothing might happen, but it's also true that you might get enough additional settlement to prevent the door from operating. Then you'd be put to all sorts of trouble. Why take the chance? You're not in any particular hurry, are you?" The last was to Hanley.

"No, but we don't want to let it go too long. The door is very difficult to operate, you know—" He broke off. "Well, let's go down." He led the way out of the office but paused outside the door. "By the way, I suppose you'll be interested in hearing that we've got a line on the shortage that was troubling us last week." The remark was addressed to the group in general.

All seemed to gather closer, interested.

"You don't say! I'm glad to hear that," Dickson spoke up. "It's none of my business but I'm curious to know who was involved."

"Why, we believe Jerry Done— Well, one of our assistant cashiers is behind it. He denies everything, of course, but he's very vague in his statements and can't account for himself during the noon hour of the day it happened. He's under arrest and I think he'll come clean presently."

"Didn't take you long to dig it out," Dickson commented.

"We haven't got the cash back yet," Hanley reminded him, "so we're not congratulating ourselves for a while."

Both Morton and Borden had listened interestedly but neither made any comment. They all went downstairs to the vault. Old Jeremy was inside, seated at his small desk. His face bore a gray pallor, his eyes were sunk and listless. He appeared to have aged ten years in the four days since the men had seen him before. He looked up at them with curious apathy for a moment, then turned his face away, with only a nod for greeting. In a chair beside him sat Maxwell Fenner. He had been talking earnestly to the older man but stopped when the engineers came in.

"Oh, you're here early this morning." Hanley pretended surprise at finding Fenner there. The latter quickly got up.

"Am I in your way here?" he asked, playing up to Hanley's pretense.

"No; not at all. Sit down. We shall only be a few minutes." Fenner let himself back into the chair.

"Set up your level and try the corners again," Dickson instructed Borden curtly. He turned to Morton. "No change in the condition of the cracks that I can see." Obviously it was his intention to establish at the outset that the operations of his company across the street had caused no further damage.

Morton only mumbled an unintelligible reply, not proposing to commit himself until he had had a chance to look the situation over.

Borden spread the legs of his tripod and set it up in one of the rear corners and attached his level. Dickson opened a folding rule and held it in turn in the four corners of the vault for Borden to read. The results indicated that the vault had tipped no farther.

Fenner sat beside Jeremy's desk gazing around vacantly, idly drumming the desk top with his nails or twirling his gold-capped pocket pencil. His wandering gaze missed not the smallest detail. Morton moved around the walls.

"I can't see any difference in any of the cracks," he finally conceded to Dickson. "None of them seem to have opened up. I think we may safely assume that the settlement has stopped. Just the same I think we would do well to postpone any underpinning for another ten days."

The remark precipitated a brief discussion between Hanley and Dickson and himself as to ways and means of shoring the vault. Fenner got up and moved over to Borden.

"Quite an instrument you have there," he remarked. "How does it work?"

"Why, it's just a telescope with cross hairs in it and a spirit level attached. When you get the bubble in the middle the line of sight of the telescope is exactly level. That's all. You read a rule through it—in two corners there, say. You find one reading shorter by a half inch than the other, which means that it's a half inch higher. That's what we did the other day, and now today we find the same difference, which means the vault hasn't moved."

"Pretty delicate machine, I suppose?"

"Yes, they get out of whack easily; but not if you're reasonably careful with them. They get out of adjustment more from the knocks they get being lugged around than they do from actual use. The cases are pretty well padded, though."

The talk between Morton and Dickson and Hanley terminated abruptly. At a sign from Dickson, Borden dismantled his instrument and collapsed the tripod.

"Why, this looks like the machine you had over at Knoeckler's. It isn't the same one, is it?" Fenner suddenly asked Borden.

"No; same model, though," Borden answered. "I suppose we won't be able to get the other back for a few days. There'll be formalities, I presume?" He looked at Fenner as if he would like to ask him more but thought it unmannerly.

"Well, I shouldn't think it would be long. The coroner's verdict will be returned in a day or two. Knoeckler's physician, it seems, reported that the old chap was a victim of ailments that would make a fatal stroke a likelihood at any time."

"Poor devil! Well, he's just about as well off. I think his business had pretty nearly gone to pot. But I notice by the papers that he had a daughter. I didn't know he had any family at all. Sort of had a notion he was all alone." Borden strapped up his level box as he spoke. The others started out and Borden had to hurry after them before Fenner had a chance to reply.

When Fenner felt sure they would all have had ample time to leave the bank he came up from the vault. To his faint surprise he found Morton and Dickson still in the entrance lobby. In a rapid, even voice, scarce above a whisper, Morton was addressing his companion. The latter, apparently much exasperated but not quite beyond control, seemed continually about to break into violent protest, but Morton gave him no chance to interrupt. Catching sight of Fenner's approach, Morton stopped speaking instantly. Dickson, turning to ascertain the cause of Morton's abrupt silence, unexpectedly encountered the detective's gaze and crimsoned deeply. Neither Morton nor Dickson spoke and Fenner merely nodded and passed on up into the bank. The pair watched him out of sight but the interrupted discussion was not resumed. Instead, with a shrug of his shoulders and not a word of farewell, Dickson turned and went out into the street. Morton made his way up to Hanley's office.

"I want a little legal advice," Morton began when Hanley had admitted him. "Perhaps you or one of the bank's legal staff can give me a few pointers. As you no doubt gathered from yesterday's—er—discussion, my secretary is the late Mr. Adolph Knoeckler's daughter. His death, coming as it did, has been frightfully trying for her. I'm sort of looking out for her, and among other things I want to relieve her of all the troublesome details connected with winding up her father's affairs and settling his estate; though I'm afraid it may develop that the estate is a negative rather than a positive quantity."

He smiled a little ruefully but went on, "Now first I want to find out the proper legal steps for taking over her father's affairs or her affairs, or however you want to put it. For reasons of my own I'd rather not have my firm's attorneys handle this."

Hanley pondered a moment. "I think the proper step is to apply to the Probate Court to have yourself appointed executor of Knoeckler's estate," he answered. "I'm not sure, and I'm not familiar with the legal and technical details. I'll tell you what I'll do; I'll put you in touch with a firm of very good lawyers who will be glad to take care of the whole thing for you. They are excellent, reasonable, and—er—discreet. Don't you think that would be the best way to handle it?"

Morton did, so Hanley wrote down a name and address on the back of one of his business cards and handed it to him. Morton pocketed it and went out.

2

As Morton left Hanley's office, Fenner, entering, met him at the door. He stood aside to allow the engineer to pass. Inside he tarried only a moment. Hanley could not conceal his curiosity as to the results of the morning's experiment, but Fenner would offer him no satisfaction. Instead, he questioned the banker shortly regarding Morton's visit. When Hanley had briefly outlined Morton's request, Fenner only grunted.

From the bank he went to Police Headquarters where he closeted himself with Bryce.

"Do you suppose that Morton or Dickson or Borden have any idea they are being watched as closely as they are?" he asked the inspector.

"I don't have any notion Morton suspects anything—unless he would just naturally expect it and think nothing of it. He's given no sign he's aware of anything, but we've only been tailing him since yesterday noon, you know. I wouldn't be surprised if Dickson and Borden are wise, though. The boys say both of them are getting a little self-conscious lately. Murphy caught Dickson looking at him rather queerly yesterday."

"That's too bad. It defeats the whole object of watching them."

"I suppose so," Bryce agreed discouragedly, "but it's not an easy thing to shadow a man who suspects he's being watched without having him wise up, at least, after a short time. I could put some new men on. That's not so good, though, because these fellows have become accustomed to their habits and are quick to sense a deviation from them."

"But you think Morton is all right yet?"

"I think so; yes."

"Well, how would it be to keep right on with him as you're doing, and with Dickson and Borden you could simply switch your two pairs about?"

"I'll try that," Bryce agreed.

"Now, one other thing. Do you still have a man in Knoeckler's shop?"

"No; we took him off when the girl came back, but the place has been locked up tight since then and the man on the beat keeps an eye on it."

"Miss Knoeckler's not staying there, of course?"

"No. She took her clothes yesterday. She's staying uptown with a sister of Morton's—up near Columbus Circle."

"Oh, of course. You told me yesterday. I can't say I exactly blame her for getting out of those quarters above the shop. It must have been a cheerless enough place before, and now it would be positively gruesome."

"Me either," the inspector agreed.

"Going to stay with Morton's sister, eh? That rather puts a new light on our gay Lothario, doesn't it? Maybe he's going to 'do right by our Nell' after all."

"Maybe."

"Will you let me have the key to the shop?" Fenner requested, rising. "I'd like to poke about there a bit."

Bryce produced a key from his desk drawer. "Not quite satisfied, eh?"

Fenner did not reply but only held out his hand for the key. "I'll return it in an hour or two. Our friend, Mr. Morton, will probably be after it soon. But not this afternoon. He'll be all tied up with Knoeckler's funeral this afternoon." Fenner took the key and left Bryce, accustomed to his eccentricities, only mildly astonished but more than mildly curious.

In less than two hours, true to his promise, he was back. He tossed the key on Bryce's desk with a brief "Thanks."

Bryce dropped it back into the drawer. He shoved the drawer shut slowly, looking at Fenner the while.

"You've got something up your sleeve now. I can tell," he said. "I know you wouldn't spill it till you got ready so I won't even ask, but if you should need any help let me know. The police might come in handy. We *do* cover a lot of ground, you know." He swung his chair around as if to get back to work.

Fenner felt the mild reproach in his attitude. He said: "I've got a hunch almost strong enough to make a pinch on, but hunches aren't of much use in court. There are too many gaps in my theory to act upon it yet, and the most important missing link is the little canvas sack full of Uncle Sam's promises. It wouldn't do to be too precipitate and lose that."

"Hardly!"

"To sit tight a while—that's still our ticket; and to keep track of everybody every minute." He broke off. "Now, 'home and so to bed,' as Samuel would say. I still have great faith in the efficacy of sleeping on all of these puzzling little matters. Things are dormant now—suspiciously so. The lull before the storm, you know. Watch out!" With this cryptic if theatrical admonition the investigator took his departure, homeward bound.

Bryce was as much encouraged as puzzled. He knew from experience that this unwonted volubility betokened a discovery or development that put them many steps ahead. He knew, too, that in plenty of time he would learn what it was all about.

6
WEDNESDAY
APRIL 6TH

1

Fenner was awakened later than usual the next morning, Wednesday, by the bright sunlight streaming through the open windows. He bathed and, still sleepy, went downstairs to breakfast.

He had gone to bed with a brain full of queries; his rest had been troubled and fitful; now his waking was haunted by the same puzzling questions, gaps in his theory that required spanning. Yesterday's visit to Knoeckler's shop had been fruitful enough, but there still remained wide openings to be bridged, whys and hows that demanded their answers.

And then there was the major distraction of T. Jerome Hanley. There had not been what Fenner considered an opportune occasion to draw the bank manager out upon either the subject of Sunday evening traffic on the Belleville Turnpike, or the quaint un-American custom of covering brokerage margins with unexpected cash. It would require all his finesse, Fenner mused, but he would have to get it over with today.

At Police Headquarters he went straight to Bryce's office and reviewed the latest additions to Bryce's cumulative biographies of the principals in their case. The inspector had little to tell him but Fenner was not surprised. He settled down on the edge of Bryce's desk and lighted a cigarette.

"I switched the men about on Dickson and Borden last night," Bryce presently said. "I think they'll be all right now. These are some of my best boys. Neither Hanley nor Morton have given any

129

sign they're wise. As for old Donegan—he's too broken up about his boy to notice anything."

"How'd Knoeckler's funeral go off?" Fenner asked.

"All right. Miss Knoeckler and Morton were the only mourners. It was all very brief and to the point. By the way, you were right about the key to Knoeckler's. Morton phoned about it already this morning. He's going to be co-executor, along with the girl, of the old man's estate—if there is any such thing."

"Hanley said that Morton was planning something of the sort."

"I bet his wife would be tickled to hear that," Bryce remarked grimly.

"Have you met her?"

"No; but I talked over the telephone with her—last Thursday, you know, when we were looking for Morton—and if she's as bad as she sounded, I'm not sure I blame the man for taking the air."

Fenner only smiled. Marital difficulties were things of which he had only indirect acquaintance.

"That may be part of the reason," he said. "Miss Knoeckler is a damned attractive girl; at least, to my way of thinking, she is."

"I think so, too; but if Mrs. Morton is as much a shrew as she sounded, it makes the old boy's lapse a little more excusable."

"It makes it a little more understandable," Fenner corrected. "How about the girl? Where does she get off in the long run?"

"Maybe Morton'll get a divorce and marry her," Bryce suggested cheerfully. "He certainly has made no effort to conceal the fact that he thinks enough of her."

"Maybe he will, but I'm not sure I'd bet that way." Fenner slid off the desk and stretched himself, complaining through a sigh: "Ho-hum; I suppose I'll never get rich sitting here chewing the fat. I'm going to my own office for a while. Then I'll drop in on Hanley after lunch. You can reach me in one place or the other, in case any of our super-exemplary candidates should forget himself."

A slow, sardonic smile broadened on Bryce's face as he watched his friend depart. "I can just picture you hanging over the phone waiting," he flung after him with good-humored sarcasm.

2

Several hours later this same morning in Randolph Morton's office Stephen Coles found his first opportunity since her return to confront Elsa Knoeckler alone. She had been in the office for a few minutes on Monday afternoon, but Morton had been awaiting her and they had shortly gone out together.

Morton had previously told Coles of Mr. Knoeckler's death but had communicated just the bare fact.

It had been a strange conversation, Morton speaking quite impersonally of Elsa as if there was nothing whatever between himself and the girl, Coles wondering if he was actually expected to believe this or if Morton simply chose to put that face on the matter as the least embarrassing way for both of them. Certainly the latter, Coles had concluded, inwardly boiling; and had thought to himself furiously: "If the son of a — really thinks I'm that dumb he'd have fired me long ago!"

On Tuesday Elsa had not come to the office at all, nor on Wednesday until now—almost noon. If the shock of her father's death had affected her much, it was not reflected in her appearance. To Coles she seemed more desirable than ever.

"Hello, Steve," she said simply upon entering the office.

"Hello, Elsa! How are you?" Coles got slowly to his feet. He wondered, incredibly, if she too would take the line that nothing had happened. He hurried on: "The boss told me about your father. I was awfully sorry to hear it."

"Thanks!" Elsa made no other reply, but looked away. She was half sitting on the edge of her desk peeling off her gloves. Coles could not take his eyes off her. He thought of Morton and his smoldering anger flared up.

"You were away, weren't you?" The question was natural enough, but there was a bitterness in the tone she could not miss.

Elsa ignored the query. She asked casually: "When do you expect Mr. Morton back?"

"At noon. Don't worry; he'll be back in time to buy you a lunch!"

"I asked a civil question. There is no reason for being nasty. You might at least give me a civil answer."

"No reason! No; I suppose not. You take me for an awful sap, don't you, Elsa?"

"I don't take you for anything. Let's not argue."

"Oh! Let's not argue! No; of course not. Look here—you went home Thursday because you 'didn't feel well.' You must have improved a lot by evening. I stopped in to say Hello. I was going to chin with your dad, too, but I didn't see him around. I suppose he approved of your little jaunt?" Coles leered over her.

"What do you mean?" Elsa gasped.

"Aw, can it! Let's quit stallin'. You went away with Morton. I'm not blind."

Elsa slid off the desk to her feet. "If I did, what of it? It would be my own affair."

"Oh, God! Elsa, you know how I feel about you. It breaks my heart to see you taken for a ride by that dirty bas—" His anguished protest was cut short by a strange shadow that passed over Elsa's face, a blending of anger and hurt and pride. She started toward the door.

"Wait a minute, Elsa. I'm sorry."

"I don't want to hear any more."

"I love you; I always have. But right now I'm only thinking of your own good. He's married; he's too old for you anyway. Can't you see he's only playing around and—"

"Stop it! Stop right now! You don't know what you're talking about and it's none of your business, anyway. I'm perfectly capable of leading my own life."

"You think you are now. When he gets tired and gives you the air you'll sing a different tune. Hell! When I think of it I could strangle him with my bare hands." Coles paced the room to work off his fury, waving his clenched fists melodramatically. He rambled on: "For a while you and I got along pretty well—till he started handing you his smooth line. Then I wasn't good enough. Oh, God!" He covered his face with his hands.

As Elsa watched him, her mounting anger gave way to compassion.

"I'm sorry you feel as you do, but it's not my fault," she said. "I'm sure you'll get over it if you try. Don't worry about me. Besides—" She paused.

To Coles her sudden pity was more galling than her anger.

"Besides what?" he insisted savagely.

"Randolph and I are going to be married as soon as he's free. I shouldn't have told you that, I guess."

"Oh, it's 'Randolph' now, and he's going to marry you?" Coles sneered. "Well, I'll say you shouldn't have told me that. It hurts me when I laugh! Oh! I could kill the dir—"

A metallic clank outside warned them that the elevator had stopped on that floor. They heard footsteps in the corridor approaching the door. Coles sat down quickly and picked up a pencil. Elsa slid back onto her desk and started searching in her handbag for a compact. Thus Morton found them when he opened the door.

He beamed at the girl, apologizing. "Sorry to have kept you. Been here long?"

"Only a moment."

Morton addressed Coles: "There'll be a lot of pier holes ready to inspect at the Consolidated job this afternoon. Are we pretty well cleaned up here?"

"I think so."

"Meet me at the job, then—say, at two-thirty."

"Two-thirty. Right."

Morton held the door for Elsa and they went out. Coles watching them half rose from his chair, gripped the arms of it, white-knuckled, rigid—pulled himself down again. As he relaxed, a great wave of self-pity rose from within him, blinding, suffocating, engulfing his reason. For a long moment his dull eyes stared at the closed door; then mechanically he resumed his tasks.

3

At the Consolidated Bank, as had seemed to happen often lately, Fenner found that Hanley was not in his office. A secretary informed him that the manager had gone across the street to conduct several members of the bank's directorate through the site for the new building. He was expected back momentarily so Fenner decided to wait.

He perched himself on a window sill and lit a cigarette. From where he rested Fenner could look almost straight down into the excavation for the new building. From that height—Hanley's office was on the ninth floor—the narrow street separating the new site from the old building seemed narrower than ever.

The crosslot bracing divided the lot into neat little squares. The men working in the bottom were out of Fenner's view but there were a few whose duties kept them up on the bracing or on the edge of the excavation. Fenner watched the tiny figures interestedly. Most of them were signalmen who guided the dirt and stone buckets as they were hoisted or lowered.

The job noises blended with the street noises to form a low, variable clamor. Fenner had been seated at the window a short time and his ears had begun to accustom themselves to the din when above the racket a human voice was raised in a shrill cry. Other voices joined the first and a minor tumult swelled, but as quickly dwindled to the former steady hum. Curious as to the cause of the disturbance, Fenner flicked the ashes off his cigarette and leaned out of the window better to see down into the lot.

The men had flocked across the timbers to a point near one corner of the job where they fringed the opening through the bracing, leaning over each other in their endeavors to see into the bottom. Presently a man—a foreman or superintendent of some sort, Fenner concluded—appeared at the head of a ladder leading up from the bottom. With effective gestures and, Fenner imagined, appropriate language, he dispersed the group, then disappeared into the green shanty which housed the job office. A few moments later he came out, shouted some commands to one of the derrick signalmen and disappeared down the ladder.

Fenner was about to decide that the whole disturbance was a false alarm when he saw one of the empty stone skips being swung around and let slowly down through the opening around which the crowd had been congregated. He decided that someone had been hurt and his conclusion was verified only a few minutes later when the hollow clang of an ambulance bell floated up clearly above the other noises. He saw the machine pull up at a ramp on the far side of the lot. Two white-coated attendants hopped out and a gateman waiting for them spoke a moment and pointed into the cellar. The attendants scrambled down stairways and ladders in the direction indicated and disappeared beneath the bracing.

After a seemingly interminable wait, for Fenner's curiosity was mounting rapidly, one of the attendants reappeared. When he reached the bracing level he glanced back hastily, then hurried up to his ambulance. At the same time the stone skip came again into view, rising slowly, carefully, up from between the rows of timber bracing. Fenner saw that it was freighted with a human cargo. The ambulance attendant and the foreman he had noticed before were squatted in either end of the skip; between them lay an inert figure, the head swathed in bandages, the clothing disheveled.

Fenner's eyes followed the skip as it swung up and out with its triple burden until it came to rest at the ramp where the ambulance waited. In a twinkling the figure was bundled into the car and with a peremptory shriek of the siren whisked away. A crowd of passers-by which had collected around the waiting ambulance melted swiftly; the foreman turned back to the job; the incident was closed.

Fenner turned from the window vaguely disturbed. Another small item in the cost of these mammoth structures, he reflected— a human item, difficult to evaluate. He wondered for a moment how much of this sort of intangible cost was ever recorded upon a builder's books. The reflections were cut short when the office door swung open and Hanley burst in, white and trembling.

"There's been an accident," he said weakly. "Randolph Morton's been hurt—maybe killed."

Fenner started up with surprise. "What! Was he the man they just took away? Good Lord!" He seized Hanley's arm. "Tell me more quickly." Already questions were seething in Fenner's brain, doubts.

Hanley sank into a chair. "There's little to tell," he said. "A chunk of iron fell on his head—brained him. The ambulance surgeon has little hope. They took him to the Broad Street Hospital."

Fenner seized the telephone and put a call through to Bryce. He told him in a few moments what had happened and asked him to come to the job. He turned back to Hanley.

"Tell me what you know," he demanded. "I'm going to meet Bryce downstairs in a few minutes."

Hanley had regained most of his composure. "Why Bryce?" he asked, and then at Fenner's insistence went on: "I was down in the bottom showing Mr. Spencer and Mr. Whitehead—they're directors and both big stockholders—through the job. We came across Morton and Dickson and Borden and the superintendent. They were having some sort of a discussion—or rather, had been, for it looked as if they had about finished. We had seen all we wished, so I took my guests up to the street gate and parted with them there. Then I went back down as far as the top of the bracing, thinking I'd wait for Morton to come up, as I wanted to talk to him. I'd only waited a moment when I heard a lot of yelling and the men all came running over. I gathered that someone had been hurt but I didn't know it was Morton until the superintendent came up to call the ambulance. When he told me who it was I went back down into the cellar again."

"What did you say happened to him?"

"An iron bar, a sort of sawed-off crowbar, fell from somewhere and caught him on the head. A glancing blow, it must have been, or it surely would have killed him outright."

"Where did it fall from?"

"Nobody knows. The superintendent suggested it had probably been left on one of the upper layers of bracing and either rolled off or got knocked off. No one seems to have seen it happen. One of the laborers working near by heard a noise and turned around and saw Morton stretched out on the ground."

"Who was down there when you got back to the bottom again?"

"Four or five laborers and foremen and Mr. Dickson and—well, quite a crowd. Borden came along, too, right after I did. Morton was unconscious and to me he looked about gone. The superintendent had put something on his head to stop the bleeding. The ambulance men dressed it before they took him away."

Fenner got down to the street just in time to see Bryce round the corner toward the job entrance. He ran a few steps to overtake him and together they went to the office shanty. Bryce inquired for the superintendent, and a plan boy went down into the job to find him. While Fenner and Bryce were waiting Dickson walked into the shanty. He seemed little surprised to see them and remarked: "It certainly doesn't take you fellows long to get around when there's any trouble."

"Trouble?" Fenner looked at the engineer for a long, searching moment. It struck him as odd that Dickson should so readily take their presence for granted.

"Mr. Morton, I mean. Of course you've heard?"

"Oh, yes; we heard," Fenner replied. "But you flatter us as to the speed. I was right across the street in Mr. Hanley's office when he came in with the news, so we stepped over. What happened to Morton, anyway?"

"A bull point fell on him. That's all we can find out," Dickson replied tersely.

"Anybody see it happen?"

"I guess not. One of the rockmen working a few feet away says he heard a noise and turned around and saw Morton lying there. He'd seen him standing looking around a few seconds before. Why, I had been talking to him myself not five minutes before."

"Did Morton usually spend much time down here on the job?" Fenner asked after a moment.

"Quite a little, lately. He likes to inspect all of the pier bottoms before they're concreted."

"Was that what brought him down to the job today?"

"Yes. There are several pier holes in which the rock strata slope sharply. Morton had been quite insistent that we level them off, so we had him down to look them over before we poured them."

"I see." Fenner hesitated, then went on almost apologetically. "We'd like to have a look around. Could you show us the way down there?"

"Certainly; no trouble at all." Dickson was surprisingly agreeable.

He led the way outside and down a series of ladders to the bottom of the excavation. Fenner and Bryce, unaccustomed to climbing, followed him gingerly. To Fenner the scene at the bottom of the huge hole presented a thrilling and interesting spectacle. The

raw rock floor and sides, rough and rugged as the blasters and drill-
ers had left them, reminded him of a deep stone quarry into which
he had once made a trip. Through the openings in the network of
heavy timber bracing overhead he could see, four stories above him,
the painted fence he knew to be at street level; down in the bottom
the timber posts supporting the bracing stretched away in even
rows like tree trunks in an open forest. Little streams, channels in
the rough bottom, led the ground water which seeped up through
the fissures in the rock, rippling away to a sump pit. Absorbed by
the interesting closeup of the bowels of the earth, Fenner for a
moment almost forgot his gruesome errand, but Dickson brought
him rudely back to the time and the place.

"Right here's where we found him," he announced, pointing to
a location a few feet from several small, rectangular depressions
in the rock. Fenner could see a telltale discoloration of the glistening mica schist where Morton's head had rested. Dickson pointed
to the depressions. "Those are the pier bottoms we had been discussing. Morton wanted them leveled off a little more, so we put a
man on them. You can see they slope away a little. I suppose Morton
thought he'd hang around and see that they were done the way he
wanted them." There was a trace of scarce concealed impatience
in his voice that led Fenner to conclude that the discussion of the
pier bottoms might not have been a wholly amiable one.

"How long after your talk here ended did Mr. Morton get hurt?"

"Not more than five minutes," Dickson answered positively. "I
had started up to the office shanty to use the telephone and hadn't
even reached it."

"Who else was down here with you and Mr. Morton?"

"Why, Borden and Quinn, the foundation outfit's superintendent. Oh, yes; and Steve Coles. That's Morton's assistant."

"Did they leave him when you did?"

"Quinn left a few minutes before. We had decided about the
piers, and he is a busy man—always in a hurry. Coles stayed with
him. Borden left at the same time I did. He had a lot of his routine
data to collect. Here he comes now."

They saw Borden picking his way through the cluttered lot toward them. The younger man only paused to exchange a word or two with Dickson and then started for the ladder.

"Did you want to talk to him?" Dickson asked Fenner as Borden moved away.

Fenner looked mildly surprised at the question. "I hardly think it's necessary. I should like to talk to this chap, Quinn, though, if he's around—and also to Coles."

"He's around, all right," Dickson assured them. "Find Coles and Quinn and send them down here, will you, Borden," he commanded.

A few moments later the foundation superintendent joined them. He acknowledged the introductions of Fenner and Bryce pleasantly enough but seemed to turn a shade cooler when he learned that the latter was connected with the police and was inquiring into Morton's accident.

Accidents on foundation construction were as inevitable as the law of averages, and Quinn had been dealt his share of them, but this was the first one in his experience that the police had investigated with anything except casual formality. Of course in this case the victim was not some obscure laborer, which made the prompt inquiry a little less surprising, but Quinn knew nothing of Morton's possible connection with the recent bank robbery.

"What's your idea about the affair?" Fenner asked him abruptly.

"I don't know what you mean. Mr. Morton was hit by a bull point. From the position in which he was found it seems likely the bar fell off one of the upper layers of bracing of that row." He pointed to a range of timbers the edge of which came approximately over the spot where Morton had been hurt. "Of course I haven't any idea how a bull point could have got up there on the bracing. We're very careful to leave nothing lying around on the timbers, just to avoid this very kind of accident. And I haven't any idea what could dislodge it. One of these Guineas probably kicked it off and is scared to open his trap."

"What is a bull point used for?"

"Mostly wedging out rock and getting out loose bowlders. Loosening the hardpan," Quinn explained.

"There'd be no use for one up there?"

"No. Some lazy ba—d probably left it lying there. Too lazy to take it back to the tool room. The men walk around on the bracing a great deal."

"Where's the bull point now?"

"Up in the office. I kept it in case the insurance inspector should want to see it."

"I'll look at it when we go up. Thanks very much," Fenner concluded. He turned to Bryce. "I think we had better go now. I'm anxious to get over to the hospital. But wait! Where's Coles?"

Quinn interrupted: "He left as soon as Morton was put in the ambulance. I imagine you'll get him at the hospital or at his office—or maybe here, later. He's coming back to inspect these pier holes. I'm going to concrete them on the early night shift, and ordinarily he or Morton would have to see them before they're poured."

They started up to the street.

"I suppose you've notified Morton's office and family," Fenner suggested casually.

"I called our own main office. They're taking care of it."

In the job office Quinn handed Bryce the bull point. It was simply an iron bar about two feet long and an inch and a half thick, pointed at one end. Bryce took it in his handkerchief. Fenner smiled and pointed out: "It's been handled by a dozen people, I'll venture."

"Perhaps, but this is a good habit," Bryce countered. He balanced the bar in his hand, estimating its weight. "This wouldn't have to fall far to kill a man if it caught him right. I'd hate to have it come down on my cranium from even a foot or two." He passed the bar to Fenner who examined it briefly and handed it back to Quinn.

As they left the job to go to the hospital the inspector felt someone at his elbow. It was his man, Quade, whom he had placed on the job as assistant timekeeper. When they had put a long block between themselves and the job, Bryce motioned for Quade to overtake them.

"What's up?"

"Maybe it's nothing, Chief. About a half hour before he was hurt, Mr. Morton was having some kind of a row with Borden. I couldn't get what it was about, but they seemed pretty hot. Dickson and Quinn came along and joined in."

"You know Coles? How about him?" Fenner interjected hastily.

"He came along later. He hung around the others but didn't get in it."

"Where were you when Morton was hurt?" Bryce asked.

"In the shanty. As soon as I heard the yelling I ran out, but by the time I got down to the bottom everybody on the job was hanging around. I couldn't find out much."

"All right, Quade; see what you can pick up between now and evening and let me know."

4

At the hospital Fenner and Bryce, without disclosing their identity, secured Morton's room number from the desk nurse. As they made their way through the cool, white corridors, the heavy scent of ether and Lysol assailed their nostrils. The particular odor had always been a sickening one to Fenner, and in some way disconcerting. He caught himself wondering, heavy hearted, if they would find Morton alive; if the man would ever again open his eyes and look upon the light of day. The thought unnerved him.

For a brief moment there flashed through Fenner's mind the things he had learned about the man in the short few days he had been working on the case. In spite of an innate conservatism Morton had been a hard liver in his day. There was no doubt about that, but he had also been a hard worker, a hard player and withal a gentleman with his share of gentlemanly attributes. Fenner could not help feeling a grudging admiration for the man. Suddenly he wondered about Elsa Knoeckler. What would become of her if Morton died—if he was already dead? Had she heard? It would probably be for her the final, crushing blow. Then he thought a little wearily that he would be glad when the case drew to its conclusion, for he realized, disconcertingly, that he was on the point of allowing his feelings to color what should be purely intellectual, cold-blooded processes of reasoning.

Their scarce audible footsteps echoed softly down the long corridor. Bryce, who was more or less familiar with the layout of the hospital, led the way.

"They've certainly done the best they could for him," he whispered to Fenner. "This is the most expensive wing of the place—private rooms and private nurses." He was scanning the room numbers. "Ah! Here we are."

The door stood partly open and they glanced in. There was an anteroom between the hall and the patient's room. A rather dapper-appearing individual, in a semi-reclining position suggestive of the ultimate of solid ease and comfort, lounged in one of the armchairs with which the room was furnished. He looked up when they entered and, upon seeing Bryce, sprang to his feet.

"Oh, hello, Chief," he said and waited. "Anything?"

The man shook his head. He appeared to be a person of few words.

"This is Mr. Burke, Max—Mr. Fenner," Bryce said.

"I've heard of you. Glad to meet you, sir," the younger man acknowledged. Burke, Fenner inferred, was one of Morton's stalkers. Taking advantage of the incapacitation of his quarry, he brazenly lolled there at his ease instead of hovering discreetly around some corner.

"What's the latest on Morton?" Bryce asked. Burke nodded toward the door. "Two doctors and a nurse in there now. He was still unconscious when the nurse was out here a few minutes ago."

"Anyone been here?" Fenner asked.

"Not a soul."

"Morton's been here less than an hour," Bryce reminded him.

"I rather expected to find Coles here," Fenner mused.

Just then the door to the sickroom opened. A white-gowned elderly surgeon stepped through and closed it carefully behind him. He looked at the men inquiringly.

"What's the word on Mr. Morton, Doctor?"

"Whom do you represent?" the physician countered coolly.

Bryce turned back his coat in true detective fashion, displaying his shield, and answered crisply: "Police Headquarters."

"Oh, I see. We have to be careful in cases of this kind." He hesitated, looking from one to the other of them, but then went on: "Mr. Morton's condition is more than critical. His skull has been fractured and he's had a severe brain concussion. There is a chance that he will recover, but it is distinctly a remote one. However, miracles have happened before this. At present he is in a state of coma from which he may emerge in an hour, or a week, or never. Everything that is humanly possible is being done for him. That's all I can say at this time—except that in any case he can't be seen for at least two days and probably longer."

The doctor took a step back as if to return to the sickroom, but the door swung open behind him and the nurse coming out pushed past him. Over one arm was draped the mud-stained clothing they had taken off Morton. In her hands she carried a porcelain tray upon which were spread what appeared to have been the contents of his pockets.

"Excuse me," she murmured as she slipped between Fenner and the physician and started briskly across the room.

"Just a minute, young lady!" Fenner spoke sharply. The girl turned in surprise at the incisive command. The doctor paused, too, his hand on the door knob.

Fenner walked across to where the girl waited uncertainly.

"Here, Bryce," he said; and to the girl: "Whose clothing have you there?"

"Why, the patient's, of course." She was puzzled by the question the answer to which must be so obvious.

"And the articles on the tray—where did you get them?"

"From the pockets of the suit, naturally." She had recovered from her surprise and the answer came a little tartly.

"What are you going to do with them?"

"It's customary to lock those things up in the hospital office," the doctor explained. His gaze fell on Bryce. The detective was standing beside the nurse, his eyes riveted upon the contents of the tray she held, stupefaction written plainly upon his face. His eyes followed the inspector's to the tray, as did those of the other people in the room, except Fenner who when she first came in had observed the small object which held Bryce's fascinated gaze. The tray contained a leather wallet, a fountain pen and a small gold pencil, a watch and chain, a cigarette case and a small jeweled lighter, some loose change, a soiled handkerchief, a spectacles case, and upon the top of the pile in naïve innocence a small, metal-rimmed, fiber tag with a tiny hole in one end.

Bryce picked it up gingerly. The blank lines were all filled in. He read:

> Date . . . . March 30, 1931
> Consignee . . . . Park Avenue Branch
> Amount $180,000.00
> Checklist ML2-6202
> Packed By . . . . J. Donegan

"Put the tray down for a moment. I want to ask you one or two questions." Fenner's tone was more conciliatory now that he had had time to recover from his initial surprise at the sight of the tag. Even so, the girl seemed about to protest but the doctor spoke up.

"Do as they say, Miss Farrell," he instructed. "It's all right. These men are from the police."

"Did you, yourself, remove these articles from the patient's suit?" Fenner first asked her.

"Yes; just now."

"Can you recall from which pocket each article was removed?"

The nurse hesitated, then said uncertainly: "Why, just about, I think."

"Will you please tell me?"

Obviously mystified the girl complied with his request. "The pocketbook and pencil and pen were in his inside coat pocket. The lighter and cigarette case and his watch were in the vest. The handkerchief and the change were in his trousers." She stopped.

"And the little tag—?"

"Oh, that was in his side coat pocket—that and the case for his glasses."

"You're sure?"

"Yes; I remember them distinctly."

"Very good. That's all. I'm going to take this tag." He suited his action to his words. "The other things you may put away as you intended. Now one thing more: You will save yourself and others a lot of trouble if you mention this to no one. Do you understand?"

The girl nodded meekly. Fenner looked at the doctor. "The same applies to you, sir, if you don't mind."

"Of course not."

The doctor went back to his patient, Burke resumed his arm-chair and Fenner and Bryce went out. It was somewhat after five o'clock and the sidewalks were crowded with office workers going home. Bryce moved to the curb, bit the end off his cigar, and spat meditatively.

"A good thing we happened to be there when the nurse walked out with that tag," he observed. "Looks like the answer, doesn't it?"

"Perhaps; but we needn't be precipitate. There's no danger of Morton running away. It's odd that—but never mind. We'll have to dig up Coles now. We may as well try Morton's office first. It's only a few blocks from here."

They went there only to find the door locked, the place in dark-ness, and received no answer to their knock.

"At the new building job, I guess," Bryce commented. He looked at his watch. "Maybe we can catch him there before he gets away. Otherwise we can talk to him in the morning."

"I'd much rather see him now." A puzzled frown darkened Fenner's countenance.

A few moments later they approached the building excavation. It had become quite dark by then and the flood lights which illu-minated the site for the night work were blazing in all their glory. In spite of their glare the lot abounded with dark spots and shad-owy corners and presented altogether an eerie spectacle. In the street a concrete truck, its rotating barrel-like body tipped sharply, was spouting its load of concrete into a hopper whence it was led away in chutes to the piers and walls that were being poured. A number of similar trucks lined up along the curb awaited their turn. Fenner and Bryce watched for a moment, then turned into the gate.

They paused in the doorway of the job office. Quinn was changing into his street clothing. Dickson and Borden were still there, too, leaning over a plan table in session with the night-shift superintendent. Quinn looked up from tying a shoelace, nodded curtly and asked: "How's Morton? The hospital won't tell us much."

Dickson and Borden also looked up, waiting for the answer.

"Not so good. Small, fighting chance, maybe," Bryce answered shortly. "Seen his man around? Coles?"

"He was here a little before five and O.K.'d the piers and walls we're now concreting. I haven't seen him since, though he may be around the job somewhere. Wait a minute; I'll let the timekeeper look around for him." He stepped to an adjoining smaller shanty, spoke to its occupant, and came back.

Dickson straightened up from the plan table, lighted his pipe and joined them. Fenner stood in the doorway looking about the lot.

"Seems to be a lot of activity," he commented. "Does the work keep going like this every night?"

"Oh, yes," Dickson volunteered the answer. "Twenty-four hours a day. Not always this busy at night, though. Just happens we've got some unusually large concrete pours to make this evening."

There was a moment of silence, Dickson hovering at Fenner's elbow. He seemed about to ask him something but not quite able to make up his mind.

"I shouldn't think your men would be able to see what they're doing in that uneven light," Fenner remarked.

"They get used to it. Where it's too dark they rig up more lights; that's all."

"Excuse me." Borden mumbled the apology as he and the foreman squeezed past the group in the doorway and went down into the cellar.

Fenner watched them walk out on the bracing. "Many accidents at night?" he asked.

"No more than by daylight. Maybe not so many," Quinn grunted. Just then the timekeeper came back and reported to Quinn: "He's not around, Boss. Guess he's gone home."

Quinn turned to Fenner with a little shrug. "I guess Coles has gone for the day—or night, rather. You might find him here some time tomorrow."

"Much obliged, anyway. It's not important. We'll see him at Morton's office in the morning."

They bade their host good-evening and left.

"Very enlightening, wasn't it?—Not!" Fenner moaned when they were once more in the street. "Well, how about something to eat? I want to hop around to the hospital again, but not so soon. There's this tag thing to go over. Come along!" They went into the India House but neither spoke until the waiter had taken their orders and gone away to fill them.

"Now then, what do you think of it?" Fenner asked.

"It looks to me like my original hunch on Morton wasn't so wet after all."

"Perhaps—and then again, perhaps not," Fenner said enigmatically. "But if you're right, maybe you can answer two questions that have fretted me for the past hour. One, assuming that Morton robbed the bank, why the devil would he still be carting that tell-tale tag around with him? And two, assuming he had some reason for carrying it, why wouldn't he slip it into that ample wallet of his instead of carrying it loose in his side coat pocket? Also, you might tell me how he disposed of the loot and when."

"I don't know about the tag. Carelessness maybe. But he certainly had the whole week-end in which to cache the money. He had more opportunity than any of the others for that. And good Lord! What more proof could we want?"

The answer convinced Fenner not at all, but for the moment he refrained from reiterating his disagreement.

"I only hope Morton revives, and soon!" he said fervently.

"What good would that do? The doctor says it wouldn't be safe to talk to him for two days. I'm not waiting! Besides, the chances admittedly are that he won't come around at all. No, sir! On the strength of that tag I'm going to get a warrant out, and I'm going to take a half dozen men and go through everything Morton's got with a fine-toothed comb—his office, his apartment—that camp out in Jersey—everything. And I'd almost give you odds we net something." Bryce rapped the table softly to emphasize his conviction.

Fenner looked at him with studied coolness. "You feel that we're pretty lucky, don't you?"

"What do you mean?"

"Well, the Consolidated Bank theft occurred a week ago, lacking a day. Randolph Morton, who had both ample motive and at least a possible opportunity along with three or four others, and is therefore justifiably under suspicion, was out of our sight and free to do as he pleased for three days succeeding the robbery, and has been under observation in only a general way since then. We had absolutely nothing on him. Now, out of a clear sky, that little tag pops out of his pocket like a rabbit out of a magician's hat—and in circumstances that make it improbable for us to miss it and impossible for him to explain it. If the thing is genuine it would be for us a phenomenal piece of luck. Why, the chances of such a thing happening in the normal course of events would not be one in a million! I'm not quite ready to believe my luck is that good. Why, I'd quit this business and play the market. No, sir! Somewhere there's an Ethiopian among the kindling! The whole thing strikes me as an inspired piece of business."

Bryce's jaw dropped, but he was not prepared to alter his program and said as much.

"Oh, no; of course not," Fenner agreed. "It's the only thing you can do. You'd be failing in your duty if you did any less. But at the same time I'd not be too sanguine. Above all, the thing is to not let up on the others for an instant; double up on them, if anything. The more I sniff at it, the more this 'accident' assumes the bouquet of a great big wide red herring."

"You mean it's not an accident? Is that what you're saying?"

"I mean it might not be; that's as far as my thinking has taken me; but I'll tell you one thing: if there was a prodigious amount of 'coincidence' in old Adolph Knoeckler's timely demise, there's twice as much here!" He stopped and looked away, lost for a moment in a maze of ideas.

Bryce pondered this new slant of Fenner's, his cumbersome thinking processes feeling at and around it, slowly, methodically, where Fenner's, rapierlike, were darting to the core. At first it seemed wildly fantastic, but upon more thoughtful analysis it seemed no more illogical than his own hasty assumption. But who—?

"You know," Fenner went on, "the 'accident' itself wasn't so bad. I think I'd have swallowed that in a little while if nothing else had turned up to the contrary, but this tag business is spreading it a bit too thick. Unless—" He stopped a second. "Unless the accident was an accident and somebody simply took advantage of it to plant the tag on Morton. But that's not so good either. That would be granting our culprit almost as much pure luck as we are unwilling to assume ourselves to possess. Oh, Lord! Still, there's a chance—"

For a moment Bryce felt almost resentful that Fenner had implanted the seed of doubt in his mind. He would search Morton's possessions and affairs—that would have to be done—but he knew there would not be the zest he would have put into it had he been definitely convinced of a fruitful outcome. Inwardly he heaved a sigh. It would be a relief, when this case was solved (he had not yet begun to doubt that eventuality), to get back again to something straightforward and tangible.

"Well, then, what's the answer?" Bryce put the question a shade impatiently.

"The answer's not far to seek. It's the same watch and wait, especially watch. Our clientele is unchanged. Any of them could have planted the tag, especially when they were getting Morton up to the ambulance, except the Donegans. Rather, except Jerry, for old Jeremy might have put it on Morton yesterday morning at the bank. I think you can leave that out, though, because Morton would have doubtless found the tag between then and now and dropped it like a hot potato. The rest are as eligible as ever, though."

5

In due course they finished their supper. Bryce went to Headquarters to attend the technical formalities which would permit him to conduct his search of Morton's affairs. Fenner went back to the hospital.

In the little waiting room he found Burke and Elsa Knoeckler. Burke had retired to a corner of the room and was apparently absorbed in a newspaper. Miss Knoeckler sat quietly, wrapped in her own thoughts. Her eyes were heavy and her face drawn but in spite of her tired pallor she retained a surprising charm and attractiveness. The emotional experiences which had been crammed into the preceding few days had left an undeniable impress upon her countenance, but the effect was not detrimental; rather, it brought into relief certain qualities of courage and stoicism. Anew Fenner thought he understood and appreciated Morton's feeling for the girl. Out of deference to her feelings he called Burke out into the hall.

"Any change?" he asked.

"No, sir."

"When did the girl come in?"

"About half an hour after you and the chief left."

"She come alone?"

"I believe so."

"What is she waiting for?"

"The doctor, I think. Both doctors went out before she got here. The girl talked to the nurse a minute and from what I could overhear one of the doctors is expected back later in the evening."

"I see. Thanks. You're going to stay here, are you?"

Burke nodded.

"And keep Bryce posted if there's any change in Morton's condition?"

"That's right."

They went back into the anteroom. The girl was sitting exactly as she had been before. Fenner leaned over Elsa's chair and addressed her in a low tone.

"I'm glad to see you again but I'm sorry it's under such trying circumstances," he said. Elsa looked up at him but did not reply and Fenner continued: "Mr. Morton is only an acquaintance as far as I'm concerned; I know that to you he is a very dear friend. That's what prompts me to speak to you about him. The doctor told me this morning that he had a fighting chance. I have a feeling that he has that and more, but it might be a long pull. There's little you or I can do to help him now. But when he gets well he's going to have another battle to fight. In that connection it may be that you can be of use."

The girl had returned his gaze steadily throughout this long introduction. Bewilderment was registered in the deepening frown wrinkling her face. Fenner drew a chair close to her, sat down, and hurried on before she could ask the questions on her lips. "This may be a waste of your time and mine. In that case little will be lost. On the other hand, you may be able to tell me things which, taken with what I already know, will be of immeasurable help. Then much would be gained. I simply want to learn all I can about Randolph Morton—his plans, his associates, his financial condition, his domestic affairs—all the little intangible things you probably can tell me. I'm going to take you into my confidence and in return I expect you to take me into yours."

Elsa thought over what Fenner had said for a long moment before replying: "I think you were right when you spoke of wasting your time. My own I don't care about. The truth is: I hardly know anything at all about Mr. Morton." She looked away.

"Am I right in supposing that Mr. Morton is a wealthy man?"

"I suppose so. He never seems to worry much about money, though he has lost a lot in the last year or two."

"Do you know anything about his domestic life?"

"I know he plans to secure a divorce," Elsa said firmly with a challenging lift of her chin. "He has asked me to marry him when he obtains it."

"Do you know a Mr. Hanley at the Consolidated American Bank?"

"I've heard the name; that's all."

"Has Morton ever told you how well he knows him or anything about their connections?"

"No."

"Did Mr. Morton tell you about an—er—misunderstanding at the Consolidated Bank in which he was believed to be involved?"

"Why, no." Elsa seemed properly surprised and Fenner judged that she was speaking the truth.

"Did you ever hear him speak of 'Dickson' or 'Borden' or 'Donegan'?"

"Why, there's a Mr. Dickson he consults with once in a while about the foundations at the new bank building. I don't remember the other two names."

"Did you ever see this before?" Fenner placed the fiber tag on the arm of her chair.

Elsa looked at it curiously and said: "Not that I know of."

"Do you know what it is?"

She looked at it again. "No."

"Well, I'll tell you. It's an identification tag belonging to a dispatch bag containing a hundred and eighty thousand dollars which disappeared recently from the Consolidated Bank. This tag was found in Mr. Morton's coat pocket after he was hurt."

The girl visibly flinched but soon regained her calm. She straightened up in her chair. "There must be some mistake. If what you say is true Mr. Morton will have an explanation for it when he recovers—if he recovers." She added the last in a lower tone.

"I hope you're right. For reasons which I can't go into at this time I believe you are. But in the meantime his position is an uncomfortable one."

Elsa nodded mutely. Fenner made a last appeal. "You're still quite sure there's nothing you can tell me to help us?"

The girl only shook her head wearily.

"If anything occurs to you, come to me." Fenner got up and picked up his hat. "I suppose I need hardly tell you to say nothing of this."

Again she only nodded. Fenner saw that she could not trust herself to speak. He bent over her and murmured: "These things have a way of straightening themselves out. Keep a stiff upper lip."

Elsa Knoeckler, he reflected, had yet a bitter cup to quaff.

7
THURSDAY
APRIL 7TH

1

A CLEAR, SERENE SKY, pure molten turquoise, flawless, greeted the rising populace in general and our principals in particular as Thursday dawned upon greater New York. The air was fragrant, soothing, mild.

The flawless sky held no meaning for Elsa Knoeckler when, the brilliant sun already three hours high, she came suddenly awake from tossing, fretful slumber and with but a glance at her unaccustomed surroundings reached anxiously for the bedside telephone. Nor held it meaning for Randolph Morton, who still slept on. Stephen Coles' eyes were open but he did not see the sky.

Jeremy Donegan might have seen it, but his haunted eyes were nowadays continually cast down. Jerry sensed the brilliance of it and sniffed the morning air, but his barred window opened on a gray stone court wall. T. Jerome Hanley noticed it as he stepped into his limousine and thought, strangely enough, of a South Sea Island and peace.

Philip Borden, on the upper deck of an Erie Railroad ferry, bared his head to the fresh breeze and with keen appreciation watched the nearing skyline block out the translucent blue. Christopher Dickson, in the slaty atmosphere of the smoking cabin on a Staten Island ferry several miles down the bay, had real need of fresh air and blue sky, and morose desire for neither.

Inspector Bryce glanced at it perfunctorily for a key to the weather and found it eminently satisfactory. Maxwell Fenner, who

154

would have altogether failed to notice it under no conceivable circumstance, gave it a scantily appreciative glance with but half a thoughtful eye.

It was shortly after nine when he knocked at the locked doors of Marten, Morton & Purcell, and as on the previous evening elicited no response. He went downstairs to the building lobby and telephoned Quinn from whom he learned that Coles was not at the job. Fenner went out of the building and turned toward the Consolidated Bank with a half-formed idea that he would spend an hour talking with Hanley and later try Morton's office again, but before he had walked two blocks he faced about, impelled by an urge he could not have defined, and went back to seek Coles again. The place was still locked and quiet as a morgue.

Fenner had given no particular thought to Stephen Coles and at first sought him hoping only to learn more of the details of Morton's affairs, but this persistent, inexplicable absence whetted Fenner's natural curiosity and set his mind to working in strange channels: Morton and Coles—partners in crime. Impossible? Elsa Knoeckler, too, might be involved. Preposterous! Still, could anything be considered unbelievable in this fantastic case? That brief visit to Knoeckler's shop on Thursday evening might not have been only for Elsa's clothes. What more innocent than to give Elsa a package to keep for him? And what more obscure, secure place than Knoeckler's little shop to leave it temporarily? And what more plausible explanation of Morton's solicitous assumption of the burden of the old man's affairs? And what more hideous, mortifying finale than that Coles had taken advantage of Morton's accident to run out with the loot—had even arranged the 'accident'? And what more likely than that Stephen Coles was at the very moment lulled by the click-clack of rails rapidly putting miles between them, or standing in a stern somewhere watching a churning wake reflect the morning's flawless sky and steadily add widening miles of water behind him while Fenner pondered before the locked door of Marten, Morton & Purcell?

The fabric of theory, born during the impatient moment of waiting, crystallized in a twinkling and galvanized Fenner into action. He sprang into the hallway and pushed the elevator button. In the lobby below he telephoned Bryce.

"Coles hasn't showed up yet," he told the inspector curtly. "I'm worried about him. He's not at the job, either; I talked to Quinn." Over the wire Fenner heard Bryce's perplexed grunt and went on: "Why don't you hop over here to Morton's office? The building superintendent will admit us. Maybe we can dig up something. In the meantime I'll try to get the girl down here."

Bryce agreed.

No sooner had he hung up the receiver than doubts sprang into Fenner's mind. The idea of Morton's having committed the theft ran so directly counter to Fenner's conception of the man's psychological makeup that he still found it hard to accept. Equally, his other theory, while far from complete, so logically fitted the human equations involved that he was reluctant to abandon it. Nevertheless, Coles' mysterious flight at this particular time certainly could not be overlooked, and, taken together with the discovery of Morton's possession of the tag, might properly be considered conclusive circumstantial evidence against the pair.

For several thoughtful moments Fenner stood in the telephone booth weighing these pros and cons. Absently he dialed the number of Morton's sister's uptown apartment. Elsa was just about to leave for her vigil at the hospital when Fenner's call came in. Puzzled and vaguely worried she agreed to go to Morton's office instead.

Arriving there she found, in addition to Fenner whom she expected, Inspector Bryce whom she did not; and her uncertain doubts increased. Fenner had outlined his idea to the inspector while they waited, and, inasmuch as it once again fell in with his preconceived notion of Morton's guilt, Bryce found it easy to accept.

"Good morning. We're looking for Stephen Coles," Fenner opened abruptly when Elsa came in. "Thought you might be able to give us some help."

"Why, isn't he here?" It was then ten o'clock.

Fenner glanced about the room and replied good-humoredly: "It seems that he isn't."

"He should be. That is, he's usually in by this time. Did you call his house?"

"His name's not listed. I've been fishing through his desk looking for an address but haven't yet run across one."

"He has a room in the Bronx." Elsa went to her own desk, took a small address book from one of the side drawers, leafed through it for a moment, and read off Coles' address and telephone number.

Fenner called the number and asked for him. He learned from the proprietress of the boarding house that Coles had not been there at all during the previous night. It was very unusual of him. She was surprised and mildly grieved. Had he contemplated going away? No; not that she knew of, and he usually advised her. There was nothing secretive about Coles. He was one of her steadiest boarders. Who was calling? Oh, Mr. Coles' employer. But wasn't he at work? Well, she was sorry but she didn't know where he was nor where he was likely to be found. Presently Fenner disconnected and turned to Bryce with a shrug.

"Gone," was all he said.

Elsa had listened, first with interest, then with bewilderment, then with quick, cold dismay. Her last conversation with Stephen Coles, which in the excitement of subsequent events she had almost forgotten, came quickly to mind. Steve's mood, his jealous, impotent rage, his thoughtless threats, assumed a new and hideous significance.

"Did you want Steve—Mr. Coles—about Mr. Morton, or what?" She gasped the question. "Is anything wrong about—him?"

They could not fail to observe her agitation, and Fenner particularly was puzzled. He was not yet convinced of any guilt on her part.

"'Wrong about him,' Miss Knoeckler," he led her gently. "I'm not quite sure just what you mean."

"Are you looking for Mr. Coles because you think he had something to do with Mr. Morton's injury?" she asked frankly.

"I'm sorry. I can't give you a direct answer to that. We naturally want to find out what he knows. Also, it's an odd time for him to disappear."

"There's something—I haven't told you." She was addressing Fenner haltingly now, feeling her way along. "Believe me, I had simply forgotten about it. It didn't seem important at the time and it didn't occur to me until just now." She stopped.

"Well, what is it?" Bryce snapped.

Fenner waited patiently.

"It's about Steve and Mr. Morton. Oh, I don't quite know how to put it. You see, Steve thought he was in love with me. When he found out about us—Mr. Morton and me—he was—well, quite upset."

"And so—?" Fenner suggested.

"That's all. But I thought I ought to tell you."

"Coles made threats against Mr. Morton?" Fenner suggested shrewdly.

"I don't think he meant what he said, but he seemed to feel pretty strongly about it," Elsa admitted.

"When did you last see Coles?" Bryce put in.

"Yesterday, just before noon—here in this office."

"Is that when he made the threats?"

"They weren't exactly threats," Elsa demurred.

"Can't you recall exactly what he did say—his words?" Bryce insisted.

Elsa hesitated. "I'm afraid not. You see, he raved on so—"

Bryce waved an impatient hand. Fenner cut in sharply: "Tell me this, Miss Knoeckler: Do you yourself think it likely that Coles had anything to do with the accident which befell Mr. Morton?"

"Why, no. I can't say that I do; unless—"

"Unless what?"

"Why, unless he went crazy."

"But you do think it's possible or you wouldn't have told us anything," Fenner finished.

Bryce got to his feet and announced savagely: "We'll go after him!" The black book opened in his hand as if by magic. "This is as good a place to begin as any. Let me have that address again, will you?" To Fenner he said: "I'll send a couple of men out to that room. Maybe we can pick up a picture." Bryce relit his cigar and the man-hunt was on.

Elsa excused herself to go to the hospital. No sooner had the door closed behind her than Bryce started, a drawer at a time, methodically going through the contents of Coles' desk. Fenner watched for a second, then proceeded in the same manner to go through Randolph Morton's. Primarily Bryce was looking for any sort of a clue or paper which might give him an inkling as to Coles' probable whereabouts or the direction in which he would most likely flee. Fenner was seeking he was not sure what. When they had finished with the desks they tackled the files, then the bookcases. Two hours later they left the office.

"It seems," Fenner remarked caustically as they walked away, "that we've taken the proverbial one step forward and two steps back."

"What d'ye mean?"

"Well, for a brief moment after it became apparent that Coles had 'taken it on the lam,' as some of your estimable colleagues might put it, I thought that we might be on a pretty tangible track. Now it appears that Mr. Coles, even if guilty of violence toward his benevolent ex-employer, was subject to motivating influences of a different sort of which we were hitherto unaware. In other words, our smart calculations seem to be knocked galley-west."

2

It was just after noon when Fenner and Bryce walked up the slight ramp to the timekeeper's shanty at the new Consolidated Building job. They found Quade alone.

"Anything new?" Bryce asked.

"Not much. From what I can gather, that argument Morton had yesterday was about leveling off pier bottoms. Dickson and Borden and Quinn were all peeved at him—thought he was too particular and was wasting time and money. It seems Morton finally hung around down there himself because he was afraid they might not do things the way he wanted."

"Find out any more about Coles?" Bryce had telephoned Quade as soon as he had learned from Fenner that Coles was missing.

"He was last seen by the night timekeeper a few minutes after eight last evening. It seems he came back after dinner to have a last look around. Quinn saw him, too. He told him that you and Mr. Fenner had been looking for him. Coles made some wisecrack answer about tomorrow being another day. Quinn says Coles might have been a little the worse for having had his dinner in one of those speakies in Pearl Street."

"Drunk?"

"Oh, not badly."

"You've seen nothing of him today, of course?" Fenner put in.

"Nope."

"Well, keep your eyes peeled." Bryce's gruff parting admonition was more from force of habit than from intent.

"He seems to have beat it, all right," the inspector meditated aloud as they reached the street. "I wonder where he got the guts to brain Morton. I'd never have put him down as the violent type."

"He isn't. He's anything but, if my judgment, based on two brief interviews, means anything. But a person crazed with jealousy steps beyond his type characteristics."

They trudged to the Police Station where Bryce assembled the last reports of his various aides and read them off for Fenner's benefit. Randolph Morton had spent the largest part of the previous (Wednesday) forenoon in Knoeckler's shop in Fulton Street. In the afternoon he had gone to the job where later he had been hurt. He still hovered at the brink of eternity, but today the doctors held forth a faint ray of hope. Elsa Knoeckler was spending most of her wakeful hours at the hospital. Dickson and Borden were going about their daily tasks in quite the usual prosaic way, both being at the Consolidated job a great deal of the time. Hanley had been to the theater last evening. Jeremy, together with a young lady, presumably Jerry's fiancée, had visited Jerry at the jail. It had been the usual session of mutual condolences and reassurances, with Jerry showing most courage of the three. Nothing had been learned from it. There was the whole story.

"A lot of chaff but not an ounce of grain in it anywhere," Bryce concluded; then added hopefully: "When Morton wakes up maybe we'll get something."

"When Morton wakes up?"

"Well, I'm still thinking that tag is going to be hard for him to explain."

"Suppose he simply looks at it and tells you he's never seen it before?"

Bryce had no ready answer.

"Have you uncovered anything more in connection with Morton's affairs?"

"Not so far. We went through his apartment last night. Two of the boys are out at that camp of his in Jersey today but I haven't heard from them yet." They were silent for a moment.

"I've been wondering," Bryce presently resumed, "why couldn't everything we supposed this morning about Coles and Morton be true and this 'jealousy' slant be just additional reason for Coles giving Morton the works?"

Fenner did not reply at once. His instincts had from the start apprised him of some intangible fallacy in the whole idea. Now that he had found another explanation for Coles' disappearance he was glad to drop the other. Presently he suggested: "If that was the case I don't think Coles would have taken a chance on getting drunk last evening—even slightly. Neither do I think he'd have come back to the job at all. He'd have cleared out, pronto!"

"Maybe so."

3

The day wore on. About midafternoon Bryce went to the hospital. Morton had taken a turn for the better.

Fenner made his way to the Consolidated Bank. There were still one or two matters which he felt duty-bound to discuss with T. Jerome Hanley. Curiously, he was vaguely relieved to find the manager gone for the day.

With hardly conscious guidance, Fenner's steps carried him across the street to the truck platform overlooking the new building excavation. For no reason he could define, the job attracted him like a needle drawn by a powerful magnet. He leaned over the rail and gazed down into the busy lot, peering as if to discover somewhere therein the key to his confusion.

His instant reaction upon learning of Morton's injury, he reflected, had been that the engineer had met with foul play. This notion he had not for a moment abandoned. All the circumstances surrounding the accident were unnatural. Most startling of all was the fact that every one of the people under suspicion in connection with the vault looting except the Donegans was on the job and without a real alibi at the time Morton was hurt. He ticked them off on his fingers: Dickson was on his way up from the bottom, Borden was somewhere about the job bringing his records up to date, Hanley had left his guests and gone down to look for Morton. The obvious explanation for any attempt to kill him would be that somebody wished to silence him. If Morton was not himself involved in the bank theft, he must have known or suspected who was. Therefore, when—if ever—he was able to speak, he could disclose his suspicions and name his attacker. This had been Fenner's first conclusion and hope.

Now it appeared that Morton might have met his misfortune at the hands of his own assistant and for a reason in no way related to the Consolidated Bank. It seemed almost incredible to Fenner that events should conspire to produce this particular distracting effect at this particular time; yet if this was not the case, then why should Coles have fled? And if this was the case, then whence and wherefore the tag in Morton's coat?

Once again Fenner took himself back to the beginning, retraversed the case as it had unfolded step by step, reconstructed the nebulous theory his intuition had prompted and which had seemed to be filling in until today, and once again he arrived at the same impasse: Morton, by any reasonable deduction, was attacked by the perpetrator of the vault theft and the tag left upon him to direct suspicion to him. Yet Coles, who had equal opportunity but an independent motive, was gone. Mildly at first, then devastatingly, a horrible suspicion obtruded itself. . . .

The sun had dropped behind the tall buildings to the west and their long shadows extended themselves completely across the site before a sobered Maxwell Fenner roused himself from a speculative reverie and betook himself back to Bryce's headquarters. Here another surprise was in store for him.

The inspector looked at him with grim satisfaction, waited deliberately until it was apparent that Fenner had nothing to disclose, then remarked with an abortive effort at casualness: "I know you've had something up your sleeve on this case since Tuesday. I don't know how Morton's accident yesterday affected it, but see how this fits in: The bird we've been looking for, who went to Knoeckler's shop ahead of Morton and the girl last Thursday evening, was none other than Stephen Coles. He was looking for his lady love."

"No!"

"No less! I got it from the girl a while ago. I ran into her at the hospital and buzzed her a little about him. I asked her when Coles had first started being obnoxious about Morton. She said it was only since the week-end. She'd played sick to get away from the office Thursday and he'd come around to the store that night and hadn't found her. That's what started him off. She says he raised hell when he saw her Wednesday morning."

Fenner sat for a moment assimilating the disclosure, attempting to relate this new fact to the maze of other facts already known. Presently he said slowly: "This may be precisely the fact I've been looking for. It wasn't quite crystallized in my mind, but now I realize that the puzzling thing up to this moment has been Coles' connection to the case. The jealousy motive was strong enough, but unconnected unless we assume pure coincidence. There has been too much of that already. But this may tie him in. I don't see quite how, yet, but I feel that it does." He paused, lost in thought, then went on, slowly voicing the thoughts: "Morton was attacked—killed as far as the attacker's intentions went—as a direct result of the vault robbery and the tag was left upon him to attract suspicion; whereupon Coles, who it now appears has become involved in the case, disappears completely. The inference is obvious." Again he paused. "In fact, it's too utterly obvious."

Fenner got up and paced the floor. "Any leads on him yet?"

"The boys found a couple of good photos in his room," Bryce replied. "Some papers and letters, too. His home's upstate near Rochester. They're on the lookout around there. We're getting out a circular, too."

"Well, I suppose it can't do any harm," was Fenner's enigmatic comment.

8

FRIDAY
APRIL 8TH

1

AT HALF PAST EIGHT the next morning, unconscionably early for Fenner, he sat again in Bryce's office. He was attempting, though without much success, the role of Pollyanna, for he had found the inspector in low spirits indeed. Bryce made no effort to conceal his mortification at the turn the case had taken and at their slow progress.

"We certainly muffed this up," he moaned. "I wish to God I had stuck to my original hunch on Morton. He'd be in a cell instead of the hospital, and while I don't know where the bank's dough would be right now, it's a cinch it wouldn't be halfway across the continent or maybe in Canada with Stephen Coles."

"If I was convinced that that was the case I'm not sure I wouldn't feel better about the whole business than I do," Fenner confessed soberly. He forced a lightness into his tone. "From your remarks, Inspector, I gather you haven't yet put the bracelets on your fugitive."

"Not so's you'd notice it! Not even a decent lead so far."

"And," Fenner pressed, "having slept upon the matter, do you feel he's gone because he double-crossed Morton and took the money or because he brained him in a fit of jealousy over the girl?"

"He's gone. What difference does it make?"

Fenner shrugged his shoulders. Next he asked: "What's the word from the hospital this morning?"

"A little more encouraging. He's still in a critical condition but the doctor says that, having come through the night, his chances are now definitely good."

"Has he become conscious?"

"He came out of the coma late last night but they put him to sleep again. The doctor says it'll be about a week before we can talk to him."

"By that time we may tell him more than he tells us," Fenner commented hopefully.

"Yeah? I wish I could share your optimism."

"Let's get down to cases. Anything out of order yet in our 'little daily stories'?"

Bryce opened his book. "I see from this report that Miss Knoeckler spent a pleasant quarter of an hour in Morton's office with us yesterday. I suppose that might be considered compromising. That's about all." He turned serious. "Were you able to get anything out of her at the hospital the other evening?"

"I'm afraid not," Fenner replied. "Morton hasn't taken her into his confidence much. She knows less of his financial affairs than we do. She did tell me he's planning a divorce so he can marry her. I flashed the tag on her and told her where it came from. Thought I'd frighten something out of her, but no such thing! She insists it's either a mistake or Morton can explain it. When this is all over I'm going to congratulate the man upon his selection of mistresses. She's loyal if ever a girl has been."

"I imagine he'd be delighted to hear you refer to her in those terms," Bryce said dryly.

"I didn't use the word disparagingly," Fenner objected. "The more I see of Miss Knoeckler, the higher my opinion of her becomes. She's taken a lot of hard knocks these last few days, with scarce a whimper. As for her affair, it's just that—her own affair."

Bryce regarded Fenner curiously. "If I had never met Mrs. Fenner I'd be inclined to suspect you of falling a little for the girl yourself."

Fenner laughed. "Nonsense! But I never professed to complete insusceptibility. That's a state I reserve for older age than I hope to attain. But let's get back to business. What next?"

Bryce turned back to his notes. "From Morton's office she went to the hospital and was there until dinner time. Had dinner up-town at a tea-shop near where she's staying and then went in. Not out yet this morning.

"Now, here's the Donegans: Jerry in fair spirits and apparently resigned to waiting for something to happen. Sticks to his original story and told me yesterday that inasmuch as he was innocent he wasn't worrying because certainly no one could prove him guilty. Sounded fairly convincing. His father went to see him again last evening. Their talk was very restrained. I believed they suspected they were being listened to. Sometimes I have a feeling there's something fishy about the old gent, but I can't quite pin it down. But anyway, he's followed his routine so regularly that you could almost set a watch by his movements. Then, of course, his record is so long—"

Fenner waved his hand as if to discard the entire suggestion. "To my way of thinking he's out. If I'm mistaken, then this is simply going to settle into one hell of a protracted wait. He can wait forever. Go on."

"Now Dickson and Borden: Both of them stayed on the job until late in the afternoon. Dickson called up the hospital several times during the day and Borden also called once or twice. They both seem concerned about him, though I suppose it's natural. Dickson went to his main office about half past four. He went home by the usual route and wasn't out of the house all evening. He left home at the usual hour this morning. Here's something that gave me a start for a minute: When Borden left the job yesterday he went around the corner to a pay-phone booth and talked for five or six minutes. That was about ten minutes before six. McFadden—he's one of the men on him—got the number from the operator but it turned out to be only his house phone. Borden went home, had dinner, went to the "Y" for his Thursday class, then home as usual. He left the house at the usual time this morning and is on the job now."

Bryce closed the book and settled back into his chair, folding his hands across his ample girth resignedly. "That's all except Hanley. The morning dope on him hasn't come in yet, but if there was to be anything special I'd have heard by now." He sighed his

disgust and pushed the book away from him, concluding wearily:
"If you can find anything in any of that you've got a better nose
than I have."

Fenner got up and walked to the window. The sky had been
heavily overcast since dawn; now a steady drizzle was falling. He
stared into the gloomy murk speculatively. "You know," he said
slowly, "that bit about the pay phone intrigues me. Let me have
the time and the telephone number of the booth, will you?"

Bryce leafed through the notes and read off the phone number.
"At five-fifty P.M.," he added as Fenner jotted it down.

"Perhaps we can make something of it. Anyway, 'No stone
unturned,' you know." Fenner folded the slip of paper and tucked
it into his vest pocket. He picked up his hat and umbrella and went
out into the rain.

2

Bryce turned to his desk after Fenner had departed and began
going through the small daily quota of routine work that accompanied his position. After a brief, desultory attack, however, he thrust
the sheaf of papers aside, unable to focus his attention upon them
and unable to expel from his thoughts the perplexities of the
Consolidated Bank case.

Inactivity had always irked him. Fenner's theories of watchful
waiting had always rasped upon a certain spot of raw impatience
in his makeup, but seldom quite so exasperatingly as on this particular morning. And yet he could not deny their proved effective-
ness in the past, nor at this moment could he suggest any practi-
cable substitute.

Laboriously he got up out of the chair and moved over to the
window. The old station building with its massive, forbidding walls
and barred windows was a gloomy place at best, but on days like
this when the skies were grayed with storm and the feeble play of
daylight that somehow found its way in was dimmed, the place
assumed a deadly repressiveness that the yellow electric lights and
bustling activity could never quite allay. Even Bryce, casehardened,

immunized by years beneath the heavy atmosphere, sometimes felt its pressure.

On this morning he could feel it, a somber, intangible heaviness, as he watched the wind and rain swirling in the dismal courtyard, splattering maliciously against the high windows, dripping monotonously off the stone sills. Through the gates at the end of the court he could see an occasional dray rumbling along the river front, the driver soaked, the horses steaming in the foggy morning. Heavy trucks thundered ponderously along; lighter ones sputtered in and out among them. The steady rush of the wind and rain against the window panes was punctuated, with monotonous regularity, by the shrill blasts of a traffic policeman's whistle around the corner, as often by the strident squawking of taxi horns, and now and again more pleasantly by the melancholy throatings of tugs and freighters making their steady way up the East River.

Bryce thought of Fenner out in the rain. He wondered what his colleague could have hit upon to take him forth into such cheerless weather. Borden had called up his home from a pay-telephone booth, superficially not a suspicion-inviting departure from normal action, for if he suspected the job phone was tapped and used an outside phone for that reason surely he would know by the same token that he himself was under surveillance and would do nothing quite so obvious.

The more Bryce pondered the matter, the more perplexed he became. His first inclination would have been to dismiss it from his mind, but he knew that if Fenner attached significance to the event then suspicion was extremely likely to be justified. But his puzzling got him nowhere and gradually the subject slipped out of his thoughts.

He went back to his desk and resumed his work, but without enthusiasm and again not for long. The distracting question that ran through his mind this time was why Fenner had said nothing to Hanley of the discovery of the tag. Fenner had not seen the bank manager since the event—that Bryce realized—but certainly the development was of sufficient import to warrant getting in touch with him. Perhaps Fenner suspected Hanley of possessing firsthand guilty knowledge of the tag and was waiting for an overt slip. Hanley had been in the excavation when Morton was hurt. He had had as much opportunity to plant the tag as anyone, if Morton was being framed. Yet if Fenner suspected Hanley of any duplicity, he would not put the man on his guard by failing to report a find which Hanley, if involved, would certainly know had been made. Quite the contrary, he would have immediately rushed to him and disarmed any suspicion by telling him all about it and probably would have discussed the find and its implications at as much length as Hanley desired. On the other hand, if Fenner was sure of Hanley, why had he not reported the incident as would have been the natural thing to do? Bryce found no answer, and with a mental note to quiz Fenner he turned back to his papers.

Thus the morning limped on—a long morning, boring, endless, with Bryce conscious of the passage of every minute of the time. Noon approached and he was becoming more and more impatient for some word from Fenner when the phone bell at his elbow jangled. He picked up the receiver, nervous, a vague premonition assailing him that something at long last had happened. It had. The voice at the other end of the wire was that of his aide, McFadden.

"Say, chief," he reported, "we ain't sure yet, but it looks like Borden might've give us the slip."

"Given you the slip? When? Where? What do you mean?" Bryce bit the words off savagely.

"Well, you see," his lieutenant explained, "it's rainin' like hell down here—has been all morning. All these fellows have got on yellow oilskin slickers and hats. From ten feet away or from behind you can't tell one from the next—laborers, bosses, everybody. Borden was hangin' around the office shanty keepin' dry most of the morning. Quade says he acted like he might've had something on his mind. About half past ten he put on a slicker and went down into the job. Quade give me the high sign and I seen him go down the ladder. Then the rain got so bad the job knocked off. The men come on up and checked out, but not Borden. I got hold of Quade right away and he slipped down and took a walk around the bottom. He says there's not a soul around but a few pump mechanics. Bert is over watching the restaurant Borden generally uses. Maybe we'll pick him up there. It's almost noon—" McFadden hesitated, awaiting an outburst from his superior, but the storm failed to materialize.

Instead Bryce simply instructed: "Hang around there. I'm coming over. If Borden's not on the job we'll pick him up somewhere. Tell Quade to stay there too. I want to talk to him."

The inspector hung up, thought a moment, then phoned Fenner's office but was not surprised to learn that his colleague's whereabouts was unknown. Bryce pressed a button, issued rapid instructions to the lieutenant who appeared, and went out into the rain, knowing that even as he crossed the threshold his handful of brief commands had set into motion the ponderous machinery of the law, that already its tentacles were extending and spreading, swiftly, implacably; that many wires were humming in the vast city network, that dozens of watchful eyes were waiting alert in railway stations, ferry houses, and at a hundred strategic points in the department's ramified system. But the knowledge afforded Bryce only a limited measure of comfort. The system was good, he knew, but to the wary fugitive a thousand loopholes offered. At least, Borden hadn't had much of a start. Coles had had a whole night, which made a great deal of difference. Still, if Borden was staging a planned getaway, their chances were not better than average, but Bryce was not convinced that this was the case. McFadden and Quade were not infallible. Borden could have very well quite unconsciously walked out of their ken. In that case he might shortly just as innocently walk back in again.

Bryce found McFadden waiting across the street from the job gate. He had no more than arrived when Quade also put in an appearance, sauntering up the ramp and across the street to join them. With the noonday throngs reduced by the weather to a hurrying minimum, and the clamor stilled that ordinarily rose up from the new building site, the street assumed an unaccustomed holiday quiet. Bryce and his two aides huddled in the shelter of a building entrance. In a low voice and in scarcely more detail McFadden repeated what he had told his chief over the telephone. Quade could add little to the account. Borden, he said, had stayed in the office shanty most of the morning, passing the time of day with the superintendent and doing a little figuring over the plans but mostly watching the rain pour down. It had been decided to "knock off" the job for the day if the rain did not subside by eleven o'clock. A quarter of an hour before that time Borden had donned one of the company issue of oilskins and had gone down into the cellar for a final look around. The men had checked out and gone home, but Borden had not appeared. Casual inquiry by Quade had elicited the fact that the superintendent had not seen Borden after he left the shanty. Quade had taken a hasty walk through the cellar and had then communicated with McFadden. Since then he had made a more thorough tour, examining every nook and corner. He was satisfied that Borden was no longer on the job.

Bryce digested this information for a moment, then turned to McFadden and commanded: "Chase around to that restaurant. He may have come in there by now. I'll be either here or in the phone booth in the lobby."

When McFadden had gone, Bryce telephoned the construction company's office and talked to Dickson, asking for Borden. The engineer was not a little curious as to this sudden burst of official interest in his assistant, but he could give no clue as to Borden's immediate whereabouts, stating only that Borden was supposed to be at the job. When Bryce countered that the job had been shut down on account of the rain, Dickson somewhat testily suggested that in all likelihood, then, Borden was at lunch or on his way up-town to the office.

"It's quite possible," Bryce agreed dryly, and added peremptorily: "Be good enough to have him get in touch with Mr. Hanley or myself when you hear from him, will you?" Abruptly he rang off leaving Dickson more mystified than ever and no less ruffled. When he came out of the booth Bryce found McFadden already back.

"No luck, Chief," the latter reported soberly. "Bert is still there, though, and it's not twelve-thirty yet. There's still a chance." Bryce stepped back into the booth and called Fenner's office but found that there was still no word from him either. Somewhat at a loss as to where to turn next, he started back to headquarters, but as he passed the Consolidated Bank entrance he remembered that he ought to notify Hanley that Borden might call him up.

The bank manager welcomed the inspector warmly, almost excitedly. He was, he said, "hungry for news." He'd not seen Fenner since the afternoon of Morton's accident, and then only for a minute or two. Mr. Morton, he understood, was thought to have a good chance now. He'd tried several times during the morning to get Fenner on the telephone but had been unable to. Were they getting anywhere? Was anything new? There was to be a Board meeting during the afternoon. He'd like to report some sort of progress if such a thing was possible.

Bryce acknowledged both statements and questions with only slow nods and thoughtful rolling around of his unlit cigar between his lips. When Hanley seemed to have finished, he said with cheerful irrelevance: "Young Borden may call you up. We lost track of him this morning. I left word with Dickson to have him call you or me. I can't say I expect him to call but I wouldn't be surprised if he did. On the other hand, if he doesn't show up soon I'll begin to suspect something fishy." Bryce watched the bank manager's face as he made these remarks but detected nothing untoward in the latter's reception of them or in his bearing.

"But what the devil shall I tell him?" Hanley naturally wanted to know.

Bryce ignored the query for a moment. A little thing like that ought to be easy for a bank manager. But presently he replied: "Oh, tell him you want to see him about the vault. Tell him anything. If he calls at all, that lets him out, which will mean it won't make any difference what you tell him. If he doesn't call or show up, it won't be very long before we pick him up."

Hanley whistled between his teeth, mildly amazed. "So that's it! Well, this is something. And have you given over your suspicions of Mr. Morton?"

Bryce looked at the banker sideways, wondering if the question was as innocent as it sounded. The tag! Who could tell?

"Why, we haven't exactly given over suspecting anybody," he replied cautiously. "This is one of those damned cases where everybody is guilty until proven innocent, you know."

Hanley's only reply to that was a grunt. He looked at his watch.

"Will you come upstairs with me and have lunch?" he suggested. "We have quite a dining room. It would be better than to go out in this rain."

Bryce looked out at the gray streets and troubled skies. The rain, which had somewhat abated before he came in, had renewed its violence and was coming down in great swirling sheets that he could hardly see through. The thought of a comfortable lunch tempted him but, more intriguing, there was the remote possibility that his host might become carelessly expansive. He would certainly be one up on Fenner if anything of that sort could be brought to pass. "Why, I suppose I can, if you like," he assented to Hanley's invitation.

Before they went up he telephoned his headquarters. He found, though with no surprise, that the wide net had so far yielded up nothing.

3

Throughout an unusually hearty and protracted lunch, Hanley, much to Bryce's disappointment and disgust, kept the conversation strictly upon politics, prohibition, the weather and musical comedies. At the conclusion of the meal they returned together to the manager's office.

Hanley opened the door for Bryce, but the inspector did not enter. Instead he stood rooted to the threshold, frozen in astonishment. Hanley glanced over his shoulder and saw within, seated in his most comfortable leather guest chair, Maxwell Fenner. The dapper investigator presented a picture of solid comfort. His knees were crossed, one leg swinging idly; his cigarette drooped at just the proper nonchalant angle; his whole attitude reflected the acme of indolence.

Before him on one end of Hanley's desk was placed a small tan suitcase, unopened. At the window, gazing meditatively out, sat Philip Borden. A uniformed policeman standing by in one corner of the room lent an air of grim reality to the scene. Fenner nodded to Bryce and Hanley.

"You've both met Mr. Borden," he said amiably, exaggerating the courtesy. Hanley and Bryce, taken aback at the unexpected amenity and not sure of the irony, both managed nods. Borden returned their bows gravely.

"Mr. Borden and I have been having a very interesting discussion of the matter of the trifling shortage that came up last week," Fenner explained. "A little one-sided to be called a discussion," he amended, "because Mr. Borden very modestly prefers to let me have the floor."

"Oh, yeah?" from Bryce.

"It isn't always that we have the chance to review intelligently our theories and earmark our mistakes for future profit," Fenner went on.

Hanley's eyes were on the suitcase; he hardly heard the remark.

Observing this Fenner said: "I haven't opened that yet. Mr. Borden will supply you with a key, I believe. I think it would be poetic justice to have old Jeremy and young Donegan check it over, though I haven't the slightest doubt you'll find your consignment quite intact."

Borden shook his head. "I'm sorry I can't help you," he said. "I have a knife, though, that will make a monkey of that grip if you care to use it." He drew a heavy clasp knife from his pocket, opened it slowly, and held it out for Hanley.

The manager crossed the room to take it, moving as in a daze, hardly comprehending what was happening, hardly able to believe he was awake. He hesitated, undecided as to how to attack the lock. Bryce impatiently took the knife from him and with several swift slits ripped a whole side out of the grip. Within they saw the small canvas dispatch bag, comfortably crammed as it must have been on the day, little more than a week past, when it so mysteriously disappeared from the vault.

Hanley looked at Fenner bewilderedly, then sideways at Borden, then across the room at the policeman, finally at Bryce. Fenner replied to his questioning glance by announcing: "Mr. Borden has expressed an intention to refrain from discussing his part in this affair pending advice of counsel. This is his privilege, of course, but I believe I can outline the principal points without his assistance." Fenner's eyes bored into Borden as he expressed this conviction.

Borden returned his glance coolly for a moment, then turned away to resume his watch through the window.

"In the first place," Fenner continued, "I suppose you're all curious as to where this little bag of tricks has been hidden for the past week. Well, it has been just about five blocks from here tucked away in the Hudson Terminal Parcel Room. You must have had some anxious moments; those places are far from infallible." The last remark was addressed to Borden.

The younger man broke his silence.

"Not me," he said laconically. "I knew nothing about it. A parcel check was handed to me Wednesday morning by Mr. Morton. He asked me as a personal favor to get a bag he had left there, to keep it for him for a couple of days, and to keep my mouth shut. At first I thought it was liquor he'd got while he was in Detroit, but for my trouble he promised me a month's pay if a deal he was trying to put across went through, so I knew it couldn't be that. I never saw that bag until this morning. I had no idea what it contained when I went for it, though I did begin to suspect it when you brought me here." He paused and then went on: "I suppose even if Mr. Morton recovers I'll have a hard time making anyone believe my word against his."

"Why do you so quickly assume Morton will deny your story?" Fenner asked quickly.

"Why not? Do you think I can't see I've been taken for a ride? I'm the sap! To think I was going to take care of all of that loot for him for four hundred dollars. I suppose he was afraid to offer me more—I'd get too curious." He broke off. "I'm talking too much." He said it almost apologetically.

"Yes, you are," Fenner agreed. "It's a pretty plausible story, though; but I should be very surprised if you got by with it, even if Morton never wakes up to talk." He looked Borden over appraisingly and said icily: "You have a remarkably quick head in emergencies. It's a shame your talent was diverted out of honest channels. You might have made your mark in the world. Since the moment I tapped your shoulder at the Hudson Terminal this noon you've been deliberating your chances. You were caught with the goods and knew it. You might have made a break but decided that the odds would be too much against you. You had to shift the blame and there was Morton all stretched out to receive it. You're taking a chance on his passing out, but not such a bad chance at that, because it would still be your word against his if he recovers. But that's not all." Fenner's tone was low but incisive. "You banked on one more circumstance—this." He drew from his pocket the fiber tag and tossed it clattering on the desk. "You knew Morton had it on him when he was taken away."

Hanley started up out of his chair at the sight of the tag but settled back again. Borden looked at it with mild curiosity, then turned away uninterestedly. Fenner could not help admiring the man's control. He resumed his remarks with slow, firm deliberation, directing them all at the impassive Borden as if to hammer down his reserve. "You hope that Morton dies so there will be no one to deny your clever cock-and-bull story. You had better pray that he lives. Murder is a damned sight more serious than larceny." He hesitated. "Suppose I were to tell you I had an eye-witness who saw you drop that bull point on Randolph Morton's head? Would you want him to get better then?"

It was a shot in the dark and utterly failed of its mark.

Borden's gaze shifted for a second; then he cleared his throat and said evenly: "You can have no such witness because I did no such thing."

"A man cool enough to do that is of course cool enough to deny it," Fenner observed dryly.

Bryce interrupted, suggesting: "Suppose we go around to the station. Maybe Mr. Borden'd feel more like loosening up there."

"It would be of no use whatever," Fenner replied impatiently. "Can't you see that here's a fellow whom your third degree would never faze? It's going to take more than a beating up with a length of hose or a few teeth knocked out to make him change his story."

Hanley had watched and listened with growing bewilderment. He picked up the tag which Fenner had tossed upon the desk.

"What? Where?" he started but Fenner interrupted him.

"I'm going to run through this whole thing from the beginning as I have reconstructed it. I venture, Mr. Borden, you'll have damned few corrections to make; and when you've heard the whole business and realize how tight you're sewed up, maybe you'll come to your senses and decide to come clean.

"Now let's get back to last Thursday morning. You went into the vault with the party. You carried your level in its box and carried the tripod under your arm. You were mildly interested in the workings of a bank, not having been around them much before, and kept your eyes open in a natural, normal way, but for the most part you tended to business. When you got into the vault you were naturally impressed with the proximity to such vast wealth. I dare say every member of the party had somewhat the same feeling somewhere in the back of his mind. It would be unnatural not to. When you went to set up your instrument you had to get back in the corner behind that money truck.

"You unpacked your machine and did your job. However, when you were through and glanced down, you saw your level case standing invitingly open and sheltered from view behind the truck loaded with sacks of money. The juxtaposition was too much for you. In a flash you decided to take a chance. You stooped over and flipped one of the sacks from the truck into the level box. No one noticed. I can imagine your elation. Whether you picked a sack at random and just happened to get the particular one in the whole load most suited to your purpose, or whether you took time to glance at the tags, you can tell me when I'm through.

"Anyway—so far, so good. You had made a perfect beginning on what was going to be a grand coup. You were troubled by no conscientious scruples, no moral sense of right or wrong. A bank with all the wealth of the Consolidated could well spare some of it to you, if you were clever enough to take it. It was just a game, with the odds against you but the prize worth winning if you could bring it off. You might have even started mentally enjoying your gains, but I suspect not. There were other things to keep your brain busy. You felt pretty sure you'd get out of the building, but you had no idea how long it would be before a hue and cry was raised.

"You might have walked out of the bank and disappeared. When I think it over I believe that would have been your wisest course. But you preferred not. It would have meant becoming a fugitive, uprooting your life and its associations. You thought you knew a better way: to cache your loot and go about your normal way of life and wait—years, if necessary—until the thing blew over and it was safe for you gradually to draw your stake back into use."

He paused for breath, still looking at Borden. The latter had not altered his bearing a whit. He simply sat and listened, politely curious. Fenner was not discouraged. He went on: "So you schemed to make yourself a chance to get away as soon as the party broke up. Your instrument was a little out of shape. You exaggerated the difficulty you were having with it and arranged to take it to Knoeckler's shop to have it fixed. That gave you a plausible reason for leaving the party and, more important, carting your loot along with you. You put the level telescope in the box on top of the sack and squeezed the lid shut. It must have been a tight squeeze because I later tried it in the same box with a sack not quite as large and was just able to make it. The bracket you crammed into your coat pocket. When you left the bank you walked as far as the corner with Mr. Morton. You didn't know how much time you had, but you feared it would be the minimum. To get up to your own office in the normal time, with a reasonable allowance for lunch, that was your object.

"You went into a store—there are a number along Nassau Street where a valise like that can be had—and bought that grip. Hastily you transferred the sack to the grip and packed the level and bracket properly. Then you went around to Knoeckler's and left the instrument for repairs. A general overhauling, you asked him to give it, because the specific condition you complained of to Dickson probably would not have even warranted the repairs. Then you took your little grip and walked over to the Hudson Terminal and checked it. You had lunch at the Exchange Buffet there—I imagine you put it away in quite a hurry—and went on up to your office where you very innocently put in an appearance at just about the time you should have.

"But even then you were not safe. You could not leave the grip at the parcel room indefinitely. You did not even fell like keeping the check about you, so you mailed it with a plausible note to your friend, a Mr. Arthur Lowman, from whom you obtained it this morning. Then you sat back to wait.

"You didn't have to wait long. In a few minutes Hanley called you downtown. You came along, anxious to do everything you could for us, and with a plausible, reasonable account of your actions since leaving the bank. Since that time you've hardly been out of our sight, but you've known it all along and acted with corresponding circumspection."

Fenner stopped again. The room was so tensely quiet that even breathing seemed to have ceased.

Hanley and Bryce waited in rapt absorption. Borden seemed, if anything, a shade more thoughtful. Fenner turned back to him and went on: "There is little I've told you so far that can not be specifically proved. You might get out in from four to six years, counting on good behavior, if that was all of the story. Unfortunately I feel impelled to outline some additional conjectures which will be turned over to the district attorney. I believe a little investigation, especially if Mr. Morton's testimony becomes available, will bring out certain circumstances which will result for you in something more serious than four to six years up the river."

He waited for some sort of response. Borden was silent for a long moment; then he said: "I'm sorry, sir, but I'm afraid I don't know what you're talking about."

Fenner shrugged his shoulders. "So that's to be your line! Well, we shall see." He turned to the others and apologized: "I shall try to make a long story short." He drew his chair around so it more squarely faced Borden and picked up his discourse where he had left off. "When we finished talking to you Thursday, you went back to your office. You had hardly got there when you had a telephone call from Adolph Knoeckler. He was very insistent that he see you about your level. You knew there was nothing about the repairs to it that couldn't be settled over the phone, so you smelled a rat and went down to see him. Mr. Knoeckler was not so dumb. He showed you that little tag. I don't know how much he asked you for, but I imagine it was plenty. Incidentally, you can thank me at least partly for that call of his. I'll tell you why. When you transferred the sack from the box to the suitcase you were in a hurry. The tag got caught in one of the brackets in the box and you yanked the sack out and left the tag there. It probably wasn't wired very securely. Old Adolph found the tag and thought nothing of it. A little while later he read in the afternoon tabloid of the robbery of $180,000 from the Consolidated Bank's vault, and that some engineers were being questioned. He might not have thought much of that either, but when in a few minutes I came in and quizzed him about your stop there, the time, and whatever else I could find out, he put two and two together. He was poor, in ill health, and tired. He saw a chance to fix himself for life, so he called you up.

"As I say, I can't even guess how much he wanted; but however much or little it was, you realized that your secret was no longer your own. I don't know whether you bashed him in the head and carried him down cellar or shoved him down first and then bashed him. The result was all the same. You should have left the cellar light on, though. It would have looked much more natural if he had been found with the light on—as if he'd started down for something. Still, I suppose one instinctively leaves a job of that sort in darkness, and you weren't thinking very clearly just then.

"When you started out of the store you were probably really panicky. But you saw the flatfoot loitering across the street and came to your senses. You walked a few steps, then turned back and opened the shop door and called something back, presumably to someone within and came out chuckling. It was an excellent bit of play acting and fooled Murphy completely—fooled us all for a while.

It was late in the afternoon and the back of the store was dark. With that sort of a business there would probably be no more customers that day. There was a good chance that nothing would be discovered until it was too late to tie you directly to it; but, even so, I imagine you had a bad night. After all, old Adolph was rather a feeble old gentleman, and murder wasn't exactly a part of your everyday routine—even the murder of a pathetic old amateur blackmailer. But once you start this business, one thing follows another and it's hard to know just where to draw the line."

Fenner paused upon this observation and glanced around at his listeners. Borden returned his glance impassively when their eyes met but mostly he stared out of the windows or around the blank walls. Hanley, whose rapt attention had been centered upon Fenner throughout the long discourse, relaxed a little and allowed his glance to sweep furtively over Borden. The uniformed policeman who from the background had listened avidly to the denouement of a larceny mystery such as he was not likely to encounter again in many a year, shifted his weight and settled himself into a more restful position against the wall. Bryce, who had listened to his colleague with ungrudging admiration, now addressed Borden:

"What have you got to say, young man?" he urged. His notebook was open on his knee.

Borden regarded him with ill-concealed disgust.

"I have only this to say—that I don't know what you're talking about," he replied. "It's obvious enough that some sort of a frame-up is being put over and that I'm to be the goat. I've got nothing to say until you get Morton down here or take me to him so I can face him. Aside from that I guess I'd better get a lawyer to do my 'saying' for me. I know my limitations and they don't include debating with a bunch of clever sharks and getting myself locked up or worse for something I know nothing about."

"Well said! Damned well said!" Fenner applauded. "You belong in the 'Talkies,' but you're not kidding me." He resumed his serious tone. "Furthermore you won't be able to kid the judge or a jury. Your 'or worse' is the more likely.

"Now I'm going ahead from where I left off. Correct me from time to time if anything occurs to you. Last Thursday night and Friday you went about your business in quite the normal way. Friday afternoon I asked you to come to Knoeckler's. The old man had been found dead. Now here was your first bad slip. Aside from leaving the tag in the level box, of course. Do you remember our interview? Probably not in detail. Well, the point is that you came in and went out of that shop without once demonstrating any normal curiosity as to where or how Mr. Knoeckler had met his end. You acted properly shocked and surprised when we told you he'd met it, but you didn't bother to ask how or where. At the time I attributed this omission on your part simply to excitement, but I've since observed that you're not the excitable sort. The obvious explanation was that you felt no curiosity about the details of Knoeckler's death because you already knew all about it. As I say, that was your first bad break. Also, I observed you looking over that bench and desk in the shop with a great deal more than ordinary curiosity. Whether you were seeking anything in particular or just checking over to see that you had made no omissions or left anything incriminating in your wake on the previous evening, I do not know.

"Ever since the theft, but especially since Friday afternoon you have been a watched man, but you guessed that everyone who had been in the vault would be watched, so you weren't much disturbed. For five or six days you have gone about your business. Our little gesture of arresting Donegan was a quite futile sham so far as you were concerned. It didn't fool you for a second. How long you would have continued simply to go about your business I do not know. I had nothing but conjecture to go on and would have had to wait however long you decided to make it.

"Wednesday morning you learned that Mr. Morton had in some way become suspicious of you. That altered everything. You had to act and act quickly. You were too closely watched to salvage your loot and make a getaway. There was only one alternative. Morton met with an 'accident.' Then you conceived the brilliant idea of laying the ghost forever by planting the tag on him. When it was found, he would be beyond reach of our questions. The mystery would be forever sealed. The first indication that your scheme had miscarried came when Morton was taken away in an ambulance instead of a morgue wagon. Your iron bar had struck him only a glancing blow, but, even so, almost sufficient to do away with him. Since Wednesday you have been keeping posted almost hourly as to his condition.

"Late yesterday the indications were that he had a chance to pull through. You made preparations for a quick exit by telephoning your friend, Lowman, to bring the parcel check with him to the city today so you could get it. To be sure you were not on a tapped wire, you used a pay phone. Then you covered your tracks by making a call to your house. The ruse fooled McFadden. That was the number they gave him when he traced the call. It might have fooled me, too, if you had picked a booth farther from the job and had made the thing look more like an afterthought—something you'd forgotten. But to go right around the corner from your own job telephone—that's a little too pointed.

"That small piece of bad judgment was probably the factor that spelled the difference between success and failure for your escape, for you were in the clear when you visited Lowman's place this morning. I had traced the call and was on my way to see him, but perfectly innocent of any pursuit of you, when you barged in. I don't know how you managed to give McFadden the slip, but you did. The rain was in your favor, and with practically every man on the job decked out in a yellow slicker it shouldn't have been so terribly difficult. I was in the lobby of the building where Lowman works when you came in. It was pure luck I glimpsed you before you saw me. I went to the street and found neither McFadden nor his partner in sight, so I knew something was wrong and decided my little talk with Lowman had better be postponed. When you came down I followed you to the Hudson Terminal. When you went to the parcel room the whole situation dawned on me.

"As soon as you're safely incarcerated I'm going back to see Lowman. I expect him to confirm certain details that will make the case a little more airtight. I believe he will, too. His wife was fairly communicative over the telephone while I was tracing up your call this morning."

With a little nod, almost a bow, Fenner got up, indicating that insofar as he was concerned the meeting was adjourned.

"Inspector, I'll turn this lad over to you. Between you and the district attorney he ought to get transportation up the river—with a one-way ticket. Too bad!"

Next he turned to Hanley.

"As for this stuff," Fenner indicated the grip, "I'd like to see old Jeremy when you tell him to check it up, and Jerry too, if we can get him over by that time."

Hanley pushed a button on his desk.

"You can have that pleasure in a very few moments," he said. "I'm as anxious as anyone to get this nightmare over with." He turned to a boy who had unobtrusively responded to his summons. "Ask Mr. Donegan, Sr., to step up here a moment."

When the boy had gone Hanley went on: "It's going to be a gratifying privilege to announce the outcome of this affair at the Board meeting this afternoon. Mr. Fenner, I'm going to insist that you be present to receive the personal congratulations of the directors and whatever other form of appreciation they may decide upon."

"Thank Bryce as much as me. It's the steady pressure of the system that really brought this to a head."

Bryce was busy at the telephone. He was instructing that Jerry Donegan be brought to the bank. Hanley got to his feet. It looked as if the meeting would break up. Only Borden remained seated. Now he spoke up:

"If I'm to be detained I'd like to use your phone to get in touch with Mr. Dickson. There are a number of matters at the job that he will have to attend to."

"You're to be detained, all right," Bryce assured him grimly.

"Well, I'm not sure it will be for long," Borden countered airily, "though I can see that a lot of explanation is indicated. But Mr. Fenner's tissue hypothesis is more ingenious than plausible, when you take it apart. For instance, the assertion that I planted that tag on Mr. Morton is ridiculous. Mr. Hanley himself was by Morton's side before I reached him after the accident occurred and stayed with him until after he was taken away. I believe he will in ordinary fairness admit Mr. Fenner's claim is quite impossible. Even if I had been so minded and had possessed a tag, there was never a second when Mr. Morton was not observed by at least two or three people." He looked to Hanley appealingly.

The bank manager hesitated, apparently recalling the details of the previous afternoon. Finally he said with an air of reluctance: "I can't say. There may be something in that, Fenner. I remember, now, that Dickson and Quinn and myself were down by Morton before Borden showed up; and after that—well, I don't see how he could have done it without someone noticing."

Fenner shrugged his shoulders. "That's only one item in a long, long chain," he pointed out. "I can't pretend to reconstruct every detail. On that particular item we may as well wait for Mr. Morton to recover. In the meantime—" He waited suggestively.

"In the meantime you're under arrest," Bryce finished. He seized Borden's elbow. The policeman moved over to Borden's other side and they proceeded out. Going out they saw Old Jeremy coming down the corridor toward Hanley's office. The old gentleman, glum as had been his wont of late, little realized the pleasant surprise in store for him.

When he entered the office Hanley crossed the room to meet him. He took the old man's arm, saying: "I've got a job for you I think you'll enjoy. I want you to check over the bag there against Jerry's list. Jerry's coming over directly. Then I want to have a talk with the two of you."

"Where did it come from? Is everything all right now?" Jeremy asked dazedly.

"Yes, Jeremy, everything is all right. You two have been first victims of circumstances, then tools we reluctantly but of necessity used in our efforts to catch the thief."

Jeremy took the canvas sack out of the grip, handling it as a father would a new-born child, and went down to his vault. When

he returned a few moments later to announce that the consignment was intact he found his son in the office. Father and son
greeted each other with surprising matter-of-factness.

Hanley addressed the two of them.

"You men have been through a lot," he said. "This bank owes
you apologies for what it has imposed on you. You were arrested,
Jerry, purely with the object of stimulating the real thief to some
sort of action that would betray him to us. Whether or not the ruse
was particularly successful or useful is neither here nor there. In
any case, the whole mess is over now, and I'm as glad for the sakes
of you two as for any other reason."

He looked at his watch. The afternoon was wearing on. The
meeting would be called in an hour. His desk was full of matters
requiring attention. To Jerry he said: "I want you to take a month
off. Draw your pay in advance. When you come back I'll have some
good word for you. As for you, Jeremy, I'll see you later." He nodded significantly, and father and son, accepting the hint, departed.
Hanley watched them go out. When the door had closed behind
them he turned to the detective.

"If I remember correctly you said you believed Jerry lied about
his actions during that noon hour," he remarked. "You said as much
to his father here Monday afternoon. Have you changed your mind
about that?"

"No; I haven't; but I think I can guess why he lied. I believe
that at the beginning he wasn't sure his old man wasn't trying to
pull a fast one. In his confused way Jerry was attempting to take
the blame if it later appeared that the old fellow was going to be in
trouble. This is only a surmise." Fenner settled his hat on his head
and picked up his umbrella.

"You're not going?" Hanley asked.

"I am indeed."

"But the meeting—it'll be within an hour or less. Why don't you
make yourself comfortable here? Then you won't have to come
back. Look; it's still raining like the very devil out."

"Who said anything about coming back?"

"But the Board will want to thank you."

"Nonsense! The $180,000 involved in this case is considerably less than the bank's average commission on the smallest security issue they underwrite, or most other deals they put over. It's chicken feed! Why should they bother?"

"Well, a great deal of human interest attaches to this sort of thing. They'll all be anxious to see you and glad to meet you."

Fenner thought a minute, then shook his head slowly as he said: "No. No, for two reasons. In the first place, I abhor obsequies— post mortems of any kind; in the second place I don't relish the thought of being an object of curiosity, even though my method of making a livelihood is perhaps a little more glamorous than some others. Nope! You give the Board my felicitations and deep regrets.

"Besides, this case is not over yet. You've got your money back but Borden is not convicted—which reminds me of something—" He reached for the telephone and called the hospital and inquired regarding the condition of Mr. Morton. Presently he hung up and smiled at Hanley. "Patient improved and doing nicely," he quoted sententiously. "That means he probably isn't any worse. I can't quite decide whether his recovery will make things harder or easier for Borden. You know, there's still a lot in this case that doesn't meet the eye. I'll be glad when Morton can talk." He broke off. "Well, I'll be on my way. I shall pop in on you in a day or two."

"Very well, if you insist. In the meantime, many thanks until you're better paid."

4

From Hanley's office Fenner went directly to the building where Borden's friend, Lowman, was employed, and up to his office. A boy at the door obligingly pointed out Lowman to him. Borden's friend, like a dozen others in the large room, was busy over a drafting board. Fenner crossed the room and stood by the table until the man looked up, a celluloid triangle in one hand, a pencil poised in the other.

"Mr. Lowman, I believe?" Fenner smiled.

"That's right. What can I do for you?" The question was put abruptly. Lowman obviously had no time for insurance agents or anything of the sort.

"You can tell me if you recall the number on the parcel check you returned to your friend, Philip Borden, just before noon today."

The triangle dropped from Lowman's hand, clattering to the table. The pencil he laid down slowly. "Parcel check? What do you mean?"

"Just what I say—parcel check. Borden came up here and got it just before noon." Fenner was coolly insistent.

"Why, I— See here; who are you, anyway? What's the idea of coming in here this way and—"

"I'm from the police," Fenner interrupted. "Would you rather answer one or two simple questions here or come down to the station and answer under oath?"

Several of the other men working at the adjoining tables were beginning to notice the altercation. Lowman glanced around; he whitened a little, taken aback at Fenner's invitation.

"I'll answer anything I can," he said in a moment; "but what's it all about?"

"You'll find out in plenty of time. Now about the check—?"

"I've never seen any check or anything of the sort," Lowman responded promptly.

"What was Borden's errand here this morning?" Lowman looked away and rubbed his hand over his mouth thoughtfully.

"Why, we just talked about our plans for the week-end."

"With the telephone systems perfected the way they are, Borden came four blocks through a drenching rain just to talk about your plans for the weekend? Remember; he only stayed about thirty seconds. Come again, only a little more plausible this time, please."

Lowman countered with a question.

"Where is Borden? Why don't you see him?"

"Borden is in jail without bail and likely to be there for some time. Nothing you can say or fail to say will alter that fact. The best way for you to stay out of trouble is to be perfectly frank with me. The truth always comes out eventually. Might as well have it now. What do you say?"

"I say I've never seen such a thing as the parcel check you speak of," Lowman replied doggedly.

"Then why was Borden here this morning?"

Lowman hesitated a long moment; finally he cleared his throat and spoke:

"I gave him back a sealed envelope I'd been keeping for him; that's all. I don't know what it contained except it was bulky, like about a four or five page letter folded up."

"Where did you get it and when?"

"Borden mailed it to me a week or so ago."

"And you've no idea what it contained?"

"No; Borden said there were several papers which would be embarrassing if found on him but which he valued highly. He asked me to keep the whole business under my hat. I told him I wouldn't say anything to anybody."

"Don't censure yourself. You're acting wisely. You might have become an accessory after the fact without realizing it. That's about all I want to know for now. I may ask you to confirm what I've told you at a later date. When I do, I'll get in touch with you." Fenner went out leaving Lowman half mystified, half astonished, and with a guilty suspicion that, in spite of himself, he had talked too much.

Highly gratified that his surmises had been so accurate, Fenner thought of going to see Borden again. Perhaps when he told him the results of his interview with Lowman, Borden would realize the hopelessness of his situation and throw himself upon the mercy of the law. But Borden could not afford to do that, Fenner decided quickly. The theft was bad, but the murder charges Borden could never own up to. If Morton died there would be two of them. No; Borden would simply have to brazen it through to whatever end was in store.

Fenner knew that when the district attorney received the facts as he had outlined them in Hanley's office, he would begin building his case at once. He knew, too, that Bryce was already probably turning over the scanty facts he had and digging for more.

The whole ground would have to be gone over more thoroughly. He, Fenner, would be called upon first to help in the arrangement of the case, later to testify. It would all be very drawn out and infinitely boring.

He reviewed the afternoon briefly. One fact caught his mind and held it: it was that Borden had taken the pains to deny the one particular accusation in the chain which Fenner felt least sure of— the planting of the tag on Morton. Fenner wondered if he could safely infer from this that in the other particulars he was correct. He knew, of course, that he was right in a general way, but there were many details and loose ends to be explained.

But if he was right in everything else and wrong about the tag, then where did the tag come from? Rather, how did Morton acquire it? Borden perpetrated the theft. Where did Morton's trail cross Borden's after that event? At Knoeckler's shop first, Fenner remembered. In the excitement of having killed Knoeckler, Borden must have failed to get the tag back. Of course, and Morton could have found it there, either on that fatal evening a week past when he waited for Elsa, or since then while he was going about the business of straightening out the old man's affairs. That would account for Morton's suspicions of Borden, too. Only why had he not come directly to the police with his information? Odd thing! Also, where would Morton's missing assistant fit into that picture? Fenner decided that here were some angles worth a few mental gymnastics. He concluded that, rather than go around to the jail to talk further with Borden, he would allow that gentleman to stew in his own juice over night, while he, Fenner, went home and forgot the case until his mind cleared so that he could do it justice.

5

But if he thought he was so easily to forget the case, even for only over night, he was mistaken. His way to the Subway took him within a block of the Consolidated Bank job. When he should have been half way up to the Pennsylvania Station, he was there at the truck gate peering in. A murky dusk was falling and the rain still persisted. A few oilskin-clad figures moved soddenly about beneath the pale glow of the flood lights. The soaked timber braces glistened.

Fenner remained for only a moment, an indefinable but strong conviction upon him that somewhere in the dark pit before him was concealed the key to his puzzle, and equally strong presentiment that only fate in its good time would reveal it. He faced about and started for home, changed his mind for the second time and turned his steps toward Centre Street and Philip Borden's cell.

Bryce was not in his office but arrived almost upon Fenner's heels.

"Upon second thought," Fenner explained, "I'd like to talk to Borden again."

"Glad you came back. He looks to me like he's about ready to give in now. Shall we have him up?"

"Please. Have you been third-degreeing him?"

"Oh, not to speak of." Bryce pushed a button, issued a curt order to the officer who responded, and in a few minutes Borden was brought in. He was pale and visibly less assured than when he had left the bank, but there were no visible marks of violence upon him.

"Well, my boy, the inspector tells me you've decided to come clean. I think you're wise."

Borden stiffened and for a moment it appeared that an angry retort was framed upon his lips, but as suddenly he slumped into his chair and dropped his gaze to the floor. There was a moment of tense silence.

"Well, how about it?" Fenner urged kindly.

"I suppose I may as well," Borden agreed in a low voice. "There isn't much that you don't already know about the money. I took it just about as you figured out; but as for the rest—I know nothing about it. Knoeckler and Mr. Morton, I mean."

"Then why did you go to Knoeckler's shop that afternoon?"

"He phoned me. I'd dropped the tag there. He read the papers and doped it out as you said. He wanted half."

"Well—" Fenner's gold pencil appeared in his hand and he twirled it meditatively.

"I saw I was in a hole and there was nothing I could do about it," Borden continued. "I dickered with him and we settled on fifty thousand. I told him he'd have to wait a month or two, and he said he'd keep the tag."

"Sounds fishy to me," Bryce put in coldly.

"How did you leave Knoeckler? Did he seem much disturbed?" Fenner asked, ignoring his colleague's comment.

"I left him sitting at his desk. He seemed—well, no more excited than you'd expect under the circumstances. I swear to God I never touched him! I don't remember about the next day, Mr. Fenner. When I came in the store and you sprung it on me he was dead, it sort of took my breath away. At first I was glad and relieved. Then I thought of the tag and that he must have left it about the place somewhere. I didn't know what to do. I looked around as well as I could and didn't see it, so I decided I'd have to take a chance and let things ride. That's all I know."

"What were you and Mr. Morton arguing about on Wednesday afternoon a short time before he was hurt?" Fenner asked after a moment's thought.

"About leveling the pier bottoms. Morton was too particular and it was slowing up the job."

"That all?"

"That's a lot of boloney, Max," Bryce cut in gruffly. "From what Quade told me, they were having it hot and heavy, and they wouldn't get that way over pier bottoms."

Borden said shortly: "That's all we discussed."

"How do you suppose Morton got that tag?" Fenner next inquired.

"I don't know. He must've found it in the shop. He was the old man's executor."

"How did you know that?" Fenner snapped.

"Coles told me," Borden replied evenly.

"Where's Coles now?"

"I don't know."

"When did you see him last?"

Borden rubbed his chin. "Wednesday afternoon about five or five-thirty, I think."

"Do you know Coles well? Did he tell you anything else about himself or Morton?"

"I didn't know him so very well. We used—"

He stopped for Fenner's gold pencil had clattered to the floor. The detective, leaning over to recover it, grunted: "Go on."

"We used to talk once in a while on the job. Wednesday afternoon while we were waiting for Morton to show up, Coles seemed to feel like unloading his chest. He told me that Knoeckler's daughter worked at their place and that Morton was making a play for her. I guess Coles had a yen on her himself. Anyway he was pretty sore. Spoke of him as a 'dirty buzzard' and talked of quitting his job."

Fenner thrust the pencil into his pocket. Bryce chewed his dead cigar. Borden glanced furtively from one to the other.

"Now will you be good enough to tell us just why you decided to clear out when you did?" Fenner resumed.

Borden hesitated only a moment. "Well, when I found out Morton was interested in Knoeckler's affairs, I got worried about the tag. I knew that if he found it he'd wise up the same as old Adolph had. So when it began to look as if he'd soon be out and around, I thought I'd better go."

Fenner got up. "We'll get all of this down in black and white tomorrow morning and you can sign it. That will be all for this evening."

A guard took Borden's arm and conducted him out of the office.

"What do you think of it now?" the inspector asked warily.

"Not a bad yarn if he can stick to it. That remains to be seen. Now let's do a little summing up: If what he says is true, then Borden committed the theft, Knoeckler reasoned it out and attempted to blackmail him, to which Borden agreed to submit. Knoeckler later, presumably from the intense excitement, had a stroke and fell downstairs. That ends it as far as Borden is concerned. Morton either had a genuine accident or Stephen Coles dropped the bar on him and cleared out. Fits together pretty well

at that. The only thing that could really upset it would be for Coles
to come back. This Borden is as clever as they come!"

"Or for Morton to give us something new," Bryce amended.

"Yes; that might happen." Fenner looked at his watch and found
that it was after seven o'clock. "There's one thing more; then I'll
run along. Look in your notes, Inspector, and tell me when Borden
left the job on Wednesday evening."

Bryce looked and in a few seconds announced: "About quarter
after eight. He went out with Dickson."

"And it must have been about six-thirty when we left, wasn't it?"

"Something like that."

"Coles wasn't there then but he must have come back. Quade
told us that the night timekeeper had last seen him about eight
o'clock, slightly inebriated. Borden says he didn't see him after 'five
or five-thirty.' Funny, isn't it? Then so far as we know he was last
seen by the timekeeper. I'd better talk to that chap right now. He'd
be there at this hour, wouldn't he?" He reached for his hat but did
not get up.

Bryce made no immediate reply and Fenner fell into a brown
study from which he emerged only when the inspector remarked:
"Maybe we'll get a break and turn up Coles in a day or two. Then
we'd be finished and, believe me, there'd be no regrets."

"I'd not count on learning anything from Stephen Coles. Not
unless you've got a couple of good spirit mediums on your staff."

Bryce sat up. "What do you mean?"

"I don't know how it was done or where he is, but ever since
he's been gone I've had a strong hunch poor Coles is quite beyond
our 'turning him up.'"

"You think he's done in, too?" Bryce gasped.

"I think he might be. If Borden is telling the truth, he doesn't
even know that Coles is missing. Yet a few minutes ago when I
asked him about Coles he replied: 'I didn't know him very well.'"

"What of it?"

"Wouldn't the natural answer have been: 'I don't know him so
very well'?"

"But when could he? How could he? Remember one thing, Max: Borden hasn't been out of our sight till this morning for a week."

"That's not literally true. Out of your ken, is what you mean."

"All right; have it your way; but when? Where?"

Fenner turned up his palms in a gesture of negation. "That's what we must find out." He got to his feet. "I really am going, this time. I must stop at the job. I'll ring you up if anything develops. Otherwise we resume in the morning, *n'est-ce-pas?*"

9

SATURDAY
APRIL 9TH

1

A FEW MINUTES after eight the next morning Joe and Giuseppi Spinelli, among a gang of seven or eight carpenter laborers, swung off the ladders into the bottommost depths of the Consolidated Building excavation. It was Saturday, a half-holiday, pay day, and with spring in the air to boot. Small wonder that in the hearts of Joe and Giuseppi there swelled a warm flood of the joy of living. This morning they would strip forms; this afternoon and tomorrow they would congregate and argue, yell at their women, lap up Guinea Red, and sleep.

Stripping forms consisted of demolishing the temporary wood encasement into which the concrete for the walls was poured, after the material had hardened. The small gang spread in pairs along the basement wall and with wrecking bars and crowbars attacked the wood panels. To the accompaniment of noisy splintering of timber, the heavy clank of hammer and bar, cheerful small talk, and occasional brief bursts of Venetian melody, the new concrete wall was gradually exposed, glistening in its smooth, gray newness. As it dried out it would become white.

A board at a time, the forms came down, Joe Spinelli at one end, Giuseppi at the other; the wrecking bars thrust behind an edge, a quick wrench, and off the planks flew. There was an easy rhythm to the men's movements; the boards clattered to the growing pile with mechanical regularity.

Abruptly the rhythm ceased. Joe had pried his end free but the loosened board did not fall off. He looked up and saw his brother, rigid, spellbound, staring at the wall exposed by the removal of the fast board. He moved over to Giuseppi, then stopped, frozen in his tracks. The outline of a human hand, palm out, fingers spread, like a fearful grisly warning, faced them from the surface of the concrete wall. Timidly Giuseppi reached out with his bar and touched the palm. It was soft, pudgy, yielding before the iron and allowing several small bits of concrete to flake off from the edge of the pattern.

"Mother of God!" His teeth chattered and he crossed himself.

"Tony! Benito! Here; look!" Joe came to his senses and called to the others. They gathered around, awestruck, gesticulating. Finally one, cooler than the others, ran to the ladder and up.

Soon he returned with a labor foreman and the superintendent. Quinn examined the find briefly and said: "Here; chop out a little concrete around it and let's see what we've got."

All the men hung back. Quinn looked up impatiently. "Don't stand there like a God-damned bunch of dummies. Here! Gimme that bar!" Suiting his actions to his words he seized a bar from the man nearest him and with a few deft strokes broke out enough concrete to reveal a man's hand and wrist. He looked for only a moment, then stepped back and, gauging from the position of the hand and wrist, started cautiously cutting into the concrete at a point several feet away. The concrete, still comparatively green, broke away without great difficulty. After a quarter of an hour of cautious exploration an unusually large chunk pried out revealed, about a half foot back from the wall surface, a small section of matted hair. Five minutes more of feverish activity and a face—misshapen, stone gray like the fresh concrete, one glazed eye open, the other hideously mutilated—was exposed. Quinn recognized the mortal remains of Stephen Coles.

He straightened up and issued crisp instructions: "Go on with the forms, boys. Martin," this to the foreman who had come down with him, "get a couple of air drills down here. He'll have to be cut out. Better rig up a frame and hang a couple of tarpaulins on each side, or the whole damned job will be demoralized. You better get some level heads on those drills, too. We want him out in one piece. You'll have to figure on taking out about two feet of concrete all around. Snap out of it, now!"

Quinn went up to the office shanty and asked Quade to notify the police. This was about half past nine. Inspector Bryce at the time was in his office, together with Murphy, McFadden, a stenographer and Philip Borden. The stenographer had just prepared a transcription of Borden's detailed confession. The latter, haggard and worn from a long night of questioning, slumped in his chair at one end of the desk. His story as he had related it the previous evening to Fenner and Bryce remained unchanged. Ten hours of sustained, intense grilling had not shaken him from it, and Bryce had reached the reluctant conclusion that his colleague's doubts had been ill founded.

When the phone buzzed Bryce picked it up, acknowledged himself, and listened while Quade told him what had happened at the job. He eyed Borden's dejected figure grimly as he hung up the receiver and said: "You'd better not sign that thing just yet. There will be a few additions. Believe it or not, Stephen Coles has come back!"

He called to the guards: "Take him away, boys. I've got to go out."

2

Two hours later the clay that had been Stephen Coles was transferred from its snug, torrid grave to a refrigerated slab in the city morgue. The head had been bashed in; otherwise the cadaver seemed intact.

Fenner and Bryce came to headquarters together. Fenner had come to the station late that morning and had overtaken the inspector just as he reached the job. It had been a gruesome two hours. The removal of Coles' body from the wall had been a grisly, nauseating task. It had been there less than three days, but the heat generated by the concrete as it hardened had stimulated the processes of putrefaction, and the men operating the chipping hammers and breaking away the concrete could work for only short periods without relief. One, indeed, collapsed and had to be taken away, shaky and vomiting.

Fenner paced the room nervously but Bryce flopped into his chair.

"Let's get Borden up here and get this thing over with," the inspector suggested impatiently. "You say you're sure, now?"

"Yes, I'm sure now. Borden said he last saw Coles about five-thirty Wednesday. The night timekeeper told me last night he'd seen Borden and Coles standing together on the bracing a little before eight o'clock on Wednesday. The spot he pointed out was almost directly over the place he was found. They were concreting that section of wall on Wednesday evening. Yet it's still circumstantial. Borden might not break down."

"If we throw all that in his face he'll break down, all right."

"Better still," Fenner suggested, "we might take him around to the morgue to review the handiwork. That ghastly sight would break him down if anything would."

"We'll get him up, anyway." Bryce lifted his telephone receiver. "Bring that fellow Borden back here, Clancy," he ordered curtly.

Bryce lit his cigar and Fenner walked over to the window to wait. Five minutes passed, five minutes of somber quiet with both men lost in their thoughts. Bryce roused himself, realized the elapsed time, and reached impatiently for the desk buzzer. A rattle of shots in the next wing of the building cut the movement short. There was a noisy shuffle, shouts of excitement, then more shots. Bryce sprang to his feet and ran from the room, Fenner following. The stir of clamor in the building died as quickly as it had risen.

In the next wing they found a group of officers carrying one of their number to the emergency hospital room. The guard, Clancy, with the assistance of two of his companions, limped along in the rear. Philip Borden was stretched upon the floor, a police surgeon kneeling over him.

"How is he, Doc?" Bryce asked quickly.

"He's alive, but he won't be for long."

"What happened?"

"You'll have to ask Clancy. I came when I heard the shooting. He tried to make a break; that's all I know."

"Where's Clancy?"

"Got a bullet in the thigh—not serious. I sent him to the hospital. The other had one in his chest. He's a little worse off but he'll pull through."

"Will this bird talk any more?" With his foot Bryce indicated the figure on the floor.

"Very unlikely. He's riddled. He can't possibly live two hours."

"He going to the hospital, too?"

"Yes; they've gone for a stretcher."

"Come on, Max." Bryce led the way. In the emergency ward they found Clancy seated upon an operating table, his wounded leg stretched out before him, the other swinging idly.

"What happened, Clancy?" Bryce asked. Clancy hung his head.

"Go ahead; spill it!"

"Well, I was bringing him up like you said when all of a sudden I felt a yank and he had a rod in my ribs. He told me to keep my trap shut and lead him out of the place or get plugged. I steered him into the ante-room where some of the boys was waitin' to go out on their beats. They wised up but he got the drop on 'em. He started to back out and then, somehow, the shooting commenced."

"Your gun he had, Clancy?"

The guard looked up soberly. "Yeah. Yes, sir."

"Let's see it."

Clancy indicated his trousers and holster belt draped over a chair. Bryce drew the gun from its holster and broke open the chamber. "Was it fully loaded, Clancy?"

"Yes, sir."

Bryce held it up and remarked to Fenner: "It's a damned lucky thing Borden wasn't handy with one of these. He got off six shots before they stopped him."

There was a shuffling in the hall and two men came in bearing Borden on a stretcher. They lifted him to a table and the same surgeon went to work over him. Presently he straightened up and signaled to Bryce. "I think he's coming out of it now but he won't last long." As he spoke Borden's eyes fluttered open. Bryce and Fenner moved to the side of the table.

Borden made a limp motion with his hand and wrist, smiled feebly, and muttered something terminating in "—bungled it up!" He sighed and relaxed. The surgeon pressed a glass of stimulant to his lips and he opened his eyes again. They met Fenner's. He whispered hoarsely: "Guess I'm done.—Listen!—I didn't brain Morton but I stuck the tag in his pocket when we found him. Tell him I owned up. Tell him to keep an eye on my mother." He looked at Fenner pleadingly, then his eyes drooped shut and his head fell back. Again the surgeon forced the liquid between his lips but this time could obtain no reaction. He put his ear to Borden's breast, raised up and shook his head, murmuring: "He's washed up!"

Fenner and Bryce went back to the inspector's sanctum.

3

Fenner drew a handkerchief from his breast pocket and blotted beads of perspiration from his forehead. Bryce sat down heavily, mechanically drew a match from the desk stand and struck it, held it poised six inches from his dead cigar while he stared vacantly into space. Roused when the flame reached his finger tips he cursed softly, struck another match and lighted the cigar.

"A swift, clean-cut finish," Fenner observed meditatively. "That's as it should be."

"Yeah; clean-cut for Borden but not for us. Too bad he couldn't have talked more. There's plenty we're in the dark about yet."

"Details, but little else. His suicide—for it was certainly no less than that—I regard as tantamount to a confession. He certainly knew before he made his break that he had about one chance in a thousand of getting away with it. But what puzzles me is: what prompted him to try it just then? It's almost as if he knew we'd found Coles."

Bryce looked up quickly. "Oh! But of course he knew it. He was sitting right where you are when Quade telephoned this morning. Borden was getting ready to sign his statement. I told him not to bother, that we'd have some additions for it, that Coles had come back. That was before I went over to the job. Thought I'd give him something to think about."

"Ah, well that, of course, explains it." There was a note of reproach in Fenner's voice. "It appears he thought about it quite seriously—and perceived that he had come to the end of his evil way." Bryce did not reply and Fenner went on: "Borden was an unusual criminal type. We—or I, rather—grossly underestimated his subtlety, his keenness, and most of all his utter ruthlessness. I realized from the start that we were matched against a quick, acute brain, but I hardly expected such a cold-blooded devil and least of all such a mentally agile one. He has twice hopped from one setup to another, a step ahead of us and outguessing us each time. At first we had Morton brained and the tag planted to direct suspicion to him and away from the others, including Mr. Borden. But Borden guessed that we would reason just that way so he took the next step and supplied a potential criminal, Coles.

"If Morton appeared to be the victim of a frame-up and Coles was missing, we could be depended upon to make the desired deductions. With only Morton found accidentally killed but in possession of the tag, any suspicion which Borden might share with the others would be lulled, but without the money returned it would never quite die. However, with Morton patently framed and Coles missing, suspicion would be so strongly focused upon him that Borden would certainly be relieved of it, even if neither the money nor Coles were ever seen again. At first we reasoned just about as Borden planned. Our reactions on Thursday when it became apparent that Coles was gone were exactly what Borden counted upon. But I had previously developed such a strong theory presuming Borden's guilt that, even in the face of the new evidence, I couldn't quite abandon it. Then, too, the jealousy motive confused the issue." Fenner paused for breath.

"He sure stuck to his story overnight," Bryce interposed. "The boys were after him pretty strong, too."

Fenner suppressed a shudder. He had visions of a brutal third degree, and he knew that third degrees are never quite so vicious as when they promise from the outset to be futile. No sympathy, however, was due Borden. He replied: "He could well afford to. It was a good story. When I first nabbed him yesterday, if you remember, he was innocent as hell and his feelings were deeply injured. But the goods were on him and he was 'in a spot.' His first play was to pass the buck to Morton on the long chance that Morton might not recover. When he learned I was going to get in touch with Lowman, he realized the game was absolutely up as far as the theft was concerned, so last night he figured he'd take as short a rap as he could get and deny the more serious charges. There's no real proof of Knoeckler's murder and Borden knew it. We won't know about Morton until we can talk to him, but the chances are he never knew what hit him, so Borden figured that even if he recovered to talk there would still be nothing but conjecture against him; and of course there'd also be the highly diverting fact that Coles, who also had a motive, was missing.

"Borden alone knew where Coles was and counted upon him never to appear and upset the story. That wall was five feet thick. It was only by the purest, fortuitous chance that Coles landed with one hand against the forms. That hand needed only to have been an inch back from the surface and that Wop would never have had the chance to snatch Coles back from the limbo. Yes; all in all Borden had a pretty good story.

"But once Coles is found the yarn collapses like a house of cards. An accidental fall into a body of soft concrete wouldn't damage a person much. The most superficial autopsy must disclose the head injury and the fact that Coles had suffocated. Borden saw he was licked. He knew his goose was cooked and he preferred the end he met to burning in the chair. And of course there was always that thin glimmer of hope that by some colossal fortune he might win free." Fenner stopped and looked away, traced odd designs on the desk top with the gold pencil which had somehow found its way between his fingers during the long discourse.

Bryce produced his notebook and leafed through it. "I'm glad," he said in a minute, "that Borden gave in and opened up about the tag. It certainly simplifies matters as far as Morton is concerned."

"How is he today?" Fenner quickly asked. "I'd sort of overlooked him in the excitement."

"He was much better this morning. They feel pretty sure of him now." Bryce turned several more pages. "Now how about Knoeckler? Where does this leave him?"

"It leaves him murdered in cold blood. Borden practically confessed it. His story last night was that they'd agreed on a blackmail payment and that the old man had kept the tag. Today he admits that he, Borden, subsequently planted the tag on Morton after he was hurt. Well, you know old Knoeckler wouldn't have given him the tag, and Borden wouldn't take it and leave the old fellow alive to talk."

Fenner thrust the gold pencil into his vest, thus figuratively placing a concluding period after their discussion. He got to his feet.

Bryce settled back more comfortably in his chair. "What's your hurry? Sit down a while. There are a lot of loose ends that need tying together. How'd you happen to run into Borden yesterday?"

"From the list of calls for that pay phone Borden used I found the one to his house and the one just before it to an Arthur Lowman in Orange. I called the number and learned from Lowman's wife that Borden was one of her husband's best friends. I got Lowman's business address and went to see him. As I was scanning the directory board in the lobby, Borden came in. I happened to see him in time to duck up the stairs out of sight until he got in an elevator. When I saw neither of your men, I realized something was wrong so I waited for Borden to come down and tagged along after him. Sleuthing—in a literal sense, I mean—is out of my line. It's a wonder Borden didn't spot me right away, but I guess he felt sure he was safe. When he went to the Terminal I thought he was going to leave the city and I decided to pinch him on suspicion, so I picked up the officer on the corner. Then when he headed for the parcel room I suddenly saw the whole thing. I waited until he got the grip and then we nailed him.

"He came along as meekly as you please. Before we came away I got the parcel check from the clerk. The grip had been there just eight days—since twelve-forty-five last Thursday. The tag was stamped and Borden had just paid the extra seven days' storage. That clinched it. The rest you know. I brought Borden to Hanley's office where you found us." Fenner lit a cigarette and smoked thoughtfully.

Bryce shifted in his chair and looked at his colleague accusingly.

"You must have been pretty sure from the beginning that Borden was our man," he said. "Why didn't you let me in on it?"

"On the contrary, I knew nothing of the sort. There was nothing tangible to go on for quite a while. If the possibility of connection between the robbery and the death of Adolph Knoeckler was ignored, Borden did not head my list. As a matter of fact, they all looked pretty much alike; or at least there was something unnatural about the conduct of all of them. Jerry started off by lying about his noon hour. Dickson's disappearing for three or four hours on Thursday afternoon made him eligible, even if it later appeared he'd been hanging around a bucket shop. Morton's dropping out of sight completely the way he did made him a more likely candidate even than the others. The dispatch bag was small; Morton and Dickson both wore coats; Dickson went out carrying his over his arm. Morton had a briefcase and Borden the level box, though to tell you the truth I didn't attach proper weight to that box at the start. None of them would be subjected to much scrutiny in the company of Hanley, and any of them might have gotten away with it. Then of course, there was always the possibility of an inside job—involving Old Jeremy or not, as you please."

"But what led you to Borden when you did pick him out?" Bryce persisted.

"A sort of hybrid process of elimination, I suppose. My investigation at the bank brought me to the point where I was ready to discard the inside job theory. Morton and Miss Knoeckler turned up on Monday and we learned that Morton, too, had been to Knoeckler's shop on Thursday evening. That seemed to double the likelihood that the theft and Knoeckler's demise were connected in some way, so for a starter I assumed just that.

"That left it between Morton and Borden, but with the odds in favor of Borden. I'll tell you why: From even the most casual inquiry it became apparent that Morton was by nature a cautious, planning sort of person. The chap we were looking for must have been just the opposite—an opportunist, a quick thinker, and with it all an unusually cool-headed person. Borden more nearly fitted that description than any of the rest. Remember the day we saw Borden and Dickson down on the crosslot bracing—when the chain on the stone-pan broke, you know? Dickson was scared out of his wits, but Borden never turned a hair. That little incident demonstrated as completely as anything could have that Borden possessed the attributes of quickness and coolness that the fellow we were looking for must have needed. Also it showed conclusively that Dickson did not have them, which let him out.

"After that it became a question of motive and method. For the theft, the motive was obvious. For Knoeckler's murder, it could only be to silence him. That Knoeckler attempted to blackmail Borden was at first a pure guess, but why else would he call Borden down there when he suspected something rather than get in touch with the police or the bank? Knoeckler was a pretty shrewd Dutchman. The tag was at some time in the shop—I found positive proof of that on Tuesday. What with the tag and the tabloid article and my calling to question him about Borden, the fellow couldn't fail to see it. But when he confronted Borden he made the fatal mistake of underestimating his man. Borden, with characteristic quickness, decided to eliminate him for good, and did.

"My theory was considerably bolstered when I reflected back upon Borden's conduct that afternoon we called him to the shop. Though he simulated a natural amount of surprise at Knoeckler's death, he was not curious as to how it happened, or when or where. The excitement might have caused him to fail to ask the questions one would normally expect, but he being otherwise such a level-headed chap, that seemed hardly likely.

"As to Borden's method of perpetrating the theft itself, I staged an experiment to get a line on that. A reenactment. Hanley arranged a second inspection of the vault on Tuesday morning for my special benefit. If I had conducted the same experiment earlier I'm not sure it would have helped so much, for one thing was very evident: that under the circumstances any one of the party, with care and perhaps a little better than ordinary luck, could have filched the sack and gotten away with it. The sack could have been concealed beneath a coat draped over the arm. Dickson and Morton both had them. Besides, Morton carried a briefcase that would have held it. But I was looking not for anybody's method, but for Borden's method, and the answer was absurdly simply—the level box, of course. Just to be sure, I went around to Knoeckler's shop Tuesday afternoon and tried putting a sack of the same size into the level case Borden actually carried. It was a snug fit but it worked.

"That took care of the method. While I was there, I found something else." From his pocket Fenner drew a short length of light white-metal wire, doubled and bent into a loop. "It's a wire the bank uses to attach the tags to their sacks. The sample sack I had obtained at the bank had a tag attached with such a wire. After trying it in the box I had tossed it to the bench. When I went to get it the similarity between this piece of wire lying among Knoeckler's things and the one on the bag caught my eye. I straightened them out and found they were exactly the same. There was little doubt they were part of the same cut and meant for the same purpose. For a minute I was quite excited. I had visions of some sort of connivance between Borden and the old man, but I concluded that this was entirely unnecessary from Borden's point of view, so that plain blackmail was the only explanation left. And the wire indicated pretty conclusively that the tag had been at the shop. I concluded that, after killing Knoeckler, Borden recovered the tag but overlooked the wire.

"Now we come to Morton: At first when he was hurt I thought he had in some way come to suspect Borden and had rashly confronted him—that heated argument in the excavation, you know—and that for his pains Borden had scrambled up onto the bracing and given him his 'accident': and that Borden had then played his ace of trumps by planting the tag and forever exorcising the finger of suspicion. Now it appears, if Borden's dying statement is to be believed, that I was right only about the last half of it." Fenner concluded his long explanation with a sigh of relief. He stretched himself and got up.

"And Coles?" Bryce suggested.

"Coles was an afterthought when it occurred to Borden that the planting of the tag on Morton would be seen through. He encountered him, half-drunk, on the bracing there, brained him, and dropped him into the wall they were pouring. In the dark it should have been relatively easy."

Bryce who had listened patiently now spoke up sharply: "You conducted your 'reenactment' on Tuesday morning. You got the key from me and went to the shop and confirmed your findings in the afternoon. You must have been morally sure on Tuesday evening that Borden was the chap we were looking for. Why didn't you pinch him then? It would have saved Coles' life."

"Not too fast," Fenner protested. "There was certainly nothing upon which Borden could be convicted. My conclusions were based altogether upon circumstantial evidence. The length of wire was the only really tangible thing I'd found, and, since both Morton and Borden had been to the shop, it didn't prove anything conclusive against either. More important, I had no idea until yesterday as to how Borden disposed of the money. If we pinched him, we stood a chance of losing it, for if he had cached it in such a way that it could lie for a long period unattended, he might figuratively thumb his nose at us, even if we got a conviction of sorts. Not literally, of course. He would naturally stick to a story of innocence and bide his time."

"I suppose that is true," Bryce agreed, "and the way things have turned out the state is saved the cost of prosecuting him, and—"

"And I," Fenner concluded happily for him, "am released for a much-needed tour of some Canadian countryside."

Bryce had no answer for that except an unintelligible grumble.

4

It was with a definite sense of relief that Fenner left Police Headquarters and headed for his own office. In the back of his mind he
had a vague notion that he would clear up whatever odds and ends
awaited him there and get away before anything new could turn
up, although anything of that sort need hardly have been feared
on a spring Saturday afternoon. He hailed a cab, though the distance was only a half dozen short blocks, and settled into the cushions lazily while the cab rolled through the quiet streets of the
deserted financial district.

He wondered if Bryce was satisfied and would regard the Consolidated Bank case as a closed volume. Of course Morton's possession of the tag had not been satisfactorily explained, despite
Borden's dying testimony. The more Fenner thought of it the more
he realized that the assumption that Borden had placed it on
Morton could not be reasonably made. In the first place, according to Borden's earlier claim, which was substantiated by Hanley,
Borden had had no opportunity to do such a thing. Assuming that
the opportunity had existed, however, Borden had had no way of
knowing that the opportunity would present itself on that particular day; and, knowing himself to be under observation, he would
certainly not risk keeping the incriminating tag upon his person
except for a limited time and for a definite purpose.

Then too, the fact that Borden at first selected that particular
accusation to deny specifically kept recurring to Fenner. It was not
unreasonable to infer that it was the one charge which, being
erroneous, Borden knew could not be proved. He had probably
picked it in the hope that when it was proved false doubt would be
cast upon the other charges also.

The cab drew to a halt and Fenner paid the driver and got out.
He went up to his office, still musing, tossed his hat on the desk
and settled into his chair. His combination stenographer, office
girl, bookkeeper and telephone operator glided in with a sheaf of
papers and notes but Fenner, with an absent, careless gesture,
waved her away. He had Morton on his mind and knew he would
not rest easily until he had made some mental disposition of him.

The tag! If Morton had found the tag at Knoeckler's, then Borden must have left it there. In the stress of having just killed the old man he must have lost his head and gone off without it. Then it would be the tag that Borden must have been looking for when he so anxiously scrutinized Knoeckler's bench and desk the next day. But if Morton found it there, it must have been on that fatal Thursday evening when he waited for Elsa Knoeckler; for if Adolph had threatened Borden by means of it, and had gotten himself killed on the spot, there certainly would have been no opportunity for him to secrete it anywhere, and if it had been lying in the open the police or he himself would have found it after Knoeckler's death.

By the same reasoning, Fenner suddenly perceived, Morton idling about the place could not have failed to find it. Furthermore, Morton with an idle quarter of an hour to wait for Elsa, could not have failed to read the tabloid article spread invitingly on the counter as Adolph had left it. Morton would have remembered that Borden intended coming to the shop from the bank. It was even simpler for him to put two and two together than it had been for Knoeckler.

Why had not Morton come forward with his find? But that was not all. Fenner suddenly realized that Morton, knowing himself to be wanted, or at least strongly suspecting it, for the newspaper article left little doubt, had deliberately absented himself until the following Monday. The question occupied Fenner for but a second; the answer was not far to seek. Elsa! She would be the answer. Morton had anticipated this trip with her; his heart was set upon it and he would naturally be reluctant to change his plans. Well, that was not a difficult thing to understand.

Then with time to dwell upon the particular chain of circumstances which had thrown into his lap the opportunity to share in Borden's ill-got fortune, he must have succumbed to the temptation to recoup his recent losses. He must have decided, quite unconsciously, to steal a leaf from Adolph Knoeckler's book. There was no doubt Morton needed the money. Fenner wondered if Morton, knowing Borden to be a thief, suspected him also of being the murderer of Adolph Knoeckler. He suspected not, for Morton might then have thought twice before attempting his blackmail scheme—might even have dropped it and turned over the tag, for it would have been simple to say that he had found it among Knoeckler's effects.

But if Morton had attempted blackmail, Fenner realized, then Borden's last statement must have been altogether false. This would not be a hard supposition to make; there had been an inspired air about it, anyway. Fenner recalled the words: "I didn't brain Morton but I stuck the tag in his pocket when we found him. Tell him I owned up. Tell him to keep an eye on my mother." Garbled and meaningless in any ordinary interpretation, but once assume that Morton blackmailed Borden, and the words become filled with significance. The tag had been found on Morton, embarrassing at best. This confession of Borden's would let him out! But what object? "Tell him to keep an eye on my mother." Obvious! Fenner recalled that Borden had lived alone with his mother. He twirled his pencil in silent amazement at the only reasonable inference. Throughout the case Borden had consistently lied to serve his own ends. Now he had simply gone out, true to form and with his wits about him, lying to indebt Morton to him on the long chance that the latter might repay the debt by doing something for his mother. He had not even bothered to depose one way or the other about Adolph Knoeckler or Coles because the denials would be purposeless, but had denied the attack on Morton for the same reason he had falsely admitted placing the tag upon him. Fenner felt a grudging admiration for the man's adroitness.

If Morton had stolen a leaf from Knoeckler's book, Fenner reflected, he had also come perilously close to copying its concluding page. He wondered if that was not punishment enough, and found it easy to persuade himself that it was. Besides, there was the practical consideration that he, Fenner, had nothing but his own deductions to go on; and, in the face of Borden's dying statement, it would be difficult to substantiate any accusation against Morton. Fenner was not sorry that this was true; he had always preferred that the dead or sleeping be let lie. Also, there was Elsa Knoeckler—

But Bryce— Would he be content to let sleeping dogs lie? Fenner feared he might not, and that the inspector might by his more cumbersome mental processes sooner or later arrive at the conclusions he himself had just reached, Fenner believed not unlikely. Bryce might grill Morton without warning; it might work. Some sort of preventive was obviously indicated. Fenner was debating its most feasible form when his secretary tiptoed in and announced a caller. Close upon her heels followed Elsa Knoeckler.

Fenner got up to offer her a chair, then resumed his place and waited gravely for her to explain her errand. Elsa sat for a short time silently twisting her gloves, then she began: "I don't know quite why I came. It's silly to be bothering you. I've been worried sick ever since our talk the other evening. Please don't misunderstand me. I haven't for one minute believed Mr. Morton was mixed up in that bank business. He's always seemed—well—wonderful to me." She spoke almost with reverence. "And he's been so kind and thoughtful, especially since Father died. He's had so much trouble— But anyway, I read in this morning's paper that they'd arrested somebody and got the money back. Does that end it?" She looked up anxiously.

"Practically," Fenner admitted. "I hope so."

Elsa's countenance visibly brightened. This was the reassurance she had come to hear.

Fenner went on: "Now then, there's one other thing I may as well tell you. You'll read it in the papers tonight anyway. Stephen Coles was found dead at the job this morning." Elsa blanched but said nothing. "His body was found in a concrete wall when they took the forms off—been there since Wednesday. It was an unfortunate accident but we couldn't keep it quiet. Now the tabloids have got wind of it and their reporters are swarming and snooping all over the place. It's the sort of a thing they eat up. I'd advise you to lay low for a few days and keep out of their way."

"I will," Elsa promised. "Poor Steve!"

"How is Mr. Morton?" Fenner changed the subject.

"He's getting better all the time. The doctor says I can probably talk to him a minute on Monday." Elsa smiled a little wanly.

Fenner saw her eyes light up softly as she spoke. The mere
thought of talking to Morton seemed to warm and animate her. He
pictured Morton and wondered with a twinge he recognized as envy
what there was about the man that could stir a girl to such devo-
tion. Randolph Morton, a potential blackmailer! What could he
bring her except ultimate unhappiness? Still—there was a chance.
The experiences of the past few days might prove chastening.
Fenner resolved to do what he could toward giving her that chance.
It occurred to him that her visit at just this time was opportune.
He said: "I'm glad you came. There is something you can do better
than anybody else. You will possibly talk to Mr. Morton before
anyone does except the doctors and nurses. Make it a point to do
that. Then give him this message from me; tell him this: that he
has never seen the fiber tag I showed you the other day; that he
knows nothing of such a tag; and that if he is ever confronted with
it he is to view it with natural curiosity 'for the first time in his
life.' You see, Mr. Morton may have unwittingly made himself an
'accessory after the fact.' We may as well spare him embarrassment. I haven't the slightest doubt that a certain ponderously efficient friend of mine will sooner or later—probably sooner—make
it his business to interview Mr. Morton about the tag in question.
Is that all clear?"

"It's not at all clear, but I understand what you want me to do,"
Elsa answered.

"Perhaps Mr. Morton will sometime make it clearer." Fenner
turned away, an almost curt dismissal in the gesture.

Elsa rose and waited awkwardly. Fenner, too, got to his feet.
He held out his hand. "I wish you every happiness."

Elsa accepted it timidly. "Thank you—uh—Good-by."

"Wait a moment; there's something else." It had suddenly oc-
curred to him that Randolph Morton might suffer a change of heart.
Fenner decided grimly that he would obviate that possibility. "Tell Mr.
Morton that on the day he leaves the hospital he will hear from me."

Elsa nodded bewilderedly. Mystified but somehow reassured she left the office.

Fenner seated himself again before his desk. He drew a blank white card before him and poised his pen over it for a moment, formulating his message; then he wrote rapidly, nearly filling the card. From his pocket he drew the fiber tag and enclosed it with the card in an envelope which he sealed and addressed to Randolph Morton.

He rang for his secretary and when she appeared held out the envelope and said: "Now listen carefully. This is the only important thing you'll have to do while I'm away. First, put this envelope in the safe; then every morning before you do another thing call up the hospital and inquire about Mr. Morton. On the day when he is to leave there take this envelope and deliver it to him personally. Deliver it to him alone. Clear?"

The girl nodded.

Fenner's tone lightened. "All right, then. Now bring on that other stuff you waved at me when I came in. I want to get out of here."

EPILOGUE

A WEEK ROLLED BY; a leisurely, unforgettable week for Fenner who had driven past the blue waters of the St. Lawrence and wandered up into the Old World of Quebec, passing old landmarks, viewing with sleepy interest the scenes of romantic legend.

For Bryce in the city it had been just another week; a week crammed with a little more than its share of bustle and activity; a week in which he begrudged himself even the solitary hour he had wasted in going to the hospital and interrogating, quite futilely, Randolph Morton.

For Elsa Knoeckler it had been a lagging week but blessed in that each day brought a steady betterment in the condition of the man she had, from blended admiration, pity, and her own need, learned to love.

And for Randolph Morton it had been a peculiarly enlightening week, for he had discovered how lonely and unhappy and restless he could be by himself, and how secure and calm and contented he could be by simply having Elsa near him. More and more his convalescent days divided themselves into the happy, living periods of Elsa's visits and the shadowy periods of only anticipation or remembrance.

On this, his last day, he struggled into his clothing. For several days he had been sitting up; the day before he had walked the corridors; today he was to be discharged. The surgeons assured him that with a few weeks of rest he would be quite himself again.

216

Morton was glad to get out. In his heart he knew that he was lucky to be out—out and a free man. Fenner had perceived the truth about the tag. Morton wondered how, but much more he wondered why the investigator, through Elsa, had warned him. It was a warning well taken, he reflected, for Bryce had been curiously insistent with his questions. Even yet Morton dared not feel absolutely sure that the inspector was wholly satisfied. But why? What had he ever done for Maxwell Fenner? For the hundredth time he put the perplexing question from his mind, unanswered. He would see Fenner at the first chance and try to find out. That was all he could do.

They had refused to disturb his mind with details, but he had learned that Borden, arrested for the bank theft, had been killed in an attempt to escape. That was all he knew and he was not unnaturally consumed with a tremendous curiosity for more details.

There was a warning tap on the door and it was pushed cautiously open. A girl, a stranger to Morton, thrust her head through the opening and, seeing him alone, asked: "Is this Mr. Randolph Morton?"

"Yes," Morton affirmed, curious.

She crossed the room and held out an envelope. "Mr. Maxwell Fenner instructed me to hand you this."

Morton looked at the envelope, then at its bearer. She nodded and without another word backed out of the room, closing the door softly as she left. Morton held the envelope on his knee for a moment, then slowly slit open the flap. He drew out first the fiber tag and, seeing what it was, thrust it hastily into his coat pocket. Then he drew out a white card and read:

Randolph Morton—
You are on the road to recovery.

I am returning a certain article recently appropriated from among your effects. You and I alone know where and when it got there.

Before he died of gunshot wounds at the Police Station a short time ago, a mutual acquaintance left the following message for you: "I didn't brain Morton

but I stuck the tag in his pocket when we found him
. . . tell him I owned up . . . tell him to keep an eye on
my mother." You and I alone know what he meant.

Blackmail is a hideous thing and not infrequently
incurs its own punishment, yet I unhesitatingly re-
sort to it in, I hope, a subtler form when I tell you
that this note and all its implications are tendered
as a wedding present to you and another of our mutual acquaintances.

Best wishes,
Maxwell Fenner.

Morton read the cryptic message slowly, then again, then a third
time. A slow frown darkened his brow but gradually faded. Uncertainly he smiled. He smiled to think that Fenner, with all his astuteness, had believed the message necessary.

He tore the card into tiny bits which he dropped into the waste
basket. When Elsa came to see him a short time later she found
him standing before the window gazing serenely out.

BROKERS' END

TO
L.A.B.

FOREWORD

THE F. W. STRONG CASE, as Fenner called it, is the second from his files that he has permitted me to fictionize. Innately opposed to personal publicity, Mr. Fenner overcame his scruples when I pointed out that the case had its origin in certain malpractices, not uncommon at the time, of which the public needs to be informed.

L. F. B.

CHARACTERS

Sigurd Strong	*Chairman of the Board,*
	F. W. Strong Company
Margaret Purcell	*Mr. Strong's Secretary*
Shirley Strong	*Mr. Strong's Wife*
Martin Hoyle	*Treasurer of F. W. Strong Company*
Abraham L. Behrmann	*Counsel of F. W. Strong Company*
Winthrop Parness	*Director of F. T. Strong Company*
Anthony Wheeler	*Director*
Maurice Parker	*Director*
Judge Francis F. Spar	*Director*
Robert A. Hood	*Director*
John Bartlett	*Reporter, the* Globe
Detective Inspector Bryce	*New York Police*
Quade	*Bryce's Staff*
Meehan	*Bryce's Staff*
Murphy	*Bryce's Staff*
Burke	*Bryce's Staff*
Maxwell Fenner	

PROLOGUE

THIN BLUE SMOKE from a half dozen cigars, lingering despite the most advanced scientific ventilation and air conditioning, created a perceptible haze over the huge oval board room table.

"You've heard the Counsel's report?"

"Move it be accepted."

"All in favor, Aye. Contrary, No? So ordered."

The drone seemed somehow without beginning or end. It was only mid-April but the heavy languor of spring, stealing between the tall open windows, had settled over the assemblage like an invisible fog, enervating, anesthetizing, relaxing.

A dull buzz of whispering from one end of the table terminated abruptly at the peremptory rap of Sigurd Strong's paper knife on the plate glass top. The Directorate of F. W. Strong Company shifted in their chairs and gathered, listlessly, their scattering attentions. There had been Secretaries' reports, Treasurer's reports, Real Estate reports, Sales reports. The burden of their song had not been light, but their tenor was becoming an old story to the board. There had also been overindulgence at lunch, which contributed not a little to the general lethargy.

When his rapping had secured attention, Sigurd Strong, Chairman, swarthy, leonine of gray mane, scarce looking his fifty-odd years, rose heavily to his feet at the head of the table and addressed his fellows thoughtfully.

"Gentlemen, we have reached a point where I'm beginning to question the advisability of continuing to support these sour loans.

We may as well face facts. The defaults are piling up in such proportions that an early showdown is inevitable!" He paused for
emphasis and looked around. "We all realize that the sooner we
stop footing these interest and principal payments, the less our
resources will be depleted when that time comes." There was less
than the customary measure of pomposity in Mr. Strong's manner
of speaking, and this in itself lent weight to his words.

His listeners stirred uneasily. Some straightened up in their
seats. F. W. Strong Company sold Real Estate Bonds. They had
probably sold more dollars worth, nominally, than any other firm
in that business. They had become an institution with a far-flung
sales organization that permeated every city, town and hamlet in
the country. The firm name was the watchword for Security. "Forty-
five years without loss to any investor"—this was the F. W. Strong
Company slogan. "Forty-four—" it had been last year, "Forty-
three—" the year before that, and so on back. Small wonder the
directorate sat up! To fail to support sick loans was of course a
novel idea. The issues would be in default. The long maintained
record—expensively maintained these last months—would be definitely relinquished. That such a course would be ultimately un-
avoidable had not, until recently, even occurred to most of the
directors. Until this moment it had scarce been spoken of above
a whisper. As a body they looked at Sigurd Strong. He avoided their
glances and hurried on, his voice flat and dry.

"This Romaine Hotel defection will be the last straw! The May
first interest will be ninety thousand dollars, and a two hundred
thousand amortization payment is then due. Parness says they'll
have less than sixty thousand—"

He looked toward Winthrop Parness, immaculate, third from
the head of the table on the left, who removed his cigar just long
enough to nod.

"And so—" Sigurd Strong was speaking slowly now, feeling his
way—"we'll have to announce a default. Mr. Behrmann and I have
selected a Protective Committee for the Bondholders of this issue.
We shall have to work out a reorganization plan—" His voice now
definitely faltered. His glance had accidentally come to rest upon

an oil portrait of his father, the founder, hung over the fireplace at the opposite end of the board room, and for a fleeting second Sigurd fancied he read scorn in the somber eyes.

These pronouncements were falling with varying effect upon the seven men gathered about the table. Upon Abraham Leroy Behrmann at Strong's right, Counsel for F. W. Strong Company, they fell without effect, for they were quite expected. He had been discussing the whole problem with Strong for several weeks and had helped lay out the course upon which Sigurd was now embarking. Behrmann, a few years younger than Strong, almost completely bald, wizened of mien, slight of build, bandy legged, looked more the part of a small-town tailor than one of New York's most eminently successful corporation lawyers. His gentle, intelligent eyes alone belied the first impression.

Upon Martin Hoyle, Secretary and Treasurer, seated opposite Behrmann at Sigurd's left, they fell with mixed effects. Partly he was incredulous, partly he was puzzled as to possible repercussions affecting him personally. Martin Hoyle had been snatched from the firm's accounting department several years before and made Secretary and Treasurer. He had never quite overcome his surprise, and even now in little secret moments he marveled that he, Martin Hoyle, should actually be an officer of the great house of F. W. Strong and, more unbelievable, that he should be getting away with it!

Next to Hoyle sat Anthony Wheeler, scrawny and popeyed, and next to him Winthrop Parness, a veritable tailor's model, both of the firm of White, Wheeler, Parness and McClintock, Real Estate. Neither was quite prepared for Sigurd's program. It was the Spring of 1931; the depression was a year and a half old. Surely, they argued, it must have nearly run its course. Now if F. W. Strong and Company would only carry on for a few more months—. Spring, full of promise, was in the air. It was easy to be hopeful.

Opposite Wheeler next to Behrmann there was Judge Francis Fenwick Spar. He had been roused from a tranquil post-lunch slumber by the sharp rapping of Sigurd's paper knife, but he had not come completely awake in time to catch the portent of Sigurd's words, so of course their effect upon him was little more than mild puzzlement.

Next to the Judge and opposite Parness sat Maurice Parker, Senior Vice President of the County Consolidated Bank and Trust. He was a rotund but solid individual, bald on top, double chinned and heavy jowled, with little swells of flesh bulging above and below the temple bars of his spectacles. He leaned forward, his elbows and forearms on the table, humorless, seething with dignity. Prone to deliver himself of long, portentous expatiations upon the most trivial occasions, he now found himself quite at loss to comment at all.

Last, at the opposite end of the oval from Sigurd, and most profoundly disturbed of the lot by his words, there was Robert Alanson Hood, 3rd, Director of Sales. Much younger than the others, his spare, powerful figure scarcely softened by expensively artful tailoring, he leaned anxiously over the table. The deft regularity of features that might have been lifted bodily from a collar ad was hardly marred by the perplexed frown. Scion of an old family, Hood had taken the traditional step from college football to bond selling upon his graduation some eight years before. From the start his success had been phenomenal, for a short time in selling bonds himself, but mostly in training and inspiring others to sell them. It must be admitted that the era had been in his favor and that distributing any sort of security to the hungry market had degenerated at that time almost to mere order taking. But the missionary zeal displayed by Hood, the fervor with which he and his aides converted thousands of people from other forms of investment to the security of F. W. Strong bonds had won him at the age of thirty a Junior Vice Presidency and a place on the Board of the F. W. Strong Company.

Absolute safety of principal and assurance of interest, these Hood knew to be ninety-eight percent of his department's stock in trade. The merits of individual issues mattered little. People bought an income assured by the F. W. Strong name. Now that name seemed threatened with impairment. Incredibly innocent, it had never occurred to Hood to question the soundness of the issues his men peddled. They were F. W. Strong Bonds, synonym for impregnability; that was enough. Apparently, if he correctly gathered the import of Sigurd's words, it had been considerably less than enough!

With opening eyes and growing bewilderment Robert Alanson Hood, 3rd, for the first time really examined his fellow directors. His glance swept from Sigurd Strong, so glacial and formidable, to Counsel Behrmann, crafty and shrewd; from Treasurer Hoyle so precise and businesslike, to Winthrop Parness, airy and worldwise, and Anthony Wheeler, unbelievably dull. It swept on over Judge Spar to Maurice Parker, heavy and as solid as his bank. It ended upon the glass table top between his own forearms. Suddenly to him all these men seemed old and experienced and he by contrast young and ill-qualified. He felt anew a vague bafflement that had troubled him often, a sense of polite exclusion from their inner circle that he had been obliged to accept and pass over. He remembered many meetings, usually perfunctory affairs, at which his suggestions were received with good-humored tolerance and then quietly forgotten.

But this meeting was no perfunctory affair. On the contrary, the mere attendance of the entire directorate, in itself a rare circumstance, attested the importance of the event. They must have sensed, Hood perceived, that something unusual was due; he hadn't at all. And Sigurd Strong's brief dictate, demolishing at a stroke a policy, a reputation, and a slogan forty-five years in the making, apparently was to go unchallenged. Reluctantly Hood pushed himself halfway to his feet.

"Mr. Chairman, I think there should be some discussion."

In unison all eyes swept from Strong to the Sales Director.

"Of course," Sigurd agreed crisply. "You have the floor."

"Well, we don't want to go off half-cocked—" Hood's tone was apologetic. "The safety feature is ninety percent of our sales argument—there's no denying that, especially since the other markets have been shot to pieces." His initial nervousness overcome, Hood became more glib. "Frankly, I'm afraid that abandoning that argument will have a tremendously adverse effect upon our sales volume."

"Without doubt it will, but we have no choice in the matter."

"But surely this one payment—"

"It isn't a question of this one payment," Sigurd interrupted curtly. "It's a question of policy. These defaults are only starting! We simply won't have funds to keep covering them. Besides, until things improve, our sales are going to be curtailed anyway. That's another fact we may as well face. There won't be any new issues under present conditions, and by May first we should be pretty well cleared out of what we have now." The last remark was more a question than an assertion.

"I should hardly say that," Hood demurred. "There are almost a half million of the Romaine Hotel First Mortgage issue available yet, and three hundred thousand of the Junior Participation Bonds. We're pushing them as hard as we can but they're not going over so well. Of course, if they're in default—" Hood shrugged his shoulders.

"They're not in default," Counsel Behrmann corrected sharply. "They can't be declared in default until the interest date arrives."

"Mr. Chairman!" Without troubling to bestir himself from the depths of his chair, Winthrop Parness suggested suavely: "I move that we defer action upon this matter until next month. At that time we shall be better able to size up the sales situation. If it should appear advisable perhaps some arrangement could be made for managing the quarterly interest payment. The amortization we can let ride. That would give us three months extra in which to distribute whatever we have left on our hands." Parness' accents suggested an American actor, possibly a somewhat inferior American actor, playing an English role.

"Second the motion!" It was not definite who spoke up.

Mechanically Sigurd repeated the motion and put the question. It was passed with a few mumbled "Ayes". As simple as that! Judge Spar dozed off. Hood sank back into his seat. Martin Hoyle leafed through his papers. Winthrop Parness examined his nails. Behrmann blew rather poor smoke rings. The drone resumed.

So devious in its windings, so mysterious in its ways, so inevitable in its continuity yet so intangible and faint the ineluctable thread from cause to effect, that no one of the eight men gathered

in the drowsy board room could possibly know that his listlessly
mumbled "Aye" marked a definite focal point, his own minute contribution to a weird pattern of events that would result in untold
misery for scores of people, precarious happiness for a few, and in
violent death for no fewer than half of their own number.

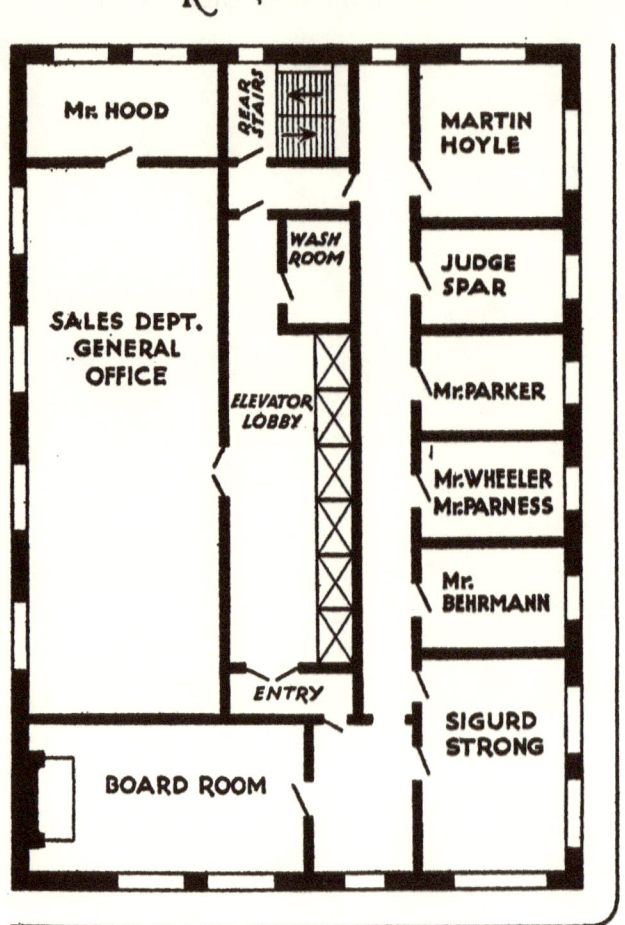

SECOND FLOOR PLAN—F. W. STRONG BUILDING

1
CORPORATE DEMISE

EIGHTEEN EVENTFUL MONTHS passed quickly. Instead of spring with its fair if elusive promise there was the crisp threat of fall. As the packed seasons whirled by, dislocations in business generally, and in the field of F. W. Strong Company particularly, rather than abating had become steadily more acute, but the drone in the board room had persisted in its biweekly spasms until early October, 1932.

Superficially the scene was little changed. The same eight men surrounded the oval table. The impassive eyes of the founder still gazed serenely from the canvas over the mantel. The tall windows were again open, but upon overcast skies; the breeze which rustled the hangings was cool and unfriendly. However, lacking was the haze of cigar smoke and missing, too, the air of languor.

The general inattention this time arose not from lethargy but from individual absorption in individual affairs. The men seldom exchanged direct glances and an air of manufactured optimism and forced humor pervaded the place. Each seemed to talk with his tongue in his cheek, a sheltering palm over his lips, a furtive eye cocked on his fellows as he mouthed calculated or unconscious falsehoods and watched their effect.

By hook or by crook, by high-pressure campaigning, by raising salesmen's commissions to unheard of proportions, by artfully maneuvering trades with clients for their holdings of stronger and more seasoned bonds, the bulk of the Romaine Hotel bond issue had been cleared from the shelves of the F. W. Strong Company, the actual legal default of the enterprise having been deferred on three successive quarterly interest dates to make this possible. The effort, however, had proved abortive. Once the floodgates were opened this default and scores of others swept over the firm like a tidal wave.

Now Counsel Behrmann is on his feet reading the Company's swan song.

In varying degree the listening directors show the impress of the devastating period they have passed through. Sigurd Strong is grayer than before and his heavy shoulders are now slightly stooped. Martin Hoyle, Treasurer, gets more and deeper wrinkles as his books show fewer current assets. Anthony Wheeler is duller, his eyes more protuberant, his face and figure generally more scrawny, his attire more shoddy. The once Apollo-esque features of Robert Alanson Hood are furrowed and careworn; he has aged ten years in one tenth of that time.

Winthrop Parness, too, has aged and he has taken on a little weight. His neat mustache is waxed into somewhat more precise points and his suit, this time an Oxford gray with a delicate pin-stripe, has changed just enough to keep abreast of the changing mode. Maurice Parker still exudes dignity but it is with a more conscious effort. The bald spot has extended itself many degrees and now leaves exposed a sizable polar area. The puffy flesh still bulges at his temples, but without spectacle bows to emphasize it. Instead, tortoise-shell nose glasses cling precariously to his bridge, insured only by a fine black tape draped over one ear and thence to a breast pocket.

Judge Spar, stifling mental yawns, is a scarce perceptible degree more awake; otherwise he is less changed than the others, except Behrmann. Counsel Behrmann seems least changed of all. His quietly correct clothing is no more noticeable, his wizened face not a day older or dryer. He reads aloud from a formidable, legal-appearing document bound in a light blue cover. Behrmann flops over the long pages as he finishes them. The paper is titled:

PEOPLE OF THE STATE OF NEW YORK, Plaintiff

vs:

F. W. STRONG & COMPANY, Inc., et al, Defendants

Behrmann's voice was not loud but distinct and penetrating. Occasionally he glanced up over the paper, eying his audience quizzically. As he approached the meat of the long communication he secured emphasis by slower and more careful enunciation. ". . . and due deliberation being had, it is ordered, adjudged and decreed as follows: That the said defendant, F. W. Strong and Company, incorporated, a New York Corporation, be and they are hereby permanently enjoined from buying, selling, or otherwise dealing in securities in and from the State of New York, provided that this injunction shall not apply to sales made by the Receiver of F. W. Strong and Company, a New York Corporation, hereafter appointed for the purpose of liquidation."

There followed a lengthy decree appointing permanent receivers for the company with numerous provisions outlining their function and conduct until eventually Behrmann's reading concluded: ". . . due deliberation being had, it is further ordered, adjudged and decreed that the defendants, Sigurd Strong, Abraham L. Behrmann, Martin Hoyle, Francis F. Spar, Anthony Wheeler, Winthrop Parness, Maurice Parker and Robert A. Hood be and each of them is permanently enjoined from acting in the State of New York on any committee organized for the protection of holders of securities sold heretofore by or through any of the defendants in this action"—a quick pause for breath—"and it is further ordered, adjudged and decreed that either party may apply for such remedy in the premises as the nature of the cause may require.—Enter.— Ralph Horne, Justice of the Supreme Court. Dated October 2nd, 1932."

The dry rapid crackle of Behrmann's voice ceased abruptly. Without any comment or explanation he folded up the document and dropped into his seat, leaving his audience expectant, quite suspended, wordless. The tense, empty silence continued for a few

moments then was gradually dissolved into the swish of uncomfortable bodies shifting in leather chairs, the shuffle of feet on the
plush carpet, and finally by Sigurd Strong's voice speaking as in
a vacuum, unheard, unattended, for they all suddenly knew that
everything had been said.

In an adjoining room, an anteroom separating the board room
on one side from Sigurd Strong's private office on the other, Johnny
Bartlett, news gatherer par excellence of the *Evening Globe*, leaned
familiarly over the desk of Miss Margaret Purcell, Secretary to Mr.
Strong. Mr. Bartlett was not gathering news. He was absorbing
from as nearby as he dared the fragrance of Margaret's hair, and
he was urging upon her with as much vehemence as he could command, without too much raising his voice, the desirability of his
company for dinner.

"It's pay day, Peggy. Comes only once a week on Friday! Gala
occasion and all that! Now I know a place where—" At the sound of
shuffling feet in the next room Johnny suddenly straightened up.
The meeting seemed over.

"Guess I'll brace the old boy now," he whispered.

The door opened and Strong stepped in, going toward his own
office. At the sight of Johnny his manner unconsciously bristled,
but he knew the value of a friendly press. His voice said cordially
enough:

"Ah; how are you, Mr.—er—?"

"Bartlett, sir."

"From the *Globe* if I remember?"

"That's right."

"Glad to see you again."

"Do you care to make any statement about the action at Special Term, part four, this morning? The District Attorney says—"

"I do indeed want to make a statement," Sigurd interrupted.
"It was the most outrageous travesty on justice ever perpetrated
in this state. We intend to appeal this decision to the highest court
in the land. Of course the damage to our reputation, carefully built
up and nurtured over a period of forty-five years, is difficult to

estimate and will be more difficult to mend. However, in the long run justice will prevail."

Bartlett scribbled industriously.

"I understand the injunction affects the bondholders' protective committees, too, Mr. Strong. What about that?"

"That is as unfair to the bondholders as the rest of it is to us. It is our sincere belief that we are better qualified than anyone else to reorganize properties that find themselves in difficulties; that we better than anyone else are able to protect and conserve the interests of the first mortgage bondholders!" Sigurd's voice had risen to a sonorous, oratorical pitch. Suddenly he seemed to come back to earth. "Be good enough to quote me to that effect in your paper, young man."

He turned away and passed into his own office, saying over his shoulder as he left, "I'll need you in about five minutes, Miss Purcell."

Bartlett waited until the door had clicked behind him, then indicated her departed employer with a contemptuous thumb.

"The old s. o. b. almost believes that blarney himself, doesn't he?"

"Hush up!"

"How about tonight?"

"I might not get away until all hours tonight, Johnny."

"I'll wait. Say, Peggy; when this outfit gets through folding up will you marry me?"

Numerically this must have been at least the twentieth time that Johnny had put that question, so Margaret was neither surprised nor moved, and before she could reply Martin Hoyle came in from the board room and had scarce crossed the office to Mr. Strong's door when the sharp summons of the buzzer at Margaret's desk obviated the necessity for the answer Johnny had by now learned to expect. She gathered up her pencil and notebook and fled.

2

MR. HOYLE GOES ON A JOURNEY

THAT FINAL MEETING, marking the corporate expiration of F. W. Strong and Company, took place on a Friday afternoon. About half past eight the following Monday morning a certain Willie Sidensticker, aged fifteen, became suddenly and certainly the most surprised office boy in the Metropolitan area; probably the most terrified, too.

It was his duty each morning immediately upon his arrival to make the rounds of the executive offices of the F. W. Strong Company, a cheese cloth in one hand for putting the finishing touches on the glass desk tops cleaned by the charwomen the night before, a supply of sharpened pencils and fresh memo pads in the other. Willie adjusted the patent desk calendars to bring them up to date, filled inkwells, wound desk clocks and, upon occasion when he was early and time hung heavy, snooped in the desk drawers.

Usually Willie had finished his chores before any of the office occupants arrived. On this particular Monday, however, Willie found Martin Hoyle at his desk. Martin had been there since Saturday. He was slumped forward over the desk, his head resting upon it, a horrid hole in his right temple, a brown smear down his cheek and chin, and his jaw the center of an irregular dark stain on the glass top. Mr. Hoyle, even from the distance of six paces which the horrified Willie tremblingly kept, was obviously, unmistakably and thoroughly dead!

A black .38 caliber automatic, which Willie had remarked several times during explorations of Mr. Hoyle's desk, lay beside the swivel chair. That was all Willie had time to notice. He did not even pause to close the frosted glass door in his flight down the corridor.

And so it was that the officers and employees of F. W. Strong and Company, as they filtered in an hour or so later to attend to their final duties in connection with the obsequies of the firm, found themselves confronted by detectives and uniformed police-men. The hallman (dispatcher, he called himself; Senior-Vice-President-in-charge-of-errands, the boys called him), to whom Willie had come running with the news, had told Mr. Hood, who happened to arrive early that morning. Mr. Hood had taken one careful look through Mr. Hoyle's door and had telephoned the police.

Plain-clothes Sergeant Roberts, arriving promptly with two patrolmen, had taken one look also—a closer look. He had crossed the threshold far enough to assure himself that Hoyle was dead, had surveyed the disposition of the body and the weapon, had scratched his head for an uncertain moment and had then decided to play it safe. He had backed out of the room, closed the door carefully, leaving the patrolmen on post there, elbowed his way through the silent group of gaping office boys and stenographers and had telephoned the precinct station house. Whereupon there had shortly descended upon the scene Inspector Bryce of the Homi-cide Squad, an assistant, a deputy medical examiner, a photogra-pher and a stenographer.

Methodically each had gone about his business, and by the time Sigurd Strong put in his appearance, shortly before ten o'clock, their preliminary or field work was well under way. The photogra-pher had taken pictures of the room, of the body from several points of view, of the gun as it lay, and was preparing to photograph a few fingerprints he had found on the desk top, the telephone re-ceiver and the furniture. The Medical Examiner's man had scruti-nized the body and placed Hoyle's demise at "sometime Saturday afternoon or evening," and attributed it, pending an autopsy, to "a bullet wound in the right temple, fired from a gun held very close by, possibly within a foot and slightly lower (there were slight powder burns around the wound) and probably self-inflicted. Death had been almost instantaneous."

Inspector Bryce and Sergeant Roberts had been gathering facts, and the stenographer had a quarter of his book filled with their questions and other people's answers and statements. From Willie Sidensticker, questioned first, they had learned that he had discovered Hoyle at about half past eight when he came in to arrange the desk, and that he had run immediately to Huffman, the hallman. The office door, like all the others in the row of executive offices, had been shut but not locked. He had touched nothing. In fact, he had hardly entered the room. Willie had last seen Mr. Hoyle some time Saturday morning when he had been sent out by him for a tin of pipe tobacco, they learned.

Mr. Robert Hood could tell them little, either. He had been called hurriedly by Huffman almost immediately upon his arrival that morning, had gone with him and looked into Hoyle's office but upon seeing Hoyle's body had decided not to enter the room. He had telephoned the police and then Mr. Strong at his home. Mr. Hood had last seen Martin Hoyle about mid-morning on Saturday. They had talked for a few minutes, but only about business matters. Mr. Hoyle, though not cheerful—none of them were during the last few days—had not seemed unusually depressed nor had he acted in any way abnormal.

From Margaret Purcell they learned that Hoyle had dictated several routine letters at about eleven o'clock on Saturday morning, that he had gone out then and had given her instructions to type them up and leave them on his desk, informing her that he would later return and sign and mail them. She had not seen him after that, having left the office herself shortly after noon. The carbon copies of the letters, which Miss Purcell readily identified, were in the file basket on Mr. Hoyle's desk and the originals and addressed envelopes were missing, so it was presumed that Hoyle had come back on Saturday as he intended.

From the building superintendent they learned that the offices were cleaned each weekday evening and on Saturday afternoon, usually fairly early. There would be no occasion for any of the building staff to be on that floor at all on Sunday. The charwoman assigned to that particular wing on the past Saturday lived somewhere on the lower east side. There was no telephone but they had her address and would be glad to send for her. She would be on duty again at five in the afternoon. Bryce wrote down the address and handed it to an assistant, who immediately left to question her.

And it was at this juncture that Sigurd Strong, summoned abruptly from a late and leisurely breakfast by Hood's telephone call, burst in upon Bryce's examination. Huffman, the center of a hushed group of awed office employees, cut short his eleventh and best detailed depiction of the events of the morning to conduct Mr. Strong to the scene. With an artful combination of deference to each, he presented Inspector Bryce.

Sigurd looked over Bryce's shoulder to where the assistant medical examiner was finishing his preliminary examination of Hoyle's body. Strong shuddered and turned away, his gold headed cane tapping out an agitated tattoo; then, seeming to gather himself together, he said:

"Terrible, isn't it! And Martin, of all men! I'd never have believed it." He paused. "When did it happen, officer?"

Before Bryce could reply the two men came in with a stretcher.

"What are they going to do now?" Sigurd, asked.

"We'll take the body to the morgue."

"Oh, I see. Is that—we want Martin to have—well, wouldn't an undertaker be better?" Sigurd finally stammered.

"There'll have to be further examination," Bryce said curtly.

"Is that necessary? I mean—there is no doubt about Mr. Hoyle's suicide, is there?"

"Superficially it appears to be a fairly clear case of suicide. However, an autopsy in cases like these is quite customary."

Sigurd only grunted. He looked more calmly now, almost meditatively, at the preparations being made to move Martin Hoyle.

Bryce broke in upon him.

"Do you know of any reason why Mr. Hoyle should have killed himself?"

Strong shook his head.

"No," he replied slowly, "no more than any of us. The firm, as you're probably aware, has had more than its share of stormy weather. We've all been distressed, but Mr. Martin no more than any of us. He seemed all right Saturday."

"When did you see him last?"

"Let's see—Saturday morning we had a talk, about ten-thirty, I should guess. I didn't see him after that."

"What was discussed?"

"Oh, business." Sigurd made a little noncommittal gesture. "The details of turning over the books and funds to the receiver."

"Did Hoyle say anything about going anywhere?"

"Going anywhere?"

"Yeah; a trip or anything like that?"

"No; nothing of the sort."

Bryce hesitated a moment, then said bluntly:

"He was Treasurer, wasn't he? His books all right?"

Strong appeared about to bristle, then replied steadily: "I'm sure he had nothing of that kind to worry about."

Bryce shrugged his shoulders.

"People don't kill themselves for fun. Was Hoyle married?"

"His wife died several years ago. I believe he had no close relatives." There was a moment of silence.

The camera man had packed up his paraphernalia and stood chatting with the deputy medical examiner and one of the patrolmen. Hoyle's body had been disposed upon a stretcher and two attendants, upon a nod from the Inspector, started to remove it. Sigurd Strong involuntarily shrank back as the gruesome, blanket-draped form was carried past him.

"This room will have to be undisturbed for a day or two," Bryce informed Strong. "I'll leave a man here. There will be a few more formalities—" His voice trailed off as he took a last slow look back about the office. Almost absently he remarked, "I'll be back."

One of the uniformed men settled into a chair by the wall; the rest of the party filed out after the Inspector.

Early that afternoon Mr. Bartlett of the *Evening Globe* cautiously insinuated himself into the post-lunch lassitude pervading the anteroom office of Mr. Strong's Secretary. Margaret had some work to do, but not much, and had not been occupying herself with it anyway, so the intrusion was less unwelcome than it might have been. Nobody in the offices of F. W. Strong had done any work all day, and there seemed to be a sort of tacit understanding that nobody would. It would take more than that day for the office routine to recover from the demoralization caused by the discovery of Martin Hoyle.

All morning the clerks and stenographers had been congregating in constantly fluxing, whispering groups. There had been two principle topics of hushed conversation, quite unrelated—the Treasurer's untimely demise and the probable effect of the receivership upon their various tenures of employment. A few alien faces, objects of furtive scrutiny, moved about outside the little groups, orienting themselves and getting settled into the desk space assigned to them. They were auditors and clerks employed by the newly appointed receiver.

Margaret had avoided the groups. Her own reflections weighed heavily upon her. Across Fifth Avenue the shop windows, just visible from where she sat, reminded her that winter was in the offing. She had a good position and this would be an unfortunate time to lose it. Margaret had been Sigurd Strong's secretary for several years. She was discreet, and capable in an unassertive way. The work and surroundings were pleasant. Mr. Strong was always agreeable. Mr. Behrmann, who gave her more work than Mr. Strong, was a more exacting task master but usually patient. Mr. Parker and Judge Spar seldom had any work and seldom noticed her. Mr. Wheeler and Mr. Parness usually did most of their detailed work in their own real estate offices. Altogether, it was a comfortable, congenial position.

Mr. Parness had made himself something of a problem at first but that hadn't lasted long. By an affected obtuseness and a studied indifference she had evaded his subtle advances until his attentions had presently subsided for lack of fuel.

Recently and until a few weeks past, Hood, too, had been casting self-conscious glances in her direction. They had culminated
in several clandestine meetings (mixing of business and pleasure
was definitely discouraged by the F. W. Strong Company personnel director) with dining and dancing or movies, and had then
unaccountably ceased. Margaret often wondered why. She thought
with a wry smile of the bewildered creatures in the b.o. and halito-
sis advertisements.

She was in a brown study on this afternoon pondering Mr.
Hood's remissness when Johnny Bartlett slid into her office. This
perhaps accounted for a certain coolness in her manner. Actually
Margaret was fond of Johnny, enjoying his company and relishing
his never-failing, gay humor.

He draped himself across the end of her desk, hauled out his
notebook and started reading with mock gravity: "'We all regret
deeply the loss of Mr. Martin Hoyle, our late Treasurer. To the
Board of Directors and to his friends in F. W. Strong and Company, cognizant of the strain under which Mr. Hoyle has labored
for the last several years, it was quite understandable that a human
will might break. We remaining may simply labor more devoutly
in order to bridge the gap Mr. Hoyle's departure has left. Signed.
Sigurd Strong, Chairman.' Not bad, eh? That's what the old boy
handed me before lunch."

Bartlett shut the book and thrust it back into his pocket. "Isn't
that the cat's meow, Peggy! I think it's swell, only you need quite a
sense of humor. The only trouble is the City Editor can get that
stuff over the telephone. If I handed in just that he'd fire me and I
wouldn't blame him. There's a better story around here, Peggy, and
I'm going to be on hand when it breaks."

"Story? All you think about is stories. You'd murder your grand-
mother to write up her funeral!" Margaret's tone was more acid
than her words. Her temper with Johnny had not been wholly natural since Mr. Hood had withdrawn into his crisp businesslike shell.

Bartlett eyed her sharply.

"Stories are my living, Peggy," he reminded her gently. "They'll
be *our* living one of these days when you get over—"

"Oh, shut up!"

Before Bartlett could undrape himself from her desk Margaret touched his arm.

"I'm sorry, Johnny. I didn't mean to be nasty. Everything has gotten on my nerves."

Bartlett, from whose broad good-nature rebuffs flowed like water off a duck, wisely changed the subject.

"Mark my words about the story, kid. You know who that white-haired guy is—in there now with Strong?"

"It's someone the bonding company sent over about poor Mr. Hoyle."

"And why should the bonding company send him over about poor Mr. Hoyle?" mimicked Johnny. "Because they're sympathetic, huh? No, ma'am! It's because they're plenty worried. They think there's something fishy. Whom do you think they've sent over with their condolences? That's Maxwell Fenner."

Margaret's only acknowledgment of this important announcement was an innocent blank stare.

"Never heard of him before, have you?" Johnny urged. "Neither have a lot of people. He doesn't advertise. Well, he's a slick gent, and he wouldn't be wasting his time here if there wasn't something up."

This was, of course, a gross exaggeration. For every baffling or intriguing case in Maxwell Fenner's career of larceny investigations there were a score of prosaic and uninteresting ones.

"Therefore," Bartlett concluded airily, "it behooves little Johnny to poke about a bit."

"Mr. Strong might not enthuse over your snooping," Margaret suggested. She rocked back in her chair, folding her hands behind her head and stretching luxuriously. At twenty-six her serious beauty was just finding its bloom. Her dark eyes, clear, limpid, were cast absently up toward Johnny's face. Her smooth round arms raised, her dark blouse was drawn by the motion snugly across mature breasts.

Johnny's eyes widened.

"Don't *do* that, woman—just when I'm learning to be good!"

Margaret rocked forward, laughing, and Johnny resumed:

"As a matter of fact, the Old Boy might not like it, but then he's on the way out, anyway. The receivers are the babies in the driver's seat now." He got to his feet and looked down the long private corridor which led from Margaret's room back toward the rear of the building. On one side at regular intervals six doors with frosted glass panels led into the various executives' offices. All of them were shut.

"Which office was Mr. Hoyle's?" he asked Margaret.

"The last one; but you may as well save your time and a walk. It's locked and there's a policeman there, besides."

"Who uses all of the other offices?"

"The first door is a side entrance to Mr. Strong's room. The next is Mr. Behrmann's. The one after is used by Mr. Wheeler and Mr. Parness when they're here. Then comes Mr. Parker's and then Judge Spar's."

"They all officers?"

"Mr. Behrmann's the counsel. The rest are vice presidents, except Mr. Parness. He's a director, though."

"I suppose the whole bunch were in on Saturday? I don't see many around today," Johnny observed.

Margaret covered a yawn and turned to her desk. "Listen, Deteckative Bartlett; if it's all the same to you I've got a half dozen letters to get out now. I'll be seeing you."

Johnny accepted the dismissal with even more than his usual equanimity.

"You'll be seeing me, all right. I'm nature's original remedy for Secretary's sore eyes—or any other blighted areas. Toodle-oo!"

3

ENTER MR. FENNER

WHILE ON THE ONE SIDE Margaret and Johnny Bartlett flipped incon-
sequential trivialities, on the other side of the heavy door to Mr.
Strong's sanctum that gentleman, A. L. Behrmann and Maxwell
Fenner were in serious discussion. Sigurd Strong, his voice buzzing along in a low, confidential monotone, was doing most of the
talking—apologetic, almost, and softening as much as he could a
tentative indictment of his late associate.

"Against our every instinct and natural inclination from our
years of association with Martin, we've come to the reluctant conclusion—the almost unbelievable conclusion, I might say—that
something is wrong somewhere. A cursory check of his accounts
and bank balances reveals certain irregularities—er—peculiarities,
perhaps I had better call them. How significant or extensive they
are only a more thorough audit will disclose. We hope and still
believe they will prove to be of small import. However, Mr.
Behrmann and I, immediately the matter was brought to our
attention, concluded that it was only proper that your people be
instantly apprised." He looked thoughtfully, almost watchfully, at
his visitor and then at Behrmann whose face wore a peculiar little
half smile.

Such thoughtfulness, Fenner told himself sardonically, merited
more than casual appreciation, or scrutiny. Aloud he murmured:

"Of course, of course. Perhaps, as you suggest, the irregularities will be found to be of minor nature. Let's hope so."

Sigurd, his tone now less equivocal, resumed:

247

"Mr. Hoyle as Treasurer was bonded for one hundred thousand dollars. In addition, I believe there is a blanket Officers and Directors Bond for a like amount which would supplement the other in case of deficiency, or perhaps even operate first. Now if these irregularities prove to be of serious proportions your firm undoubtedly will be presented with claims." He switched his glance from Fenner to Behrmann for approbation, as a small boy might who had been illy coached.

Behrmann nodded slow agreement, a mirthless smile wrinkling his face. There was an ageless character to his dark, parchment-like complexion receding into the equally dark, almost bare skull. He might have been a prematurely bald forty-five or a youthful sixty. Actually Behrmann was about halfway between, but he had scarcely altered in appearance during the last dozen years and probably wouldn't for many to come. He agreed tersely with Sigurd.

"Just so. For that matter, the receiver's auditors are already installed and getting to work. Any basis for a possible claim will probably be all the more promptly ferreted out and, if I know Judge Horton, all the more vigorously prosecuted."

Maxwell Fenner appeared less disturbed than he felt. He had visions of grossly juggled books, terrific shortages, and the bonding company, his client, holding the bag to the extent of their coverage. He asked:

"When was your last audit made?"

"The books were closed June thirtieth for the semiannual statement. I believe your firm was supplied with a copy of the auditors' report at that time," Behrmann answered.

"By whom was it made?"

"By Langhorne and Simmons."

"They've done all our work for years," Strong chimed in.

"Exactly," Fenner murmured caustically, and before Behrmann or Strong could take exception to his comment he went on briskly, "I shall bring several assistants in the morning. I suppose there will be no trouble about access to the records—what with this receiver moving in?"

"None, I'm certain," Behrmann promised.

Fenner airily switched the conversation as it threatened to languish.

"Awfully sudden, wasn't it? About Mr. Hoyle, I mean," he said, and thought to himself that if the same asinine remark had been addressed to him he would have been tempted to reply that people didn't often shoot themselves by degrees.

"Yes; we were thoroughly surprised," Sigurd answered. "Martin was the last person in the world of whom one would expect anything of that sort, even with strong reasons."

"Did he leave any family?"

"No close relatives that we know of. His wife died several years ago. There were no children. I believe he had a half-sister and some cousins somewhere in the Middle West. We're making inquiries."

"And he shot himself in the head? Have the police had anything to say?"

"Anything to say? I don't understand." Sigurd seemed genuinely puzzled. "They were here all morning looking things over and getting statements. I suppose there's little that could be said. Martin was simply in over his head and took the easiest way out. You know"—Sigurd turned to include Behrmann in their conversation—"he's never been quite the same since his wife died. That may have had something to do with unbalancing him. He brooded a lot over her. Not long ago he said to me—it was just after Shirley, that is, Mrs. Strong, had been here and the three of us had had a drink together—that he couldn't see that he had much left to live for. It surprised me very much for, as I say, he was usually very matter-of-fact."

Mechanically, as if his own mention of the subject had been the stimulus for a definite reflex action, Sigurd leaned toward a cupboard-like arrangement beneath one end of his huge desk and produced a decanter and a tray of glasses.

"You'll have a drink, Mr. Fenner? I don't mind admitting I've found a shot or two helpful today. You, A. L.?"

He poured three drinks without waiting for answers, corked the decanter and set it back in the desk. Fenner picked up his glass but toyed with it absently while the others gulped their down.

"Hoyle killed himself Saturday," he thought aloud. "Isn't it unusual that he shouldn't have been found until this morning? Surely someone—"

"That doesn't surprise me as much as that no one heard the shot," Behrmann broke in. "So far as we can learn Martin came back after lunch Saturday. The cleaning on Saturday is done as soon as everyone clears out, which is usually by one P.M. or a little after. So Martin must have come back after two, or perhaps even later in the afternoon. The woman who cleaned this row of offices saw no one about and she finished about two. There would be no reason for anyone to be in these offices from then until this morning, so I can see that Martin mightn't have been discovered. But how the devil a revolver could be fired without being heard by the starter or the elevator man on the first floor, or by any other occupants of the building, or even by people in the streets, is more than I *can* figure out!"

Fenner shrugged his shoulders.

"These Fifth Avenue busses backfire once in a while, you know." He tossed of his drink, placed the empty glass beside the other two, and got to his feet. "I wonder if I could have a look about Mr. Hoyle's office?"

Sigurd and Behrmann exchanged glances. The former said, "The Police have ordered that the room be undisturbed. In fact, Inspector Bryce left a man on duty there."

"Inspector Bryce! So much the better. The officer will see to it that I meddle with nothing. I'm sure he'll permit me to glance around."

Before his firm if gentle persistence they could only assent. Sigurd led the way out of the office and down the corridor to the easterly door. Margaret Purcell from her desk in the anteroom watched the procession curiously.

They found the door locked and upon knocking heard the sound of a chair being tipped down away from the wall against which it had leaned, heard the guard moving and saw his shadow behind the frosted glass door. He opened it but barred the way.

"May I come in, officer. I'm sure it will be all right with Inspector Bryce."

At the use of his superior's name the officer looked doubtful but he held his ground.

"My orders, sor, was to admit nobody. Maybe, now, if ye was to get ahold of the Inspector—"

Footsteps hurrying down the corridor, as if in response to the suggestion, caused them all to look around. "Speaking of the devil—" ejaculated Fenner.

Inspector Bryce looked at them curiously.

"Hello, Max," he said casually, extending his hand to Fenner. To Strong and Behrmann he simply nodded. He returned the patrolman's salute with a brief wave.

"You time your arrivals nicely, Inspector," Fenner remarked. "Your man was just about to heave me out on my ear. Not out, exactly, either, because he wouldn't let me in." The officer looked his appreciation. The complaint was as pointed a compliment as he could have asked.

"I was just after tellin' him to get ahold of you, sor." He moved out of the way. Bryce did not enter; instead he faced Strong and Behrmann in the doorway.

"Anything turn up in the way of a motive?" he asked brusquely.

Sigurd's palm crossed his chin and he looked at Behrmann for counsel. The lawyer spoke cautiously.

"There might be. We're checking up as fast as we can," he said. "In fact, we may as well admit that Mr. Hoyle's books don't quite balance. That is why we have called upon Mr. Fenner—or rather, why Mr. Fenner has called upon us," he corrected, his face breaking into his suave, inscrutable smile. "Until we have some facts and figures, however, we can't really say anything."

"No; of course not. Well, you should know in a day or two?" The statement was at once a question and a dismissal. "Come in, Max. I want a final look around before this place is cleaned up." Bryce moved as he talked, quickly and directly, without lost time, words or motion. Sigurd and Behrmann passed reluctantly down the hall. "Terry, close the door and stay in the hall. Let me know if anyone comes moseyin' around."

The policeman disposed of, Bryce turned to Fenner. "Glad to see you,—especially here and now! This ought to be right up your alley."

"The arithmetic, the dollars and cents balance sheet; that's my 'alley' as you so elegantly phrase it, in this case," Fenner reminded him.

"But you wouldn't turn up your nose if I told you there was something screwy about this suicide, Max."

"Homicide, instead of suicide, eh?"

"Not that necessarily, but it's not all as simple as it seems."

They eyed each other warmly. Maxwell Fenner and Inspector Bryce had been thrown together on a number of important cases and together had shared a gratifying average of success. Their last case* had been brought to an abrupt and violent termination early the preceding April, and they had been more or less out of touch for the intervening six months, so each welcomed the sight of the other.

Bryce and Fenner were as different in temperament and method as two individuals following the same calling could very well be, but this never hampered them when they were engaged together on a case; rather, the methods and tactics of each supplemented those of the other to perfection. Bryce had a long record of police service and was thoroughly steeped in the police method and imbued with the police point of view. "Action!" was his motto; and, given something to start from, he pursued his course with a relentlessness and vigor that left no stone unturned until he either arrived at an answer or reached an impasse that balked further inquiry. More often the former was the case.

Fenner, on the other hand, had a languid, easy-going way about him, sometimes partly assumed but more often genuine, which,

---

* The $180,000 robbery of the main vault of the Consolidated American Bank, with several attendant homicides, recorded in *The Bank Vault Mystery*.

though it irritated Bryce, usually deceived their quarry and was invariably effective. "Give them time," he sometimes said, "and they all make the breaks that hang them. The odds are so overwhelmingly on our side it shouldn't be necessary to do more than to be sure that we miss no tricks." His idea was to sit back with his finger tips alertly on all the aspects of a case, to prod gently here and there when things became too quiet, and to wait for the opening that experience had taught him would inevitably occur.

Aside from possessing a trained, reasoning brain in a strictly intellectual sense, Fenner was possessed of a deep insight into the mental and psychological processes of his fellow men, and it was more often by the application of this insight to specific situations than by any marvels of deductive reasoning that he produced the remarkable solutions for which he was known.

Fenner had served his apprenticeship with the New York City Police years before, but the driving pressure one moment, alternating with political hampering the next, had irked him until he had resigned to initiate a practice of his own. His success and reputation (among a limited circle permitted to know of his exploits) had grown slowly and steadily until, after twenty leisurely years, he was regarded as the leader in his particular field. Fenner specialized in larceny work and confidence cases, and was retained by several of the larger insurance companies and bonding houses. In his experience, however, he had also been called upon from time to time to investigate murders and other crimes of violence, and was an ardent student of criminology in all its phases.

4
BAGS AND BULLETS

"WHAT'S THE STORY?" Fenner asked the Inspector. "All I've been told is that Martin Hoyle committed suicide, with a veiled suggestion that it might have been for financial reasons. He probably had them!"

"Until half an hour ago I thought that was all there was to it. It looked like an open and shut case; finger-prints on the gun check, bullet track and powder marks on his head check, motive probable, opportunity O. K., in fact, everything in apple-pie order—so perfect I felt leery about it at the beginning. Anyway, the Bureau of Ballistics just sent me their dope and that's why I'm back. The bullet taken out of Hoyle's head was so badly flattened and deformed by its encounter with the bony structure of the cranium that the rifling marks are useless for purposes of comparison. They can't even say it was fired from Hoyle's gun, or rather from the gun found, which presumably was his. They don't say it wasn't. On the other hand, they say the shell we picked up positively was from that gun, but from its position"—he pointed with his toe to a slight chalk mark on the carpet—"they say it must have been moved or else ejected from a gun fired in a different part of the room, say—here."

He consulted a diagram and indicated the far side of the room near the window. "Nice little riddle, eh?"

"The shell might have been kicked before it was picked up this morning," Fenner suggested.

"I suppose it might have been, but it's damned queer. Ejected from Hoyle's gun, pointed as it must have been when he shot himself, that shell should have been found out in front of his desk somewhere. Now the office boy that discovered him and that fellow, Hood, both say they scarcely came inside the door. The officer they called went directly from the door to Hoyle's chair and back, not around in front of the desk at all. He wouldn't have kicked it, anyway." Bryce stopped talking and fell into an almost morose study.

Fenner moved to the window and glanced out. It opened upon the side street. Three floors below taxis, cars and trucks in a slow procession moved toward Fifth Avenue, snaking their way carefully between the cars parked on one side and a small excavation where several men were repairing a leaking steam main. Small wisps of vapor floated upward and there was a sustained tiny hissing scarcely audible above the noise of the traffic. Cars, he reflected, must have been moving in just such a slow procession on the previous Saturday afternoon, their occupants shopping bound, matinee bound or homeward bound, and quite unaware that three floors above them and slightly north—a scant forty feet—a Mr. Martin Hoyle was dying from a bullet in his brain. He said presently:

"Their work—the Bureau of Ballistics—is it quite positive now?"

"Almost one hundred percent. With the equipment that has been developed for comparing them, the rifling marks on a bullet or the hammer indentation on a shell are almost as dependable in their way as finger-prints."

"Speaking of finger-prints," Fenner switched abruptly, "are your men all through? I want a look through Hoyle's desk if it's all right."

"We're through. Mostly his own prints, we found; a few of the scrubwoman's, and some others which we're looking into now." He produced an envelope from his pocket and withdrew from it a bunch of keys which he handed to Fenner. "Hoyle's keys. You'll need them. You can dig into the desk all you please. Maybe you'll dig me up some sort of a point of beginning!"

"Maybe I will. I'm not sure I want to, though. You know, all together, Martin Hoyle was bonded for some two hundred thousand dollars. If he's very much short there's going to be weeping and wailing and gnashing of teeth all up and down William Street."*

Fenner sat down at Martin Hoyle's desk, yanking the swivel chair sideways and disposing himself fastidiously so as to avoid the dark stain which still blemished the plate glass top. He started methodically going through its contents. Before long he called sharply to Bryce:

"Was this drawer closed when Hoyle was found?" He indicated the shallow center drawer which he had just pulled out.

Bryce came over from a tall wardrobe locker which he had been scanning.

"Yes; they all were."

"Then, Bureau of Ballistics or no Bureau, shells or no shells, someone else was in this room after Hoyle was shot. Awfully soon after he was shot, too."

The irregular stain on the desk top converged at a point where the small pool had flowed over the edge and dripped to the floor. Partway back from the front of the drawer two small dark spots overlapped each other on the drawer bottom. It was to these that Fenner referred. When the drawer was opened about halfway the spots came directly beneath the extending finger of stain where Hoyle's blood had dripped from the desk top.

"This drawer was opened and closed while Hoyle was still bleeding. If you knew who opened it you'd probably know why Hoyle shot himself, or *if* Hoyle shot himself. If we even knew what was being sought for in the drawer we'd have a good start."

Bryce stooped closer. "It's blood, all right," he said. With the sharp limber blade of his knife he carefully pried loose a flat splinter of the drawer bottom, including the two spots, and thrust it into an envelope. "The Medical Examiner can tell damned quick if it's Hoyle's or not."

Bryce had not seemed much surprised; now he abruptly straightened up.

"Say; wasn't that drawer locked?"

*William Street is known as Insurance Row.

"Yes; I just unlocked it."

The Inspector appeared relieved. He said:

"I thought I had tried them all this morning. Every drawer in the desk was locked then, and—Cripes! Whoever locked the drawer put the keys back in Hoyle's pocket! That's where we found them. What the devil do you make of that?"

"The desk wasn't examined this morning?"

"Nope; too many around. I knew I'd be back. I saved another item for this trip, too, in the wardrobe, a Gladstone bag. From its weight it's fully packed. It's locked, too, but I expect the keys are with the others." Bryce took the key ring from the desk where Fenner had tossed it and moved back to the wardrobe. Fenner joined him.

"Is that bag just where it was? Did you move it at all?" he asked over the Inspector's shoulder.

"Not a whisker. I lifted it to be sure it wasn't empty but set it right back. Why?"

"I only wondered. Rather odd, isn't it? Its position looks unnatural." The suitcase was set across the short direction of the wardrobe about four inches from one end. "If you or I or ninety-nine people out of a hundred put that there we'd set it in one corner, or at least lengthwise against the back of the wardrobe," Fenner observed.

"So what?"

"So would Mr. Hoyle if there hadn't been something else already in that corner; another bag, for instance, which isn't there now."

"Kind of far-fetched, isn't it?" Bryce scratched his head.

"I'm not sure it is. It would require almost conscious effort to open that wardrobe and set that bag down, alone, as it's now placed. It just naturally goes into the corner."

Bryce looked at the space between the Gladstone bag and the end of the wardrobe. "Maybe you're right. It must have been an awfully skinny grip, though."

"A briefcase, perhaps, or maybe nothing. It's purest conjecture."

"Whatever it was—or wasn't—it's gone. Let's take a look at the bag we *have* got." Suiting his actions to his words Bryce selected a key on Hoyle's ring and, at first attempt, opened the bag. They found it well packed with clothing, toilet accessories, a few books and papers. Martin Hoyle had evidently contemplated a trip of some duration.

"Do you suppose he was getting ready to lam?" Bryce wondered. "He must've changed his mind."

"Maybe he was simply going on a business trip."

"Not officially. I asked Strong that this morning after I'd noticed the bag."

"Well, he went on a longer trip than he expected." Fenner let his glance wander about the room. "All that remains is to determine why, or what, or who, altered his plans, who possibly expedited his final journey," he finished airily.

"Yeah; that's all!"

"And of course there's the little matter of proving it." Both were silent for a moment. A speculative look crossed Fenner's face.

"To start off with," he pondered aloud, "someone was here, possibly with Hoyle or possibly attracted by the shot. In either case it must have been someone familiar with the run of things here, probably someone connected with the company."

"Correct," Bryce said laconically. "I got about that far. Everybody of consequence in the outfit is being picked up and watched. We've got two dozen men on it already."

"But officially this is a definite suicide?"

"Oh, yes. Whether it was or not, there's no sense making our work any harder."

"And if it was," Fenner went on, "someone providentially took advantage of it. It could be anybody who happened to be in the building late and heard the shot, but it would have to be someone familiar enough with Hoyle's affairs to figure it worth while to do some snooping, also someone clever enough and careful enough to have covered his tracks as well as he apparently did.

"And if it *wasn't* suicide, we're looking for the same person, except that in addition he will be cold-blooded enough to have planned and executed a deliberate murder, and thorough and painstaking enough to have arranged this almost perfect suicide

stage set. Also he'd have to be at least moderately familiar with fire-
arms. Those requirements should narrow the field considerably."

"What about motive? Do you suppose—?"

"That will develop when we get into these books. From the little
I've learned of Martin Hoyle it probably wasn't women. Per se, it
must have been money. Elementary, what!"

"But this outfit didn't have any money left," Bryce protested.

"That remains to be seen. For my client's sake I hope there's a
little."

Fenner resumed his examination of the contents of Hoyle's
desk. Bryce paced the floor, chewing his cigar, and permitted his
mind by a profound, if slow, process of ingurgitation to absorb the
background of the peculiar case.

It was late in the afternoon when they called the patrolman back
to his post and left the office. In the elevator lobby they were
promptly pounced upon by Johnny Bartlett who had waited with
commendable patience for several hours.

"I'm from the *Globe*, Inspector. I understand the Police aren't
satisfied about Mr. Hoyle's death. Anything to say?"

"Where the devil did you get that?" the astounded Inspector
countered, and added hastily, "Anyway, there's nothing to it."

"I only wondered," Bartlett went on innocently. "Was he much
short?"

"I think you'd do better to see Mr. Strong," Fenner broke in.

"I've already seen him, Mr. Fenner. Say, look here," Bartlett
hurried on impulsively, "I'll print whatever you want me to now if
you'll give me a break when this story opens up."

Fenner and Bryce exchanged doubtful glances.

"What did Mr. Strong tell you?" the former asked.

The reporter handed him a copy of Sigurd Strong's unctuous
statement. Fenner perused it in silence. He handed it back and laid
a friendly hand on Bartlett's shoulder. There was a winning understanding and a tacit promise in the gesture.

"For now, son, you print just that."

CONCERNING A TALK WITH MARGARET AND
SOME GENERAL REMARKS BY YOUNG MR. HOOD

PRIMARILY FOR REASONS of convenience but not without an eye to the bizarre, Maxwell Fenner established himself early the next morning in the erstwhile office of the late treasurer of the F. W. Strong Company. A rich, maroon suede cover was spread over the desk top, effectively concealing the stain and harmonizing so well with the warm hues of the Circassian walnut furniture and trim that Fenner almost persuaded himself of a flair for decoration. Otherwise nothing in the place was touched or changed.

This gruesome selection of temporary headquarters was made advisedly. In the first place, most of Martin Hoyle's personal papers and record files were there; also access to the other offices was convenient. But another consideration, less tangible but not less important, actuated Fenner. This room had been essentially Martin Hoyle's. He had spent half his waking hours in it for the past several years. He had worked in it, lived in it, dreamed in it— probably, Fenner mentally qualified—and at last had died in it. Fenner had a theory, vaguely defined and one he would scarcely have attempted to defend by any process of reasoning, that some people impart to places they inhabit certain aspects of their own personality; and conversely, that a room or a house or, as in this case, even a business office might, for those who frequent it, lend a perceptible degree of color and shape to the tiny, unrealized motivations that influence their conduct. Simply by occupying this space so abruptly vacated by Martin Hoyle, Fenner felt he would absorb, if only subconsciously, a certain tempering of sensory impression which would enable him better to place himself in Martin Hoyle's shoes, better to perceive his thought processes and habits of feeling, more easily to understand and vibrate into sympathy with them.

In nine cases out of ten Fenner would have stopped considerably short of such a refinement of procedure. Much of his work involved only pure arithmetic—so many dollars in the till theoretically, less so many dollars in the till actually, equals so many dollars defalcation. Motive? Avarice, greed, women, or perhaps sheer boredom. Perpetrator sufficiently inept, careless, inexperienced or for other reasons so obvious as to require no particular astuteness to detect and only ordinary police routine to apprehend. A bill to the client and on to the next.

But this affair from the outset had presented possibilities indefinably intriguing. There was at once a complexity of pattern and setting, an interweaving of motives and diverse personalities that made the inevitable truth attractively obscure. Here was the F. W. Strong Company, one-time Gibraltar of financial integrity and security, legally defunct only for several days, but morally insolvent for many months before they were finally enjoined from peddling worthless real estate securities to an unwary public. Here was Martin Hoyle, widower, age forty-two; staid, respected treasurer, dead by (with reservations) his own hand, under circumstances quite natural considering his own and his employer's straits. Here was as heterogeneous a board of directors and officers as could anywhere be found, and among them possibly the answer to the peculiar mislocation of two tiny drops of Martin Hoyle's blood, a .38 shell on the carpet where it shouldn't have been, and a queer unnaturalness in the position of an unaccountably fully packed bag. The more Fenner resolved these things, the more savored the environment.

His first act on Tuesday morning, once he was esconced, was to request the attention of Margaret Purcell.

"About the two letters, Miss Purcell, the last ones Mr. Hoyle sent, you know," he began when Margaret came in, somewhat uncertain and shaky, for it was her first visit to the room since Hoyle's death.

"Yes?"

"Will you tell me if these are the file copies of the letters you typed for him Saturday morning and left for him to sign?" Fenner handed her the two sheets which had been found in Hoyle's desk basket.

Margaret glanced at him and assured him that they were. Both were routine communications, one to a midtown bank, the other to the Lex-Strong Building Management Corporation, a subsidiary formed by the Strong Company to operate certain properties thrown back on their hands.

"Were the original copies mailed?"

"We suppose so; Mr. Hoyle signed them and they aren't here," Margaret replied.

"How is the mail here handled?"

"There's a chute in the hall. The boys clean out the desk mail baskets several times each day. Mr. Hoyle, when he worked late, would sometimes drop his mail in the chute as he went out."

Fenner appeared satisfied and dismissed Margaret. By two brief telephone calls he learned that both of the letters had been received by the addressees on the previous morning and consequently must have been mailed on Saturday. The envelopes naturally had been thrown away, necessitating a third call to Inspector Bryce who sent two rookie detectives scurrying upon their trail.

Fenner swung about in Hoyle's swivel chair, folded his hands across his chest and leaned back so that his half closed eyes faced only the undistracting ceiling, a position which experience had taught him was conducive to most facile cerebration. For fully half an hour he scarcely moved a muscle. Finally, his limbs somewhat cramped, he straightened up and touched the button which would produce Miss Purcell. When she reappeared, notebook in hand, he indicated a chair.

"You won't need your book. I want to talk a few minutes about Mr. Hoyle."

Margaret slid into the chair, only nodding.

"Do you do all of his work here?"

"Only lately. He used to have a girl of his own from the steno-graphic department."

"Ever do any personal work—anything other than this company's business? Did he have any outside interests?"

"No; that is, not that I know of. Mr. Hoyle was treasurer of the different operating companies too, you know. There has been quite a little work for them—letters and reports—but you'd hardly call that 'outside.'"

"No; quite right. How long have you been here?"

"Three years. More than that—almost four."

"Was Mr. Hoyle here when you started?"

"Yes; he'd just been made treasurer."

"Did he have many personal friends call on him here—people not connected with the firm?"

"Hardly any. I can't remember any at all."

"I see. Ah—your room is the entryway from the main hall for people who come and go. I observe also that your desk commands a view of the private corridor down this line of offices. Can you recall if anyone came in to see Mr. Hoyle on Saturday? Any time Saturday?"

"I don't remember anyone. Of course you can get in or out of these offices without using the elevators or main lobby at all. The door across from this one goes to a stair hall that leads down to the rear lobby. It opens into Fiftieth Street."

"But even so, you might see them step across the corridor."

"If I happened to be looking, I might. If I didn't I wouldn't." Miss Purcell seemed restive. "Of course I'm not at my desk all of the time."

"Did any of the other officers have any outsiders in on Saturday?"

"I don't particularly remember about Saturday. There are a great many people going in and out all the time. They're in and out of their own offices, too—passing back and forth."

"I suppose so." Fenner waited.

"Mr. Horton was here Saturday morning. He was in Mr. Behrmann's office with Judge Spar and Mr. Strong. Mrs. Strong

was here, too, late in the morning. There were others—several—
but I don't remember them."

"'What time on Saturday was the place pretty well vacated?"

"I went out myself only a short time after noon and I think
everyone was gone then. Mr. Hoyle had gone out about eleven with
Judge Spar. Mr. Strong and Mr. Behrmann and Mr. Parker went
out a little before I did. Mr. Parness and Mrs. Strong went down in
the elevator with me. Mr. Wheeler wasn't in on Saturday. Of course
a lot of people were left in the general offices and down on the
main floor."

"How about Mr. Hood?"

Miss Purcell flushed slightly, but not so slightly that Fenner
failed to remark it.

"His office is in the Sales Department in the other wing. I don't
know about him." This was only part of the truth. All too well she
remembered Hood passing through her room about half an hour
before noon, hat and coat on, obviously ready for the street. He
had opened Parness' door, then apparently changed his mind and
closed it again. He had come back and passed out into the lobby
without so much as a word for her. It had left her with a distrait,
almost sickening, forlornness.

"Then, so far as you know, you were the last person to leave
this particular row of offices Saturday, and that was very shortly
after twelve o'clock?"

"Yes, sir; that's right."

Fenner leaned back. "Thank you. For now, that will be all." He
resumed his brown study.

Meanwhile several skilled accountants, previously coached,
were ferreting their way through Hoyle's books and papers, drawing off statements and analyses which they now began to bring for
their master's review. Fenner digested them as they accumulated
and not without growing relief, for it became more and more apparent that the quick assets of F. W. Strong and Company had so
dwindled that if poor Hoyle had been one hundred percent short
of them the loss would not have been formidable.

Somewhat after mid-morning there came a lull. Fenner got to his feet and wandered idly into the long corridor. At the far end where it opened into her office he could see Miss Purcell busy at her machine. He opened the first door he came to, that labeled "Judge Francis F. Spar," and glanced in. The office was empty, so he passed on to the next, Mr. Parker's. It, too, was empty.

In the next, used by Anthony Wheeler and Winthrop Parness, he found both present, and also Mr. Hood, ex-sales director. Wheeler was at his desk, Parness lounged upon one end of it, Hood stood by the window staring moodily out. They were engaged in a not too amicable discussion which died abruptly as Fenner insinuated himself into the room. All three looked up at him curiously and there was a moment of strained silence. Young Hood broke it by first offering Fenner a cigarette and then inquiring with a flippancy so obviously affected that no offense could be taken:

"Not to begin on a sour note or anything like that, Professor, but what's the bad news—or have you had time to find out yet?"

"Bad news?" Fenner looked up naïvely.

"How much was Martin into the company for?" Hood asked the question with such brutal candor that both Wheeler and Parness shifted uncomfortably.

"Take it easy, Bob," the latter admonished, and apologized to Fenner, "Mr. Hood's a little upset."

"Upset, hell! I just asked a perfectly natural question. Martin didn't shoot himself for fun. It hasn't been enough that every issue we've peddled for the last four years has gone sour. Martin was just capping the climax!"

Parness essayed the role of pacifier.

"Listen, Bob; don't go off half cocked. Wait till you know what you're talking about. Besides," he added with a shrug of his shoulders, "I can't see what difference it makes now." He said "cawn't" and his London accent, which had never seemed natural to Bob, now added to his irritation.

"That's just the point. Nothing makes any difference now. But it's easy for you to talk. All you've been doing, you and everybody else around here, has been to sit back on your heels and concoct these lousy issues. I've been selling 'em! Selling them with all my heart and soul, by the thousands, to every friend I've got. Selling them in good faith, too, but who in God's name will believe that now? *You* don't have to listen to the poor suckers that come wanting their money back. I *do!* I hardly dare show my face on Fifth Avenue any more. Now Martin—" He waved his hand, a gesture of mingled disgust and despair.

"The trouble with you, Bob," Parness went on suavely, ignoring the personal implications in Hood's outburst, "is that you try to take on your own shoulders the responsibility for things actually caused by conditions beyond your control—general business and economic conditions that no one could be expected to foresee. Well, if you want to feel that way and get yourself all hot and bothered it's your own affair, but please don't expect the rest of us to."

There was enough acerbity in his tone to inflame Hood further.

"That sounds good, that 'general conditions no one could foresee,' but it's a lot of hooey and you know it! A year and a half ago the Romaine Hotel and a dozen others were—"

Anthony Wheeler rose out of his chair and placed a restraining hand on Hood's arm.

"Pull yourself together, Robert. Maybe you're partly right; maybe you're all wrong. Anyway, there is nothing you or I or anybody else can do about it now. The receivers are taking over the assets; let them take over the worries, too. In a way I'm not sorry it's all over with." The older man's shoulders drooped. His tired voice calmed Hood as quickly as Parness' had infuriated him.

Fenner had maintained a discreet silence. Now their glances returned to him and he spoke up.

"There's really nothing I can say yet," he told them. "Superficially it would appear that Mr. Hoyle's records may have been somewhat confused. However, I think any actual shortages will develop to be of very slight extent. So slight, in fact, that they would certainly not furnish sufficient motive for suicide. Tell me: do you know of anything else in his private life that might make him want to end it?"

"Martin was a quiet duck," Parness presently replied; "but 'still waters flow deep,' you know. I, for one, don't know a thing about his personal life. I only knew him here."

"I'm afraid none of us knew him as well as we thought we did," Wheeler volunteered. "Now that this has happened we realize it. Maybe Martin was lonesome. None of us were too clubby with him. But on the other hand, he certainly didn't invite it."

"Probably a gregariously inclined sort of fellow, but not enough so to encourage advances," Fenner echoed sententiously.

"Exactly," Parness and Wheeler agreed.

Hood had moved apart from the group, making no effort to rejoin the conversation. Now he unceremoniously left the room.

"When will the funeral be held?" Fenner paused in his own departure to ask the question.

"It was to have been today from a parlor on the west side," Wheeler answered, "but there seems to be a little hitch with the police. Mr. Strong expects to know by noon."

6

FENNER LOOKS OUT OF A WINDOW

BACK IN HOYLE'S OFFICE Fenner paced the carpet. The mention of funerals had sent him off anew upon a maze of speculation concerned with bodies and death, thence to bullets and shells and ballistics, and had definitely relegated to the background the more prosaic matter of a few missing dollars.

Who would move a shell and why? Nobody, deliberately; and probably not the person they were looking for, accidentally, for he had shown himself capable of the most meticulous care in the matter of otherwise covering his tracks. Two tiny blood spots in a desk drawer, that was all he had left in his wake.

The Bureau of Ballistics had said that the shell, from its position, had probably been ejected from a gun fired near the window. Fenner moved to the window and turned and surveyed the room. Martin Hoyle could have by no stretch of the imagination been shot from there. It was inconceivable that he had met his end anywhere except in the chair in which he had been found. Perplexed, Fenner leaned against the window and looked out.

The cars still trooped in an unbroken line toward the Fifth Avenue intersection. It was as if they had not stopped since he looked out the day before. The small street excavation where the steam main had been leaking still stood open but the repairs had apparently been accomplished, for no steam escaped and there was no noise. Two men appeared to be gathering together tools and equipment and packing them into a two-wheeled, trailer toolcart. The third laborer, for prolonged periods between listless shovelfuls, contemplated with supreme insouciance the sizable pile of dirt he was starting to throw back into the hole.

Fenner watched one or two slow spadefuls. Suddenly, as if snapped from a spring and with amazing agility for a man of his years, he seized his hat and dashed from the room. A moment later he could be seen in the street engaged in subdued conversation with the foreman of the trio. The other two were huddled close. A careful observer might even have seen something green and crinkly pass from Fenner's hand to that of the foreman. For the time the activity of backfilling and repaving seemed suspended.

Upon leaving the workmen Fenner observed that it was almost noon and decided not to go back inside. A brisk turn down Fifth Avenue to the Library and back, or even to the new Empire State Building, the steel frame of which could be seen thrusting its way skyward a mile south, would both improve his appetite and clear his fogging brain. So it was not until almost two hours later that he reappeared at the Strong Building.

He strolled to the side street entrance and paused there a moment, an enigmatic smile lighting his face as he watched the three laborers engaged absorbedly in a most unorthodox process of backfilling a street excavation, for each shovelful was being carefully screened through a course sieve. And, most surprising of all, for in New York City street audiences are more easily attracted than in the most provincial town in the land, the unusual performance was apparently completely escaping the notice of all passersby. Fenner cut his self-congratulation short when from a corner of his eye he saw Johnny Bartlett lounging in a nearby doorway.

"Shine, sir?" A voice at his elbow aroused him from his reflections. He was about to decline mechanically but a glance at his feet revealed that the suggestion was not out of order. The boy placed his box so that Fenner could lean against the building and went to work. Fenner's gaze swept down upon him, at first absently and then with more care. The boy was about fourteen years old. His own shoes shone, which was surprising enough, but—more unusual—he wore a reasonably clean shirt and necktie. For a coat he wore what at one time had been the jacket of a porter's uniform. "F.W.S." embroidered in gold letters emblazoned each lapel.

The shine was a good one, expeditiously but carefully performed. When he had finished the boy folded his shining cloths methodically, restored them to the box, and waited.

"How much is it worth, son?" Fenner's hand was in his pocket.

"A nickel, sir."

"A nickel! You're a hell of a business man! When anyone asks you that you say, 'It's worth a quarter, Mister, but on account of the competition I sell them for five cents.'"

"Yes, sir." The youth grinned.

"Are you connected with this building?" Fenner was fingering a silver half dollar.

"My old man has the cigar stand in the back lobby. I help him and I shine through the building."

"That's why you wear that jacket, eh?"

"Yes, sir."

"How long have you been shining shoes through the building?"

"Oh, for a couple of years."

"Know the men there—any of them?"

"Yes sir."

"Know Mr. Strong?"

"Oh, yes sir."

"Mr. Hoyle?"

"That bumped hisself off? Yeah." The boy brightened up. "I shined him Saturday." There was awe in his tone.

"You don't say! What time was that Saturday?" Fenner handed the youngster the half dollar and waved away the change.

"About this time. Maybe a little earlier, sir."

"You don't work Saturday afternoon?"

"I was just ready to quit. I was closing up the stand."

"Was Mr. Hoyle going out or coming in? Where'd you shine him?"

"Inside. He was coming in."

"'Was he alone?"

"Yes sir."

"Why didn't you tell someone about this before?"

"Nobody asked me."

"Tell me, sonny; did Mr. Hoyle act funny, like he might if he was going to bump himself off—or anything?"

"No sir. He gave me a quarter. That was more'n usual."

"Did he say anything?"

"Nope. Just went upstairs."

Fenner reached again into his pocket.

"I want you to try to remember something, son," he said. The boy's eyes followed the motion and he looked hopeful. "Was Mr. Hoyle carrying anything when he came in—a suitcase or grip?"

The boy answered instantly:

"Yes sir; he had a black grip. He put it down beside him while I was shining him. He had a newspaper, too." Fenner slid the coin into the boy's hand.

"I want you to keep mum about this whole business, son. Understand? I'll talk to you some more later. You're usually at the stand in the back lobby?"

"Yes sir." The boy's astonished eyes followed Fenner through the door.

Fenner went through to the main lobby and for several moments engaged an obliging elevator starter in conversation that bordered upon polite cross-examination. From there he proceeded upstairs where he found Bryce waiting impatiently. A sheaf of empty F. W. Strong Company envelopes, some torn and wrinkled, others neatly slit and clean, lay on the desk. There were ten in all, seven addressed to Lex-Strong Building Management Corporation and three to the midtown bank.

"The ones at the bank were easy," Bryce remarked.

"There was only one sack of waste paper to go through. But that other dump! My Lord! They must have let their stuff accumulate for a week and emptied the whole works last night. There were four big burlap sacks, chock full. Murphy said he'd be in that cellar a week if he had to go through it alone, so I sent him some help. I guess the envelopes are what you're looking for." He shoved them toward Fenner.

Fenner picked up the envelopes and sorted them. All of them were postmarked at the Grand Central Post Office Branch at some time Saturday morning, except two, one each to the bank and to the Lex-Strong Corporation. These were postmarked at 4:50 P.M. at the Hudson Terminal Branch. He pulled them out of the group. "All that remains is to be sure that these particular envelopes were the ones for Hoyle's letters, though it would certainly be the height of coincidence if they weren't. All of the others are postmarked earlier than Hoyle could have mailed his."

Fenner compared the envelopes with the letter copies still on the desk. Certain idiosyncrasies common to both, caused by trifling irregularities in the letter dies, were at once apparent. Both envelopes had been addressed on Miss Purcell's typewriter.

"But even if this bird for some damned-fool reason took it upon himself to mail Hoyle's letters, why not in the chute right in the hall? Why all the way downtown?" Bryce wanted to know.

"The chute is in the main lobby. Hoyle came back, by the rear lobby and walked upstairs. Whoever else was here left by the same way and wouldn't pass the chute. Besides, did you ever hear letters popping into a box from one of those chutes? It makes quite a racket. Not a racket you'd ordinarily notice but certainly one that would be noticed after hours when the building was supposed to be empty. This chap would think of that. No—he probably simply got all of the way downtown before he happened to remember the letters."

"Maybe Hoyle himself mailed them after all," Bryce suggested. "He might have gone downtown in the afternoon and come back later."

"Possibly, but not likely. I'll tell you why. At three o'clock on Saturday afternoons they lock the rear street door. I just had a chat with the elevator starter. After that, and also in the evenings, everybody going in or out is required to register, even the outside tenants from the upper floors of office space. The starter keeps the register in the front lobby. He didn't see Hoyle at all on Saturday afternoon. That's half of the story; the other half is that Hoyle had no key to the rear lobby on his ring. He must have returned a little before two and didn't go out after that."

Fenner crossed the room to the window, glanced out and returned to the desk. Then he asked:

"Have you been able yet to find out much about the crowd here?"

"Give us time. We only started yesterday afternoon. Anyway, you can find out more snooping around here for one day that my boys can by tailing them all week. How's the money look now?"

"Well, the brutal truth is that for quite a few months there hasn't been enough for anyone to worry about. The company has been going along, living from hand to mouth, and managing to peddle enough bonds to meet their overhead payroll from the proceeds, but that's about all. It's really criminal but I suppose as long as people are what they are nothing can be done about it. They should have been out of business two years ago. I don't know about the various subsidiary companies; we haven't got to them yet, but I rather imagine we'll find the same condition all the way through."

The door opened and one of Fenner's assistants, without comment, placed several typewritten sheets on the desk. Fenner picked them up, murmuring an apology to the Inspector, and started to read them. Suddenly he got up, again went to the window and looked out.

"What in hell's eating you? What have you got out there, anyway?" Bryce followed Fenner and looked out also.

"I'm playing a hunch," Fenner answered. "I'm playing it for twenty dollars, so far. If it pans out I get forty from you; if it doesn't I'm just out of pocket, that's all."

"Forty from me! Try and get it! What the devil are you talking about?"

"I'll tell you if I collect." Fenner resumed his perusal of the papers. When he had finished he clipped them into a sheaf of others and swung his chair around. "By the way, Mr. Hoyle brought a small grip with him when he came back Saturday. We weren't so wet about that, after all."

"How'd you find out?"

"A bootblack saw him—in fact, shined his shoes for him in the rear lobby about two o'clock Saturday. Hoyle was on his way back here. He gave the kid a quarter which was 'more'n usual.' Now where does that fit into the pattern?"

Bryce shrugged his shoulders and fished in his breast pocket for a cigar. "We're looking for a guy that must've been here; now we're looking for a grip, too; that's all."

Fenner stretched himself, paced the floor a moment, looked toward the window and quizzically at Bryce. Then he moved over and glanced out. This time he turned away abruptly and remarked, "I collect. Back in a moment." There was a gleam of suppressed excitation in his eyes that belied the calm tone. He rushed out of the room without even stopping for his hat, which lay within easy reach on the desk. For Maxwell Fenner, accustomed model of sartorial perfection, such a lapse betokened haste indeed. Bryce heard his footsteps take the stairs three at a time and fade away below.

Soon he was back, his keen face pink with exertion, excitement and not a little satisfaction. He was shaking a small object in the hollow of his closed fist much as one shakes a die, and when he tumbled it out on the maroon desk cover it rolled in a small arc, wobbled and stopped, gleaming dully. It was a bullet. Bryce picked it up.

"Thirty-eight. Where'd you get it?"

"Bought it for forty dollars. Sell it to you for forty-eight. That's ten percent for overhead and ten percent for profit, quite the customary arrangement, I believe."

"I can get 'em for less," Bryce announced sagely.

"Seriously, I did pay forty dollars for it. If your Ballistics Bureau finds it was fired from Hoyle's gun you'll admit it was a good buy, won't you? Come here." He took Bryce to the window. "If for some reason or other you wanted to fire a shot out of this window in the middle of a Saturday afternoon, without anyone noticing, where would you shoot?"

"Up in the air."

"No good. The buildings across the street are so high you can't shoot up in the air without reaching out of the window where you'd be seen. There are people and cars passing continually. Everything in sight from within the room is stone or glass or pavement. A bullet might break a window or ricochet and kill someone. The only suitable thing in range from here is, or was, that pile of dirt where they've been digging up the street. From here you could fire right into it—and on Saturday afternoon the men weren't working."

"But—"

"Wait. The Bureau of Ballistics failed to identify positively the bullet found in Hoyle's head as from his gun. They did identify the shell but said if it hadn't been moved it must have been ejected from a gun fired near the window. Those two facts seemed stuck in my head; I couldn't get rid of them. While I was looking out this morning it suddenly occurred to me that Hoyle's gun might actually have been fired over here but not at him. If he had been shot and the murderer wanted to make it appear that he'd killed himself he'd have to arrange to discharge Hoyle's gun. Also he'd pick up the shell from his own gun and leave that from Hoyle's. After all, it's pretty common knowledge that hammer indentations on a shell are sometimes identifying. Now if this fellow shot out of the window I figured that it was ten to one that he fired into that pile of earth. They were just starting to fill up the hole when I grabbed the foreman. I slipped him twenty and told him what to look for, and to keep his mouth shut. I promised them another twenty if they found it. And I knew they had a moment ago when they stopped screening the earth they were throwing back."

"Maybe this foreman isn't so dumb. Maybe he made sure of the other twenty by going round to a sporting goods store this noon. Thirty-eight slugs aren't exactly rare." Bryce fingered the bullet.

"That'd give you a laugh for many a day, wouldn't it? Well, you take it to your Bureau. Let them look it over. Incidentally, the lid's going to be off as far as the newspapers are concerned. That reporter, the chap who braced us in the hall last night, has been loafing in a doorway out there taking things in since noon. The foreman might keep his mouth shut but one of the men is almost sure to talk."

"Won't do much harm now. If that bullet is from Hoyle's gun then the one in his head wasn't! And if we're sure Hoyle was murdered we can take off the silk gloves and go after it right. It's still likely it's an insider, someone known to Hoyle and familiar with this place. A few stiff grillings might bring out a lot; enough to start putting two and two together." Bryce wrapped the bullet up and slipped it into his pocket. "I'll take this along and let you know as soon as I can. Maybe the Medical Examiner will have something on the blood spots, too. He's making some counts."

7

ALIBI PARADE

IT WAS LATE IN THE AFTERNOON, and skies appropriately overcast made it seem even later, when Bryce returned. He was accompanied by four men, one the police stenographer who had been there the day before, one an assistant prosecuting attorney, the others detectives of Bryce's division. Fenner needed no more than the fact of their presence to grasp that his conjecture as to the bullet had been correct. The Inspector read his thoughts and nodded curtly. Now that he knew where he was headed he had taken on a new aggressiveness.

"The sky's the limit now," he said. "Let's get ahold of Strong first. We'll keep the whole bunch around for a while."

"It's nearly five," Fenner pointed out.

"They can stay all night if it takes that long to answer the questions I'm going to ask," Bryce replied grimly.

Fenner shrugged his shoulders. He slid the telephone toward Bryce.

"You call him. I'm a spectator here."

"You've been handy to have around; I guess we can put up with it." Bryce smiled. He picked up the telephone and asked for Mr. Strong. Miss Purcell took the call first but passed it on to Sigurd Strong, whom Bryce without overmuch ceremony asked to step into Hoyle's office.

In a moment, first heralded by his rapid, heavy footsteps in the hall, he appeared in the door. He seemed slightly ruffled by the peremptoriness of Bryce's request but otherwise was quite in possession of himself. He looked from Bryce to Fenner inquiringly, a suave dignity in his manner that disdained a direct spoken question.

"Who around here stands to profit by Mr. Hoyle's death?" Bryce fired the question with what was intended for disconcerting abruptness.

"Martin *didn't* kill himself, then? He really *was* murdered?" There was not the faintest trace of surprise in Sigurd's tone or on his countenance, and from his inflection he might have said in so many words: "I suspected that all of the time."

Bryce sat stupified and Fenner was more surprised than his expressionless face showed. He looked at Sigurd Strong as if for the first time. He saw again the thick shock of iron gray over the broad, high brow, the neatly clipped mustache, the high arched nose—perhaps the only definitely Semitic feature in Strong's aging face. He had registered them all before, but he perceived, for the first time, a somber intelligence smoldering momentarily behind the dark eyes, an intelligence that would quite make mockery of all the solemn inanities and unctuous pronouncements Fenner had heard issue from Sigurd Strong's lips. It puzzled Fenner but set his wits on edge. The brief flash of fresh insight into the old Jew's make-up thrilled him, abstractly, as a connoisseur of a difficult sport is thrilled by a flash of subtle or obscure play.

There was a moment of silence, then the Inspector bludgeoned along:

"Yeah, he was shot, all right—and the way we's got it doped out he was shot by somebody from right around here. You got any ideas on the subject?"

"I can't say that I have. Martin Hoyle was well liked. So far as I know he hadn't an enemy in the world."

"Why haven't you said before that you suspected Mr. Hoyle had been murdered?" Fenner suddenly asked Sigurd, not accusingly but only curiously as if his interest was purely academic.

"I didn't, necessarily."

"Then why did you answer as you did—as if you had known all along?"

Hesitating only a moment Strong replied thoughtfully:

"Did it seem that way? I'm sorry if I misled you. You see, I've not been quite able to imagine Martin committing suicide. He wouldn't do it! And yet he had! So when I came in just now and saw you all gathered here, after everything was supposed to be settled, it seemed obvious and natural that my first reaction had been right. That's all."

Fenner and the Inspector exchanged glances. The explanation seemed straightforward and candid and simple, but it was somehow less than either had expected.

"How do you know Martin was murdered—and why by someone here?" Strong asked.

Bryce ignored the first query; to the second he replied: "We know he was shot on Saturday afternoon. From the circumstances he must have been shot by someone familiar with this place and the routine of the building."

"His life seemed centered here. Isn't that true?" Fenner added. "He had no outside interests and few outside friends. It seems more likely that someone here is involved."

Strong shrugged his shoulders.

"I think you're taking a lot for granted. However, if there's anything I can do to help matters or to facilitate your inquiry I'll be only too glad to. I'm sure everyone here will feel the same way."

Fenner suggested:

"It will be necessary for the inspector to ask some questions, an inevitable part of the official routine—quite personal questions, perhaps, but no offense may be taken. The sooner this is done, the better. Perhaps you could arrange for the office force to stay for a while, the people most closely associated with Mr. Hoyle, the department heads and of course the building staff."

"When?"

"Why, right now. Why not?"

"I'll be glad to do that. I'll see that everyone is available as soon as I can get them and for as long as you need them."

Sigurd reached for the telephone, thought better of it and stepped to the door. Before it could close behind him he had come back. At the end of the long corridor, artlessly limp in a chair by Miss Purcell's desk, he had glimpsed the by now too familiar figure of Mr. Bartlett of the *Globe*.

"I say, Inspector"; Strong said anxiously, "do you suppose we can avoid any more publicity? The firm is—"

Bryce shook his head.

"It's not possible now, and the more you try to duck it the worse breaks you'll get. It's best to give them a simple statement and let it go at that. But you needn't worry about it. We'll take care of that."

Strong went out and was gone for perhaps ten minutes. When he came back it was as if he had re-donned his protective crust of pompous dignity. He had made, he informed them, "the requested arrangements." Mr. Hood, Mr. Parness and Judge Spar he had been unable to reach, but efforts were being made to locate them.

Bryce had relit his cigar. Seated at Hoyle's desk he occupied the center of the stage. The lights were on now, soft indirect illumination such as befitted the ultramodern executive offices of F. W. Strong and Company, gently flooding every nook and corner. In addition, a bronze desk lamp cast to the blood-red desk cover oblique rays which, reflected up past the Inspector's heavy face, emphasized the bushy brows and lent him a most forbidding aspect.

Fenner had withdrawn unobtrusively to the background of the window ledge, whence he stared out into the gathering murk. The assistant prosecutor and the police stenographer were seated across the desk from Bryce, so Strong, perforce, dropped into the only vacant chair in the room, that at the end of Hoyle's desk.

"When did you last see Mr. Hoyle alive?" Bryce asked the first question quite mechanically as if it were part of an often repeated ritual.

Sigurd answered carefully, "Last Saturday morning about ten-thirty."

"Where?"

"Right here in this office."

"What were the circumstances?"

Sigurd looked puzzled but answered patiently, "We bad some matters to discuss, matters pertaining to the firm, and we discussed them. That's all."

"Was Mr. Hoyle insured?"

"I'm not sure but I believe not. I believe that he discontinued all of his insurance when his wife died several years ago."

"Had he any enemies? Do you know of anyone who would profit by his death, or anyone who might have wished him harm?"

"None. Absolutely no one!" Strong was very positive.

"Had there been any disagreement or friction between Mr. Hoyle and any of the others here?"

"Not that I know of. Certainly nothing of a character that would lead anyone to kill him."

"Where were you last Saturday afternoon?"

Strong was quite undisturbed by the question.

"I was at the Urban League Club most of the afternoon. Mr. Behrmann and I had lunch there. We sat in the lounge for an hour or so. When we parted I went to my room and slept until late afternoon. Mrs. Strong called for me there and we drove out to Larchmont for dinner."

"You live in Larchmont?"

"No; my brother does. We were having dinner there."

"And the Urban League Club?"

"I have a room there. I stay there occasionally when my town house is closed."

Bryce took a new tack.

"Do you know whether or not Mr. Hoyle planned going on any sort of a trip?"

"I told you once before that so far as I know he did not. His duties here would not have permitted his absence—not for a week or ten days at least. Why do you ask that?" There was a faint edge to Sigurd's tone.

"His bag was all packed; that's all."

Strong shrugged his shoulders.

"I don't know anything about that."

The corridor door opened noiselessly and Abraham Behrmann appeared. He glanced about the ring of faces, his countenance expressionless. Bryce squinted out at him from the glare of the desk lamp.

"You're just in time, Mr. Behrmann. We were about to send for you next."

"Yes? That's good, then. So you're not satisfied about Martin?"

"No; we're not," Bryce agreed bluntly. "Maybe you can help us. Where were you Saturday afternoon?"

Behrmann and Strong looked at each other, almost furtively. The lawyer cleared his throat.

"No offense, Mr. Behrmann," Fenner spoke up from the background. "It's an inevitable part of the inquiry."

"I understand perfectly," Behrmann said drily. "It's the first question one naturally asks. Why—I was at the Urban League Club. I had lunch there with Mr. Strong." He inclined his head slightly toward Sigurd. "We talked for a while. The rest of the afternoon I spent in the library there. It's a rather good one. Now that isn't an altogether air-tight alibi but I imagine if you inquire you'll find enough people who saw me browsing around there to bear me out. But see here; what made you change your minds about Martin?"

"A number of details," Bryce evaded. "By the way, where is this Urban League Club?"

"In East Fifty-third Street, just off Madison."

"'That's only a few blocks from here."

"That's all. A five-minute walk."

"Do you know anything about Mr. Hoyle's private life—his affairs other than here?"

"I can't say that I do. I know nothing whatever about him personally. I *do* know that his work here, especially lately, was enough to pretty well fill up any one man's existence."

Fenner spoke again from the background.

"I believe Mr. Hoyle acted also as treasurer for a number of so-called 'Bondholder's Protective Committees.' What did that entail? Can you tell me a little about it?"

"Certainly. Protective Committees are groups we organize to take over or otherwise reorganize properties behind our loans when they become in default. Mr. Hoyle was naturally the logical person to handle the funds of these committees."

"And the other members?"

"They were selected from among the officers and directors. I, myself, acted as counsel for the committees."

"In other words, they were pretty much F. W. Strong Company affairs?"

"I suppose that's true," Behrmann conceded.

"We have felt that we are better qualified than any outsiders to reorganize these properties as they find themselves in distress; that we can accomplish such re-organization more quickly and efficiently than anyone else possibly could," Sigurd Strong chimed in, unconsciously quoting the company's stock arguments.

"Quite all right, Mr. Strong," Fenner agreed brusquely. "This is neither the time nor the place to debate your company's business policies. I only wondered if that angle of Mr. Hoyle's activity might have injected some distinctly outside element. Apparently that has not been the case."

"When did you leave the Urban League Club Saturday, and from there where did you go?" Bryce resumed his interrogation of the lawyer.

"I went home—it must have been around half-past five—to my apartment. We had dinner in and some friends for bridge. I wasn't outdoors again at all until late in the day Sunday," Behrmann answered straightforwardly and with good grace.

"O.K., Mr. Behrmann. Thanks." Inspector Bryce by his manner terminated the interview and turned to his notes. He leafed through them a moment and then asked Strong, "Is Mr. Parness about yet?"

"He may have come in. I'll see." Strong went out.

"Is Mr. Parness an officer of the company?" Fenner asked Behrmann while they waited.

"He's on the Board; that's all. Mr. Parness and Mr. Wheeler are our real estate experts—White, Wheeler, Parness and McClintock, you know."

Fenner had heard of the firm.

"What about Judge Spar?"

"Judge Spar is a vice president. Mr. Parker, too."

"Mr. Parker's with the County Consolidated Bank and Trust?" Fenner ruminated.

"That's right. He's senior vice president over there."

"So you have some talent in every direction, eh?" Fenner led on. "Quite a nice setup."

A wry smile wrinkled the little lawyer's face.

"It was a nice setup," he corrected. "Times have changed. The real estate market—"

The arrival of Winthrop Parness cut short what Fenner felt would have been a fruitless dissertation, anyway. The newcomer dropped into the chair opposite Bryce with an extreme ease and assurance that stopped just short of being offensive.

"I just got in. Sig told me about Martin. Sorry if I've kept you. Anything I can do? Just say the word."

From his seat at the window Fenner studied Winthrop Parness. He saw what at least superficially appeared to be the acme of physical and sartorial perfection. Parness in his early forties was tall and erect of figure. He had dark, even features with stormy eyes and matinee-idol lashes, a not too small, neatly clipped mustache somehow faintly reminiscent of the gay nineties, and clothing straight from Bond Street.

Bryce went through more or less the same list of questions as he had with Strong and Behrmann and elicited more or less the same responses. Parness had last seen Martin Hoyle "in this room late Saturday morning." He and Judge Spar had talked to Hoyle for a quarter of an hour. There had been nothing unusual in Hoyle's manner or actions. So far as Parness knew Martin Hoyle had no enemies and there was no reason in the world why anyone should wish him harm. But when the questions took a more personal turn Parness' assurance surprisingly dwindled.

"Now would you mind telling us just how you spent Saturday afternoon?" Bryce had suddenly asked.

The answer, delayed for several moments of careful thought, took both Bryce and Fenner unawares.

"You mean—you want me to establish an alibi? I'm sorry, but I can't."

"You can't! Do you mean to say you can't tell us where you were on Saturday afternoon?"

"Exactly—or rather, I won't." Parness' lips closed firmly as if his last word had been spoken.

"Isn't that a little irregular?" Fenner drawled from the corner. "Murder, you know, is a serious thing."

"So far as I've been made aware I've not been accused of murder—or anything else."

"No, no, of course not," Fenner responded gently, "but suppose we put it this way: We know that Mr. Hoyle was shot and we have reason to believe the crime was committed by someone associated with him here. In the interests of justice and to simplify the work of the police and the law every one of you has a definite moral obligation to establish his innocence. Of course an easily verifiable alibi is the simple, obvious way to do it."

"I can see that. I agree with you but I'm unfortunately unable to do anything about it. I can assure you, of course, that I was nowhere near here, if that assurance helps you any. I was driving all afternoon—I got up beyond Bear Mountain. I was back in time for dinner with some friends and we saw a play. That part you may satisfy yourselves about very readily."

"In other words, you've got an alibi for the evening but not for the afternoon," Bryce suggested disagreeably.

"Not at all, and don't get me wrong." The Winthrop Parness veneer seemed to fall away. "I've got a very good and undisputable alibi from the time I left here Saturday noon, but I can't substantiate that portion which applies to the afternoon. If the worst comes to the worst I suppose I should have to, but until then I prefer not to. Of course you have my word that I was nowhere near here, that I last saw Martin in excellent health before noon on Saturday right in the chair you're sitting in." And that was that, as far as Winthrop Parness was concerned.

From Anthony Wheeler they learned nothing whatever of Hoyle. As to his own whereabouts on the previous Saturday they learned, as Fenner had already discovered from Miss Purcell, that he had not been to the office at all on Saturday. He had been in the city, however, having visited his broker's office on lower Broadway during the latter part of the morning. He had done some week-end buying at Washington Market and had gone home early in the afternoon. The balance of the day had been spent "doing things around the house."

To Fenner, listening, this bit of testimony seemed the first thing he had heard or learned of Anthony Wheeler which was really in keeping with his external appearance and character. It was much easier to picture him, with his careless clothing and gaunt homeliness, bent over meat counters and vegetable bins in Washington Market, or at home taking down screens and raking leaves, than to imagine him consummating important real estate transactions, or having anything whatever to do with brokerage houses.

Maurice Parker came last. Neither Mr. Hood nor Judge Spar could be found, so their catechism was perforce deferred. The pudgy banker mopped tiny sweat beads from his brow as he took his seat opposite the Inspector. He wielded his handkerchief with one hand while he held his glasses with the other. Their trembling lenses caught the lamplight and set two tiny blurs of light dancing on the far wall, betraying his nervousness before he spoke a word.

"Shocking! My, My! Horrible!" he kept repeating half to himself, and then, "A man never knows when he's safe any more. Martin murdered. I can't get over it! When Sig told me it just about bowled me over." He made one last dab at his forehead, pinched his glasses carefully onto his nose and peered at the Inspector. "Have you done anything about it, Officer?" he inquired petulantly. "Are you going to arrest somebody?" His uncomfortable bulk seemed to squirm in the chair and his eyes shifted quickly to Behrmann who had remained in the room, then at the stenographer with his book, then back to Bryce's heavy face, grim above the red desk top.

Bryce viewed him up and down, first with good-humored tolerance, then with quickly narrowing interest. The man was so obviously completely unnerved and his condition was such a severe contrast to Anthony Wheeler's sorrowful calm or to Parness' callous assurance that the Inspector was puzzled.

"Mr. Hoyle was a pretty close friend of yours, Mr. Parker?"

"Yes, of course. That is, not intimate, but we were very friendly."

"You had quite a visit with him here Saturday morning. What did you talk about?"

"I don't know what you mean by 'quite a visit.' I don't know what you're driving at! I was here for fifteen or twenty minutes. Bob Hood was here, too, and Mr. Behrmann was in and out. We talked about the only natural thing under the circumstances, the District Attorney's injunction and what we could do about it—or couldn't do. Martin seemed pretty disgusted, as we all were."

"Did he say anything about his plans?"

"No. In fact, he distinctly said he hadn't any. He said he hadn't enough money to plan anything. Bob told him to buy a farm!"

"At what time did you last see Mr. Hoyle—alive?" Bryce injected a malicious pause before the 'alive' but the innuendo completely missed Parker. He thought a moment.

"It must have been about eleven Saturday morning. He was going out. I saw him in the washroom. I came back into the office and he went out into the elevator lobby. That's the last time I saw him."

"Do you mind telling us just where you were from then on for the rest of the day?"

Parker looked up somewhat angrily but Behrmann cut in:

"We're all in the same boat, Maurice. It doesn't mean anything. Just tell the Inspector what he wants to know. It appears to be the most we can do."

Parker wet his lips.

"Well, let's see—I left here a little before noon. In fact, Sig— Mr. Strong and Mr. Behrmann went down at the same time. They asked me to come to lunch with them but I had some matters to take care of at the bank so I couldn't. I went to the bank and stayed for several hours; then I went home."

"Where's that?"

"I live in Montclair."

"No lunch Saturday, Mr. Parker?" Fenner spoke in a mild, half-absent manner.

"Oh, yes; I stopped at the oyster bar at the Lackawanna Station in Hoboken."

"So then?"

"I was home for the rest of the day and evening."

During the interview Parker's nervousness seemed to evaporate and by the time he and Behrmann went out he had quite regained his composure, and with it that pompous dignity which usually characterized him.

Following this Bryce and Fenner again questioned the elevator starter, the building superintendent, and the charwoman who had cleaned up the offices the previous Saturday, only to learn nothing that they did not already know.

"Here again! I might have known," Margaret had sighed when Bartlett slipped in thirty seconds behind Bryce and his party.

"Yeah, you might've," Johnny agreed; "but there's nothing you could've done about it. Say! was I right, or was I right!"

"What are you raving about now?"

"In ten minutes you'll know, and in the morning the whole wide world will know—exclusively through the columns of the *Globe* and the astute news-nose of one, John Timothy Bartlett—that Martin Hoyle was murdered."

Margaret sat up.

"Really, Johnny?"

"Officially, lady. What a scoop!" He bent over anxiously. "Say, any of the other boys been around?"

"Not a soul. But what's it all about? How do you know?"

"Inspector Bryce and Mr. Fenner and I are just like that." Johnny held up a pair of crossed fingers. "The gory details aren't released."

Margaret leaned back.

"You enjoy tantalizing me, I suppose?"

The reporter grinned and was about to reply when down the narrow hallway the door to Hoyle's office opened and Sigurd Strong stepped out. He hesitated, seemed to reconsider, and stepped back in again. In a moment he reappeared and hurried up the hall and into his own office without noticing them at all. Soon Margaret's phone tinkled. She answered it and Bartlett could hear the buzz of Strong's voice coming through the receiver and the louder rumble of it through the closed door at his back.

Margaret's contribution seemed to be limited to several "Yes, sirs" and an "I understand, Mr. Strong." She hung up and turned from the phone. "You'll have to excuse me, Johnny. I've got to locate some of the men for Mr. Strong."

Bartlett got up and said, "I'll be around. I guess I'm not so popular with that guy, am I? Anyway, I haven't told you anything, see?"

Several hours later Fenner and Bryce were not surprised to find themselves buttonholed in the hall.

"Any clues as to who killed him, Inspector?" Bartlett's pencil was poised.

The Inspector and Fenner traded quick glances and Bryce snorted, "At it again, eh? Where'd you get that?"

"You're doing more with this case than an ordinary suicide would warrant. And there's that extra bullet. Well, it looks mighty interesting, Mr. Fenner."

Bryce cut in crisply:

"It's true that the department isn't completely satisfied about Mr. Hoyle's death and is still working on the case. There are several angles that need to be investigated. However, no one is under any suspicion, and unless and until something more definite is uncovered there will be nothing more to say. Now don't make too damned much of it!"

8
CONCERNING FOOTBALLS AND HIGHBALLS

WEDNESDAY MORNING broke open clear and crisp and abruptly colder. Robert Alanson Hood, 3rd, parked his two-year old roadster in a side street between Fifth and Madison a short distance from his office. He surveyed it critically as he stepped away from it, noting that it was beginning to show its forty-odd thousand miles and remembering ruefully that it would have to do him for some time to come. He glanced at his watch—he felt he couldn't even afford to have parking tickets fixed any more—then hurried toward the F. W. Strong Building.

The brittle air had a tonic effect and for a brief interval Hood forgot F. W. Strong Bonds, receivers, business and its worries, and even that slumped over figure of Martin Hoyle! Football weather! Why wouldn't it be a good idea, as soon as this mess was cleaned up, to take a crack at one of the 'pro' leagues? In a week or ten days he could accomplish what remained to be done in connection with the F. W. Strong Company. He was still in fair physical shape. A couple of weeks of conditioning and he'd be able to take it with any of them. They took a terrific beating in the pro games but he'd be good for at least a couple of quarters. The complete change would be good for him, and the physical contact and frenzy of contest would be an outlet, a blessed relief for jagged nerves. He hoped the season wasn't too well started for him to break in. By the time he reached his office he was bending his mind to ways and means of realizing his sudden inspiration. He knew several sports reporters, and then there were three or four of his own ex-team mates who still picked up more than spending money each fall on the professional gridiron.

"See Mr. Strong." The curt direction stared up at him from the otherwise blank memo pad on his desk. Hood hung up his hat and coat, glanced at the few letters on his desk without sitting down, then sauntered out through the general sales offices toward the executive wing.

There was a subdued tenseness in the atmosphere, an indefinable expectancy. The whispering knots of employees who had been continually in evidence on Monday and Tuesday were quite dissolved, and in direct contrast to the semi-holiday air that had pervaded the place the first two days of the week, everyone now was quiet and tending to their own knitting—unnaturally quiet, it suddenly occurred to Hood.

"Mornin', Mr. Hood." "Good morning, sir." Nods and greetings from the salesmen and office help quickly banished the impression and brought to Hood's heart an alien, warm glow. He liked these people sincerely. They liked him, too, just as sincerely. There was scarcely another officer in the company who could say as much. Yet he'd harmed them irreparably. Almost everyone of them was loaded up with worthless bonds that he had urged upon them. "F. W. Strong Company"—"Invest in your own organization"—"If it's good enough to get a living from, it's good enough to put your money it!"—"Put your heart and your savings in your work!" It had sounded swell. Banana oil! Romaine Hotel! Parness and Wheeler had made more promoting that lemon than the property would ever pay anyone again!

"Morning, Miss Purcell. The boss in?"

Margaret had looked up at his approach.

"He's in. He's expecting you."

He looked at the closed door. There were voices; Sigurd Strong was not alone. Hood paused at Margaret's desk.

"What's on his mind; do you know, Peg?"

He hadn't called her "Peg" for days.

"I don't know. I suppose it's about Mr. Hoyle."

"What about him?"

"Oh, haven't you heard?"

"The funeral?"

"No; it isn't that. It's the police. They think he didn't kill himself."

"Didn't kill himself! What do you—? When did all thus turn up?"

"Yesterday afternoon. They were asking everyone all kinds of questions. It was in the late *Globe* last night, and in all of the morning papers, too, but not much in them. I tried to get you for Mr. Strong. You weren't here."

Hood only whistled between his teeth.

He found Maxwell Fenner and Sigurd Strong bent over reams of papers and reports spread on Strong's huge desk. "—now taking the incomes from these properties as we have them set up—" Strong's voice stopped in mid-air upon the arrival of Hood, then continued in the same level tone only now addressed to the sales director: "The police think Martin was murdered, Bob. Better stay available until Inspector Bryce gets here. He has been questioning everybody. You weren't around yesterday afternoon?" He raised his brows slightly making the last comment.

"I left early. There was a dinner at the armory I was obligated to attend." Hood held a captain's commission in the artillery reserves. "Why do they think Martin didn't commit suicide?"

"I don't know that. Oh, by the way, have you seen the Judge yet this morning? He wasn't here either."

"Judge Spar here at nine-thirty! Your jest is unseemly." Hood's voice turned facetious and Fenner looked up sharply. "But seriously, Sig, what am I supposed to know?"

"Inspector Bryce is inclined to interview everyone who knew Martin at all."

"Oh, I see; and it wouldn't be very flattering to be left out, would it? Well I'll be right here, and if I see His Honor I'll tell him to stay awake long enough to pop in on you." Without ceremony Hood went out.

"Disrespectful young cub, isn't he?" Fenner suggested guilelessly when the door had closed.

Strong flashed him a quick sideways glance before replying:

"He's not quite himself. He's been very much disturbed at the turn affairs here have taken."

A half hour later Inspector Bryce arrived and went directly to Fenner's headquarters in Hoyle's office.

"Mr. Hood's here if you want him this morning," Fenner volunteered.

"I know. He left his apartment at 8:50, parked his car in East Forty-eighth Street, and entered this building at 9:20. Judge Spar is here, too. He lives with a married daughter up in Bronxville. He got the 8:45 down and walked up from Grand Central, making one stop on the way for an eye-opener. He arrived twenty minutes ago." It was then about a quarter after ten.

"You're very thorough, Professor. How about the others?"

"We have an eye on them but they're not covered so thoroughly now. I especially picked up Hood and Spar when they couldn't be found to talk to last night. But let's get Hood in."

"Talk to the Judge first; he's least promising," Fenner suggested.

They sent for him. In a few moments he came in accompanied by Mr. Behrmann. The Judge had seen the morning papers. The lawyer said:

"I've taken the liberty of explaining the situation to Judge Spar, so you may fire away at your convenience.

Judge Spar made an impressive figure. He was portly but very erect of figure, and his rather ruddy face was set off by neatly brushed, snow-white hair and white eyebrows. He wore correct morning attire and an old-fashioned, turndown cravat.

"I await your pleasure, gentlemen," he announced gravely.

"It's anything but a pleasure to be compelled to question you, Your Honor." Bryce unconsciously summoned a friendly tone and used the court room address. "As Mr. Behrmann has told you, we have reason to believe Mr. Hoyle was murdered. We've naturally got to explore every possible source for dope on him, and these sources seem to be pretty much limited to his associates here. Could you tell us anything that might shed any possible light on Hoyle or on his death?"

"I'm afraid not. I don't know what your evidence is, of course, but it would take a lot to convince me Martin was murdered. What possible motive could anyone have? I can't imagine Martin involved with women; I can't imagine him associated with any sort of money racket. When you've eliminated those two you've removed ninety-five percent of your causes for homicides. On the other hand, there is plenty of explanation for his ending his own life, just in general conditions, to say nothing of what you may have discovered in connection with his accounts or his stewardship of this company's funds." The Judge's glance slid inquiringly from Bryce to Maxwell Fenner.

"Not at all," Fenner differed. "There's little or nothing to say about the books; and as for general conditions—why, Martin Hoyle was anything but the sort of a person who would take his own life for reasons of business disappointment."

The Judge did not reply.

"When you talked with Hoyle Saturday did he seem perfectly normal?"

"So far as I remember, he did. I may not have been particularly observant."

"Now—uh—how did you spend your own time after you left here?"

Judge Spar was not surprised or disturbed by the question. Behrmann had prepared him well.

"I went up to the Polo Grounds to the football game. Fordham was playing Georgetown. It was an unusually fine day, if you recall, and it turned out to be an exceptionally interesting game."

"You went alone?"

"Oh, yes. It was more or less a spur-of-the-moment idea. Things had been anything but pleasant around the office. I wanted to get away from it for a few hours—get out of myself, don't you know. And I succeeded, for, as I say, it was a splendid contest. From the game I went directly home—that is, to my daughter's home in Bronxville where I am temporarily making my abode."

That was that. For some twenty minutes more the learned jurist rambled, discoursed, deplored, slyly questioned and commiserated, but nothing was developed which it is worthwhile here to record. Fenner hopefully let him ramble, encouraging him and subtly leading him on whenever he seemed about to run down, attending keenly every word, but all to no purpose.

Next they sent for Hood. He was not at his desk and it was some time, perhaps fifteen or twenty minutes, before he returned and responded to their summons. In fact, Bryce was about to go out for him personally when he came in, slightly flushed and apologetic. Their talk with him was very different from their conversation with Spar, but ultimately no more enlightening.

"We won't need to stand on ceremony with you," Fenner had remarked as soon as Bryce had outlined what they wanted. "I rather imagine that you prefer we didn't."

"It's all right with me, but I'm damned if I know what you think I can tell you."

"How'd Hoyle stand with the gang here? I know from experience that an outfit like this never runs without friction."

"Well, Martin wouldn't have wearied his neck carrying his brains around but he wasn't a bad egg. Everyone liked him—at least no one disliked him. I always hit it off with him all right, though we didn't have a great deal of direct contact."

"Who did?"

"No one, really. Mr. Strong was his only direct superior. Mr. Parker probably knew him as well as anyone. We did most of our banking with the County Consolidated—that's Parker's outfit—and of course Hoyle handled that end of things."

"Did Hoyle and Mr. Parness get on well?"

"Well enough. Parness was of the opinion Hoyle was too small for the job he had. Of course he didn't air those views around Martin, but he made cracks from time to time. On the surface, though, they were always agreeable."

"How about Mr. Behrmann?"

"Well, A. L. is Mr. Strong's right hand. When he opens his mouth around here it's the same as Sig Strong speaking, or was. I guess he gave Martin his orders to a certain extent, and Martin never argued with him. Martin was pretty good at agreeing with everybody and heading straight down the middle of the easiest road. Around this place a disposition like that was invaluable. I should know; I developed a swell one!" Hood looked away ruefully.

"And it helped you out?" Fenner encouraged with faint sarcasm.

Hood turned bitterly flippant. "Oh, tremendously! Made me what I am today." He slumped in his chair and covered his face with his hands, then slid them back over his hair, in the single deliberate gesture recovering from his momentary lapse. He faced them squarely. "Anything else?"

"Yeah," Bryce replied. "Just tell us where you were and what you were doing last Saturday afternoon."

Hood, in contrast to Judge Spar, was obviously uncoached. He caught his breath audibly.

"Why—what do you mean?"

"There's nothing particularly obscure about the Inspector's question," Fenner baited. "Where were you Saturday afternoon? That seems relatively a simple thing to grasp and answer."

Hood waved aside Fenner's irony.

"No-no. It's sort of sudden. Do you mean that you think I might have had something to do with Martin— with his death?"

"Not necessarily, but we *are* asking you, as we have asked everyone else here, to establish an alibi."

"Well—" Hood kept them waiting for a long moment, then broke into a low laugh. "Your question isn't as simple to answer as you think. It may sound incredible, but the fact is I don't *know* where I was Saturday afternoon—that is, not *all* Saturday afternoon. I know where I started and I know where I finished up, but there's a pretty long blank space I can't tell you anything about."

His inquisitors stared at him blankly.

"You see, I was feeling rather low Saturday. I had been right along, but on Saturday several things occurred which seemed to top off the load, so I guess I went on a bit of a binge. I left here before noon and stopped at a speakie on Forty-third Street East of Lexington. I had a few drinks and intended getting lunch there. They must have been pretty powerful because I don't seem to remember about any lunch. There were two men, hail fellows who seemed bent on getting shot, too. I had some more drinks. We harmonized a little but that wasn't so good so we went back to the drinking. They talked about a card game and the way I was feeling I was all for it. I thought I could trim the pants off the best poker player in the Metropolitan area. We left the place and went somewhere in a taxi. It must have been west of Broadway because I vaguely remember the cab getting snarled up in the theatrical district traffic. I remember arriving at some place, an inferior sort of dive, and sitting down at a round table with this pair and a couple of others already there. That's about all. When I woke up Sunday I was in a different place, a cheap hotel on Ninth Avenue below Forty-first. I'd been pretty well rolled—not even my watch or fountain pen left. The clerk said I had come in with two men on Saturday evening. They'd left in an hour or so and paid for my room for the night. My head felt as big as a church so I got a cab home. The superintendent of my apartment building staked me with enough to tide me over the rest of Sunday. He will be glad to confirm what I've told you. Also the hotel clerk will remember me. I doubt if I'd ever find that other place, though."

"Did you report the matter to the police when you found you'd been robbed?"

"No. I'd been taken over rather easily and wasn't very proud of it. I was only out about seventy-five bucks so I thought the best thing would be to keep quiet. I *did* go back to Forty-third Street. The bartender there, whom I know well enough to believe, had never seen either of these birds before. I'd know them, though—anywhere. Some day I'll run into them and—" His silence was eloquent and left no doubt as to the savagery of his intent.

"I'd like to be around when you find them," Fenner smiled, and added: "Too bad it happened when it did. Too bad it happened at all, of course, but particularly unfortunate that it had to be last Saturday afternoon."

Hood got to his feet.

"You can't mean that you really have an idea I might have killed Martin!"

"Oh, no; but wouldn't it be simpler if you had a nice, air-tight easily verified alibi? Now wouldn't it?"

"But for what reason? What would I have to gain by killing Martin? I can't understand—" His protest died wearily.

"You're not being accused," Fenner explained mildly. "I believe every word you've told us. I'm just remarking, academically, so to speak, that you're not eliminated. Sit down a minute. I think we can talk to you. Maybe you can help us. I assume that if you knew Hoyle had been murdered you'd want to see justice done."

Hood let himself slowly, almost warily, back into the chair.

"Of course. But I—you see, this is all very sudden. I hadn't any idea until I walked in this morning that there was any doubt about Martin having shot himself."

"Well, he didn't!" Bryce put in flatly.

"Now starting from there," Fenner continued, "do you know of anything in Mr. Hoyle's relations with anyone here that would have engendered any sort of ill feeling?"

"Not that would lead anyone to kill him. Nothing that strong. We all got along. Parness used to get irritated with him, but very tolerantly. Behrmann became impatient with him once in a while. But Martin was really an expert accountant, and pliable enough— don't quote me—to be just the bird they'd want in that spot."

"Could you enlarge on that a little."

"Well, there's nothing to enlarge on; nothing specific. What I mean is that Martin could always be counted on to play along with the crowd."

"In their financial schemes, you mean?"

"Yes. Nothing illegal," Hood insisted hastily, "but sometimes on questions of valuations, or on the disposition of the funds coming in, or on matters of our own compensation—things of that sort which might be subject to differences of opinion or criticism."

"Was there any clique or group, or even individual, who wasn't inclined to 'play along with the crowd,' as you put it?"

Hood reddened. "I'm afraid not."

"We seem to be rapidly getting nowhere," Fenner remarked suddenly, and abruptly terminated the interview. "Never mind, for now. As things shape up I may want to talk to you further. Please remember that our conversations are confidential."

When Hood departed he left the room a well of silence. Fenner glanced at his wrist; it was eleven-twenty. After perhaps five minutes Bryce broke the quiet striking a match to light his cigar. He said, "Well?"

"I was about to make the same illuminating remark, myself," Fenner answered.

"What do you think of the young fellow?"

"I'd be satisfied about Hood except for one thing: A person with the ability and personality to get as far as he has at his age doesn't go about with his remorse pinned on his sleeve. Yet if it's an act, what's it for? This company has been pretty grossly mismanaged, depression or no depression. Whether or not anyone will ever be held criminally responsible it's too early to say. Maybe Hood anticipates something of that kind and is building up a background for himself. That might account for his penitent airs."

"Uh-huh. Weren't you pretty chummy with him?"

"If he's on the level he'll be a help to you. If he's not there's still no harm done."

Bryce pondered this until Fenner presently suggested:

"Now that the returns are all in does anything strike you as funny about this case? It seems almost incredible that not one—not a single one—of the people we consider as possibly guilty has provided a really one hundred percent airtight alibi. Not one! Almost too much for coincidence! Look at your notes to be sure my memory serves me. Mr. Strong was sleeping in his club room not five minutes walk from here. It's certainly not inconceivable that he could have slipped out and back in again unobserved. Behrmann was 'browsing in the library' there; the same thing applies to him. Mr. Parness was driving in the country. He claims he can, if necessary, produce his companion, but his reluctance may be a stall for time. He probably could dig up someone to testify for him. Mr. Parker was at his bank and then home, but he didn't leave until on a mid-afternoon train. Lots of spare time there if he moved that dignified bulk of his rapidly. Mr. Wheeler was first downtown, then

shopping at the market, then home puttering around. I'll wager
when you've dug into that you'll find he was home *alone!* Still, he's
the one I'd worry over least. Judge Spar was forgetting about his
troubles at a football game, alone! Now no one can argue about
that. A football mob would be one place where you couldn't blame
a man for not having been noticed if he didn't run into someone
acquainted with him. And now along comes young Hood with the
most unique story of the lot and just as difficult to check up on.
It's all too inconceivable, yet there it is!"

"But looking at it the other way, they *might* all be O. K.," Bryce
pointed out. "We're checking up as fast as we can. The doormen and
flunkies at the club place Strong and Behrmann there for lunch, and
Behrmann in the library at least part of the time. They place the
time when Mrs. Strong called for Strong at about the time he says.
They place Behrmann's departure at five-thirty. In fact, he talked
for a few minutes with the library custodian. And we can't find a
soul who saw either of them go out in that time. Wheeler *was* at
his broker's until after twelve o'clock. He *was* at Washington Market soon after that. He's apparently a regular shopper there. A clerk at
one of the cheese counters remembers waiting on him some time
Saturday noon. Mr. Parker *was* at his bank though nobody seems to
have seen him leave, and he actually *had* an oyster stew in the Lackawanna Station. The counterman picked his picture out of several."

"Still, it's all fragmentary, full of loopholes. It's singular—more
than singular—that not one of the stories is positively and continuously confirmable."

Bryce drew deeply on his cigar, removed it from his lips and
contemplated it soberly.

"Somebody shot him," he backtracked cheerfully. "Somebody
probably from right around here. Your inquiry ought to turn up a
reason. Maybe Hoyle had something on one of them, one or more
of them, that would be bound to come out now. Someone might
have wanted him unable to blab. Anything like that?"

"Not yet. We've scarcely scratched the surface, though, and—"

The door flew open. Sigurd Strong stood there, his dark countenance ash-gray.

"Wheeler's dead! Shot!"

9

MR. WHEELER VIEWS THE RIVER

STRONG HAD BURST IN upon Bryce and Fenner at eleven-thirty. Here we must digress.

An hour and a half earlier Anthony Wheeler had boarded the 9:58, New York bound, at Glen Ridge, New Jersey. Only four other commuters, scattered along the platform, got on with him, for the 9:58 ran well after the morning rush hour was done. A sixth passenger hurried down the winding sidewalk leading to the Erie station and barely scrambled aboard the last car as the train pulled out.

At Jersey City Mr. Wheeler, together with a handful of others who did not cross the river by tubes, boarded the 10:25 ferry to Chambers Street. He went upstairs and out to the rear deck, seating himself from long habit at the end of the continuous bench which runs around the upper cabin. The same crisp breeze which had so opportunely pepped up Mr. Hood earlier in the morning now blew over Anthony Wheeler's gaunt brow, but it affected him quite differently, investing him with a subtle chilliness and a scarce-conscious, vague melancholy at the imminent approach of winter.

Wheeler was getting old; worse, he *felt* that he was getting old. But with the mellowing years he was acquiring a philosophical tolerance that would have seemed impossible in his younger life. Consider, for instance, the state of affairs at the office. It didn't bother him much; he refused to let it bother him; but only a few years back it would have driven him frantic. And without doubt he would lose a great deal of money before the year was done, but he'd make it back next year, or in two or three when things picked up. In the

meantime he'd not have to worry about being comfortable, which
in these trying times was something!

Presently the boat pulled away from the slip. Wheeler, watching a pair of gulls, forgot business. Circling and dipping in swift,
graceful arcs, they hovered over the path of the ferry and scanned
the churned-up wake for edible refuse. Their effortless suspension,
poised on the air current, fascinated him. Here the science of avia-
tion could obtain pointers aplenty. So absorbed was he that when
a man suddenly sat down beside him it was as if the fellow had
appeared from nowhere.

"Hello there, Wheeler. I thought I'd find you back here. Getting some fresh air, what?"

Wheeler looked up.

"Oh, good morning! You rather startled me. But what are you
doing here? You're way out of your beaten path, aren't you?"

"I had some business to attend."

"So early in the morning?"

"Yes; it had to be at this time. Nice morning, eh?" He sniffed
the air. "You always ride out here. I remember you're telling me
once. Very nice on such a day as this."

"I was watching the gulls," Wheeler said. "They must have a
remarkable sense of balance. That one fellow has hardly batted a
wing since I've watched him."

"Yes; they don't waste much effort. If you and I, now, could be
half as efficient—" His voice trailed off as several of a group of boys
and young men who had been skylarking on the rear deck darted
around the corner, almost tripping over Wheeler's projecting
ankles. They had been throwing wads at someone on the rear deck
below and from their high glee one must have registered a hit.
Wheeler's companion watched them for a few moments with growing annoyance.

"Why is it, do you suppose, that adolescents seem so much more
obnoxious at some times than at others?" he queried.

Wheeler smiled.

"It's probably a matter of the onlooker's mood. Take that mob
there—they don't bother me at all this morning. Some mornings

I'd have to get up and move to the other side of the deck. They just feel their oats and haven't our inhibitions. Soon enough they'll have to grow up."

"You think, then, that we have too many inhibitions?"

"Perhaps, or maybe the wrong kind."

The man only grunted and the talk lagged until presently the ferry slid between the long freight piers jutting out from the Manhattan shore. From the engine room deep in the hold came the faint jangle of the "Slow Speed Astern" signal. The few passengers on the upper deck congregated at the forward stairs.

Wheeler's companion moved restlessly and unbuttoned his topcoat. He looked about. The last of the passengers disappeared down the far steps. To the rear lay the open river with, halfway across, the only sign of life in sight, a puffing tug breasting the tide valiantly while its tow of sand barges slapped the tiny whitecaps with good-humored defiance. On one side he and Wheeler faced the blank, corrugated-iron side of the freight pier, on the other the deserted upper cabin.

"No hurry," Wheeler admonished. "If you get up when you feel the boat hit you have comfortable time to get off, and you miss all the crowding. I never hurry any more. Life's too short for that."

"That's right, Wheeler; there's no hurry. Besides, you're not going anywhere!" There was a startling quality, a paradoxical combination of deathly coldness and breathless excitement in the man's tone and manner. Wheeler turned toward his companion and his eyes widened, first in amazement and then in horror.

"My God, man! What are you—" He had started to rise but two quick dull 'Phut's stopped him. He dropped back to the bench and his gasped question died in his throat.

And just then there came the slight tremor Wheeler had spoken of as the ferry made its contact with the transfer bridge. Wheeler's figure started to topple sideways but his companion held and steadied him. He placed one of the inert forearms on the window ledge behind the bench, turned the figure somewhat sideways and adjusted the lolling head so that it rested comfortably on the arm. For all the world Anthony Wheeler was blissfully dozing.

The arrangements consumed only a few seconds. He stepped back and surveyed his work. Wheeler wore a dark brown overcoat, which was just as well. The man slipped into the cabin by the rear door, sauntered down the stairs and trailed the departing crowd out into West Street.

In due course the few passengers for the return trip to Jersey City filtered aboard. Several stood at the rail ten feet from Wheeler's figure. One, Jonathan Leininger, a wholesale soap sales-man on his way to his rounds of the Jersey City laundries, gave it a second curious glance and sat down a short distance away along the bench. He was sure Wheeler hadn't been among the few people who had entered the ferry ahead of him. The old coot probably had intended to get off and had fallen asleep. Perhaps he should rouse him. He'd better not. The fellow looked as if he needed the nap, and the round trip would only take twenty-five or thirty minutes. Mr. Leininger buried himself in the sports section and the matter went out of his mind.

Everything now was football; players, coaches, prognostica-tions. The so-called big three had all managed to win their open-ers. Colgate and, of all schools, Columbia looked promising. He'd swallow that with a grain of salt until later in the season! In the Conference Purdue looked best. They'd been rolling right along for the past several seasons. Leininger started filling in the blanks in the weekly "Guess the Scores" contest.

Ten minutes later the lurch of the boat bringing up at the Jer-sey City slip aroused him from his study. It also unbalanced the remains of Anthony Wheeler and caused them to flop into a shape-less, disconcerting heap on the deck. Jonathan Leininger forgot soap and he forgot football. He looked at the figure in astonish-ment, while his mind fluttered about. The fellow looked pretty sick. He looked more than sick! Leininger bent over and touched him and felt a cold horror. He had come through the twenty-eight years of his life without having had any intimate contact with death, but there was no doubt in his mind that Wheeler was dead.

Leininger knew he must do something. Mostly he wanted to get away. He ran to the front rail. Below, a pair of deckhands who had made the boat fast were directing the departure of a line of cars and trucks. He called to them:

"Hey! Come up here! Come up here quick!"

They looked up at him blankly.

"Come up here! Hurry!" Leininger's urge became louder and more urgent. He turned away from the rail in time to see the ferry captain step out of the pilot house to the cabin roof, and transferred his plea to him. "Hey! Captain, come down here! Quick!"

The captain took one look at Leininger's pasty face and hurried to the stairs. In a second he, the two deckhands and three or four belated passengers, attracted by the excitement, all descended upon Leininger and his gruesome exhibit at once.

"He—he's dead," Leininger stammered. "He fell off the bench when the boat stopped."

The captain knelt over the prostrate form. A slight line of crimson ran from one corner of the mouth and there was blood on the deck beneath the figure.

"He must have had a stroke, a hemorrhage. We'll have to get him down to the station master's office." He dispatched one of the deckhands for a stretcher and assistance, and soon the removal was accomplished.

Possibly because of Wheeler's dark coat it was not until a police surgeon, hastily summoned, started examining him that it was discovered that the man had been shot. Two bullets had entered his chest from the right, one lodging in his heart and the other passing completely through it and stopping in the inside of the left arm just above the elbow.

There was ample identification material in Wheeler's wallet, hence a quick telephone call to the office of White, Wheeler, Parness and McClintock, another from Parness, who had just come in, to Sigurd Strong, and hence Strong's dramatic interruption of Fenner and the Inspector.

10

BRYCE AND FENNER VIEW THE RIVER

FENNER, UPON INSPECTOR BRYCE'S INSISTENCE, accompanied him to Jersey City. By prearrangement the lieutenant from the Bureau of Ballistics, a deputy medical examiner, and several of the Harbor Precinct police were already at the station master's office when they arrived.

The scene in the dingy room was not one Fenner would soon forget. The medical examiner and the Jersey City police surgeon were bent over Wheeler's body, laid out, stretcher and all, upon a leather couch in one end of the room. Several detectives, two uniformed policemen, together with the station master, the ferry captain, and Mr. Leininger, who had recovered an astonishing garrulity, were clustered about. A group of newspaper men, kept at the door by a third policeman, blocked the entry.

They made their way in and the Inspector identified himself. The question of jurisdiction had already been raised. From the original evidence of the police surgeon and Leininger it had been deduced that Wheeler must have been killed at some time prior to the departure of the boat from the Manhattan terminal. It was assumed, also, that he had been aboard for the 10:25 trip from Jersey City, for Mrs. Wheeler had been telephoned and had informed them that her husband had left home in time to catch the 9:58 from Glen Ridge, which would connect with that boat. She had borne up well under the news of Anthony's death and was expected momentarily.

"Shot himself and managed to toss the gun overboard," had been the first offhand judgment, but that had not held water long.

306

In the first place there were no powder markings on Wheelers coat; at least none visible to the naked eye. Furthermore, according to the surgeon, either shot would have disabled him so instantly that he could not have fired the second. Suicide, therefore, was quickly ruled out, and if Wheeler was a victim of murder the question of where the crime had taken place immediately assumed important proportions. If it had happened east of a theoretical line running up the middle of the Hudson the inquiry and any subsequent prosecution would have to be transferred to the New York authorities; if on the west side it would stay in the hands of the New Jersey police.

"Let's have a look at the boat," Bryce had requested as soon as the principal facts had been outlined.

"Better still, let's make a round trip on it," Fenner suggested. "Perhaps something will occur to us we'd otherwise miss. Has the boat been in use since?"

The ferry captain replied that it had not, the station master adding a grumble or two about disrupted schedules.

Arrangements were made and they all trouped out to the boat, a relief pilot negotiating the trip as Bryce had asked that the original pilot stay with the party. A detective and a patrolman were left with Wheeler's body.

On deck Leininger pointed out the place on the bench where Wheeler had been sitting and repeated the story he had told before. Wheeler had been "sort of hunched over with his head and arm on the window sill like he was asleep." Leininger was sure Wheeler hadn't boarded the boat at Chambers Street, as he himself had been one of the first to come aboard and he had come directly there to the upper deck. He had thought Wheeler asleep and had paid no attention to him after that until he had fallen off the bench at the end of the trip. There were smears of blood on the deck where he had lain.

"He shouldn't have been touched or moved until the police came," Bryce criticized. "Let's keep clear of this area until the boys have looked it over."

"We thought he'd had a stroke," the pilot explained. "As far as we knew there might have been a spark of life left in him. Our idea was to get him down to the office and get a doctor as quickly as we could."

"Were there many passengers on the east-bound trip?" Fenner asked presently.

"At that time usually between a dozen and twenty use the upper deck. Some are quite regular. You can probably get ahold of a great many of them in the morning if you like."

"Was Mr. Wheeler one of the regulars? Had you noticed him before?"

"I believe I've seen him, yes. I can't say how often but I think fairly regularly."

The boat started across. They all waited quietly until it had passed out from the slip into the open river.

"Do you remember whether you passed very close to any other vessel on that trip, Captain?" the Inspector asked.

"I can say positively that I did not, though on the return trip I had to let a West Shore Railway ferry cut me off, and also passed quite close to one of the New York municipal garbage tows."

"This baby was shot from close up," one of the Jersey City men volunteered. "Either that or the guy that did it was a crack shot. The two wounds are too close together and too well placed to have been made from any distance by an ordinary marksman."

"You're probably right."

Bryce glanced around. He stepped to the rail and looked along the little gutter that runs along the edge of the deck.

"No shells, I suppose, Lieutenant?"

"We hadn't got up here yet."

Bryce looked again.

"Well there aren't any, anyway."

"Might've used a revolver. Why do you figure an automatic was used?" the Lieutenant wanted to know.

"The shells'd be thirty-eights, I'd bet dollars to doughnuts; and when the autopsy's made you'll find those slugs are thirty-eights," Fenner predicted. All except Bryce waited curiously, but he refused to enlarge upon his cryptic forecast.

When the ferry docked on the New York side their momentary utter seclusion was brought in on all of them simultaneously. Sheltered by the blank face of the pier on one side, with only the open river astern, as long as the upper cabin was empty they were completely out of sight.

"Right here is where it must have happened." Bryce voiced the thought of all of them. "Didn't you hear anything, Captain?"

"Not a sound."

"Is there usually much of an interval between the departure of the New York-bound passengers and the arrival of the Jersey people getting on?" Fenner asked the pilot.

"During rush hours, no. They even overlap. But at that time there might have been anything from thirty seconds to a couple of minutes. One of the deckhands sometimes walks through to be sure everyone's ashore, but we're not very strict about it. I have already found out that on this particular stop no inspection was made."

The return trip was completed without much discussion. It was agreed, not reluctantly, by the Jersey City Detective Division that the affair was more properly a New York concern, and it was decided that Wheeler should be taken to the New York City morgue where the bullets would be removed.

When they got back they found Mrs. Wheeler seated beside her dead husband. The shock had all but robbed her of her reason, and she sat staring blankly and dry-eyed into space, her earlier stoicism shattered. Sometimes she looked dumbly at the figure on the stretcher. There was nothing she could tell them except that the victim was her husband, and that he had left for business as usual that morning.

The portion of the ferry involved was photographed and carefully examined for finger-prints, though there was such a hodgepodge of them on the rail and bench that little was expected from this source. Wheeler's effects were turned over to one of Bryce's aides who wrapped them and tagged them for submission to the Chief Medical Examiner's Laboratory. The body itself, labeled with the department's identification tag U.F.95, was also soon on its way.

Leininger was released in his own custody. At first, to the soap salesman's extreme distress, they audibly considered arresting him as a material witness, but upon second thought it was decided to allow him his freedom. He started off on his belated rounds with the exciting story for all his customers, and blissfully unaware of the continual escort of at least one of Bryce's best men.

Mrs. Wheeler was removed to a hospital for observation and for treatment for shock.

Fenner and Bryce stopped at the Station Restaurant. Bryce had arranged for a police car to meet them at Chambers Street but they had just missed a boat and faced a twenty-minute wait. It was almost three o'clock and neither had eaten since morning.

"You've got a clever devil on your hands this time, old man," Fenner commented over his mug of coffee.

"You're telling me! You agree the same bird did both jobs, don't you? At least, that's what I gathered from your crack about the thirty-eights."

"The signs point that way, as I read them. Both men shot under circumstances that would require a knowledge of their habits, careful planning and precise execution; both victims involved in the same business environment—they probably had friends in common and enemies in common. Both crimes have the same, at least apparent, lack of motivation. The one difference, and it puzzles me tremendously, is that in this instance no effort was made to make the thing appear a suicide. Of course in this case there wasn't so much time. Our man may have been too rushed."

"Wait till we get the slugs—be only a few hours." Bryce became taciturn. "Wonder where the shells went. Overboard, huh?"

"They would. Seated, Wheeler would face the rail. He was shot from the right. The gun must have been pointed toward the stern. It would eject the shells right over the rail. Comforting, isn't it!"

"Funny that no one heard it."

"Silencer, without a doubt. That would account for Saturday afternoon, too. More of the careful planning."

Bryce dipped a doughnut and Fenner presently resumed, half aloud: "Hoyle and Wheeler—Hoyle and Wheeler. Of all the gang over there why just those two? What have they in common? What the devil have they got that the others *haven't* got? What the— Oh, hell!"

They drained their cups, paid their checks, and went out. In the doorway they encountered the station master. He, too, had missed his lunch, and was about to make it up. He said:

"There was a telephone call for you, Inspector, about ten minutes ago. I thought you'd gone on the other boat and told 'em you'd left. It was a news reporter—the *Globe*. I suppose he'll get you later. He asked if it was true Mr. Wheeler had been shot. I told him it was, but that he'd have to get his statements from your people or from the Jersey City cops. Is that all right? I'm very sorry. I didn't know that you hadn't left."

Fenner and Bryce looked at each other and the latter said:

"It's all right. He'll no doubt get in touch with me again."

"Yes; no doubt he will," Fenner mocked gravely. They passed out of hearing and onto the boat.

"Now where in the devil did *he* get in on this already?" the Inspector stormed.

"Same place we did. It was Parness who called Strong. Everyone in New York knows of it by now."

"I'm not so sure. Strong wouldn't tell that reporter anything, and I don't think Parness would, either. And no official reports are public yet. I wonder— Well, we'll see what he makes of it."

11

MR. BARTLETT GETS A BREAK

THEY SAW VERY SOON what Johnny Bartlett had made of the murder of Anthony Wheeler, and what they saw both explained his early knowledge and took their breaths away. They had disembarked at Chambers Street and walked out through the auto runway to West Street where the familiar little blue police runabout awaited them. A newspaper truck skidded to a stop and the driver's helper flopped a bundle of early editions on the news stand in front of the station just as Fenner and Bryce approached. Fenner's hand went mechanically to his pocket but Bryce beat him to the stand. The Inspector had glimpsed the huge scare-headline spread across the top of the page. He grabbed two papers, handed one to Fenner, and yanked him toward the car.

The front page shouted:

MANIAC MURDERS REALTOR
Anthony Wheeler Shot to Death on Ferry
Message from Crank Boasts Murders of F. W.
Strong Director and of Treasurer Last Week
THREATENS FURTHER DEATHS

A message received by the *Globe* shortly before 3:00 P.M. today dramatically broke open the mystery of the shooting of Martin Hoyle, F. W. Strong Treasurer, in the Strong Building last Saturday afternoon, confessed the murder of Anthony Wheeler, a

312

Director of the same firm, who was found shot to death on an Erie Ferry late this morning, and threatened further killings.

As announced exclusively in yesterday's late evening *Globe* the Police had not been satisfied about the apparent suicide of Hoyle and had been conducting a quiet investigation.

The maniac's letter was postmarked at 11:36 A.M. at the Grand Central Post Office Branch and was mailed within a half hour of the time Mr. Wheeler's riddled body was found on the boat. The Police are working on the case.

At the office of F. W. Strong & Co. Mr. Sigurd Strong, Chairman of the Board, declined to comment until the authenticity of the *Globe's* communication could be investigated. Of this, however, there appears to be little doubt, as the message was mailed in New York at a time when only a few Jersey City Police and the Erie Station Officials were aware of Mr. Wheeler's death.

The letter, which was instantly turned over to the Police, reads as follows:

Gentlemen of the Press and to the Public at Large:
Re: F. W. Strong & Company
THEY CAN'T GET AWAY WITH IT!

Of a half billion dollars worth of bonds sold to the American public during the last five years $335,750,000 are in default. Of the 335 million 90 percent will be lost to the investor. A small part of this loss may be ascribed to troublous times or to inept, if innocent, management. The bulk of it represents the deliberate loot of as vicious and unprincipled organized thievery as has ever been visited upon an unwary public.

Confident of the supineness of the people and the lethargy of the state, adroitly sheltered by a maze of legal technicalities in the rare instances where their brilliant record has finally penetrated the dense somnolence of the Prosecuting Attorney's Office, the perpetrators loll in luxury while the victims of their malevolent influence starve in breadlines or freeze in gutters.

More: The plundering still continues!

I repeat: THEY CAN'T GET AWAY WITH IT!

Gradually, but inexorably, these vultures are to be eliminated from the business scene. On last Saturday a certain Martin Hoyle, F. W. Strong Treasurer, because OBJECT LESSON No. 1. A few moments ago Mr. Anthony Wheeler was second to pay the penalty. Who will be No. 3? I have not myself yet decided, but be assured that the good work will be continued, and SPEEDILY. There will be no postponements by farcical, impotent courts. The list is long, scores of names in dozens of corporations, but the hooves of the lamb are agile.

May the gentlemen order their affairs.

SHORN.

Ironically enough the letter was typed on the reverse side of a printed prospectus issued several years ago by F. W. Strong & Company, describing the First Mortgage Bonds of the Romaine Hotel. . . .

The article continued with a brief outline of the circumstances of Wheeler's death as Johnny Bartlett had obtained them from the Jersey City Police, and a more detailed re-hash of Martin Hoyle's demise, and concluded with:

. . . The affairs of F. W. Strong & Company, restrained by the courts last week from conducting further

business in the State of New York, are now in process of being taken over by Receivers.

Fenner and Bryce scanned the article in but a few moments.

"Center Street," Bryce ordered, and then shut up like a clam.

"Ain't that something!" Fenner commented, and started to reread the account.

"Yeah; it's plenty! I've seen these maniac scares before. Life
won't be worth living till this baby's nailed. Cripes! Everybody from
the Commissioner down will be rode ragged."

"I hadn't thought of that angle."

"Well, I have!"

At Headquarters they found mild excitement. The crank letter
had been examined by experts from all departments. A few finger-
prints, valueless because the communication had been so much
handled in the newspaper office, were with great difficulty brought
out in the margins and photographed. The typography was that of
one of the most common makes of portable typewriters. The paper
was the rough bond frequently used for printing prospectus
circulars, and this particular circular described in anything but
modest terms the merits and advantages of the Romaine Hotel
"JUNIOR PARTICIPATION FIRST MORTGAGE SINKING FUND
GOLD BOND CERTIFICATES, SERIES B." It was dated May 1,
1929. The message had come in a plain stamped envelope of the
kind sold in post offices by the thousand, with a special delivery
stamp added.

They glanced at it but momentarily; the 11:36 A.M. time stamp
told everything. Fenner commented:

"Genuine, of course. Must have been mailed at least fifteen
minutes earlier unless it was dropped right at the post office. At
that time no one over here could know about Wheeler except the
fellow who killed him. Parness didn't get the word and call Strong
until half past eleven."

Suddenly Bryce looked up.

"When in Hell did the fellow have time to write it?"

"You know, you beat me to that question by a tongue's length."
Fenner calculated rapidly aloud: "Let's see; the 10:25 boat docked
at Chambers Street at about 10:40. It would take twenty or twenty-
five minutes to get from there up to Grand Central neighborhood.
Leaves from fifteen minutes to a half hour to write the letter and
get out and mail it. I doubt if he could do it; I doubt it very much."
He looked at the communication again. "You see, it's not a hasty
letter. There's not a misspelling or error of punctuation in it. And
it's not worded as it would be if it were just dashed off in a hurry.
It's studied, composed deliberately."

"Written beforehand, huh?"

"Looks so to me." Fenner read a moment. "The man seems
plenty hot and bothered doesn't he? He must have been stuck badly
to go off his nut like that."

Bryce paced the floor.

"You know what this means? Police protection for everybody
in New York that ever sold a bond and knows a district leader, until
this s. o. b. is pinched. It'll be a madhouse!"

Bryce was right. Already official telephones were buzzing and
Headquarters was being flooded with requests for information, for
advice, and for protection; and with protests, pleas and promises.
Bryce was called to the Commissioner's carpet and came back glow-
ering but said nothing. Fenner refrained from comment.

The Inspector carefully pocketed the letter and envelope.

"Let's go uptown," he said.

At the office of F. W. Strong Company they were welcomed with
open arms. Strong, Behrmann, Judge Spar, Winthrop Parness and
Maurice Parker were gathered in the Board Room. Strong's decanter and a number of variously empty glasses boldly adorned
one end of the large oval table. A tenseness of suppressed excitement and not a little terror filled the air. Judge Spar and Mr. Parker
had just returned from Woodlawn Cemetery where at two-thirty
they had represented the F. W. Strong Company at the hurried and
informal interment of the remains of Martin Hoyle, not the happi-
est preparation for the news which awaited them upon their return.

Sigurd Strong had essayed half-heartedly to quiet their gathering fears. After a prolonged telephone conversation he had turned to them and promised, "This crank won't be at large twenty-four hours. The Commissioner himself has assured me that every facility of the force will be devoted to his apprehension until he's caught. In the meantime he has promised us all the protection we can possibly require." It was not convincing.

Behrmann said little but his twitching, puckered lips spoke volumes. Winthrop Parness' veneer of nonchalance was as a mask half fallen off. Parker perspired and stammered and buttonholed his associates from time to time with such reassuring comments as "Poor Anthony!" "I can't believe it!" "Murdered!" "Martin—and now Anthony! Where do you suppose this ghastly business will end up!"

They all looked at the Inspector hopefully. It was Parness who spoke first.

"Bit of excitement, what!" His smile looked somewhat sickly.

Bryce could not resist: "Yeah; this nut seems to have it in for you guys!" His smile was gently malicious. In a soberer vein he said to Strong, "We're going after this thing hard. Can't guarantee anything as to how long it'll take, of course, but you're going to have all the protection the department can supply. In the meantime, there's no sense minimizing the danger. This fellow's clever and apparently means business. There's no one quite so shrewd and cunning as one of these homicidal maniacs, once he's on the warpath. Sooner or later he'll slip up, but until then you'll simply have to be very careful. Stay with other people and stay indoors." He produced the prospectus. "Can you let me have a list as soon as possible of all the people to whom this particular notice was sent?"

Strong glanced at it.

"Probably our entire mailing list," he moaned. "They went all over the country."

"But this was not a large issue," Fenner pointed out.

Strong looked again.

"The Series B? No; not so large as some. In fact, it was only a six hundred thousand dollar issue—Second Mortgage Series—but it was widely advertised."

"I think it would be better to concentrate on the actual pur-chasers of the issue," Fenner suggested to the Inspector. "The whole communication and the circumstances of both murders are dis-tinctly stagy. The man has an eye to effects. I imagine he would pick an issue he'd been burned on, to make his little play with."

Strong sent for Hood. He came in quite unperturbed and prom-ised to supply the list of original purchasers of the issue in ques-tion, immediately. Some were banks and security dealers. The names of their subsequent customers it would be a painstaking and drawn out business to procure. However, he could do it.

The afternoon wore out. Fenner got back to the more prosaic details of the purely accounting end of his inquiry. He could not, however, help contrasting the present subdued tenseness in the place with the clatter and buzz of yesterday when Hoyle's death had first been officially labeled murder.

And it seemed scarcely possible that only twenty-four hours had elapsed since Bryce first started his round of questioning, and that in that short time there had been crammed, first that amazing string of incredible alibis, then Wheeler's cold-blooded murder and the futile trip to Jersey City, and now this objectively lucid but monstrous threat.

12

MESSRS. PARNESS AND HOOD COMPARE NOTES

THE LATE EVENING PAPERS and those next morning were a revelation, even to Fenner. The yellower journals frankly abandoned their entire front pages to the F. W. Strong sensation, and even the conservative ones devoted two to four columns to it, topped with glaring heads. The more lurid sheets carried pictures of the F. W. Strong Building, arrows pointing to the office where Hoyle was found. There were photographs of the officers and directors, dug out of files accumulated during the lush years when those individuals made copy promoting properties, floating loans, and addressing chambers of commerce.

There were pictures of the Erie Ferry with the usual "X marks the spot" designation, photographs and biographies of Wheeler and Hoyle, rehashes of the Hoyle case, reprints of Sigurd Strong's statements. There were outlines of the ill-starred business history of the F. W. Strong Company, beginning with its founding and earlier creditable record, running through it's swift ascent to its zenith during the New Era period, and its subsequent equally swift descent and final dissolution in the courts. Some papers ran pictures of ex-Judge Horton, newly appointed receiver. Some had interviews with prominent leaders in the fields thought to be the intended area of "Shorn's" murderous terrorization.

All of them printed counselings of caution, reassurances by the Police Commissioner, and a statement by the Mayor, himself, to the effect that there was no reason for so much turmoil over the threats of an obvious lunatic who, "though homicidal and at large was, after all, only a single warped individual pitted against the entire mobilized forces of law and order, and who would without doubt soon be safely behind the bars of the death house at Sing Sing or of an institution for the criminally insane."

The *Globe* had again stolen a march, it alone exhibiting facsimile reproductions of both sides of Shorn's threatening message. Fenner smiled to himself. They evidently had not "instantly turned it over to the police" as their first article had professed. They had kept it at least long enough to photograph it front and back. Trust that fellow, Bartlett, to overlook no bets.

Fenner reached the Strong Building a little late Thursday morning. He pushed his way through a dozen or more plain-clothes detectives assigned to act as escorts for such of the officials as desired them. There were others stationed about the banking floor and more outside in the neighboring streets. There were also reporters by the dozen, though, by the combined orders of Inspector Bryce, Mr. Strong and Mr. Horton, they were kept pretty much outside of the building. Statements to the press by any F. W. Strong employee or official were strictly forbidden.

Margaret Purcell was at her desk, fresh as a daisy. The irrepressible Mr. Bartlett was also there, but by no means fresh. He more nearly resembled one of last season's dandelions, though the wilting was not of the spirit; Johnny had been up all night.

Fenner said, "Hello, how'd you get in?"

"That's what Mr. Strong asked me," Johnny replied blandly. "I told him Inspector Bryce wanted to ask me some questions about that letter."

"Does he?"

"He should, shouldn't he?"

Fenner pondered this. "But he's not here—or is he, Miss Purcell?"

"He'll be here soon," Johnny spoke up. "I can't get anywhere near him down at Center Street."

Fenner started into Strong's office, then stopped.

"You fellows certainly manhandled that letter before you turned it in," he said.

"What do you mean?"

"I suppose it wouldn't occur to you that finger-prints can be left on paper as well as anything else?"

"No. As a matter of fact, I didn't know that."

"Well, remember it next time. And tell your boss the same thing."

"Next time?"

"Forget I mentioned it!"

Fenner passed on and Johnny turned to Margaret.

"Did you get that? Next time! He thinks there'll be more letters."

"He thinks you bungled up the one, anyway," Margaret pointed out sweetly.

Bartlett ignored the remark. He studied her intently. The excitement and a certain amount of lost sleep had not impaired her comely attractiveness. If anything, a slightly heightened color lent a piquancy her serious beauty did not ordinarily possess.

"You're looking swell this morning, honey! These murders seem to agree with you. You'd sure be an eyeful if a war broke out!"

Margaret turned away wearily.

"You joke about the damnedest things, Johnny," she replied. "I don't mind telling you that I don't think that's very funny."

"Sorry. I guess it *was* kind of dumb. Well, I'll be getting thrown out among the common herd as soon as the Inspector gets here, so I have to make the most of my time. But seriously, this thing has been a corking break for me. My boss is tickled pink! If I can some way keep scooping them I'll be able to name my own salary in a week. Keep your ear to the ground for me, will you, Peg? You could pick up a lot around here."

"I could get fired, too, for consorting with reporters. They're not in exactly good grace right now, and—forgive me—you least of all."

Bartlett's boyish face burlesqued austere martyrdom.

"Don't be surprised if I sidle up alongside when you go out to lunch. You need my manly protection. I'll be hanging around."

Margaret turned back to her work. Now that the effect of the initial shock had partly worn off the office staff were undergoing a mild reaction from their hysteria. The release of the tension made

itself evident in the re-gathering of the gossiping groups, a resump-
tion of the normal processes, and among some even a tendency to
make morbid jests. Behrmann and Judge Spar came in, the former
with a crisp "Good Morning!" for Margaret, the latter with no salu-
tation at all. They passed into Sigurd Strong's office. A few moments later Mr. Hood appeared, a sheaf of papers in one hand and
a large folder full under his arm. He stopped my Margaret's desk
and put the folder down.

"How's things, Peg? That Cop come in yet?"

"Cop? the place is overrun with them!"

"I know. I mean Inspector Bryce."

"No, he's not here, Mr. Hood."

"Why 'Mr. Hood' when we're alone, Peggy?"

"Oh—habit."

"It's a bad habit. How's for lunching with me today? Better still,
dinner tonight? We could go to that place—"

Peggy screwed up her face in a little warning frown as Strong's
office door opened and that gentleman noiselessly crossed the corner of the room and hurried down the corridor toward the office of
the defunct treasurer.

Hood glanced at the retreating figure.

"Hell with him! This show is over! Anyway, why shouldn't you
go out with me? I've always known that was an idiotic regulation."

"Makes for efficiency, Mr. Hood," Margaret mocked.

"Perhaps I shouldn't ask you." Hood turned suddenly sober.
"Perhaps I'm letting you in for something. I might be the next one
on the spot, you know. Perhaps you'd rather not take a chance with
me."

"If *I* thought that *you* thought such an idea had even entered
my head I wouldn't speak to you for a month!"

"I didn't, but I wouldn't blame you for being a little careful."

"I'm not afraid. Oh, isn't it all horrible?"

"It's pretty bad. Have you studied that letter at all, Peggy—read
the lines and in between the lines? It's wicked and criminal of
him"—he paused after the "him" with awe in his manner—"to be
so indiscriminate, but there *is* something to his argument." Hood

tapped the folder on the desk. "I'll bet that there are several hundred names in that file who have a feeling of sympathy for this fellow—maybe even a little secret satisfaction that someone has risen up on his hind legs and tried what they themselves'd like to see done, only haven't enough guts to tackle!"

"Why Bob!"

"Sounds cold-blooded but, by God, it's true!"

"Why, Bob; whatever has poor Mr. Wheeler ever done—or Mr. Hoyle?"

Hood leaned over the desk and lectured earnestly:

"As individuals, I can't say. That's what I meant when I said that the indiscrimination was horrible and unfair. But they were willing parts of a racket and—like myself—usually in on the pay-off."

Margaret was deeply surprised. She was framing a careful reply when the lobby door opened and Winthrop Parness came in, sartorially more perfect than ever. He looked at them for just a second longer than necessary, a pause calculated to make any greeting he uttered a mild sneer. He lifted his derby.

"Good morning, Miss Purcell. Well, Bob, you've got on your bullet-proof vest, I suppose?"

Hood straightened up and moved a step away from Margaret's chair.

"Nope. I figure I can take it!"

"I was thinking less of an assassin's bullets than of Cupid's darts."

Margaret colored slightly.

Parness intended little more than a mild pleasantry and started moving toward the corridor entrance, but the remark chanced to catch Hood against the grain.

"What in the devil kind of a crack is that, anyway?"

Parness said over his shoulder, "Now don't get virile on me! It's so tiresome." He pronounced it "tiahsome." The supercilious admonition, before Margaret, was hardly designed to cool Hood off. Parness had an amazing aptitude for deftly flicking people on the raw spots, and no resistance to the temptation to use it.

Hood controlled a tremendous impulse to physical violence, but his venom found outlet through speech. He followed Parness a few steps, flawlessly mimicking the pseudo-English accent.

"Youah mornin' mannahs, Winthrop—they wouldn't possibly be from a spot of jealouseh, would they?"

"Oh, Bob!" Margaret pleaded. Once in a moment of confidence she had hinted at Parness' earlier subtle attentions.

"Don't be—be—"

"'Trivial' is the word you're looking for, Winthrop. You used 'tiahsome' a moment ago. Mustn't repeat, don't y' know."

Parness paused at his door.

"You're vindictive this morning, Robert. I suggest milk of magnesia. Besides, you're entirely mistaken. Sorry, Miss Purcell."

"I probably am, but unless I'm doubly mistaken you've got your hands full with women right now, anyway. Toodle-oo."

It was Parness' turn to bristle.

"Precisely what do *you* mean?"

"Let's step into Sig's office and chew in over," Hood teased.

Parness went into his own office without another word. Hood came back for his folder of papers.

"The fat-headed pimp! Some day I'll take him apart!"

"Bob!"

Just then Fenner came out of Hoyle's door, passed down the narrow hall and entered Parness' room.

13
MESSRS. FENNER AND BRYCE COMPARE NOTES

HOOD TOOK HIS LISTS IN TO STRONG. Close on his heels Inspector Bryce arrived. He scanned the sheets, five typewritten pages of names and addresses. Some were women, a few were institutions, but there still remained a hopelessly long list of "prospects."

He pocketed it.

"There's enough routine there to keep a lot of the boys out of the movies for some time to come," he told Fenner, who had come back. "It's something to start from, though."

Hood had lingered in the room. Fenner turned to him.

"You're in a position to hear the worst of the squawks and sob-stories," he said. "Maybe you've got a special slant on this business. There must be some particularly disgruntled investors, the more rabid ones, whom you could tell us about."

Hood thought it over before replying:

"There are, all right. Plenty of them! But Good Lord! I don't know that any of them seemed about to go off their heads."

"One of them did."

Hood said, "They used to come here in droves, but not so much lately. I guess they've learned that it won't do them any good so they don't waste the time. Some write in, but that's fallen off, too."

Bryce, reminded of something, said to Strong:

"There's another thing. Pick out of your files all of the type-written complaints or inquiries you've received and let me have them."

Hood spoke up:

"You'll have to get them from Mr. Horton. Those files have already been turned over." Under his breath he added, "Better send up a van!"

"You don't think this bird would type that warning on a machine he'd already used for letters to this company, do you?" Fenner asked. "There are no *other* indications that you're dealing with a moron."

"I don't think so, no." The Inspector was very patient. "But we can't overlook a chance."

Hood had been leaning over Strong's desk where a copy of the *Globe* with the reproduction of Shorn's letter was lying. He looked up at the Inspector and asked:

"Why do you suppose that thing was sent to the *Globe?* Why not to all the papers? But if to just one, why the *Globe?* There are several more important papers."

"No special reason, probably. Why not to the *Globe*, as well as any? It's a live paper. Does there have to be a reason?" The Inspector testily thought the question itself more puzzling than its answer.

"No-o; I only wondered." Hood shrugged his shoulders.

"The *Globe* scooped the others on the Hoyle end of it. Maybe that had something to do with its selection," Fenner suggested.

Hood eased himself out and presently the Inspector and Fenner adjourned to the ex-treasurer's office.

"That note's the real thing," Bryce said when they were alone. "The slugs were thirty-eights from the same old place. One was only a fair match but the other was absolutely unquestionable."

"After the note you could have taken that for granted. Anything more?"

"Yeah; the guy we're looking for is a short man of medium height with a brown-gray overcoat, and he's somewhere between blond and brunette, and he may or may not have worn spectacles, and he might have had a mustache, and he's over thirty and under sixty, and it's two to two whether he's fat or lean."

"Very precise. I'll know him the instant I see him. You're sure it wasn't a lady?"

"By Jeez, if we'd asked that I bet we'd have got a split vote on it, too."

"Where did you get this perfect description?"

"Four observant young citizens, age fourteen to eighteen," Bryce replied caustically. "They were on that end of the deck on the 10:25 boat. One of them happened to mention at dinner that he was aboard and his old man had brains enough to give us a ring. They all live out in Passaic. I went out myself and talked to all of them. I could very well have spared myself the trip. About all they agree on is that two men were seated together near the end of the bench."

"Very helpful."

"I asked them if it appeared that Wheeler and this other guy were traveling together or just happened to sit by each other. They all agreed that the two men were talking, but whether they looked as if they were engaged in a casual exchange of remarks or were acquainted with each other, none of them could say." Bryce snorted his disgust.

"Mr. Shorn, from his note, appears to have had plenty of material in his mind to make conversation with, if he had needed to strike one up with Wheeler, or with Hoyle either. But you may be sure he wasn't a total stranger. Whether or not Wheeler knew him, he knew Wheeler! At least he knew his habits of commuting. He must have observed him pretty thoroughly and then followed him until he got his chance."

"I wonder whom he's following now?"

"You'll probably find out soon enough," Fenner sanguinely predicted.

"I guess so. To be frank, until he tries it again we're not getting far. We're working in the dark. These lists—bah!" He took from his pocket the sheets he had received from Hood.

"Why will you be better off after the next execution—or the next? You certainly can't assume he'll get careless!"

"He'll slip up. They all do."

"And in the meantime?"

"These fellows will have to watch their step, that's all. We'll cover them the best we can with the men we've got."

"How do they take it—the idea of being escorted around?"

"Now that's a funny thing. Last night every one of them practically wanted an armored car. Today they seem less anxious about it. The first scare is wearing off now and some of them won't be bothered with protection."

"That's a natural reaction," Fenner said. "I think I can see how it would be. Yesterday the event was so close it was borne in on them regardless. Today, upon reflection, it's all so fantastic it seems incredible. It becomes almost unreal to them—so unreal that they unconsciously discount the possibility of its keeping up, or at least of its striking them."

"But wait till this nut takes a potshot at one more of them!"

"Exactly. They'll swing just as far the other way. There won't be enough cops in the State to supply the demand."

The desk was littered with reports and typewritten schedules. Fenner's scratch pad was covered with penciled figures and calculations. Bryce glanced at the jumble.

"Getting anywhere?" he asked.

"We are, now—a little," Fenner admitted. "We haven't put our fingers on it yet, how it works, or was worked, but there seems to be a good deal of the income from the company-managed properties unaccounted for. The bookkeeping setup is such that there's no automatic check. God knows how long it's been going on or what it'll run up to! Horton's crowd are working along the same lines. They'll be up to it, too, in a few days and then there's going to be Hell up Sixth Street!"

"Who's it up to? Who's involved? Would Hoyle and Wheeler have been in it?"

"Hoyle would. Wheeler wouldn't have had to be. Nobody else, necessarily. Almost anybody, possibly. They'd all have been aware of it if they'd been on their toes during the last year or two, but that doesn't mean that they were, or even that I think they were."

"But who in particular seems mixed up with Hoyle?" Bryce urged. "Anyone apt to beat it?"

"It's too early; I haven't figured how it was worked yet. I'll tell you one thing: A. L. Behrmann is far too intelligent to have missed this altogether. He's more versed in the company's affairs than some of the others."

"What about Mr. Strong?"

"He only knows what Behrmann wants him to know."

"And Hood?"

"It's not in his province. He's only the Star Boy-salesman. This tampering and appropriation is between the accounting and the setup of the books of the properties that have been taken back and are being run by the F. W. Strong Company for the bondholders. Hood has nothing to do with that. At least, I believe that he hasn't."

"By the way, that flukey story of his looks on the up and up. The boys have talked to the bartender at the speakie Hood began in, and to the jack of all trades at the two-by-four hotel he woke up in. We're trying to get the balance of it through the cabs, and I wouldn't be surprised if we turned up something in a day or two. Maybe we'll get his roll back for him."

"That would be something in return for all of your trouble, wouldn't it?"

Bryce appeared about to depart. He glanced once more at Hood's list which he had been leafing idly. He realized the tremendous volume of routine involved in checking up the people named, and knew in addition that it was less than probable that the work would bear fruit, but in accordance with his methodical, "no stone unturned" thoroughness the job would have to be tackled. Suddenly he stopped and exclaimed, "Hey, Max; what d'you know about this!" He pointed to the middle of the third page:

"- - - - - - - -

Lawrence, Malcolm J.	1764 Grove Ave., Bklyn.
Leininger, Grace E.	908 West 183rd Street, Bronx.
Leininger, Jos. W.	" " " " "
Lenihan, Michael P.	780 Centre St., Trenton, N. J.
Lindstrom- - - - - - - -"	

"Well, what of it?"

"Leininger isn't such a common name," the Inspector pointed out.

"You don't think *our* Mr. Leininger is in this! Why, you're clutching broomstraws!"

"Our Mr. Leininger lives up in the Bronx—not far from there, either."

"But he doesn't fit. That inoffensive little pipsqueak! He doesn't fit either crime or anything else. The letter—nothing!"

"He might—during demented spells, say." Bryce persisted.

"What's he doing now?"

"He's going right on about his business selling soap. Murphy says he didn't know there were so damned many laundries in the Atlantic States as appear to be in Jersey City alone. But anyway, that's what Leininger would do, innocent or guilty."

"Where was he last Saturday?"

"That will be the very next thing I find out."

"Here's another for you—while you're 'finding out things' or chasing rainbows or whatever category such activity as investigating Mr. Leininger properly comes under—each partner in Wheeler's real estate outfit carried a hundred and fifty thousand dollars worth of life insurance, payable fifty thousand each to the three surviving partners."

"Yeah?"

"White and McClintock are both in Europe."

"So what?"

"Nothing much. Where was Mr. Parness yesterday morning at ten-forty?"

"I can find out damned quick."

But he couldn't. Parness had gone. Miss Purcell informed the Inspector that Parness had been in the office for an hour or so, but had already left. Nor was he at his own real estate office. Bryce hurried out to set in motion certain wheels which he hoped would pick up the lost real estate broker quickly.

14
WINTHROP PARNESS KEEPS A DATE

SECLUDED IN ONE of the little booths that lined the perimeter of the Vladivostok Restaurant, Shirley Strong faced Parness across the red-checked table cloth. An atmosphere, artfully created, of esoteric heaviness pervaded the place. The only sound to break the deathlike stillness was the faint whir of a ventilating fan somewhere back toward the kitchen. One instinctively spoke in whispers.

The only light was a dull red glow from one shrouded ceiling fixture and a faint glare that was reflected from the foyer through the key-shaped entrance. Parness, with a practical eye, looked about to see how the air of somber mystery was produced. The floors were heavily carpeted, the ceiling padded and the walls hung, all with some heavy, deep-red stuff. There were tiny silver fleur-de-lis to break the monotony.

"Spooky, isn't it!" Shirley commented.

"Cozy, though. How'd you happen to find this place?"

A hand moved and a match flashed. The waiter who had appeared noiselessly from around the corner of the booth lighted the two tall candles on their table. From within their warm glow the outer darkness seemed more dense than ever, and the effect was of warmer intimacy and more utter seclusion. He placed two menu cards before them. One side was printed in English, the other in Russian. They ordered and he padded silently away, his maroon smock making him almost invisible against the dark background.

"Oh, Zetskaya, the cellist—he brought me here once." Shirley answered Parness' earlier question. "It's quite a rendezvous for

Russians. They gather here evenings and sit for hours. It's a haven
for the White expatriates."

"We're the only customers, Shirley."

"It's not noon yet. There will be more. Most of the crowd comes
in the evening, though."

"I'd forgotten it was so early." He glanced around. "I say,
Shirley—" Parness broke his speech off and looked at her between
the two flickering candle flames. At thirty-five Mrs. Strong looked
nearer twenty-five. Her face with its tawny, silk-smooth skin,
faintly high cheek bones and wide-set dark eyes, had more Slavic
than Jewish characteristics, including full lips, delicately arched brows,
and on this occasion overemphatic earrings. There was a quality of
sleekness in her grooming that nothing would ever eradicate—a not
altogether desirable sleekness, Parness found himself thinking,
though it had at one time fascinated him to an extreme degree.

Waiting for him to continue, watching his eyes, stony now where
they were wont to smolder, Shirley suddenly thought of herself,
saw herself clearly—what she had been, why she was there. Shirley
Goldberg had been of the lower east side, definitely. She had been
born ambitious and at an early age had begun to hold her family
and their friends and neighbors in increasing disdain.

She had schooled herself, aped the manners and pseudo-cul-
ture of the stratum to which she aspired until they became an in-
tegral part of her own character, so that when Sigurd Strong had
once miraculously met and fallen in love with her there had not
been much obstacle to their marriage. She had been eighteen,
Sigurd almost forty. That was seventeen years before. She had not
attempted to deceive herself that she was marrying Sigurd Strong
for anything but money and position, and the deception of Sigurd
had barely outlasted their honeymoon.

After the initial strain of disillusionment had subsided there
had been eight or ten years of comparative content, marred only
slightly by the fact of their childlessness. Sigurd, like many of
his race, had an innate genius for ordering his domestic life with
familiar and homely comforts, a contagious tranquility that
beguiled even the youthful Shirley. But later, with the approach of

dread thirty, this had been less effective and there had ensued what Sigurd irritably termed the "bug era." Musicians, artists of the extremist variety, fads, a poet or two, were adopted and discarded in bewildering succession. Through it all, however, she had remained technically faithful to her spouse.

Then one unhappy morning, two years before, she had encountered Winthrop Parness in her husband's office. Their affair had flared from the outset. Parness seemed externally the embodiment of all Shirley's early ideals—the Shirley Goldberg ideal brought out and refurbished in the light of Shirley Strong's wider experience. And Winthrop Parness, the sensualist, had promptly overcome Parness, the business man. The ravishing Jewess was more than he could resist, despite the fact that his native acumen warned him that he was toying with his business future. She had not succumbed immediately; she had kept him dangling with a skill that surprised even herself, so that the eventual conquest was magnified out of all proper proportion. It had progressed from lunches, dinners, drives to week-ends, an apartment with a pair of aliases, and once a cleverly contrived month in Bermuda.

The two years, despite their precarious nature, had been for Shirley a period of enchantment, and for Parness, too, though in a lesser sense because the awkwardness and unaccustomed inconvenience robbed the experience of some of its savor. Shirley could not help but detect of late a definite waning of his ardor, a waning that Parness' most gallant efforts could not quite conceal.

She suddenly came back to herself and remembered that he had started to speak.

"What were you saying, Win?"

The waiter appeared with the beginnings of lunch. Parness waited until he had moved out of earshot.

"Shirley—we'll have to give each other up for a while." He spoke rapidly, as if anxious to get the words out of his mouth. He was unable to look at her.

Shirley felt that sweetish clawing at her vitals. It had come. She hadn't expected anything so soon or abrupt or violent. She laid down her spoon gently.

"Give each other—up? For a while? What do you mean, Win? What are you saying?" She could not keep the distress entirely out of her voice.

"Don't misunderstand me, darling. It's Sig. I'm afraid he's found out, or at least has some rather strong suspicions."

Shirley was wildly relieved. Even the temporary postponement of her worse fear, that Parness was ready to discard her, left her strangely cheered.

"Why do you think that, Win?" Her question was matter of fact. It had suddenly become of small import that Sigurd had or had not found them out.

"Sig's been strange lately. There's something screwy! He's acted peculiarly and I know that's not my imagination. Then there's another thing. I've had a feeling I've been followed or watched. Several times I've tried to trap whoever it is but it never works. I took two cabs and two subways getting here today, and I'm positive that the first cab was followed."

"But Win, what for? Who'd follow you? Not Sigurd; you may be sure of that. If he ever did find out I don't know what he'd do, but I do know one thing he wouldn't do; he wouldn't tell a soul. He'd be hurt and humiliated, but he'd never make a scene."

"It's not that alone, Shirley. It's this other business, too. I haven't told you much about it and I don't know how much Sigurd has said. You see, for a while—until this crank announced himself—the police had an absurd notion Martin had been murdered by one of his associates. They poked their noses into our business and asked all sorts of questions. Went so far, even, as to ask everyone to establish his whereabouts on Saturday afternoon. You can see the situation I was in. I hadn't time to concoct anything credible so I simply told them I had been driving all afternoon but declined to tell them who with." He paused. "They finally accepted my statement but, I think, with reservations. I since learned they've been questioning the garage hands. I told the police that if the worst came to the worst I could produce my substantiation. Now that this maniac has come forward I suppose it will all blow over as far as we are concerned, but I'm not sure."

Shirley leaned forward, her eyes burning. She said with child-like naiveté:

"I wish he hadn't! I wish it had been necessary for me to step up and say, 'Winthrop Parness was with me from three o'clock on—'"

"Two-thirty, my dear."

"It was supposed to be two-thirty but I waited almost a half hour."

"Nonsense!"

"All right. 'Winthrop Parness was with me,' I'd say, 'and mostly we were in each other's arms,' I'd be proud of it! That would bring things to a glorious head, wouldn't it? No more evasions! No more of that sickening 'Mr. and Mrs. Peabody.'"

"It would bring them to a head without any doubt, but I'm not sure it would be glorious, my dear. Sigurd would probably do his best to kill me and of course I couldn't blame him. And as for you—!"

"You're wrong, Win. He knows he means nothing to me and hasn't for years. And I am meaning less to him. It's only a question of time before we'll break apart, anyway. Sigurd's fond enough of me, yet, to want to see me happy. If it came out about us his pride would be hurt terribly, but that would be the worst thing. He'd hate you, Win, but he'd never do anything that would make things any more public than necessary."

"Perhaps. Even so, until this is over I think we'll have to take it easy. Whether I like it or not I'm a public character now. Everyone at F. W. Strong will be until this maniac scare is settled. Reporters hound us every time we put our faces out of doors, and stupid, officious police want to tag along wherever we go. It's simply impossible to have any privacy, anyway, and of course I can't go through the antics I did today, to see you, without attracting suspicion."

"Do you think it will be long?"

"Lord! I hope not. I don't relish being possibly a walking target, you know."

"You must be very careful, dear. If anything happened to you, well— But they'll catch him. People don't get away with things like that in this day and age."

"He's gotten away with it twice," Parness reminded.

There was an interruption by the waiter.

Shirley said:

"Poor Mr. Wheeler! I can't help but think of his wife."

"Nor I. I went to see her last evening in the hospital. She's bearing up fairly well but the hideous injustice of it has left her frightfully bitter. She'll be all right financially, though. Did you know her?"

"I've met her once or twice. I remember her as a mousey, inoffensive little person—dowdy clothing—the sort who would know all about making jelly and her children's own clothes. She couldn't have been much of a help to Mr. Wheeler."

"Anthony was contented enough."

"But I mean—in maintaining his social position?"

"He didn't go in for that."

Their meal was finished in due course. A few couples filtered in, and here and there around the room candles sprang into mellow flame but the quiet remained unbroken. Mechanically Parness produced and lighted cigarettes.

"Bob Hood made a peculiar remark this morning," he said. He watched Shirley. She returned his look evenly.

"Yes?"

"We had words. His nerves were on edge and mine weren't too steady. I'd ragged him about one of the girls at the office. He said something about stepping into Sig's office to discuss it, or women, or something of the sort. Do you think he meant anything?"

"Probably not. I've always thought him a very attractive boy."

"What do you know about him?" Parness' crisp question contained more than curiosity.

Shirley shrugged her shoulders.

"Not much. We've had tea and a dance a time or two. He's very sweet; very—impetuous."

"I suppose Sigurd chaperoned these parties?" he added less acidly. "Why have you never mentioned this to me before?"

Shirley was silent for a moment. Parness' ill-concealed annoyance warmed her woman's heart.

"I thought you mightn't understand, Win. I really didn't think much about it at all. It was—oh—a sort of a lark. He's such a big, good-looking boy! It was all quite harmless, Win. You needn't excite yourself."

"Women are all the same," Parness observed maliciously. "You just couldn't resist the temptation. Big, good-looking boy! He's an ill-mannered, self-righteous pup, and dangerously indiscreet. If you take my advice you'll leave him alone."

"All right, Win; let's not quarrel over him. Not today. We shouldn't quarrel over anything today, Win. Must you go back? What about this evening?"

Parness looked at his watch.

"Yes; I must go back. I have a thing or two to attend to early this afternoon. I wish it wasn't necessary. If the stupid flatfeet want to play hide-and-seek with me I'd like to make it fun for them. Will you meet me early this evening—say at half past six?" Parness seemed to have recovered from his ill temper.

"Where, Mr. Peabody?"

"That Argosy place. I'll meet you in the mezzanine."

"Then?"

"Then it will have to be 'auf wiedersehen,' my dear. Now you had better wait here a while. I'll go out first."

Shirley Strong's blood tingled like a school girl's.

15

IS MR. PARNESS' FACE RED!

FENNER TOOK TWO HOURS for lunch—lunch, meditation, a turn up the Avenue, and a most interesting conversation with Johnny Bartlett. When he got back it was almost mid-afternoon.

The incident filled his mind. Bartlett had approached him as he had emerged from a restaurant a safe distance, he had thought, from the Strong Building. The reporter had walked along with him, talking from the corner of his mouth.

"Sorry to be a nuisance and all that, Mr. Fenner—"

"That's one of the inherent characteristics of your calling," Fenner had sighed resignedly.

"Well—fact is, I'm not asking a thing, not now. I've been doing some research!"

Fenner received the announcement without surprise. He looked at the reporter quizzically. The latter produced a small envelope which he handed to Fenner.

"Take a look at these," he urged. "I dug them out of the old sporting files this morning." There were five small clippings dated over the past several years, reporting the results of National Guard marksmanship competitions. In the earlier ones the name of Lieutenant Hood, and in the later ones of Captain Hood, appeared in the pistol shoots—twice at the top, once in second place, and twice third. His name also appeared, though not so well up, in the rifle results.

Fenner glanced at them cursorily.

"Why show these to *me?*"

"Just an idea. I thought you might be interested."

Fenner handed the envelope back.

Bartlett continued: "The Captain went to the armory last night. He cleaned out his locker, packed everything up in a suitcase. Reckon maybe he plans a little absence?"

"You seem inordinately concerned in his affairs. How do you happen to know all this?"

"A little birdie told me. Well, I've got to run up to Morningside Heights and interview one of the doctors on the subject of homicidal manias, or the love-life of the dementia-real estate bondholder. You'll see it: 'CITY'S FOREMOST PSYCHIATRIST DISCUSSES SHORN MURDERS.' Don't forget me at the grand breakopen of this case." He started away but after a few steps turned back and said, "The birdie told me something else. Take your money out of the County Consolidated." Then he was gone.

Fenner revolved the incident in his mind, then put it aside for more leisurely rumination and turned to his papers. His auditors were slowly uncovering a morass of the most fascinatingly obscure chicanery he had been confronted with in many a month. But his interest was scholastic and forced; his mind's eye kept forming the picture of Robert Alanson Hood, 3rd.

When Bryce came in, shortly afterward, Fenner told him of Bartlett's cryptic tip. Bryce became quite excited. "I'll have someone go through Hood's apartment. Shall we give him the works?"

"What's your hurry? If he's *it* your third degree won't mean a thing, and if he isn't you've given your hand away and gained nothing. Why not check up his whereabouts yesterday morning? Then—"

"But yesterday morning he was talking to us right here," Bryce recalled. "He and Judge Spar. We couldn't get them Tuesday evening. Remember?"

"I remember. I also remember that we waited fifteen or twenty minutes for Hood yesterday, and that when he did show up it was after eleven o'clock. I did see him earlier in the morning, though, in Mr. Strong's office."

"How early?"

"Quite early. I'd just come in."

Bryce had suddenly cooled off. He said now:

"Anyway, where would Hood fit in with that letter? He's one of the principal birds this nut will be gunning for. He *sold* the bonds. But I'll keep him covered, just the same."

"What happened to Mr. Leininger?" Fenner suddenly thought to ask.

Bryce snorted in his disgust.

"Nothing yet. I'm afraid that was a bum hunch. He's making his rounds today in Weehawken—in the smelliest laundries in Jersey, Murphy says. I didn't honestly expect much from him but I couldn't pass him up. Funny thing. He actually *is* related to those Leiningers on the list, but not closely."

"In any case," Fenner pointed out, "he couldn't possibly have mailed Shorn's letter in the Grand Central district at eleven o'clock."

A few minutes after four o'clock a call came through for the Inspector. Bryce had scarcely put the receiver to his ear when Fenner saw his face darken. The big black cigar trembled. He listened a moment and then spoke sharply:

"At his real estate office? . . . Yes, I know, Madison above Forty-fifth. I won't be five minutes. Wait unless he starts to beat it. And Quade—don't take any chances. Do you understand? If there's any monkey business plug him and argue afterward."

By degrees Bryce had gotten to his feet while he was talking. He replaced the phone and snapped to Fenner:

"Come along if you like. Quade's spotted a guy following Parness. Been at it since three o'clock this afternoon, but this was Quade's first chance to phone. Parness is up in his office now and this bird's got a cab parked across the street from the entrance."

Fenner reached for his hat.

"Parness?" he exclaimed. "Behrmann or Hood, maybe, but not Parness! Damned if I can understand it, but I wouldn't miss it!"

Bryce paused in the anteroom only long enough to recruit his patrolman on duty there and to shout hurriedly to Miss Purcell:

"Call up Mr. Parness. He's at his office. Talk to him. Tell him to hold the wire. Tell him I want him. Tell him Mr. Strong wants him. Tell him anything, only stall long enough to keep him at his desk for at least five minutes!"

Then they were off.

Shortly before ten o'clock on Friday morning Detective Quade, one of the more erudite members of the Homicide Squad, stepped out of a telephone booth in a soda fountain luncheonette on Lexington Avenue in the upper Sixties. Having learned that Sigurd Strong had arrived and was safely occupied in his office, Quade brushed a few imaginary wrinkles out of his sleeves, straightened his tie, and in five minutes was ringing the bell of the four-story stone town house, just off Park Avenue, of Mr. and Mrs. Strong. No one could have seen the slight flash of recognition exchanged between Quade and a loiterer on the far corner. There was also a patrolman at about the middle of the block.

A mildly surprised butler opened the grilled door. Calls before ten in the morning were usually at the service entrance.

"I'd like to see Mrs. Strong. I believe she's at home."

"Who shall I say is calling?"

"I'm from the Police Department."

The butler backed away.

"You may have to wait a few moments. Mrs. Strong hasn't come down yet. You had better step inside."

Quade passed through a small marble vestibule into a reception hall and sat down. The butler disappeared up a broad staircase and presently Quade heard faintly his distant voice somewhere in the upper floors. Quade collected his thoughts. This was not an assignment he would have chosen. Bryce had simply ordered:

"Go up there and talk to Mrs. Strong. Use your head. No sense in upsetting any apple carts, but find out about Parness on Saturday, and anything else you can."

The affair the preceding afternoon had been almost farcical, Quade reflected. He'd been shadowing Parness. Before noon Parness had given him the slip, whether deliberately or not Quade was not sure. Quade had gone to the restaurant Parness usually used on the chance of picking him up there. He had noticed a man loitering across the street. Later when Parness had returned Quade had noticed the same fellow outside the real estate office. There was no mistaking him. It hadn't taken long to discover that the other man also was following Parness. They had had a merry chase, Parness innocently progressing from his office to his tailor's, thence to the Romaine Hotel, thence back to his office, with the stranger carefully in his wake and himself, Quade, more carefully bringing up the rear.

At the last stop the man had obtained a cab in which he had waited across the street from the building containing Parness' office. Quade, envisaging another possible assassination upon Parness' emergence, had hastily called Bryce. Then he had posted himself in an adjoining store door, tense and ready for action. In almost no time the squad car with Bryce and Fenner and the third detective had rolled around the corner. They had leaped out, guns drawn, and had descended from both sides upon the cab's bewildered driver and the equally startled fare. Quade's practiced hands had quickly slid over the latter and brought forth a service revolver from a hip holster. Quade, Bryce and Fenner had climbed in, the third man had joined the driver, and, before two or three astonished passers-by could form even the nucleus of a crowd, the cab had whisked away, the squad car trailing it.

"Police Headquarters," Bryce had snapped.

The prisoner had recovered himself enough to say: "O.K. with me, Chief, but it ain't necessary. If you was to go around to my boss, now, you'd save some time."

"What's your game?"

"Same as yours, only not official. I work for the Mawson Agency." He had produced a shield, a wallet with his picture, and other identifying material.

"What were you doing tailing Mr. Parness?"

"You better talk to the boss. I only do what he says. This time he says, 'Get on Mr. Parness and stay on him!' Another lad an' me been at it since Monday."

Convinced, Bryce had directed the driver to proceed to the Mawson Agency. The department knew of them, Quade remembered. Their reputation was fair enough, though their operatives on one or two occasions had been involved in some rather unsavory divorce proceedings.

The talk had been brief and to the point. Mr. Mawson had explained in a very few words that he had been retained by Mr. Sigurd Strong, who evidently was suspicious of Mr. Parness' relations with Mrs. Strong. The case had been taken on Monday. At first no effort had been made to keep Parness under continual surveillance, Mawson's men usually keeping track of him at noon and from the end of business hours until he seemed 'put away for the night.' Parness had acted suspiciously on Thursday noon and had, Mawson thought, deliberately eluded them, so they had tightened up their watch. That was all.

Bryce had waited suggestively and had finally been compelled to ask:

"And how about it?"

"About what?"

"Was Mr. Strong right?"

"I'm afraid that's a matter I can discuss only with Mr. Strong."

Bryce had thought that over a little while and had said:

"All right. Now do you read the papers?"

"Of course."

"Well then, you ought to have realized you were playing with fire when you put anyone on an F. W. Strong director at this time. It wouldn't have been surprising if that lad of yours had gotten filled full of holes first and talked to afterward. Those are the orders the police now have."

"I thought of that and cautioned them. What more could I do?"

"You might have tipped us off."

"You know I couldn't have done that."

The Inspector had only shrugged his shoulders. He and Fenner had instantly concluded that it might be that Mrs. Strong was involved in Parness' peculiar alibi story for Saturday afternoon. They had debated for a moment whether, in view of the "Shorn" letters and the fact that the case now appeared to be a maniac hunt, it was any longer worth their while to check up alibis, but had decided to play safe, and Bryce had detailed Quade to interview Mrs. Strong. So now Quade waited, his hat on his knees and his eyes casting about the luxuriously furnished house.

After about fifteen minutes Shirley Strong came down, descending the carpeted stairway with a rapidity and lightness unusual in one even of her youthful appearance. Quade got up. His drawing-room manner, when he needed it, left little to be desired.

"Oliver said you're from the police?"

"Yes; that's right. Name's Quade, Miss—Mrs. Strong? I'm talking to Mrs. Strong, am I not?" His face registered flattering surprise.

"We've been horribly upset by all this. I'm sorry to have kept you waiting. What is it that you want?"

Quade looked over her shoulder into the drawing room, then glanced around.

"Could we talk somewhere, undisturbed? I won't take any longer than necessary."

"Surely." She led him into the drawing room and indicated a divan, seating herself in a chair at one end of it. She offered Quade a cigarette which he declined, lighted one for herself, and waited, curious. Quade put his hat down beside him.

"There are a few questions I must ask you," he began. "Of course, you understand that this is in the strictest confidence. You needn't worry that anything you tell me will pass beyond official lips, and of course we prefer that you repeat nothing, either."

"Yes; of course."

"We are faced with the necessity of checking up certain things— the whereabouts of certain individuals at certain times. Now we've run across one or two things that lead us to believe you may be able to help us."

Shirley Strong's heart sank. Suddenly she knew what was coming. She concealed her confusion and said:

"Mr. Strong told me even he had been questioned. I suppose it's all quite necessary, though I don't know what I can tell you that he can't."

Quade said, intending no malice:

"I guess there are a few things." He leaned over his knees and looked up at her. "We'd like to know where Mr. Parness was last Saturday afternoon."

"Mr. Parness! Why do you ask me?" She tried to look angry and haughty but the effort was less than successful.

"We thought you might know."

Shirley Strong was silent for a long moment. Apparently Winthrop's misgivings had been well founded. She realized that she must know for sure and returned Quade's searching gaze coolly.

"This is just between you and me," he urged. "You must realize that this inquiry is a serious thing. I'm sorry, but I'm afraid that people's feelings aren't going to be considered very much. Now if you're frank with me I'll see to it that as little of what you tell me passes my lips as is humanly possible."

Shirley's lips formed what was intended for a winning smile.

"I suppose you don't intend to insinuate anything, but you certainly sound as if you do. Well, Mr. Parness and I were driving— it's the sort of thing that could be easily misunderstood. Now do you mind telling me how you happened to come to me?"

"We'll get to that later. What time did you leave Mr. Parness and where?"

"He dropped me at Lord's—about five-thirty."

"When did you start driving? That is, when did you meet Mr. Parness?"

"He called for me at—rather, I met him about three. No; I think it was earlier—say about half past two."

"Where?"

Shirley hesitated.

"On Central Park West near Columbus Circle. I'd been walking in the park."

"Thank you. Now yesterday? Did you see Mr. Parness at any time yesterday or Wednesday?"

"Isn't this going rather far?" Mrs. Strong seemed about to rise. "I'm sure I want to help the police in any way I can, and Mr. Parness, too, but your attitude seems very presumptuous."

Quade became artfully humble.

"I don't intend to be, though I suppose it *does* sound that way. You see, we have to take advantage of any information that comes our way, regardless of its source, so long as it's reasonably on the level. How about yesterday, Mrs. Strong? Did you see him yesterday?"

"As a matter of fact, I did; but what is the point of this inquisition, anyway?"

"You did see him yesterday—and Wednesday?"

"We had lunch together yesterday. Mr. Parness left me about one-thirty. Why?"

"And you didn't see him again?"

Shirley paused. She had waited at their rendezvous at the Argosy for two endless hours the evening before, but Parness had failed to put in an appearance. Her early anger had given way first to bewilderment, then to despair. But she could hardly tell Quade all that. She summoned all of her poise and replied evenly and crisply:

"No; I did not."

"Did Mr. Parness mention where he had been on Wednesday morning?"

"I don't remember. I don't think so."

The rapid barrage of questions had partially robbed her of her wits. When Quade got up she remembered her purpose. She remained seated and reached for a table cigarette box. Once again she offered them to Quade and again he declined.

"Won't you sit down a moment? I've been very frank with you. Won't you be fair enough to tell me how you happened to come to me?"

"I'm afraid I can't very well do that."

"You can't do that! I'm sure I can't understand why not." She got up angrily, her eyes alight with the sudden gust of temper.

Quade relented. Some rough chivalrous instinct asserted itself. She was nice! It was easy to understand her cheating on an old horse like Sigurd Strong. She was too nice! At least too nice for a tailor dummy like Parness. And she *was* in a spot. If he tipped her off maybe she'd watch her step. Maybe she'd get a better break when the old boy clamped down on her. He said:

"I can tell you this much—someone's checking up on Mr. Parness and—and—"

"And me. Go on."

"Yes, and it isn't the police."

Shirley's face whitened but she retained her composure while she led him to the door. Quade faced her in the small vestibule. On the tip of his tongue was a friendly reassurance. He wanted to say, "Don't worry, little lady. It'll all come out in the wash!" But he forced himself to adhere to his role and said, instead, "Thank you, Madam; and please be assured that you may rely on the Department's and my personal utmost discretion."

Shirley turned back to the drawing room. She picked up the cigarette she had laid down and shook off the long ash. She had been so absorbed in her own predicament she had not quite gathered the other implications of Quade's questions. Now they suddenly sank in upon her and left her aghast. She ran to the window. It was too late; Quade had disappeared up the street.

Was it possible that they suspected—she could hardly formulate the awful thought into definite words in her own mind—that Winthrop had anything to do with the "Shorn" killings! It was too utterly grotesque. But of course not. Why, they'd questioned Sigurd, too, and everyone else. It was a mere formality. The wave of relief was short-lived. They'd wanted badly to know about Winthrop on Saturday and Wednesday. ". . . did he mention where he'd been on Wednesday morning?" She sank to the divan trembling.

She knew, of course, all of the details of the "Shorn" killings. Saturday—Wednesday. Her mind leaped from event to event. Tiny, horrible doubts obtruded themselves. She could not keep them down. Yet it was so impossibly absurd. She ran upstairs to her room, threw herself upon the bed and tried to think clearly, but was unable to focus her thoughts. She felt alone, utterly, and realized suddenly that she must see Abraham Behrmann. He was Sigurd's best friend but he was also her best friend. Nothing had ever been said, but there had always been a subtle understanding between them, something deep-seated and impersonal, something racial. It had to do, she sensed vaguely, with their common lowly origin. When she had first known Behrmann in the early days of her marriage to Sigurd, they had talked of many things but seldom of themselves, and yet, without words, Behrmann had conveyed a definite sense of understanding her. "You are an aspiring Jewess. You are young. You are beautiful and you know it! You do not love Sigurd but he is a means to your ends. It is human to be ambitious and we can only use the weapons God has given us. Sigurd is my friend; hurt him as little as you can."

Now Shirley felt she must see him. Perhaps she would tell him everything. It would be good to unburden her soul. He would be angry about Winthrop, but he would understand, and presently he would counsel her wisely.

She must talk to Winthrop, too. The doubts suddenly vanished but, illogically, she felt she must warn him. She reached for the bedside telephone and called Parness' office. She was told that Mr. Parness was at the F. W. Strong Building. Shirley hesitated for a long time. There were the switchboard girls. They knew her voice; she'd called Sigurd often. They might talk. And what if Sigurd should be in Winthrop's office—what if he should pick up the telephone and answer it? Just the thought made her go suddenly cold.

Abruptly wading through her doubts and fears she clicked the receiver bracket impatiently and called the Strong number. She altered her voice and asked for Mr. Parness. Almost instantly he acknowledged the call, suave and businesslike.

"Parness speaking."

The sound of his voice came as a sudden shock to Shirley. She seemed to be talking to a stranger. The whole affair seemed suddenly fantastic and unreal, and she felt a little irrelevant impulse to laugh at his crispness, but the detachment was gone in an instant.

"Win—I have to see you. Right away!"

"Please say nothing. It was very unwise of you to call here." His quick positiveness frightened her. Parness was, if anything, ever polite. Perhaps he was not alone.

"You needn't talk, Win. But meet me. Come to Peabody's this afternoon. I have to—"

"The wire, my dear!" Parness impatiently cut in. "Besides, it's quite impossible."

"But you must, Win! I tell you, it's important!" He cut in again hastily:

"I'll try. About three—perhaps before. Good-by!" The receiver clicked in her ear.

She replaced the telephone, feeling fresh misgivings. She hadn't thought so seriously of the wire. Still, she hadn't said anything, hadn't once mentioned her own name, nor had he. She got up and moved about the room, her thoughts darting about for something to occupy her during the long hours until afternoon should come.

16

FENNER DOES HIS SUMS

WHILE QUADE AND SHIRLEY STRONG were having their tête-à-tête in Mr. Strong's town house, Inspector Bryce and Fenner in the Strong Building were comparing notes.

"Did you talk to Strong yet this morning?" Fenner asked the question.

"Not yet, but I will."

"Going to say anything about last evening?"

"I think I will. Mawson's probably told him already. He'd be bound to. Jeez! That was a hot angle, wasn't it! Imagine old Strong with that thing under his skin all this time. He hasn't shown it, talking to Parness, has he?"

"What will you tell him?"

"I won't tell him anything, but I'll advise him to call Mawson off—at least for the present."

"What about Parness?"

"What about him?"

"You'll have to say something to him. Miss Purcell told me she stalled him along on the telephone for about five minutes as you asked her, and that he got so annoyed that she had to explain that you'd ordered her to do it."

"I'll take care of him. I'll tell him it was a false alarm." The Inspector obviously considered Mr. Parness' annoyance a matter of small moment. Suddenly he remembered something. "Did you hear the latest? Your little journalistic pal was right!"

"About the County Consolidated? Yes. I heard that the Banking and Insurance Department took them over this morning. Any excitement?"

"Not much. A run started before opening time. The line was a block and a half long. They've apparently been expecting it. Instead of opening at nine o'clock they plastered a notice on the door. The people growled a little, but they behaved pretty well. They're getting sort of used to it now, and don't get so much upset."

"I'm afraid so." Fenner's smile was grim.

"How the devil did Bartlett get that ahead of time?"

"He's got a nose for news and enough nerve to stick it anywhere," Fenner explained.

"He'll get it knocked off some day. I suppose you can't blame a guy for making a living, and that's his job; but, Max, there's something about that bird that I don't like."

Fenner raised his eyebrows but made no reply. He leafed through a fresh pile of reports his auditors had left for him and casually remarked:

"In a matter of another day or two Mr. Strong and I and some of the other gentlemen around here, if there are any left, are going to have a session. It's going to be embarrassing for someone to explain where all the income from the properties they've been managing for the last eighteen months has gone. They'll probably try to hang it on Hoyle, and maybe they can. When Horton's crowd catches up to this, and it won't be long now, he'll be screaming for indictments. He'll get them, too."

"Doesn't any of it point anywhere?" Bryce asked anxiously.

Fenner did not reply at once and Bryce insisted:

"I think you're holding out on me. Last night when Quade telephoned about Parness you made a crack that I haven't forgotten."

"What was that?"

"You seemed surprised that anyone should be out for Parness. You said, 'Behrmann or Hood, maybe; but not Parness!'"

"Did I!" Fenner's surprise was almost convincing.

"I know you'll spill it in your own good time, but why not work together?"

"That was just a slip—out of my subconscious mind, perhaps. I've been toying with several ideas, too nebulous yet to be even called theories. I've found from experience that I'm sometimes given to going off halfcocked, so in guarding against that tendency I sometimes lean too far the other way. I've had only a few of the foggiest notions, so far, and this letter of Shorn's has pretty well knocked even those galley west. Did you find out any more about the Captain yet?"

"Two men are going through his apartment today."

"It's just as well. Perhaps we're falling for something, Inspector."

"What d'y' mean?"

"Maybe Shorn's letter is a decoy. Maybe someone found that your boys tailing him around cramped his style. Are our friends here still covered?"

"Not exactly. I had to yank some of the boys off after we got the letter."

"Precisely. Maybe that's what the letter was for. Where's Parness now?"

"He's here. At least, he was in his office when I came by. Parker was in there with him. This is a fine place for a banker the morning his bank goes bust! But Parness'll stick around all right, if only to find out about last night."

The telephone jangled. Fenner shoved the instrument toward Bryce. Nine out of ten calls were for him. It was Quade, fresh from his talk with Shirley Strong. The Inspector listened to his report. He made one or two monosyllabic replies, hung up and turned to Fenner.

"Parness picked up Mrs. Strong about half past two Saturday on Central Park West. They were together until half past five. She didn't see him at all Wednesday. She had lunch with him Thursday, though, and he left her about half past one. That almost lets him out for Saturday, doesn't it?"

"It might. If he got his car in East Forty-fourth Street after two and picked up Mrs. Strong at two-thirty on Central Park West, with the Saturday afternoon traffic to contend with, he wouldn't have much time left over, would he? But he might have had enough to make a stop here. This wouldn't be out of his way. So there you are; like every other one of these alibis, so confounded loose!"

The Inspector stepped into Strong's office long enough to exchange a few words with him. He found Behrmann there. The words were brief and to the point—two simultaneous "Good morning, Inspector"s while two pairs of anxious eyes, raised curiously, met him.

"Good morning!"

"Anything new?" from Strong.

"Nothing much. Parness gave us a scare. One of the boys thought someone was following him." He gave Strong a meaning look. "We grabbed the fellow, but it turned out to be a false alarm."

"Mawson told me." Strong thus chose to ignore Behrmann's presence.

Bryce did that, too.

"I'd call him off for a few days."

"I did."

Bryce left some instructions with the staff of plain clothesmen assigned to protect the Strong personnel, then went out.

A few moments after the Inspector's departure Fenner, too, got to his feet. He stretched himself, gazed out of the window for a moment, then sauntered into the corridor. The door to Spar's office was closed. Fenner listened a moment, then tried it. The door was unlocked but the office was empty. He closed it without entering and passed on. Parker's office door stood open but that office, too, was deserted, though a hat and a folded newspaper lay on the desk.

He passed on to the next. It, too, stood open. Parness was at his desk; Parker lounged near by. The telephone buzzed as Fenner entered. Parness answered it. He appeared irritated and spoke in a low tone, his mouth close to the transmitter. Fenner waited near the door until Parness had finished but he could not help overhearing a few snatches of Parness' conversation. ". . . besides, it's quite impossible! . . . I'll try—about three, perhaps before. . . ."

Parker glanced at his watch, nodded to Fenner, and, with a curt wave to Parness as the latter finished his telephone conversation, left the office. Upon the desk there lay a jumble of canceled checks and several bank statements which Parness evidently had been going over.

"Trying to figure out where it all went, I suppose?" Fenner ventured.

"That's the general idea," Parness replied agreeably. "Unless I check up once in a while I can't believe that my money goes so fast, and I'm tempted to write the bank nasty letters." He snapped open a cigarette case and held it out to Fenner, who accepted one and in return offered a light.

"Anything new or startling?" Parness asked after a moment of uncertain silence.

"Very little. I, too, have been wondering where money goes, except that in my case it's not my own money. Perhaps you can enlighten me—give me some advance dope, so to speak."

"Advance dope?"

"Yes; in advance of a general inquiry. That's one of the questions that will be brought up at a little get-together I shall have to ask Mr. Strong to arrange—where all of the money went that has been received from the properties F. W. Strong has been operating."

"You're in the wrong pew. You see, many of the properties you refer to were formerly managed by White, Wheeler, Parness and McClintock. Having defaulted and having been taken over for the benefit of the bondholders it would hardly do for the same inefficient, unskillful management to be continued, would it? At least that was the very profound judgment of the majority of the board on each occasion when property was recovered." Parness was bitterly sarcastic. "Of course Mr. Wheeler and myself had no choice but to acquiesce, which we did as graciously as we could. Subsequent events have abundantly proved that, as usual, the majority of the board were in error. The matter is by tacit agreement no longer discussed around here."

"What do you mean?"

"If those properties were 'ineptly' managed by us—that is, by Mr. Wheeler and myself—then there aren't words to describe the bungling administration of them since. Frankly, I'm not sorry I'm clear of it."

"Did Mr. Wheeler concur in your opinion?"

"Naturally, only Mr. Wheeler had a less generous term than 'bungling' for it."

Fenner was silent for a moment, turning over these revelations in his mind. There was nothing new in their content, his auditors having arrived at the same conclusions in terms of dollars and cents, but the fact that they should come to him in this wise from Winthrop Parness was more than puzzling. He tried fitting the circumstance into the pattern of his theory about Shorn. Presently he observed philosophically:

"There's little that can be done about it now." Parness said drily:

"Horton will get the next crack at managing them. It will be amusing to see what he can do."

After his illuminating conversation with Mr. Parness—illuminating not so much in the sense that Fenner learned anything he did not already suspect as in the sense that Parness should gratuitously unbend with so much information—Fenner returned to Hoyle's room and once again attacked the ever accumulating maze of reports and audits. At frequent intervals he stopped to lean back and study for long periods the perfectly blank ceiling. Bryce, coming in shortly after noon, found him so occupied, his eyes half closed.

"Taking a little ease, Max?"

"Somewhat—and you?"

Bryce snorted general disgust.

Fenner rocked forward and got up. "Wait a minute," he said. He stepped to the door and locked it, then started in upon five minutes of what at first appeared to be the most peculiar gymnastics imaginable. Standing upon a small chair which he dragged about the room with him, he looked behind the pictures, examined the wall ventilation grating and peered at the transom and wall light fixtures. Then he stooped to inspect the area beneath the desk, crawled about lifting the carpet at its edges, and searched the wardrobe. Finally he stood up and dusted off his hands.

"Looking for a mike, huh?" Bryce correctly surmised. "What's up?"

"Yes. I can't say I really expected one, but I wouldn't have been surprised. I've been thinking about that letter. You see, it absolutely must have been written by someone from right around here."

"Huh! Why so?"

"I've been doing a little adding machine work. Of the bonds issued by this outfit in the last few years do you know how many are in default?"

Bryce was bewildered.

"How many? Why do you ask?"

"Exactly three-hundred-thirty-five million, seven-hundred-fifty thousand dollars' worth."

"Well?"

"That's what Shorn makes it, too. It's only a simple problem of addition, but you *do* have to know what to add. How did he find out?"

Bryce's face fell.

"Is that all? Why, that's all a matter of public record, isn't it?"

"In a way it is, but the various court actions are widely separated. For anyone to whom the Strong Company's records are not available to assemble all of the default data would be an impossible, or at least improbable task. For them to come out to the exact dollar would be phenomenal."

Bryce thought it over.

"It's an angle, all right. We'll begin where we left off. You think it's someone important here? Maybe one of the minor employees got stuck bad."

"That's hard to say. My hunch would be that anyone with the imagination and resourcefulness this chap has demonstrated wouldn't stay a minor employee very long anywhere."

"We'll start at the top and work down."

"You'll have to haul out the velvet gloves again. The chap you're looking for will have a perfect alibi for each of these occasions. You may depend on that—and for any future occasions, too. You can nurse this scare along and put on an ostensible night and day search for a maniac and do your real work behind the screen of that."

Bryce thought some more. He speculated presently, to himself as much as to Fenner:

"Well, now, if it's what you say—a sort of inside job, you might call it—what's it for? What's the motive? It's a cinch no one around here would be all hot and bothered about the poor investors; so if that's a stall then what's the real game?"

"That's anybody's guess so far."

"Yeah; well, what's your guess?"

"I haven't made any, and can't yet." Fenner definitely changed the subject. "I do think we ought to get everyone covered again pronto! How about the alibis for Saturday and Wednesday?"

"They're filling in. I've worked a couple of the boys in as part of Horton's crew. They mix well and have been getting acquainted with the Strong lesser fry. They're finding out a little for me already and ought to produce more as they get rooted in." Bryce produced his notebook as he spoke. "Saturday's out; none of the alibis are worth a damn except maybe Parness', which looked lousiest of all at first. Now with Mrs. Strong in the picture he looks O.K.

"Now for Wednesday morning. Take Hood first. We talked to him Wednesday right after eleven and you saw him earlier in the morning. No one remembers him coming or going, so presumably he was here all the time, but no one can definitely say that, either, so he's still in the running."

"Very definitely."

Fenner drew out his gold pencil and twirled it absently. He reached for a pad of foolscap and began jotting down notes. Bryce paused to let him catch up. The sight of the twirling pencil oddly heartened him. Its mellow gleam, flashing absently, was a familiar adjunct to Fenner's most brilliant streaks of ratiocination.

As an after thought Bryce added:

"There was nothing in Hood's apartment, though. We took the place apart inch by inch." He turned over a page. "Now Mr. Strong appears to have been in and out of the building on Wednesday a number of times, so until we get something more definite we can't say he's out. Mr. Parker has been tied up at his bank pretty steadily but when we dig into that we find it doesn't mean so much either.

In the mornings he arrives anywhere from nine to eleven. He's back and forth to this place and that, to the State Building—I guess the Banking Department has been riding him pretty hard lately—and all around the town." The Inspector paused to interject, "You know, Max; all of this could be done so much more easily and thoroughly if we could just yank 'em up on the carpet and ask questions."

"And scare half of them into the next state or Canada."

"I suppose it's better not to."

"Not yet, at least," Fenner conceded.

"Now see what you think of this: Mr. Behrmann was out, presumably with Judge Spar, on Wednesday morning. He has apparently made a point of mentioning that fact."

"Where's he now?"

"He's in his office tending to business. Don't worry; he's plenty covered now. Judge Spar was talking to us a good part of Wednesday morning so Behrmann couldn't have been out with him at that time, so I figured he'd bear some watching."

"Perhaps."

"I've inquired a little about Mr. Horton, too, but he seems to have been pretty steadily chained to his desk; and as for the minor employees,—well, it isn't possible to make a one hundred percent check in this time but they all seem on the up-and-up, and they all seem to have been tending their own knitting. They don't have the leeway to come and go like these bigger fellows."

"The general uncertainty would make them more careful, anyway."

"There's the whole works, except Parness. He's only here an hour or two each day. He wasn't here until late afternoon on Wednesday, and wasn't at his real estate office until almost noon."

"He called Strong from there when he heard about Wheeler, but that wasn't until half past eleven," Fenner pointed out wearily. "I suppose your men have been as thorough as they dared but it seems to me that the principal thing we've found out is how *little* we know." He looked at his pad and drew a few heavy lines so that the result stood out in tabular form as follows:

	Saturday P.M.	*Wednesday* A.M.
Parness	. . . E. 44th St. 2:00 P.M. Central Pk. W. 2:30 P. M.	?
Hood	. . . . Drunk ? ? ?	Office (*presumably*) ?
Strong	. . . Club with Behrmann)	In and out of office.?
Behrmann	. Club with Strong) ??	With Spar ? ?
Parker	. . . Bank, then home, D. L. & W. ? ?	Bank (Maybe) ?
Judge Spar	. Football Game ? ?	*Here with us.*

"No one's eliminated except Spar. There seems to be no doubt about him," Fenner commented. "Where's Parness now? An hour ago he was in his office balancing his checking accounts."

"He was there when I came by. I guess he'll stay until he gets a chance to get the low-down on last night." Bryce suddenly got to his feet. "I'll see you later in the day. I'll have to get the boys back on the job again, though God knows where I'll get the men! The Deputy Commish is squawking like a stuck pig now. I won't have to cover the Judge, anyway. That'll save a couple."

17

JUDGE SPAR GETS SOME FRESH AIR

Somewhat later that day, Friday, Judge Francis Fenwick Spar paused and his eyes swept down over the small pond of blank, up-turned faces. It was almost three o'clock of an overcast afternoon. The occasion was the laying of the cornerstone of the new Federal Court Building. A speaker's platform had been hastily constructed at the corner of a yawning excavation. The foundations were not yet ready for a cornerstone but it was urgent that the ceremony be consummated before the end of the term of the administration, soon to go out of office, so that certain incumbents would have the pleasure of seeing their names go down to posterity, cut in ever-lasting granite.

The stand held representatives of the city and federal governments, the architects and engineers, the contractors, the Bar Association and Tammany Hall. Judge Spar, who was making the final of the dedicatory orations, was qualified to represent either of the last two. Spar's flat voice, multiplied and deepened by three very effective amplifiers, boomed to a sonorous conclusion: " . . . and so, fellow citizens, as we dedicate this temple of the law, as we lay this first stone in a noble monument consecrated to the principles of justice and equity and order, it is appropriate that we recall the words of that earlier great American law-giver—" Spar glanced hastily at his notes—"this government of the people, by the people, and for the people, shall not perish from the earth!"

When it was apparent that he had finished, a desultory ripple of applause ran through the audience, seated down before the platform on several hundred folding chairs rented from a funeral parlor for the occasion, or standing in crowds in the rear. The clapping was sufficient to obliterate the few snickers and guffaws and here and there an "Imagine dragging that one out!" or "Lincoln'd turn over in his grave!" Hands politely covered yawns and the people shifted with mild impatience. The band, brought up from Governor's Island, arranged their instruments and prepared for action.

Judge Spar looked to his companions on the stand for a cue, and one of the architects, acting as master of ceremonies, got up and led the group to the cornerstone pier. A lead box filled with documents and pertinent paraphernalia for the curious scrutiny of whatever descendants would ultimately demolish the structure, was already in place in a recess in the concrete. The heavy granite cornerstone block swung ponderously overhead. Two stone setters, self conscious in immaculate white overalls, new for the event, stood by with their mortar pan prepared. Judge Spar was handed a silver trowel which he dipped gingerly into the mortar. He stood, slightly flustered, holding the alien object awkwardly while reporters photographed him and the news-reel cameramen ground away. Then he turned around and shook a dab of mortar on the broad base course, spreading it daintily as if he was adding mayonnaise to a salad. He stepped out of the way and the two masons, with neat gobs of mortar slung deftly into a smooth layer, quickly finished the job. One of them drew back and signaled the hoist operator. The massive stone was slowly lowered and the two men guided it into place.

As it reached its bed the band with a tremendous blare broke into "The Star Spangled Banner." There was a general commotion and everyone stood up. Judge Spar took a place by the rail, benignly looking out over the audience. He made a splendid picture with his erect figure, his snowy hair slightly ruffled by the breeze, his florid face held to a sober sternness. His black, old-fashioned cravat was set off neatly by the white piping on his waistcoat, and his silk top hat he held reverently over his heart.

It was a gray day and the wind blowing across the open square from the grim prison buildings at Center Street held promise of the first snowfall of an early winter. Judge Spar felt the bunting on the railings ripple against his legs; from the corners of his eyes he saw the flags at each end of the platform flap idly and then flutter out from the poles. He felt the cold blast on his brow and hoped it didn't bring a recurrence of his sinus trouble.

Would the band never finish? The Judge thought smugly of his speech. It hadn't been half bad. There had been some rumors of possible Communist disturbances and a score of police idled in the rear of the crowd, standing first on one foot and then on the other, unneeded but available for an emergency. The Judge hoped the Reds had noted his remarks about law and order.

His eyes swept up. From one side the Grecian façade of the County Court house, ageless in its noble simplicity and dignity, austerely overlooked the square. Carved in letters two feet high across the entablature superimposed over the row of tall Ionic columns, he read: THE TRUE ADMINISTRATION OF JUSTICE IS THE FIRMEST PILLAR OF GOOD GOVERNMENT. The inscription was ninety feet long. He reread it and wished that he had noticed it before; he could very well have referred to it in his speech.

Spar felt sleepy. The wind, he thought. It always affected him that way. ". . . the la-a-nd—of—the—free-ee And the ho-o-me—of—" The words involuntarily trouped through the corridors of the Judge's brain as the band approached the hymn's crescendo finish. But suddenly the procession stopped. Judge Spar's train of thought stopped. The wind on his florid brow stopped fanning. The interruption was the voice of Winthrop Parness over his shoulder saying, "I move we adjourn. Come along, Francis."

Spar was mildly surprised. Earlier in the day he had invited Parness to come to the ceremony, but Parness had doubted that he would be able to arrange it. Spar had not before noticed him among the group on the speakers' stand. Vaguely the Judge noticed that Parness was bareheaded. He waited a second until the final strains of the anthem died and then turned to reply, but Parness was not to be seen. The judge blinked and his eyes darted about the platform.

Parness was certainly not among those present, equally certainly no one had left. Confounded, the Judge turned back to the rail, reluctantly concluding that his imagination had been playing tricks on him, but so vivid and so real had the illusion been that the Judge was left uncertain of mind and momentarily shaky. Suddenly it swept upon him that something was very wrong. The impression was so strong and clear that it was as if the wind in a renewed icy blast had swept quite through the frock coat and white piped vest, penetrating to the very marrow of his frame and striking him with an extraordinary terror.

Recovering himself with an effort he looked nervously at his associates milling about preparing to leave the platform. There was back-slapping and hand-shaking. One, a fellow lawyer whom he knew also to be acquainted with Parness, approached and spoke to Spar:

"It's been a pleasure to have seen you again, Judge. Splendid address you gave them. In fact, the whole program went off rather nicely, don't you think?"

"Thank you. Yes; I suppose so. I'm afraid I wasn't much of a mason." The Judge chuckled and added, "By the way, did you see Mr. Parness here? I thought I glimpsed him on the platform but he seems to have gone."

"Parness? I didn't see him. I didn't know he had been here. Are you sure?"

Spar mumbled a reply and turned away, convinced but still puzzled.

The end of the hymn had signaled the end of the ceremony and the crowd, herded good-naturedly by the "city's finest," dispersed and filtered away across Foley Square.

18

MR. PARNESS KEEPS ANOTHER DATE

INSPECTOR BRYCE SLIPPED AWAY from the obscure post he had occupied at the rear of the audience during the cornerstone ceremonies. He had, he told himself laconically, always been fond of band music, which fact alone prevented the hour and a half period from having been a total loss.

The Inspector in coming to the meeting had obeyed a hunch. The affair had been scheduled to be something of a momentary focal point for the activities of the group he was studying as, according to the grapevine intelligence he had grafted into the Strong office, almost all of the executives had expected to be there. As it developed the Judge was the only F. W. Strong representative present, and his behavior had been exemplary. In Bryce's experience hunches had sometimes proved very much worth while; at other times they had represented just so much lost effort. This particular afternoon Bryce included in the latter category, but he was philosophic about it. The hunches averaged up; that was enough. He would always play them.

The Inspector had come to watch and listen and speculate. There had been only the Judge to watch, which had been fruitless enough; and dull speeches to hear, which he hadn't listened to, being occupied with his speculations. Mostly Winthrop Parness was on his mind, which puzzled the Inspector, because, more from instinct than for any reason, he had almost abandoned Parness as a suspect. Parness and Shirley Strong between them added districting elements that complicated the whole picture. And of

364

course there was still the insurance angle as far as the murder of Wheeler was concerned; and somewhere there entered in Sigurd Strong with his unsuspected knowledge of his spouse's infidelity.

At Headquarters his pique was heightened by a message from Quade, who had been reassigned to Parness at noon, to the effect that Parness had again eluded him, this time by leaving his club through a service entrance shortly after lunch. He had not yet been found. So on his way uptown the Inspector felt the increasing necessity for early and plain words with Winthrop Parness, not so much to incriminate him as to eliminate him and by so much to clarify the picture.

At Strong's he found Fenner still at the desk but its top was now quite clear. Fenner looked up at him half absently, obviously collecting his thoughts from a distance. He leaned back and clasped his hands behind his head. Bryce only mouthed his cigar, grunted a greeting and moved to the window.

"I take it from your thoroughly satisfied look and your voluble communicativeness that your afternoon has been a profitable one—no?"

"Nobody showed up."

"'Whom had you expected?"

"All of them. Parness, Behrmann, Old Man Strong—even Hood told the Judge he might be down. But his Honor was all alone as far as this outfit's concerned."

"Poor support, I calls it! It's funny, though, because they haven't been around here. The place has been like a morgue all afternoon. Maybe they're getting gun shy and hiding out. Did you get the cornerstone all laid?"

"All laid, speeches made, and everybody happy."

"Wasn't Behrmann down there? He left to go there."

"Didn't see him. Didn't see anyone from here. Parness been in?"

"Not that I know of. Why?"

"So he didn't wait to find out about last evening after all. I'd like to talk to him. That's all. He's been on my mind."

"Why I thought you'd more or less dropped him. His affairs with the skipper's better half account pretty well for his stubbornness about Saturday."

"Even so, he's always ducking away somewhere. He's not on the level. He knows we're watching him and makes it plenty hard. I heard from Quade half an hour ago. He lost Parness at his club this noon and hasn't seen him since. Four or five of the boys are trying now to pick him up but they've had no luck or I would have heard. What does he do? Where does he slip off to?"

"I should think the answer to that would be fairly obvious. Yesterday they were lunching."

Without replying Bryce picked up the telephone. He thumbed through his notebook, called a number and asked for a Mr. Flanagan. He turned to Fenner while he waited. "Flanagan's on guard duty in Strong's house until this scare blows over." From Flanagan the Inspector learned that everything was quiet in the Strong household, that Mrs. Strong was at home alone, that a half hour earlier she had taken a book to her boudoir, that no longer than ten minutes before he had heard her speaking to the maid. "So this is one time when the answer's *not* so obvious," Bryce had concluded to Fenner after repeating Flanagan's information.

Fenner rocked forward in his chair, now more interested.

"He slipped you at noon? And four or five of your men have been looking for him since? And he's not with the girl friend? This is something else again! I should say that some sort of action is indicated."

"Some sort of action" consisted of setting quiet police wheels in motion that quickly re-canvassed all Parness' known haunts and established watches at all the city's terminals. After a half hour of hovering over wires, the net result of which was no trace of Winthrop Parness himself and the negative bit of information that Parness' car was in the garage and had not been used that day, Fenner and Bryce left Strong's for the Mawson Agency on the chance that their operatives might have, during their longer watch of Parness, acquired a more thorough knowledge of his habits.

In the elevator hall they met Sigurd Strong and Parker. Strong seemed glum and nervous. In the elevator Parker eyed him curiously. He said facetiously to the others:

"I'm trying to figure out what the devil is the matter with the Chief. He doesn't look quite complete. Mustache intact; breast pocket handkerchief all right; what the devil is it? Oh! I get it—no cane. Sigurd, you look positively undressed." Strong's empty right hand opened and closed in an unconscious gesture, but the elevator stopped at the ground floor before he could reply. Strong and Parker stepped off first and left the building ahead.

Bryce said:

"What the hell's got into him? I didn't know *he* went in for that kind of rag chewing! He's been sober as an undertaker every time I've ever seen him before. More banks should fail."

Mawson himself let them in. He was preparing to go home.

"Back so soon? What can I do for you? Anyway, I'm not guilty!"

Bryce ignored the levity.

"We're looking for Mr. Parness."

"Sorry. The case was canceled this morning. As far as we're concerned he may be in Timbuctoo."

"We only want him to talk to. Where will we pick him up? Don't mention the obvious places. We've tried them all."

"What am I supposed to say?"

"Your fellows were on him for three or four days. Scratch your head!"

Mawson rubbed his chin instead.

"There's one place you might not know—the only one I can think of. It's an apartment on West End Avenue, a cheap walk-up he rents under the name of Peabody." He gave them the number. "Don't say I sent you."

After a few more words Fenner and Bryce left, but not much encouraged. From Mawson's description they felt that Parness would be unlikely to be at "Peabody's" if Shirley Strong was at home. Nevertheless, they hailed a cab and drove to the address. It was after dark when they pulled up before an old brownstone four-story house converted to inexpensive apartments. Fenner glanced up and about while Bryce paid the driver. A hard moon rode high in the heavens behind sparse wild clouds. The fall evening was cold, almost freezing. Fenner shivered and could not shake off a sense of something sinister impending.

They surveyed the place glumly. Lights here and there indicated that there was at least some life in the building. In the dim hall they scanned the bell board. There was no 'Peabody' listed, though there were several vacant name spaces. Fenner pushed the superintendent's button. They heard the distant buzz and presently the shuffle of feet along the basement corridor. A lower door opened and the janitor thrust his head through.

"Yeah? What d'y' want?"

"Mr. Peabody live here?"

"Yeah; third floor front." Without further ceremony the man withdrew.

They mounted the dim stairs. Fenner chuckled.

"Knowing apartment management, Parness must have a hemorrhage every time he passes that paragon of courtesy. Dismal dump, isn't it?"

At the third floor front they rapped. Their answer was the stillness of the tomb. Fenner sensed something amiss. He stooped to the keyhole but as quickly straightened up. "Gas!" he whispered. One glance at the heavy old-fashioned door convinced them of the futility of attempting to break it in. Bryce hurtled down the stairs. In a few seconds he was back, dragging the panting janitor behind him. The man fumbled with half a dozen keys. The third one unlocked the door. It opened only a few inches, then got jammed upon a small rug which had been folded up and tucked across the threshold. But even through the narrow opening a heavy wave of gas poured out upon them. Bryce covered his nostrils, reached down and loosened the rug and burst the door open. He crossed the dim room in three long strides and threw the two front windows open. Fenner had a vivid impression of the two bright parallelograms on the ceiling cast by the rays of the street lamp slanting up through the opened windows, then of Bryce's large figure hurrying back, silhouetted against the gray panes. The janitor fumbled for a moment at the wall and snapped the light switch, then stepped back gasping.

It was a beautifully furnished room, tasteful and comfortable, softly lighted, and almost startlingly out of place in those dingy surroundings. At the far side on a full-length divan before an old-fashioned tile fireplace Winthrop Parness, gracefully disposed, was sleeping the long sleep of the righteous. Bryce bent near the floor in the hall and took in a deep breath. Fenner imitated him. They crossed the room. Parness was stone cold, lifeless and blue-faced. Through an open door to one side they heard the inexorable soft rush of the gas, all suffusing, gently obliterating. They moved toward it together, daring not uncover their mouths or noses to speak. There was now no hurry; Parness had been for some time beyond their questions or help.

Fenner found the kitchenette light cord and yanked it. The valves for all four burners of the gas range stood wide open. Bryce threw up the small kitchen window. Fenner reached for the stove to shut off the gas but the Inspector restrained him. Touching each porcelain valve only at its tip he carefully pushed them closed. The two men then rushed out for air.

Fenner and the janitor stayed by the apartment door while Bryce went downstairs to telephone. By the time the police arrived the atmosphere had cleared sufficiently to permit them to enter, but the heavy gas odor, sweetish and sickening, still pervaded the place. The more obvious routine of the Homicide Squad, summoned by Bryce as a matter of course, was expeditiously performed, the pictures taken and the scanty facts recorded. The deputy medical examiner was hesitant about rendering a final opinion, the corpse to him evidencing more the signs of death by pure suffocation than the gas poisoning symptoms he would have expected. He deferred committing himself until he should have had opportunity for a complete autopsy. He estimated, however, that Parness had been dead for from three to four hours.

Before the body was removed to the Bellevue Morgue the janitor was called into the room for formal identification. He shuddered visibly and his teeth chattered so that he could hardly answer their questions.

"You know this man?" Bryce indicated the couch.

The janitor with an effort looked at Parness and quickly turned back to the Inspector.

"Yeah; it's Mr. Peabody."

"He lives here?"

"Once in a while. He don't stay here steady-like. They're from out of town."

"They?"

"Yeah; him and Mrs. Peabody. She stays here with him when they're in town."

"Do you know where we can get in touch with her?"

"Nope. Don't know nothin about 'em."

"They weren't here much?"

"Not much, and when they were they usually come in late."

"When did Mr. Peabody come in today?"

"I didn't know he *was* in until now."

"Whom did he rent through? Whom does he pay? Do you take care of that, too?"

"An agent—Keystone Real Estate. They take care of all that."

Bryce looked over the few notes he had jotted down. He turned back to the servant.

"All right. Now keep your trap shut. This place of yours here— well, never mind. Only if you want to keep out of trouble keep quiet. Don't run off at the mouth to reporters. There'll be plenty of them around. We'll talk to you some more later. Remember, no jabbering!"

The man stumbled out of the room thoroughly frightened. Bryce looked through the contents of Parness' pockets. There were a few business letters and papers, a Westchester commuter's time table, a wallet containing less than a hundred dollars, and credentials and membership cards in a dozen social clubs and business organizations. Bryce looked through them and packed them into a large envelope which he sealed and labeled. Upon a nod from him, Parness was removed, and most of the small group of police staff followed him out. Bryce and two assistants remained to go through the apartment more thoroughly.

From the condition of the place, the scanty stock of wearing apparel in the wardrobes, the empty bookshelves, the bare cupboards and icebox, it was at once apparent that the apartment had been in only intermittent use. There were few papers, and nothing at all of an identifying nature was to be found. It was fairly obvious, in fact, that the apartment was what it was, a trysting place pure and simple. Parness there, Fenner mused, had kept a self-made tryst with his Maker. The divan by the fireplace—what tales could it not tell! Tales of life, of love, of fused hearts, of flaming transports—tales of cooling embers, perhaps, and sordid bickering—a story finally of death, self-sought.

Self-sought? Hardly likely, Fenner answered himself, hopping back to the practical. Abruptly he was sure that Winthrop Parness would not have taken his own life. The man had ever been too self-satisfied, too filled with that languid unsusceptibility, to terminate his comfortable existence.

Fenner's interest in Bryce's examination of the place changed quickly from passive watching to active participation. He moved about the room, registering in his mind a score of details. Parness' murderer must have come in and gone out. He could very simply have come in the front door but—Fenner remembered the rug—he could hardly have departed that way. The front windows which Bryce had opened faced upon the street, a sheer drop of three stories. No egress there. The small kitchenette window opened upon a fire escape.

"Did you find this window locked when you opened it, Inspector?"

Bryce's answer came back from the living room: "Yeah; I had to unlatch it. Why?"

In just a moment the Inspector stood in the door. He eyed Fenner quizzically before he spoke:

"Me, too, Max, but how? How and why?"

"What do you mean?"

"You're leery of this suicide. So am I! Now for once, damn it, let's get together on something from the beginning. This job, you will find, is a damned sight better done than the first one was. We can't waste time or energy working at cross-purposes."

"The fellow's technique improves with practice," Fenner suggested. "I infer that you're assuming that Mr. Shorn has been about. But tell me: what makes you think Parness didn't commit suicide?"

"A hunch at first, and now the fact that the boys couldn't bring up the faintest trace of finger-prints on the nice polished-porcelain gas stove valves. The only mark on them is the small print at the very tip, where I turned them off. If the porcelain registered a print from me it ought to from anyone else. Someone with gloves opened them, or else someone wiped them off. Parness had no gloves on, and Parness had no reason for clearing up finger-prints after himself."

"Interesting! I must confess your doubts are more substantially founded than mine. I became skeptical—leery as you term it—when I tried to picture Mr. Parness calmly reposing himself there to await his beatific end. I couldn't quite do it; that's all. If Martin Hoyle was not a likely suicide type, Parness was a few hundred percent less so."

"We'll have a better slant on it when the medical examiner gets through looking him over." Bryce paused to relight his cigar.

"A slant on what killed Parness if it wasn't gas, possibly. But who engineered it and why—and how the devil did he leave this place?"

Bryce looked up, still holding the lighted match.

"There's no doubt in your mind, is there, that this is one of the regular series? I should think that could be taken for granted."

"I'm not so sure. Shorn is pretty proficient with that thirty-eight of his. I don't know why he should vary his method for this particular attack. Why the gas and all of the suicide trimmings—unless it's that he doesn't intend to claim this affair at all? I wouldn't understand that either, though, after the way he has publicly gloried in the other two."

The Inspector jumped back to the nearer, more tangible question.

"How'd he get out, Max? There's only one door and it's out. The rug jammed against the bottom of it to keep the gas in must have been placed from the inside. This window"—they were still in the kitchenette—"was latched. The living-room windows open on to nothing. The bedroom win—"

"The bedroom is out for the same reason. The sergeant had to yank a rug out from beneath the bedroom door when you first started looking the place over." And if more was needed, they found

that the bedroom windows also were latched. Baffled, they turned
their attention to other things, but a very few minutes' search revealed an astonishing lack of any sort of physical clues. Parness'
hat lay on the bed where he must have tossed it. On a chair in the
bedroom a pasteboard suit box, still in its wrapping paper but not
tied up, contained a dress shirt and white vest, not new but freshly
laundered. There were several of Parness' suits and a small supply of
other dressing accessories, but strangely enough neither the closet
nor any of the drawers contained any woman's apparel whatever.

The janitor, called up again and, a little less frightened now,
was still of no assistance. So far as he knew no one but the Peabodys
had ever used the apartment. He had seen Mrs. Peabody once, in
the dark hallway, and would not be able positively to identify her.
He had no idea at all where she could be reached. They were from
out of town and used the place only once in a while. He insisted
on this with a sly leer, fully aware that they knew that he was
acquainted with the nature of the apartment's occupancy. They dismissed him, Bryce with a gruff, "Remember what I said about keeping your mouth shut! This dump will lose every tenant in it and
you your job if I have to get tough, see?" The fellow was impressed.

They locked the apartment and Bryce posted a man there. In
the hallway Fenner stopped at the head of the stairs. He picked up
a small length of ordinary wrapping twine. Bryce eyed him.

"Saving string?"

"Mmm; comes in handy." Fenner paused at the top step, twin-
ing the string absently between his fingers. "This may tell how
Parness' murderer left the apartment. It may, I say. It's an old trick
for bolting doors on the inside from the outside. You loop the string
around the bolt knob or what-have-you and take the ends through
the crack around the edge of the door. You draw the bolt with the
string and then let go of one end and pull the string out. This is a
good, stout twine. It could have been used on the rug in the same
fashion. Bundle the rug into a small roll just behind the door. Put
the string around it and lay the ends across the doorsill. Close the
door and draw the rug up against the crack at the bottom, then
pull the string out by one end. Why not!"

"Why not? Sure; and then again, a grocery boy might have dropped it. Why not? But let me have it. I'll find out. Now we'd better get along. We ought to give Strong a ring and let him know. Maybe Parness had a family around."

"Let's find out if Strong's home. We could run up there and see him. I'd like to witness his first reaction to this. Parness, of all the mob, should under the circumstances be the one he'd least regret."

They found that Strong was at home. He was, in fact, indisposed and had gone to his room directly from dinner, an early dinner for the Strong household.

Stepping out of the corner cigar store from which Bryce had telephoned, they were not too surprised to encounter Mr. Bartlett. He munched a toothpick and walked along with them.

"You *do* turn up, don't you, son?" Fenner remarked.

"I try to get around where things are happening," Johnny replied modestly. "About Parness?"

"You know it was Parness, then?"

"All the boys will know it in a little while. They're not so close mouthed at Headquarters as you fellows are."

"So?"

"Nothing much. I was wondering if there was any question about Mr. Parness having really committed suicide. Seems kind of queer."

Fenner replied crisply:

"From any evidence we have so far discovered there's not the least shadow of a doubt."

Johnny accepted the rebuff. He explained:

"Some of the boys will raise the question in the morning editions. I thought I might get something definite."

"They'll all get the same answer from me," Bryce assured him grimly. "Now take it easy!"

At Sigurd Strong's the same butler who had admitted Quade earlier in the day ushered them into the drawing room. Strong, in a dressing gown, and Shirley Strong awaited them. Shirley closed her book upon her forefinger when they came in and looked up.

The Inspector glanced at her and then at Strong inquiringly.

"Is it important? Mrs. Strong will excuse us if you prefer."

Fenner said quickly:

"It's quite unnecessary. We only wanted to find out something about Mr. Parness. He has killed himself."

There was just a second of astonished silence.

"Oh, my God! When? How?" Strong sank into a chair. Mrs. Strong rose out of hers, white faced but controlled. She placed the book upon the table.

"He turned on the gas sometime this afternoon," Fenner answered Strong. "Has he any family? Is there anyone who should be notified?"

Strong appeared too dazed, momentarily, to grasp the question. Shirley came to his side. Suddenly he looked up at her, his face a mask. She returned his look evenly.

"Do you feel well? Shall I have Andrew bring you something?" She looked up at the two visitors. "It's rather a shock—coming on top of all of the rest."

Sigurd pulled himself together.

"Parness has—had—some relatives in Philadelphia," he said. "His office—you'll have to get their names and addresses there. But is there any reason? Did he leave any explanation?" His voice quavered over the question.

The Inspector shook his head. He outlined briefly the salient facts, omitting any reference to their doubts as to the genuineness of the suicide. Strong listened, recovering himself gradually. By the time they left, shortly afterward, he had almost entirely regained his composure. Shirley Strong did not again speak.

Bryce and Fenner talked for a moment in the street before they parted.

"That dame has got what I call 'control'!" Bryce commented. "Knowing what we do, I half expected her to pass out."

Fenner did not reply at once, and when he did it was only to murmur enigmatically, "'Control' is an apt term, Inspector."

19
JUDGE SPAR BECOMES HELPFUL

THE LEAN POPLARS that lined the street before his doorstep rustled in the morning breeze. Between the two houses across the street Fenner saw the blue hills overlying a not too distant Westchester golf course; saw them and felt their beckoning pull. He regretted F. W. Strong Company, regretted Shorn and his nefarious activities, regretted Bryce, regretted his own involvement. Saturday mornings—at least such Saturday mornings as this one gave promise of becoming—were very definitely intended by God for golf!

He stooped for the morning paper, stooped and found himself arrested, half bent over, by the giant headlines shouting up at him: "THIRD F. W. STRONG DIRECTOR DEAD." Momentarily astonished, for it had not occurred to him that Parness' death, seeming a suicide, would be fraught with such great public interest, he picked up the paper. A smaller headline explained: "Body of Winthrop Parness found in gas-filled apartment." The leading caption, however, would have instantly and inevitably established the news in the public mind not as an isolated event, but as a development in the F. W. Strong–Shorn case.

Having shot its sensational wad in the enormous headline, the article proceeded in a sort of anticlimactic fashion with its description of the suicide of Winthrop Parness. Toward its conclusion, however, it veered back with hint and innuendo to suggest that there might be more to the death of Mr. Parness than appeared on the surface and suggested that "the police are investigating several angles, including possible connection between the death of

Director Parness and the still unsolved murders of Directors Hoyle and Wheeler."

On his way to the city Fenner bought several other papers and very quickly discovered that the conservative paper to which he subscribed was conservative indeed compared to most of the rest. Most of them blithely assumed that Shorn had struck again, scoffed at the suicide theory, despite the overwhelming physical evidence, and many belabored the authorities for their failure to find the maniac and for the "inadequate protection afforded the threatened citizens."

Several of the papers had outdone their record of sensationalism following Wheeler's death. Amid photographs of Parness, of the West End Avenue apartment, of the Police Commissioner, of everyone connected with the case, there were reprints of Shorn's letter, brief biographies of Hoyle, Wheeler and Parness, and interviews with anyone, however remotely connected with any of the victims, whom enterprising reporters could dig up. One journal went so far as to print in a row pictures of Martin Hoyle, Anthony Wheeler, Parness and, last, a blank rectangle with an enormous question mark and the word "NEXT." Editorially the papers clamored for everything from protection by the police to mercy by Shorn; and one a little more original than the others produced a tabulation of statistics, actually gathered where possible and pulled out of the thin air where not, adducing a quiet but swelling exodus of scores and hundreds of the city's leading real estate financiers, alleged to have departed for the coast, Florida, Bermuda, Canada, foreign waters, or parts unknown.

The press was not universally unsympathetic but there were more than enough scathing denunciations of the police as a whole, and irritating citations of the fact that in this third instance Shorn had accomplished the atrocity after having deliberately warned the police and public, and had selected a victim presumably under police protection.

The Police Commissioner in turn issued vitriolic statements taking the press to task for its meddling tactics, ridiculing the notion that Parness had not taken his own life, pointing out that he had deliberately evaded the police to accomplish his purpose, and insisting that the Department if given a chance would prove its ability to safeguard the public.

Fenner made his way into the Strong Building through a virtual cordon of police, detectives and reporters. It was not early, but Inspector Bryce, another detective, Sigurd Strong and Miss Purcell were the only occupants of the executive wing. Miss Purcell looked pale and distrait—more so, Fenner observed, than even the harrowing circumstances so far as she herself was concerned might have occasioned. Strong and the two detectives were in the Chairman's office. Sigurd Strong had spent a sleepless night and showed it. His eyes were puffed and his cheeks and mouth drooped wearily. Bryce had not slept either; had not even been home, but his vigil had left no outward mark upon him.

Fenner had slept well. He insisted with exasperating nonchalance that in the detecting business the quarry was the one who was supposed to spend the sleepless nights and he'd be damned if he'd break the rules and do it for him.

"I see by the papers that the Commissioner's a trifle upset," he observed to Bryce.

The Inspector, in no mood for joking, only growled incoherently. Strong, appearing aghast at Fenner's levity at such a time, was also speechless.

"Poor Shorn got himself into a tough spot with his damned letter-writing, didn't he?" Fenner went on. "Every mortgage bond director's suicide for the next six months they'll try to pin on him, assuming of course—as it now appears—that Shorn'll be at large for that long."

Sigurd Strong whitened and half rose from behind his desk, but changed his mind. Bryce looked at Fenner, puzzled.

"What's eatin' you this morning?" he demanded.

"Nothing; nothing at all. I'm just thinking how swell it is *not* to have your job." He chuckled and added, "You know, only a couple more of these deaths and people will begin to figure it's serious. Maybe we'll have martial law pretty soon and then you lads can get back to your dominoes."

"Say!" Bryce screwed his face into a scowl, but Fenner cut him short.

"Forget I mentioned it! I'm just quoting one of the Broadway columnists in the morning paper. Come in when you're through."

"I'm through now." Bryce trailed Fenner out of Strong's office.

In the corridor Fenner whispered:

"Sorry, Old Man. I was performing a little experiment on Mr. Strong. The net result was zero."

"I figured it was something like that, but you needn't have rubbed it in quite so rough!"

"You can stand it." They moved into Fenner's room. "Tell me about Parness. The papers picked it up right away, didn't they? What did the medical examiner find out?"

"Enough! Parness was stunned with a blow from a blunt instrument delivered from behind at the base of the brain. Of that much the M. E. is fairly sure, as he says that the evidences of the blow are very distinct. He's got an idea about the rest, too, but he's not so sure he could sell it to a jury. He figures Parness was strangled while he was out. There are no external bruises, but he says there needn't be if the murderer had kept his grip until Parness was dead. Bruises are from slight internal bleeding, and dead people don't bleed! And there are internal bruises back of the tongue and above the larynx. What's more, there wasn't a trace of gas in his lungs and no carbon monoxide in the blood. The boys are going over the place a little more carefully for prints this morning, but if they weren't on the burner handles I hardly expect to find them any place else. We'll be talking to the other tenants and to that janitor some more, too."

Fenner had listened attentively.

"And the time?" he asked. "Did he say any more about that?"

"Nothing different from what he told us last night. Parness had been dead three or four hours. That would make it between three and four in the afternoon."

"And from three to four what do we know about our prospects here? Think it over. It can't be coincidence. They were all more or less scheduled to go down and give the Judge a hand and none of them showed up. The only one with a real 'out' from this is the Judge himself. He was perched right up before your eyes, and on his good behavior! I suppose we should be grateful for having one eliminated, anyway."

The Inspector looked at Fenner queerly for a moment.

"You're assuming that one man did all three jobs. Last night when I started talking 'Shorn' you threw cold water on it—said Shorn was getting along well enough with his thirty-eight and wouldn't change his methods. Now you're talking the opposite. What made you change your mind?"

"I didn't. Hadn't made it up and haven't yet. I was just speculating then, and that's all I'm doing now. In a case like this—"

A tentative knock on the door nipped the dissertation in the bud. It was opened cautiously and Judge Spar thrust his head in. He was unusually pink-faced and seemed mildly agitated.

"Can I come in?"

"Of course. You're bright and early this morning."

"Ah, yes." The Judge looked mildly surprised, as if he found it a peculiar remark under the circumstances. "I— that is—well, perhaps I am."

There was an awkward moment of silence while they waited for him to make known the purpose of his visit. The Judge broke it.

"Rather horrible about Parness, wasn't it?" he said at last. "Mr. Strong telephoned me last evening. He said Parness had killed himself. According to the papers this morning there appears to be some doubt about it. Is there any basis for these doubts?"

"Not the slightest shred," Fenner lied quickly and glibly. He shrugged his shoulders deprecatingly. "You know the newspapers, Judge; and I suppose you can't blame them. The people eat it up!"

The Judge looked doubtfully from Fenner to the Inspector, who evaded the direct spoken lie by remarking:

"They've got to make a good story, and this makes a better story than just another suicide. This way it will fill columns for a week instead of for only a day."

"I suppose so." The Judge was less hesitant. "If Mr. Parness killed himself what I came to see you about is probably of no significance. It was only the doubts raised by the newspaper accounts which prompted me to bother you." He leaned closer to them and dropped his voice to a confidential whisper. "I believe I can tell you the exact time Winthrop passed on. If he killed himself it's of no consequence. If he didn't, then the exact time might be an important thing to know, mightn't it?"

Fenner and Bryce waited in silent mild astonishment.

"Perhaps you will think I'm crazy," Spar went on. "I'll confess that for a moment yesterday *I* thought I was. Are you interested in or acquainted with psychic phenomena, Mr. Fenner?" The Judge unconsciously directed the question to Fenner, thinking rightly that it might be wasted on the Inspector.

"Only in the rankest, most amateurish sort of way," Fenner replied. "I've attended a séance or two, more out of morbid curiosity than out of enthusiasm, and without any sort of endorsement even in my own mind."

The Judge nodded seriously.

"I shouldn't class myself as an ardent spiritualist, either," he said, "but I've been interested in psychical investigation in a dabbling way for a number of years. Thought transference—mental telepathy, they call it—appears to be an accepted, well-established actuality. I had never until yesterday, however, experienced this phenomenon myself. In fact, I didn't recognize it at the time for what it was, and I was quite confounded! Now for some reason, it appears that this phenomenon more often and more easily takes place at the moment of death than at any other time, so last night when Mr. Strong informed me of Mr. Parness' death I—but wait: I'm getting ahead of myself." Spar smiled wanly. "Yesterday afternoon just a few seconds before the conclusion of the ceremonies downtown, Winthrop Parness appeared to me. He came up beside me and spoke to me. The band was playing and we were all standing quietly at attention. His words were very distinct, though no one else appears to have either seen or heard him at all. He said, 'I move we adjourn. Come along, Francis.' I was surprised because I didn't know he was present and hadn't seen him come. I did not answer for a moment and when I turned he was gone. It was so vivid that I was startled and perhaps a little frightened, but the moment I'd gathered my wits together I checked up quietly. No one else had seen Mr. Parness, and from the conditions there, and the inaccessibility of the speakers' stand, it was very certain that he couldn't have been there at all. The incident clung in my mind, though I should have soon forgotten it if I had not learned last night of Parness' unfortunate death.

"You may laugh at my superstitions. I've simply given you the story for what it's worth. The time of Parness' psychic visitation was, I should say, within five minutes one way or the other of quarter past three o'clock. Personally, I am absolutely convinced that it was the moment of his death."

They had listened with growing amazement to the Judge's story. Fenner without agreeing or disagreeing said:

"At any rate, Judge, that fairly well accords with the time of Parness' death as estimated by the medical examiner. It's most interesting. Too bad he didn't say—why he had killed himself." Fenner had been on the point of saying, "who killed him."

Spar apparently did not notice the defection. He got up.

"Perhaps his affairs, as they are ironed out, will reveal his reason," he suggested. "Maybe he was just fed up. We all get that way sometimes. He had no family responsibilities; and when it doesn't leave too much of a mess for someone else to clean up, I can't condemn a man for ending his life when he's fed up with living. Shortsighted, I should say, because I've found that things usually turn out better than one expects, but it's a man's own business." The Judge had risen and had been inching in the general direction of the door.

Fenner and Bryce nodded agreement with his observations, not encouraging him with a reply. He paused at the door.

"Nothing new on your search for Shorn?" he asked. "Nothing for the public, I dare say," he added with a knowing look. "Let me know if I can be of any help." He had definitely reached the door so now he had perforce to go through it.

Fenner and Bryce exchanged puzzled glances.

"Now, what in hell do you suppose that was all for?" Bryce wanted to know.

"Voluble cuss when he gets wound up, isn't he?" Fenner answered irrelevantly.

The Inspector fumbled for matches.

"So Parness' ghost walked! What do you make of it, Max?"

"The phenomenon is not unknown, and the Judge would have no reason for making that up. At least, none that I can think of. On the other hand, he's always been a drowsy codger. Maybe he dreamed it. I can imagine him having a little nap there on his feet."

"Maybe he wanted particularly to establish the exact time of Parness' death," Bryce suggested shrewdly. "He stressed that point pretty heavily, I think. I wonder what kind of an axe *he* could have to grind."

"Maybe," Fenner ventured brightly, "the man is simply telling the truth as he sees it."

"Huh! I've kind of got out of the habit of expecting that around here."

"We'll have to mull over it for a while. Now to get back where we were, where was everyone yesterday at three?"

"I'll bite! Where were they?" Bryce bit his cigar savagely. "I had the boys lined up to cover them and expected to pick most of them up at the cornerstone ceremonies. None of them showed up but the Judge. I guess he couldn't duck it! Hood came floating in here about four o'clock, so far as I've been able to learn. He hadn't been in since before lunch. Strong himself went out about two and wasn't back until almost five. Where either of them was I haven't yet found out.

"Behrmann came in a few minutes after four, just a little after Hood. He had been downtown to the County Clerk's office. We've checked that up and find that he actually was there, but only for a short time, and the clerk there can't place it within an hour. Parker was at the bank at noon and for a short time after. Murphy just missed him there. He'd gone to the State Building. He was back here about half past three, though."

"Looks as if we'd decided to get back on them about three hours too late. If Shorn's letter didn't do another thing, it was probably worth the arduous composition just for that. Cheer up! Perhaps we can worm something out of them without giving the show away. Are you going out?" Bryce had risen.

"I have to run down to Headquarters but I'll be back in an hour. I asked Strong to have the whole mob here at eleven o'clock."

"What for?"

"I'm going to give them a man, or two men, or however many men they want, apiece. Commissioner's orders."

"What if they don't want any?"

"They'll get them anyway."

"Not a bad thought. It will fit right in, won't it? Give them each a couple of rookies for bodyguards. Prime the boys to give these fellows a little rope. Then put some *good* men in the background. Maybe someone will surprise us."

"Maybe." Bryce started out.

"I say, could you have someone of your men shoot that reporter in here? There are a few questions I think he can answer. I imagine you'll find him loitering about the side entrance."

"You imagine? I *know* where you'll find him. At least I know that we won't lose him. Not until this is all cleared up."

20

JOHNNY BARTLETT BECOMES HELPFUL

Johnny Bartlett rapped cautiously before entering Fenner's sanctum. He partly opened the door and thrust his head around it. Fenner looked up from the desk strewn with papers.

"Come in here, young fellow. I want to ask you something."

"I generally do the asking, Mr. Fenner."

"Well; you do the answering this time, and don't hand me anything about a little birdie, either. Do you know that the state has a way of taking care of people who circulate rumors about banks?"

"O.K., Mr. Fenner." Bartlett was quickly abject humility.

"Where did you get your advance dope on the County Consolidated?"

"I didn't have any—not any real dope."

"Upon what did you base your remark to me?"

"A hunch, I guess. There have been a few rumors. Those things get around."

"You weren't retailing just a hunch. There was more to it than that."

"A little. I was at the bank Wednesday looking for Mr. Parker to get an interview. I couldn't get anywhere near him around here." Bartlett paused. "There was quite a little bustle and confusion— the banking floor was pretty busy—and while I was there hanging around waiting I saw Mr. Strong come in. He got in line like any depositor, which seemed a little unusual. He cashed a check. It must have been a whopper because the teller had to leave his cage for what looked like a fresh supply of big bills. I didn't think much of that but a few minutes later Mr. Hood came in. He did the same thing, only they didn't have to get any replenishments to fix him up."

"What time was that?"

"About a quarter of eleven, I think. I got there a little after ten and I'd waited more than a half hour."

"You're quite sure of the time?"

"Fairly sure; yes sir. You see, about five minutes later Mr. Parness came in and I was thinking pretty soon there'd be a quorum! He got in line, too; about a dozen spaces behind Hood. I was getting excited, especially because Parness sort of hung back out of sight, as if he didn't want Hood to see him. He'd seen Hood, too. I'm sure of it. So when Hood got his money he took it over to one of the wall desks and checked it up. Parness seemed to watch him and to keep turned away so that if Hood looked up he wouldn't spot him. Well, when three people as close to the inside as these babies are slip in within a few minutes and draw down their jack, it's a pretty good sign something's fishy! But that's all I know. You can *call* that a hunch."

"So you assumed the bank was on the rocks? But why tell *me?*"

"I don't know, Mr. Fenner, honestly. It was just an impulse. You might have had an account there."

Fenner said with faint irony:

"I'm sure I'm much obliged. I suppose you didn't discuss the matter with Mr. Parker, too, when you saw him—or did you see him?"

"Yes, I saw him, later in the day, but I didn't discuss that," Johnny replied in all seriousness.

"What, then?"

"Oh, the usual thing. I was digging for something to fill up a column or two. At first he told me he had nothing to say and started to shut the door in my face, but I argued him into letting me in. We talked along about one thing or another—about the cops. He thought they were doing as well as could be expected—said this was a job for alienists and psychopathologists rather than police. I yes-yessed him until I thought I had enough for a column. I asked him if the Shorn scare had had any repercussions on the banking business. He said not. He said that business and politics and every-thing else was in such a topsy-turvy state that it wasn't possible to trace cause and effect anymore, anyway. He said not to quote him on that."

"What prompted you to dig up that dope on Hood?"

Bartlett shifted uncomfortably.

"That was just a hunch, too."

"Hunches like that don't drop out of the clear blue sky."

"Listen," Bartlett said earnestly, "right off the bat didn't I have a hunch that Mr. Hoyle's murder was an inside job? The cops soon came to the same conclusion. Then when Mr. Wheeler was killed and this maniac stuff began I swallowed it for a while—same as you, if you did—but not for long. One time when I was talking to Mr. Strong's secretary—a week ago when the receivership was going on—she said that Mr. Hood was 'positively demented' from the way things were going. That stuck in my mind and I happened to think of it while I was talking to Mr. Parker. So that night I hung around and followed Hood up to the armory."

"Just playing the same hunch, eh?"

"Yeah," replied Johnny brightly. He did not look up quite in time to catch the cold gleam of disbelief in Fenner's eyes. "So I began to get funny ideas and prowled around and talked to some of the enlisted men. Mr. Hood's about the most popular skipper up there. There were plenty willing to talk about him. Good fel-low—athletic—fine rider—crack shot—pistol team—democratic as hell. The part about the crack shot stopped me for a minute. In the morning I looked those meets up. I thought you ought to know. I don't mind admitting that if anything comes of it I'd sort of expect a break on the release."

"Mmm—of course. I didn't suppose all that gratuitous infor-mation was from the bigness of your heart, or from any overwhelm-ing passion to see justice done. Well, we'll see. Much obliged."

It was almost eleven when Bartlett went out. Fenner waited a few moments and then he, too, got up. Pausing before the open door of the office Wheeler and Parness had used, Fenner saw within what looked and sounded like a pinochle game. Bryce's men assigned as F. W. Strong bodyguards were having their relaxation. He discovered that the reporter had gotten as far as Miss Purcell's desk, where he was bent over engaged in his customary solicitation. Bartlett looked up almost guiltily and said to Margaret: "Try to make it if you can. I've got to have important words with you." He shuffled out disconsolately.

Fenner waited until the door had closed behind the reporter. He stood drawing on his gloves and inquired lightly: "The poor boy looks all broken up—what have you done to him, Miss Purcell?"

Margaret replied equally lightly:

"He gets that way. He gets over it, though."

"An enterprising young man. Have you known him long?"

"I've known him about a year."

"Forgive my curiosity. How did you meet him?"

"He wrote real estate items for the paper. He used to be here frequently. I just got to know him. He's—good company."

"He's had plenty to write about these last few days."

Margaret, puzzled at Fenner's loquaciousness, had no reply for the last comment and Fenner went on:

"You've all been under rather a strain these last weeks."

"We've felt it."

"You work only until noon Saturdays; isn't that right?"

"We're supposed to. I don't know about today, though. I usually stay here until Mr. Strong goes out. He's been awfully busy this morning on account of the bank."

"The bank? Ah, yes; the County Consolidated. I hope you didn't get caught there personally. I observe that many Strong employees have their accounts with them."

"No, I didn't. I had a narrow escape, though. Mr. Hood warned me. I drew almost all of my money out Thursday. It wasn't much but I'd certainly have hated to see it tied up just now."

"Just now, or any time," Fenner commented laconically. "So Mr. Hood anticipated! It's odd, but everyone seems to have known that bank was going to close. Your friend Mr. Bartlett gave me a tip yesterday. I say, do you know Mr. Hood at all well?"

Margaret replied evenly:

"I think I know him fairly well."

"You must excuse my prying. You see, there's something I'm anxious to find out. I've heard rumors, the most amazing rumors, and they're the most embarrassing things to check up on." He noted with satisfaction Margaret's intensely anxious, waiting look. "I've heard rumors of Mr. Hood's being in the throes of a nervous breakdown—a serious one, to the extent, let us say, of genuine derangement. Would you say such a thing is likely?"

Margaret looked at him witheringly.

"That's the most ridiculous thing I've ever heard of," she declared. "I suppose Johnny Bartlett told you that?"

"He mentioned it. He blamed his inspiration on Mr. Parker." Fenner congratulated himself. When things seemed to be falling into the doldrums there was nothing like a judicious injection of slander to get them riled up.

"Well, it's simply absurd. Bob—Mr. Hood—may be more upset by the way business has been than some of the others. And if he is it's because he's got a conscience. He's told me some of the stories he hears from the people who've lost their savings, and I can understand him being disturbed. But as far as anything more serious goes, it's just plain nonsense. Johnny hinted at something like that to me, but I didn't think he was really serious. The idea of spreading such a thing! When I see him again I'll tell him something!"

"He probably didn't mean anything, Miss Purcell. Perhaps I shouldn't have mentioned it."

"Oh, yes he did. He's probably spreading that all around. Well, I'll tell you the truth, Mr. Fenner, distasteful as it is to me to bring myself in: If Johnny said that it's just because he's a jealous fool! I'll tell him what I think of him if I ever speak to him again."

"So that's how it is! Good Lord! I'm frightfully sorry to have dragged personalities into this. But perhaps it's just as well. We can talk frankly now."

But they couldn't. The desk buzzer sounded abruptly and Margaret got up and went into Strong's office. Through the opened door Fenner saw Behrmann and Strong bent over the desk. The latter looked up and said something to Margaret and she pulled a chair up, sat down and opened her notebook.

Whistling lightly to himself Fenner moved out through the main lobby and into the general office space of the Sales Department. The large room was quite deserted, not because it was Saturday but because the sales force had been dissolved, its last bond sold, its activity forever stopped. The long ranks of unused desks with their tops bare and glistening and their chairs drawn up close lent an air of almost mournful decadence.

Through a partly open door at the rear end he could see into Hood's private office. At first Fenner thought it also deserted, but when he had come into the line of vision of the desk he saw that Hood was there. He half lay forward over the desk, his forehead resting on his folded arms. The line of scalp where his dark hair was parted ran neat and white straight up his skull.

Fenner's heart fairly bounded. Once more death had stalked the Strong corridors. He remembered Martin Hoyle, an exact week ago, lacking a few hours! In a quick flash he thought of the new dismay that would spread—of the tabloids, of Bryce's impotent wrath, of the desperation that would haunt Strong and Behrmann and the dwindled ranks of survivors. He felt a quick compassionate pang for Margaret Purcell. He thought angrily of the pinochle game and of all of the careful precautions gone to naught. He leaped to the door and as he reached it Hood raised his head and looked at him wearily, his glazed eyes blinking. Then he straightened up, stretched his arms and yawned noisily.

"Come in. I must have dozed off. I'd a bad night last night."

Fenner stopped in his tracks. In only a second he overcame his relief and amazement.

"Phew! You gave me a fright, young man."

"A fright!"

"Stretched out over your desk you looked—well, most terrifyingly inert. I thought you were dead!"

"My God! And they try to tell me *my* nerves are on edge!"

"How long have you been here?"

Hood looked quickly curious.

"Oh, an hour. Why?"

"I only wondered. I hadn't seen you around."

Hood slid a cigarette box across the desk to Fenner. He indicated a near-by chair and suggested:

"Take a load off your feet. You seem to have something on your mind. I don't flatter myself that this is a social visit. I didn't kill Winthrop, if that's what you want to know."

"Who do you suppose did?"

"I wouldn't know. On the level, didn't he kill himself? I put all of that claptrap in the morning tabloids down to just New York journalism."

"You're one hundred percent right, so far as I know. But I wonder why he did it. He seemed to be getting a lot of pleasure out of life, in his own way. I don't mind admitting that he'd have been the last man around here I'd have expected to take his own life."

Hood dwelt on Fenner's words for a moment.

"I hadn't thought of it in that light. Maybe he wasn't as—as—" He struggled for a generous term for what he thought of as a sort of cynical selfishness in Parness. "—as indifferent, as he seemed." He puffed moodily on his cigarette.

Fenner said presently:

"You spoke of a bad night. What's your trouble?"

"Nerves, I guess. I don't sleep. Too many cigarettes and not enough exercise."

"And?"

"That's all. Well, naturally I'm not hilariously happy over business. After all, one doesn't lose a good job every day."

"You're all through?"

"The last man is fired and I turned the last scrap of paper over to Horton this morning."

"You expect to be around, however? It wouldn't look so well to start anywhere just now."

"I don't get it. As a matter of fact, I didn't have anything of that kind in mind, but still—what do you mean?"

"Until things are cleared up I'm afraid the police will want any possibly material witnesses in connection with these affairs available."

"Meaning me?"

"Among others, yes. But come along. The Inspector should be here any moment. There's to be a gathering of the klan at eleven to discuss ways and means of giving you fellows some peace of mind."

"Say, Mr. Fenner—" Hood paused and looked significantly in the direction of the door. Fenner slowed up and Hood whispered: "Where was Sig when Parness was taking the gas yesterday afternoon?"

"Fortunately for him, and unfortunately for the hypothesis you're hinting at, he was somewhere about here, I believe."

"Take it that I was simply curious," Hood answered, flushing.

"Nonsense! I'm familiar to the situation you refer to. Tell me: Is there anyone who isn't?"

21
ENCORE BY SHORN

At 10:05 A. M. that Saturday a postal clerk in the Grand Central Post Office Substation found a plain stamped envelope with an added special delivery stamp, addressed to the *Globe*. This was not surprising; every postal clerk in the city had his eyes open for just such an envelope. With the consent of the newspaper it was instantly handed to the police, removed to Headquarters and, at 10:30, in the presence of one of the *Globe's* staff sensation writers and a few of the Department's experts, carefully opened. It was handled with pincers until it was established that not the faintest vestige of a finger-print appeared on the paper. At 10:40 linotypes were clacking; at 10:55 presses revolved; and shortly after eleven o'clock newsboys were running the streets shouting "EXTRA!!" and the population was treated to another of Shorn's edifying taunts.

Bryce, who had come back to the Strong Building, was apprised of the text of the message as soon as it was opened. He wrote it down as it was given him over the telephone. Fenner at his elbow watched the crawling pencil impatiently. The message read:

Gentlemen of the Press and to the Public at Large:
Re: F. W. Strong & Company
MR. PARNESS BEAT ME TO IT!

All of the super-intelligent journalistic opinion
to the contrary notwithstanding, I did *not* kill Mr.
Parness. It is true that his turn would have come (I

couldn't consistently omit him) so this is simply one chore I am spared.

Perhaps Mr. Parness was a man of sufficient acumen to perceive that the handwriting was already on the wall. Perhaps he defeated (and served) my purpose in the only way of which he was capable. Perhaps he did not; I may have a disciple. At any rate, I must respectfully decline the credit.

I was, at the time, otherwise and less profitably employed. I was eye-witness to an example of as colossal, if disgusting, a piece of effrontery as it has been my misfortune ever to behold. No milder expression describes the spectacle of a man with the record and associations of Judge Francis Fenwick Spar dedicating any structure whatever, least of all a court building, to the "principles of justice and equity." I am indebted to the newspapers for confirmation of his exact words; I would not have dared credit only my own ears.

Scarcely less amazing was the tolerant reception accorded his wordy hypocricies by an apparently intelligent audience. Is it possible that the public has become so completely spiritless and morally insensible! Perhaps they are not undeserving of the treatment accorded them by the pack of self-aggrandizing scoundrels I have set out to destroy. I am almost tempted to abandon my crusade; there is no particular pleasure in fighting alone and unappreciated.

However, I am not yet quite convinced that we have all deserved the full measure of fleecing we've received.

Until later,
SHORN.

"Wait till the papers get a load of that," Bryce remarked as he hung up, though indeed they wouldn't have to wait long.

"Wait until Messrs. Strong, Behrmann, Spar, Parker and Hood, et al get a load of it, too," Fenner exclaimed. "You know, it's more than just the physical threat that burns them up. They haven't mentioned it, and far be it from me to bring the subject up at this time, but this fellow is calling them some pretty harsh names, and they haven't even the satisfaction of being able to call him a hundred percent liar! They're just enough tainted to be plenty vulnerable, and though they may not be quite the nefarious, deep-dyed scoundrels that Mr. Shorn portrays, they have left themselves open to criticism all along the line—more so, I'm beginning to find out, than the public is aware. That's another reason for my certainty that this chap is not far from our midst. Outsiders wouldn't *know* things were quite as bad as they are; Shorn seems to." He thought a moment. "Did they tell you anything about the letter?"

"Yeah; typed with the same machine on the back of another of those come-on sheets. Not a finger-print on it, The Post Office inspectors figure it was mailed in one of the station concourse boxes at Grand Central sometime between nine-twenty and nine-fifty."

"Are you going to have it?"

"As soon as they're through downtown."

"I'd like a look at it."

Fenner picked up the Inspector's transcript of the message and reread it.

"You'd expect this note to be anticlimatic coming at this time, but it's not," he said. "He overcomes that by introducing a new element, that the public possibly deserves their reaming. The man has a positive genius for painting the kind of picture he wants people to see. I wonder if he's getting ready to retire?"

"Retire?"

"This about being 'tempted to abandon his crusade.' It might be an effect he's preparing, establishing a reason for quitting that will square with the rest of the pretense, so that when he *does* get through eliminating whomever he wants, for whatever his reasons are, he can quit and leave the authorities still looking for a crazed, demoniacal, plucked investor."

Bryce pondered the thought, his slower but equally thorough faculties feeling around and about it.

"Uh-huh; but there'd be *some* more he figures to knock off, anyway. He promises that at the end, doesn't he, when he says he's not convinced yet?"

"Probably."

"Well, a dollar and my job says he don't!"

"Five'll get you ten, as the boys downtown so nicely put it," Fenner smiled.

"Listen; these babies are going to be so covered, whether they like it or not, that they'll have a hell of a time even taking a—bath!"

"More power to you! Only don't smother them so thoroughly that you frighten Mr. Shorn into the limbo."

"The what?"

"Nothing. If he dropped out of sight now—quit cold—you'd have one devil of a job ever nailing him."

"It'd maybe take some time," Bryce admitted.

"The easiest thing would be to catch him in his next attempt. If you make it too difficult he might lose heart and not make any."

"Jeez! Mr. Strong and the rest would sure love to hear you talking along those lines."

"They should. They're the ones that have to worry as long as Shorn's loose. But you may as well go right ahead and cover them. Whatever motive impelled him to kill two men, maybe three, will certainly be strong enough to keep him at it until he's through—and that in spite of any protection you can arrange."

"Maybe three? You think he's kidding about Parness? Why would he do that? He was frank enough about Hoyle and Wheeler."

"I think Mr. Shorn is just as frank as it suits his devilish, obscure purpose to be, and no franker. Assuming that he's connected here at Strong's and then considering the tenor of his messages, he obviously can never be convicted of over-sincerity."

It was almost half past eleven when Mr. Strong came in and told the Inspector that, as requested, everyone was present, congregated in the Board Room. Maurice Parker had been the last to arrive, having been detained at the bank. Fenner followed Strong

and Bryce out and down the corridor. Mr. Hood was in the anteroom talking to Miss Purcell, but he left her and joined them as
they passed into the Board Room. They found Behrmann and
Parker and Spar in a huddle drinking in the details of the second
message from the late extra the banker had just brought in.

"Did you see that yet, Inspector?" Strong indicated the paper.

From across the room they could read the enormous headlines:
"MANIAC SENDS SECOND LETTER."

"I heard about it."

"Is there no way in which the papers can be prevented from
printing these outrageous slanders?"

"That would be pretty hard. A sensation of this size comes about
once in a city editor's lifetime. If you try to hold them down they're
worse than ever."

"I suppose so. But these letters have done us irreparable harm.
They're spread all over the front page and read from one corner of
the land to the other. The worst of it is that many people will believe them. We try to defend our reputations and issue counter
statements and they're buried obscurely in paragraphs of print. I
feel that the authorities should exert some sort of influence on the
press—"

"Free speech, free press. You can't do anything about them,"
Bryce cut in shortly, as if to wave the unimportant subject aside. It
seemed to him that there were more vital things to discuss.

"You could do your own influencing as in the good old days if
you were still buying quarter-page ads in the financial sections,"
Fenner suggested. "Maybe you could remind some of the advertising managers and editors. They *might* remember."

Bob Hood slid deep down into one of the leather chairs and
folded him arms over his chest. He looked in their general direction but not at them and said with a semi-defiant air:

"It seems to me the press hasn't been so bad, Mr. Strong. We've
no kick coming!" He paused nervously, awaiting their combined
imprecations.

Sigurd simply stared at him, too astonished to speak. Judge
Spar snapped irritably, "Don't answer him, Mr. Strong." The

calumnies heaped particularly upon the Judge's head by the anony-
mous murderer-correspondent were not much softened by the
inclusion of the others in the general indictment.

It was Parker who finally did reply, with a plaintive, "Why Robert, what are you talking about?" His pudgy form quaked as he let
himself into a chair.

"I mean, for example, that I have yet to see a printed line in
any paper condoning this madman's operations. At least they've
spared us that, and it wouldn't have been surprising if they hadn't."

Spar turned to Strong.

"You may not be aware that that's the sort of drivel we've been
compelled to listen to from him all week," he said.

Strong had no reply but cast a furtive glance in the direction of
Fenner and Bryce. Behrmann sprang into the breach.

"Gentlemen, I think the object for which this meeting was called
is more important than either personal recriminations or the ex-
humation of a lot of past and buried actions and policies. We all
appear to be in grave, immediate personal danger. The Inspector
has asked Mr. Strong to assemble us to discuss ways and means of
combating a mad fiend who has already slain two men, and whose
threats hang over our remaining heads like the shadow of Baal. I
suggest that, for our own sakes, we place ourselves completely at
the disposal of the authorities, who are infinitely better equipped
to cope with this monster than we as individuals can hope to be.
That, at least, is my own intention. Naturally you may all do as
you see fit."

"You're exactly right, A. L.," Parker agreed.

Strong said, "Now if you'll tell us what you have in mind,
Inspector—"

"Well, of course the extreme precaution, which I hesitate to
mention because I doubt if any of you will consider it, would be to
come down to Headquarters for a few days. I don't suggest it, mind
you, but I mention it to let you know that such a course is open to
you. I don't think it would be especially suitable because there's
no telling how long it will take to clear this up. However, the Commissioner has authorized us to go to any lengths in affording you

personal protection in your movements to and fro, in your business, or in your homes. I had in mind two or three men apiece who would alternate so that one would be with you continually. What do you think of that?"

"I think it would be excellent, Inspector, and I'm sure it's appreciated," said Strong.

"I'm sure it's appreciated and I hope it's adequate," Judge Spar remarked wryly.

"If things at the bank weren't demanding such continual attention I'd accept your hospitality downtown. I swear I would." Parker spoke up. "I'm afraid that's the only place I'll feel at ease until this fellow is behind the bars."

Hood, who had watched the others react to the suggestion, now said:

"O. K. by me, Inspector, but can I ask you just one question?"

Bryce grunted assent and the others all exchanged worried glances. It was as if the mere thought of Hood opening his mouth at all alarmed them.

"What do you do with the bodyguards when you want to be alone?"

"Nothing. You don't want to be alone. You'll keep out of crowds and public places but you'll never be unattended. That will be one of the things my men will see to."

"Oh, it's to be a sort of a state of walking around under arrest, eh?"

"It may seem like that."

"Better than Woodlawn Cemetery, Bob," Parker put in. Hoyle's burial was yet fresh in his memory.

"And if we elect to decline your 'protection'?"

"It wouldn't be wise. Do you think you'll mind so much?"

"Oh, I won't mind. I guess I can stand it as well as anyone."

"What's your opinion, A. L.?" Strong asked.

The little lawyer was startled out of a reverie.

"Why, of course, it's a—splendid plan. It ought to make us all feel more secure. However—well, it's about the only thing we *can* do, isn't it—short of actually hiding in jail?"

Bryce went on:

"Tomorrow's Sunday. Our men are going to stay right with you but you can make things a little easier for them by staying close to your homes."

Fenner had been speaking in an undertone to Strong. The Chairman turned to the others with a return of some of his erstwhile pomposity.

"Before you go, gentlemen," he said, "let me request that you plan to make yourselves available Monday. Mr. Fenner informs me that his auditors have practically completed their work and that a number of questions have presented themselves. I suggest that we convene on Monday afternoon to discuss these matters."

The announcement was received with polite assents from everyone, but Fenner could feel their coldly curious glances upon him from all sides.

Bryce marshaled a dozen or more detectives and assigned them as he had outlined. Then he went back with Fenner to Hoyle's office to wait developments.

"That's that! Now, how about a little argument? I've often found that there's nothing like a good argument to get at all sides of a question."

"What about?" Fenner asked.

"You're pretty sure that Shorn is from this crowd, or at least from near by, and that all the weeping over the 'poor investor' is just to sidetrack suspicion? Then why didn't he write a letter the first time? Why did he try to make the Hoyle job look like a suicide?"

"Frankly, that puzzles me, too," Fenner admitted; "but if this was a genuine crank the same question would be in order and would be just as puzzling. Oh, I admit the theory leaves plenty to be explained, but the crank theory leaves more to be explained. For instance: Why would he rifle Hoyle's desk? Why put Hoyle's keys back into his pocket? Why start on Hoyle and Wheeler at all, instead of Sigurd Strong, who is, so far as the public is aware, the guiding spirit in this enterprise? Why Hoyle's packed bag? Why—oh, any number of things?"

"But what motive? With the crank theory you've got a definite, plausible motive. There's plenty of people been rooked out of their life's savings—plenty of 'em boiling mad. At some of the bankruptcy proceedings Strong needed police protection to keep from getting mobbed. There's plenty of material there to draw from. Any one of thousands of people could've mighty easy gone off his nut."

"Inspector, those letters aren't the work of an unbalanced mind—at least, not of a mind deranged in the sense and to the extent it would have to be if these murders are pure, insensate revenge. The remarkable thing to me is that the newspapers and public have swallowed them at their face value so quickly and so unquestioningly."

There was a knock on the door and a police messenger brought Bryce an envelope. Within was another containing the original of Shorn's second message. "Ah, there's the real thing." The Inspector took it out and flattened it on the desk. The typography and general setup was much the same as the first note, and it was typed on the back of another of the same bond-issue prospectuses. It had been folded twice to get it into the envelope.

Fenner fumbled in his vest and produced a small but high-powered reading glass. He picked up the letter and examined it minutely through the glass, particularly along the folds. Presently he handed it and the glass to Bryce and said:

"Look here, Inspector; I wonder if this looks the same to you. You can see that where the surface fibers are broken by folding, the typewriter ink doesn't run between them. In other words the letter was written *before* it was folded. Another thing: this is the second note on the *same* prospectus. Where would an outsider get a supply of the unfolded sheets? When they were originally broadcast they were folded as this is folded, to fit an ordinary large envelope, and posted probably *one each* to the mailing list."

Bryce looked through the glass, too.

"I guess you're right, Max," he conceded. "I'm no expert, but it does look that way. But who around here fits the bill? I can't picture any of these fellows killing anyone without getting sick. Besides, doesn't the time element eliminate a lot of them?"

"Let's see if it does. Now Saturday doesn't mean a thing; none of them have an air-tight alibi. Wednesday Wheeler was shot about ten-forty. I've been doing a little time table work. Do you know that you can get from here down to the Chambers Street Station in about twenty minutes by taking the East Side Subway and walking over? The boat Wheeler rode, the ten-twenty-five from Jersey City, left this side on its way over for that trip at ten-eight. It got back with him abroad at ten-forty. Add twenty minutes to each end of that and you have the period you'd have to be away from here to have turned the trick—say, nine-forty-five to eleven o'clock. Where was everyone then?

"And where was everyone from, say, two-fifteen to three-forty yesterday afternoon? That's all he'd need to have taken care of Parness. It's no more than fifteen minutes each way to the apartment in a cab. Those are the things you need to know and they won't be easy to find out. It will be especially difficult about yesterday unless we come out in the open. We should never have let up on them when we once had them covered. You'll have to proceed by the most careful indirection or you'll tip your hand and then the cards will be stacked against you." Fenner got up. "I don't know about you, but I'm going to *eat!*"

Bryce wasn't, yet.

"Did you talk to Hood today?" he asked. "I heard from Murphy. There wasn't a thing in Hood's apartment. They went through pretty carefully."

Fenner paused in his departure.

"I talked to him, but to no appreciable profit. He gave me one rather bad moment. When I went into his office he was alone and dozing. He was lying over his desk and for a second I was sure he was number four. I don't know whether I was more startled when I saw him bent over the desk or when he suddenly woke up and started talking. I questioned him. He's like two of the three monkeys: he saw no evil and he heard no evil. When it comes to the third he wasn't so hot!"

"What d'you mean?" Bryce was not up on his Oriental quadrumanous mammals.

"'Speak no evil.' I hadn't uttered three sentences before he hinted at the Mrs. Strong–Parness affair and wanted to know where 'Sig' was when Parness was taking the gas."

"Where *was* Sig yesterday, I wonder."

"That makes two of us!"

22

SUNDAYS ARE USUALLY QUIET

SUNDAY OPENED UNEVENTFULLY, an unseasonably balmy day, disarm-ingly clear and mild. It progressed as uneventfully until early afternoon when Simon Behrmann, leaving his bodyguard dozing beside a decanter of Old Bourbon, a box of Corona-Coronas and a half dozen Sunday papers, slipped out of the service entrance of his Riverside Drive apartment, hopped into a conveniently wait-ing taxi, chauffeured, not so conveniently as Behrmann would later learn, by one of Bryce's men, and had himself driven to the Grand Central Station. He bought a ticket to Beacon and got on a day coach. Another of Bryce's men sat down behind him. Two more got on at 125th Street Station and seated themselves near by.

At Harmon, while the engines were being changed, there was a whispered consultation and a telephone call to Headquarters. At Beacon Mr. Behrmann got off. He picked one of the several taxies parked at the station plaza and dickered with the driver for a few moments. Waiting until the two appeared to have reached an agree-ment, Bryce's men descended upon them. Behrmann looked at them, scarcely surprised but with no effort to conceal his discour-agement, and told the driver to shut off his engine.

"I suppose you'll want me to come back with you?"

The senior of the three nodded.

"I'm afraid so." He turned to the driver who was looking at Behrmann curiously. "Where was he going?"

Behrmann said to the man wearily:

"Tell them. It's all right."

404

"Over toward Danbury. Farm just over the Connecticut line."

"You know the place?"

"Yes. I've taken fares there a few times during the summer."

"It's a small farm I use for a summer place," Behrmann enlarged.

"What were you going there for?"

"I was going to stay there until it's safe for me in the City; that's all."

"I'm sorry. You'll have to explain that to Inspector Bryce."

The driver, partly puzzled but mostly disappointed at the loss of a lucrative, long-trip fare, watched them move away, Behrmann tacitly in their midst.

They took the next train back to New York, Behrmann at the window glumly watching the wide reaches of the peaceful Hudson slip to the rear, now closing his eyes against the reflected glare of the afternoon sun on the water, now opening them upon the shady portions of the autumnal coloration. At Grand Central a police car met them, and in Bryce's dingy office the Inspector and Fenner, who had voluntarily cut short his own late Sunday siesta, awaited them.

"What was the idea, Mr. Behrmann? You enjoy making our job harder?" Bryce asked coldly.

Behrmann shrugged his shoulders.

"I suppose I can't expect to make you understand. It's this eternal vigilance. It gets me, gets my nerves. When I looked out today I just felt that I had to get away to some quiet place; get away alone where I wouldn't need one eye always over my shoulder. So I just left. An impulse, that's all. I might have regretted it and come back tomorrow; maybe the day after. I've got that farm and I thought I'd stay there till I'd pulled myself together. That's all. I'm sorry, of course, for your inconvenience."

"I think I know exactly how you felt," Fenner cut in. "In fewer, plainer words, you were so sick of being afraid you thought you'd give in and run away. No reflection, of course. Is that it?"

Behrmann hesitated.

"It's not exactly what I mean but it will do."

"Your nerves are worn; that's one thing. But you wouldn't run away from worn nerves. These last two years must have given you plenty of practice enduring that sort of thing. You were *frightened* away. We want to know what frightened you; what over and above the Shorn operations we all know about?"

"My God! Isn't that enough to scare any man away?"

"Not a reasoning person like yourself," Fenner assured him coolly. "You wouldn't sanely argue that you'd be safer alone on a Connecticut farm than here with the entire police department concerned with your protection."

"There are things that the entire police department are powerless to protect you against."

"Now we're getting somewhere," Bryce said. "What? What is it you're afraid of?"

"I tell you I don't know. I just felt I had to get away and I went. That's all." He closed his lips tenaciously and both Fenner and Bryce realized they had definitely gotten as far as they would along this path. Fenner suddenly said brusquely:

"Let's quit beating around, the bush! What is your theory about these murders, Mr. Behrmann?"

"Theory?"

"Of course. Three men have been killed; or should I say two have been killed and a third is dead? Knowing all of them, much of their business, and the many circumstances and relationships between them, you must have arrived at some notion about the affairs. After all, murder isn't an everyday occurrence. When three happen in close succession one thinks about them! What do you think?"

"I only know what I read in the papers," Behrmann insisted stubbornly. His hunted eyes flitted from the Inspector back to Fenner.

"There hasn't been anything in the papers that would make you so suddenly take to your heels. Why is it that you're afraid to put into words the thing you're thinking—because it seems far-fetched or impossible? Believe me; for your own good and safety you would do better to voice your suspicions. You're not alone; Hood's got them, too. He said as much yesterday. And I shouldn't be surprised if the others had, only I think yours are more concrete and probably more completely formulated."

"That's just the trouble. They're nothing of the sort. I tell you I don't know!" His voice was flat, a tonelessness of weariness and despair. "I don't know anything. I have a feeling—a conviction, if you like—that this murderer who has marked us for extinction is beyond your ability or ours to cope with—superhuman, perhaps. And definite premonitions have grown upon me, grown and expanded and accumulated such weight in my mind that I'm beginning to feel—well, almost irresponsible. It's terrifying and it's shattering my nerves. That's why I thought I'd get away for a while."

"I suppose it didn't occur to you that your flight might be subject to misinterpretation?"

"It has since I started, not before. The initial impulse was a matter of feelings and instinct, not reason,"

Fenner said:

"I have an idea you may be able to gratify your sudden whim for the pastoral shortly, but please postpone any further efforts until later in the week. Besides, there's that meeting tomorrow. I believe you'll want to attend."

"Meeting? Oh, yes; the meeting." Behrmann looked up confused. "It may sound incredible but I had completely forgotten it! But, God willing, I'll be there."

In silence they watched Behrmann go out with two of Bryce's men accompanying him, heard their hollow footsteps fading away down the deserted corridor, ending in the distant slam of the door and the muffled whir of a police car engine starting. There are few places as quietly peaceful as lower New York at midday Sunday, and the complete muteness pervading the old Center Street Station would have given no indication that it was the focal point controlling the intense man-hunt under way. The Inspector spoke first:

"What'n hell do you suppose is eating that guy? Do you think he could possibly be as scared as he acts?"

"I think he could. I think he is. He'd have no reason for putting it on. And why else would he have made that break for the country?"

"He might be running out for better reasons. Does anything you've uncovered at Strong's point to him? Maybe he sees things closing in on him."

Fenner shook his head slowly.

"I don't know about things at Strong's. At best Behrmann's hands aren't spotless. But the clumsy attempt at escape which he staged is rather too obvious for a man whom we know to be as subtle and clever as Mr. Shorn. I should certainly be surprised if it was a bona-fide escape effort. But then, I've had a great many surprises during the last few days."

Bryce dragged out a fresh cigar and lit it meditatively.

"Maybe," he suggested, "he, being subtle like you say, would figure that we'd think along just the lines you have. Maybe then he'd take it on the lam, dumb like, that way just to throw us off the track."

"Maybe; but if he figured that far he'd probably figure the next step and conclude we'd see through his scheme. It's a matter of where you stop—odd or even!"

Bryce produced from his desk a sheaf of papers which he spilled out before Fenner. They were plain sheets of paper and on each was typed: 'Gentlemen of the Press and to the Public at Large: THEY CAN'T GET AWAY WITH IT!' "We went through the F. W. Strong offices last night with a fine toothed comb," he explained. "Among other things we took these specimens, one from every typewriter in the place. The boys here worked over them most of the night. None of the machines there were used by Mr. Shorn, so if he hails from these premises he's doing some home work!"

"The dirty cheat!" Fenner mocked, and added, "I think I mentioned before that you're not dealing with a moron. Find anything else?"

"Nothing of consequence. A fair collection of arms. Hood's got a forty-five that'd knock down an elephant. Behrmann and Strong both have smaller arms in their desks. Mr. Parker goes for the old western long-barreled six-gun."

"Didn't any of these fellows ever hear of the Sullivan Act?"

"Well, you can't very well clamp down on them at a time like this. If I thought a crank that had killed three people was out gunning for me I'd carry an arsenal."

"How about Parness' office?"

"Nothing there, nor in Spar's either, as far as arms goes. Spar's desk had about as complete a collection of raw photographs as I've ever seen. Funny slant you get on a guy, isn't it? The only other high spot was Mr. Strong's liquor supply."

"And everyone's been behaving?"

"They've all been sitting tight except Mr. Behrmann, and you know how long he was gone!"

"Tomorrow it may be different. We shall pry some of the chicanery out into the open at any rate. Did the medical examiner have anything further on Parness?"

"He's ready to take the stand and swear Parness was brained and strangled. They've had your twine under the microscope. There are strands of lint on it that match the nap of the rug, but he says that only indicates that they had at some time been in contact."

"Fun, eh!" Fenner got up and stretched. "I think the little that's left of this salubrious day I shall spend ambling uptown. There's a place called Toni's where I ought to drop in before I go out home. Will you join me? The air will do you good."

"I'll just open a window."

23

MONDAYS ARE QUIET, TOO

MONDAY WAS AS DISAGREEABLE as Sunday had been pleasant. A slow cold drizzle and a gusty wind to whip it had started with daybreak.

Fenner took one of the few cabs available at Grand Central. He leaned forward and looked out as they scurried up Fifth Avenue toward the Strong Building. Pedestrians hurried along close to the buildings. Some huddled in doorways or struggled with umbrellas rendered intractable by the wind. Cars splashed around corners, their horns squawking sourly, and forced the people to jump back. Rubber-clad policemen at the intersections harried the traffic irritably.

Altogether it was a dreary scene, but Fenner, sometimes susceptible to these isobaric influences, scarcely noticed the day. He had succeeded in fitting Behrmann's panic and flight into the complex pattern which he had gradually evolved out of the events and circumstances of the crowded past week. That fact and a conviction that this day would produce a crisis filled his mind.

Earlier he had discovered what he believed to be a thread of purpose, sometimes concealed, sometimes exposed, winding deviously but continuously through the accumulating series of crimes. A word here, a circumstance there, had bolstered up his theory, while alibis or other less tangible psychological factors had eliminated suspects left and right. Now in Fenner's mind all were eliminated but one. There remained only the matter of marshaling proof—proof acceptable to a jury of twelve fallible adults. This did not loom as a forbidding undertaking. Fenner had discovered long ago that the super-criminal did not exist outside of fiction, that all of them left something behind which patient exploration would uncover, that given enough latitude they would assuredly by their own acts convict themselves. Fenner went into Strong's with a sober but not a heavy heart.

He was early and found that the hallman and one of Bryce's detectives were so far the only occupants of the executive wing. Fenner spent an hour assembling and reviewing the schedules and data prepared by his auditors during the past week, and formulating his line of inquiry for the afternoon's meeting. He meant to locate and possibly to recover, to the sure relief of the bonding companies employing him, certain property incomes diverted over a period of many months, and he wanted to make one endeavor to do this by his own methods before Horton began obtaining indictments.

About mid-morning, when he had satisfactorily arranged his matinee, he sauntered out into the corridor. The door to Spar's office was closed. Judge Spar was there, absorbed in a study of a folder full of papers which he was leafing through intently. He had not heard the door open but he must have felt the slight draft, for he started up quickly and his right hand fell into the open desk drawer. When he saw who it was he relaxed. Fenner pretended not to notice the gesture.

"Good morning, Judge!" he said.

"Good morning!" The Judge looked at his visitor curiously, a paper poised in his hand, his whole manner expressing polite tolerance of an unwelcome interruption of his busy morning. Fenner blithely ignored the attitude.

"Nice morning, eh?—for the ducks." The rain still spattered maliciously against the window.

Spar resigned himself to the interruption. He put the paper down and settled back into his chair, looking out at the storm.

"I expect we needed it."

"Have you thought any more about the incident you told us of yesterday morning, Judge?"

"About Parness? No; I've been involved with some business matters that haven't left me time to think about anything else. Why?"

"I wondered whether, with the passage of a few hours' time, the experience became any less real to you; whether you might be inclined to concede the thing to an overactive imagination. I see that I'm putting this very crudely, but I suppose you get what I'm driving at."

"I do, and I don't concede a particle. Parness was there, to me, almost as if he had been there in the flesh. For a moment I had no idea that he wasn't, and until I heard in the evening that he was dead I was more than puzzled as to where he could have disappeared to so abruptly. Are the police still of the opinion that he killed himself?"

Fenner backed away. "I suppose so. I haven't seen the Inspector yet this morning. I'll leave you to your work." He closed the door and hesitated in the corridor.

The next door, that to Parker's office, was closed. Fenner opened it and found the office empty. He passed on to the next, which stood open. He saw four or five of Bryce's men congregated there and inferred that most of the F. W. Strong executive personnel must have arrived. Fenner stepped in for a word with Quade. He learned that Bryce was downtown and that there had been no developments of any importance. As he started out there were footsteps in the hall and he was in time to see Hood and Parker disappear into the banker's office.

He waited until he had heard Parker's door close, then turned the other way and entered Behrmann's office. In spite of the presence of one of Bryce's men, alert in a far corner, Behrmann and Sigurd Strong, who stood over the desk, his hat and coat still on, both jumped at the opening of the door. There was an electric air of wariness that Fenner could not help but feel.

"Everyone seems to have the jitters today. What's the matter?"

"Is it surprising?" Strong asked crossly.

"Blame it on the weather," Behrmann added.

"A bit of a change from yesterday," Fenner commented. "Nice for the farmers, what!"

From the quick interchange of glances Fenner gathered that Behrmann had told Strong of the episode of Sunday afternoon. These two apparently had few secrets from each other.

"Good for the farmers, but not pleasant for the country gentlemen," the lawyer corrected, breaking into what was intended for a smile.

Again there were footsteps in the hall. Fenner heard Robert Hood speak to Miss Purcell. Fenner said, for lack of something better:

"Have you seen Inspector Bryce this morning, Mr. Strong? Do you expect him?"

"Haven't seen him or heard from him."

"It isn't important. I suppose he'll be in during the day."

"Probably."

"The papers are quiet this morning. I was curious about the mail."

"The mail?" Both Strong and Behrmann looked up.

"Yes; I rather expected some sort of communication from Mr. Shorn. You remember his note ended: 'Until later.' I shouldn't have been surprised this morning at something apologetic for his inactivity, with the usual dash of vituperation at the status-quo in general, and at whomever he has selected for his next victim, in particular."

"The papers managed three front page columns without any message," Strong observed, "thanks to the brilliant opportunism of your Mr. Bartlett."

"Don't blame him on me. Besides, it's not his paper alone."

"You people have never throttled him very earnestly."

"We've learned that it doesn't pay. 'Power of the Press,' you know." Fenner paused at the door. "I shall see you all this afternoon, I trust."

"I've spoken to everyone."

After a pause for a few words with Margaret Purcell, Fenner made his next stop in the Sales Director's office.

Hood's guard sat by the door so that anyone coming in must pass him first. Hood was writing letters on a small portable typewriter. He did not look up when Fenner entered but went right ahead with his typing until he had come to a convenient stopping place. The guard glanced over his newspaper and then went on reading.

"Your nerves are distinctly above the F. W. Strong average for this morning," Fenner congratulated Hood. "Yours is the first office I've walked into without having people start up and jump and act generally as if they expected a visitation from Satan—Satan or Gabriel!"

Hood cocked his head indifferently.

"I've got a guy with a cannon on his hip parked by the door," he said. "Why should I do a lot of worrying when the State pays him to do it for me?"

"Very sensible. I thought you were all through here."

"I am. Oh, there are a few loose ends to clear up, but I'm practically through. I'm starting to freshen up my contacts. Have to get on some kind of a payroll again soon, you know." He indicated the unfinished letter in the machine. "May I use you as a reference as to all of my Horatio Algerian attributes?"

"Sobriety, for instance."

"That particularly!"

"You may. I'll give you a good send-off. By the way, I'm glad you came in today. You had gone on Saturday when I asked Strong to get you fellows together. There are some things I want discussed in open forum, so to speak. Mr. Strong suggested that this afternoon would be a good time. Did he notify you?"

"He didn't; but I haven't seen him yet this morning. A meeting, eh? This seems to be a day of meetings!"

"Are there others?"

"Not regular meetings. I was just talking to Parker. He asked me to come into his office at eleven-thirty. Very secret and tremendously important. He mysteriously hinted that it had to do with the identity of Mr. Shorn. Parker apparently has some hunch. I asked him why in hell he didn't come out with it if he has any notions. He said he might be wrong and wouldn't want to embarrass anyone. I suppose it's just as well that you should know, though I'd rather that you didn't mention that I'd told you. Funny thing—I think he has notions about Parness' death, too. Of course, that isn't surprising. I had them for a while, myself, Saturday; but I've thought them over since and decided that I was crazy and had been taking the tabloids too seriously. I let my personal feelings run away with my judgment. I never cared much for Parness and somehow it did look fishy for him to take the gas pipe."

Fenner had waited while Hood talked himself out. Now he got up and said simply:

"You go to your meeting. Perhaps I'll drop in."

He hurried back to his desk and called Bryce at Headquarters. His request was crisp and his tone left the Inspector in no doubt as to its urgency. He said:

"Can you come up here quickly and bring Bartlett along? He may be hanging around Headquarters, though you're more likely to find him around here. Hint that you expect a break and see how he acts. He should want to come along. If he hangs back at all then you bring him along. Hurry it up. I'll wait here until eleven-thirty. If you're later than that come directly into Mr. Parker's office."

24

MR. PARKER CLEANS OUT HIS DESK

MAURICE PARKER'S CHAIR was pushed back from his desk. Beside it on the floor a large brown traveling bag stood open. The desk drawers were drawn out and Parker was methodically going through them, examining the contents and transferring some things to the bag, consigning others to the waste basket.

At eleven-twenty Behrmann opened the door. He paused and looked nervously up and down the corridor before going in. He observed Parker's activity.

"What are you doing—breaking up housekeeping here?"

"Something of that sort. I have accumulated a few things during my stay here that I value. I'm going to get them out of here before Horton tries to tell me they're F. W. Strong assets." With both hands he picked up a heavy, handsome serpentine desk set which he placed carefully in the grip.

"You'll need a dray to get that bag home," Behrmann remarked, watching it fill up. The hands of a desk clock which went in next pointed to eleven-twenty-five.

"Scarcely that. The desk set and a few books are the only heavy items." The banker kicked the desk drawers shut and straightened up. He dusted his palms. Behrmann waited, still standing near the door. He said tentatively:

"You had something in mind, Maurice?"

"Mmm. You know what the meeting this afternoon is for, don't you, A. L.?"

"Only vaguely. I understand that Mr. Fenner wants to go over some figures."

"You know what that means to us, don't you, A. L.?"

"I expect a certain amount of explanation will be required."

"How much can you explain away, A. L.?"

Before Behrmann could answer there was a rap on the door and Hood opened it.

"Is this where the conclave huddles?" he whispered with an exaggerated air of mystery and deep plotting.

"Come in and close the door," Parker snapped. "I asked Mr. Behrmann to step in, too. We may need the advice of counsel."

Hood closed the door but his hand had scarcely left the knob when it was pushed open again. Inspector Bryce, Fenner, Sigurd Strong and Johnny Bartlett crowded in with two of the Inspector's men bringing up the rear. Though there was no outward manifestation of coercion there was a sense to those already there of Strong and Behrmann being propelled into the room by the Inspector and his henchmen.

"If we're going to have a meeting—and we are—we might as well have a quorum!" Fenner announced enigmatically. "Where's Spar?"

"At McGillicuddy's for a ball. Wanted me to go," Hood volunteered.

Fenner said to Bryce:

"We need him."

The Inspector went out. They heard the rumble of his voice in the room of the late Mr. Parness next door. In a second he was back.

"O. K.," he announced.

Fenner looked around.

"You may as well make yourselves comfortable, gentlemen," he invited. "This may develop into a lengthy session. Mr. Strong had arranged a little get-together for this afternoon, but for reasons I'll get into later I took the liberty of advancing the hour."

Suiting his actions to his words Fenner dropped into a leather guest chair by the wall at one end of Parker's big desk. He swung it around so that it partly faced the room as a whole and less directly faced Parker. The banker's desk was set diagonally across one corner of the room so that its occupant faced the door. Parker kept his seat behind it.

Hood ignored several straight chairs and a leather divan along one wall and seated himself on the window ledge at the far end from Parker's desk. Strong and Behrmann chose the divan, distributing themselves so that there was no room for Bartlett who perforce resorted to one of the straight chairs. Bryce's men lounged near the door.

The rain which had persisted since early morning poured down with increasing fury and volume, the gusts whipping it in rattling sheets against the windows. The sky darkened ominously. Hood watched the plashing drops impinge, cascade into little accumulating streams which forced rapid zigzag courses down to the sill. And it was as if the cold sogginess outside had invaded the building—indeed, the very spirits of the handful of men gathered in Parker's office. There was not a smile on any face, not a word on any lip until Fenner said:

"We needn't wait for the Judge. Perhaps, indeed, it's just as well that we get a start without him."

Sigurd Strong spoke up from the divan.

"Does the nature of this discussion require representation by the press?" he inquired. "If Mr. Bartlett's presence is not necessary might I suggest that he be excused?"

"Representation by the press is not a necessity," Fenner replied, "but I should say that Mr. Bartlett's presence is more than necessary. I should say that he is absolutely indispensable. You see, we're going to solve the Shorn mystery—lay the ghost! That is, we, editorially speaking, think we are." He looked at Bartlett contemplatively, while the reporter returned his gaze with a stare of uncertain curiosity, "And Mr. Bartlett will, I believe, be of material help," he concluded.

There were a few furtive glances at Bartlett from the others but Fenner was again quickly the center of all eyes. He hooked one knee over the chair arm, drew a smoking stand closer so that he could reach it without disturbing his languid comfort, and lit a cigarette which he toyed with and savored like an esthete. It would be hard to pick the most prominent feature of his physiognomy; perhaps the high aquiline nose, perhaps the soft, deep-set, studious eyes. His clothing, adjuring ostentation of any kind, had an inherent correctness that even his distorted lounging posture could not mar.

"It's difficult to know whether to start at the beginning, which was a long time ago, and work forward, or to take a point such as, for instance, the murder of Martin Hoyle and work both ways." Fenner's voice, deceptively pacific upon such an occasion as this, drawled melodiously. It fascinated his listeners. It had a way of disarming recalcitrant witnesses, soothing them just when his delicately assiduous questioning would have otherwise had them squirming.

"There are many things connected with the events of the past week which all of you know, a number of things which some of you know, a few things known only to certain of you as individuals. Now when all of this knowledge and information is pooled and assorted a picture will be formed which will, I am confident, be very enlightening. It is for the purpose of assembling such a picture that the Inspector and I have arranged this impromptu gathering.

"Martin Hoyle was shot to death early in the afternoon a week ago last Saturday. To all superficial appearances he had killed himself. An automatic pistol, presumably his, with one shell missing from the clip lay beneath the dead man's hand. The shell lay near by. The bullet removed from Mr. Hoyle's brain was of the same caliber. Everything at first glance pointed to suicide.

"There were two things wrong with the picture: First, from the testimony of his acquaintances here, Mr. Hoyle was not psychologically or psychically a type apt to take his own life. Second, there were unmistakable indications that someone had been in Mr. Hoyle's office and tampered with his effects subsequent to his death. His desk and wardrobe had been carefully searched. A few drops of blood had dripped into the desk drawer while it was open. The Ballistics Bureau cast doubt on the bullet removed from Hoyle's brain.

"With these questions to start from, a more careful examination was made. I won't go into all the details. It's sufficient to say that another bullet was found that undoubtedly *had* been fired from Hoyle's gun—" There was a general gasp. "Per se the bullet in Hoyle's head had come from some place else, per se Hoyle had been murdered. Furthermore, it seemed probable from the circumstances that his murderer was someone known to Hoyle and someone familiar with the layout and routine of the building. Naturally you were all requested to submit alibis." He paused to gather his thoughts.

"The next development of importance was the murder of Anthony Wheeler on a ferryboat last Wednesday morning at or near ten-forty o'clock. Wheeler was shot in much the same manner as Hoyle; so much so that, even before a letter was received boasting of the fact, we were sure he had been killed by the murderer of Hoyle. As before the crime was carefully planned, and almost surely by someone known to Wheeler. To clinch it the bullet was identified as having been fired from the same gun that killed Hoyle.

"Late Friday Mr. Parness was found dead, apparently by his own hand. In this instance there were no guns and no bullets. Parness was stunned and then strangled while unconscious. Parness was bare-handed. The gas-stove valves which had been opened hadn't a finger-print on them, though Parness' finger-prints were all over the place and on many a much less receptive surface. The medical examiner placed the time of Mr. Parness' death at between three o'clock and half past. Now that particular fact had not been made public, but Mr. Shorn, in a very wordy communication denying the responsibility imputed to him by the newspapers, naïvely states that he was listening to Judge Spar 'at the time.' What Mr. Shorn's obscure reasons are for denying this particular crime I can not quite imagine. Perhaps we shall presently be enlightened."

Fenner paused and crushed out his cigarette. In its place the little gold pencil appeared between his fingers. He waved it deliberately.

"I wonder how many of you accepted Parness' suicide at its face value at the outset."

There was a general uncomfortable shuffling. As Fenner was about to resume, Judge Spar came in, with Quade and another detective close at his heels. He looked anything but pleased.

"I thought the meeting was to be this afternoon," he complained.

"One or two things came up which made it advisable to advance the hour," Fenner explained. "Sorry to have inconvenienced you."

"No inconvenience at all, but it's not very comfortable out for running back and forth." He took off his derby and whipped the rain off it, then shed his wet topcoat and hung it across a chair back. He let himself into one of the straight back chairs and folded his hands in his lap.

"You're just in time," Fenner remarked.

"Yes?"

"We've been refreshing ourselves on the details of the several murders that have taken place—Martin Hoyle, Wheeler, and Mr. Parness. We were speculating as to what purpose Mr. Shorn could have had in denying the last one. Anyway, now that we're all here we can get down to brass tacks. I had intended approaching this thing gradually, step by step. I was going to assemble carefully a picture to which you would all contribute your respective parts, but there seems to be no point in consuming too much time. The important point is that the dreaded Shorn, the horrendous killer, the so-called maniac, the calculating, cold-blooded fiend, the man who murdered Hoyle, Wheeler and Parness is one of you mild-mannered gentlemen in this room!"

The announcement, made undramatically enough, produced naturally an almost unanimous gasp, a straightening up in chairs, an instantaneous mutual wariness with pounding pulses and criss-crossing of furtive, searching glances, but from not one mouth a single spoken word of protest. Fenner waited for a moment, then observed curtly, "The idea seems to occasion very little surprise. Perhaps you know, also, to whom I refer?"

There were no answers. Fenner sat forward.

"You don't. You may have suspicions; in fact, you do have suspicions, largely misdirected—the air has been full of them—but only two people in this room absolutely know the identity of Mr. Shorn. One of them is myself, the other Mr. Shorn. One other among you has suspicions which are accurate and well founded." Fenner relaxed again.

"But these four walls and the men at the door will hold long enough. We have time to proceed in an orderly fashion. From the circumstances surrounding these murders a few facts were evident, as the logicians say, 'from inspection.' It was almost certain that Shorn was a man known to all of his victims. He had familiarity with and probably unhampered access to these premises. Even without his edifying communications it was evident that he was conversant with F. W. Strong affairs, and with the notes the fact is undeniable. His first note stated the exact total of the F. W. Strong issues in default, a figure available to the public only at the pains of improbable research and effort. Both notes were typed upon previously unused prospectus forms which at the time had not even been folded. Last but not least, his appraisal of F. W. Strong conduct of business, if you'll forgive my saying so, was obviously the result of direct knowledge rather than of mere suspicion." No one turned a hair. For a moment it appeared that Sigurd Strong would protest, but even he thought better of it.

"The motive behind Shorn's activities is somewhat obscure. I believe that I know something of its nature but I am depending upon Mr. Shorn to enlighten me further, later on. For the time I will only assure you that it had nothing in common with the possibly understandable reasons or pardonable sentiments expressed in the notes." Fenner looked around. His audience was split between rapt attention to his words and watchfulness of each other.

"Having concluded that Shorn was in some way close to F. W. Strong Company, the next obvious step was to check up on everyone in that category at the time of each crime. An absolute alibi for any one of the times would be enough to eliminate any one person. Consider first the Saturday afternoon when Hoyle was killed.

Unbelievable as it may seem, not one of you here has an absolute alibi, even by your own accounts. Mr. Parness had one, based upon certain coincidental circumstances which we unearthed, but for that occasion none of the rest of you can be eliminated.

"Now let us consider Wednesday morning—Wednesday morning from ten to eleven, say. Think carefully, gentlemen, because each of you will have that period to account for—each of you except the Judge." He turned to Spar who sat stupefied. "If you recall, you were at that hour talking to the Inspector and myself."

Spar's relief appeared enormous. He hauled out a handkerchief and wiped his pink forehead and jowls.

"Mr. Strong—" Fenner was interrupted by a soft knock and the opening of the door. A detective entered, crossed the small room with a folded sheet of paper which he handed to Bryce. Bryce glanced at it and passed, it to Fenner who read it and folded it slowly. "Never mind, Mr. Strong; we needn't bother with the alibis now." His remarks became general again. "Everyone knows, if you will pardon a pedagogical digression, that finger-prints identify individuals. Everyone also knows that handwriting, except when most cleverly forged, identifies the writer. Some of you may know, but for the benefit of those who don't I'll elucidate, that typewriting is just as distinguishing for purposes of identification as handwriting, except of course that it reveals only the machine. There are minute irregularities in the letter dies and in the spacings that, under microscopic examination, become most amazingly positive." He waved the slip of paper. "This note is from a typography expert at Headquarters. All he says is; 'The sample is it.' The 'sample' he refers to was typed on your machine twenty minutes ago, Hood." Fenner looked up mildly.

Hood had anticipated. The discourse on identification by typewriting had set him thinking. When upon the mention of his name all eyes flashed toward him, they saw not Hood idle upon the window ledge, but a changed Hood who had slid quietly to a crouched poise upon the balls of his feet. In his right hand the black forty-five which Bryce had said would 'knock down an elephant' waved in a dully gleaming, menacing arc.

"Stand back!" he warned hoarsely. White-hot anger flashed in his eyes. There was a general effort to flatten and shrink but no place to shrink to. Fenner alone was undismayed. He signaled sharply to Bryce.

"Stand back! By God, I'm letting him have it!" The gun swung up and pointed to the corner where Maurice Parker crouched behind his desk,—crouched and whipped from beneath his armpit an answer to Hood's threat in the form of a quick spurt of flame and a deafening detonation. He answered it thus once before Bryce's blackjack descended upon his skull with an equally deafening, and for Parker all-obliterating, crash.

Hood sagged back against the wall holding his shoulder. He recovered himself enough to place his gun carefully upon the window ledge, and began attempting to divest himself of his coat, but his left arm hung limp. Quade sprang to his side to help him. Parker's bullet had entered Hood's left shoulder beneath the collarbone, not a dangerous wound but painful and bleeding freely. Meanwhile Bryce lifted Parker back to his chair, disposing him so that his head hung back, and attempted to revive him. Steel bracelets secured his wrists. The gun Bryce had pocketed.

He felt the swelling on the banker's head.

"He'll be around in a minute. I didn't conk him very hard," he said.

"Nor very quickly," Fenner added. "I warned you! Hood had a close shave."

"Quick as I could. He was fast with his rod. Took me by surprise."

The others, who had witnessed the brief tableau in stupefied, numbed silence, began to come to clamorous life. The hall door, opened by the balance of Bryce's men who had come tumbling out of Wheeler's office at the sound of the shot, revealed the corridor alive with a rapidly gathering crowd. The Inspector looked up from the still inert form of Parker long enough to thunder to his men:

"Clear 'em out!—out of the hall.. Clear them all off this floor altogether!"

Fenner quieted the babble of exclamations and questions within the room.

"It's very simple," he explained. "Mr. Parker, for reasons of his own which he may or may not be good enough to explain, has been amiably engaged in eliminating certain of your number. Until now his consummately clever schemes have clicked one hundred percent. He has screened his operations with an artfully conceived program of pretended justice executions by a crack-brained maniac. I believe that today would have concluded his activity, for the typewriter which he has been using for the Shorn notes, he returned this morning to Mr. Hood. I believe that it was his intention to kill Hood and leave incriminating evidence which, taken together with the typewriter, would convince the police and public that Shorn was simply Hood in demented moments. Mr. Hood, in a few unwise displays of conscience rumblings, has so expressed himself that such an hypothesis might readily be believed." He looked at Hood tolerantly. The younger man was pale and trembling. Assisted by Quade who, with a clean handkerchief and an office towel had roughly bandaged the wound, he was hobbling back into his coat.

"You got the point quickly enough, didn't you?" Fenner said to him. "I rather thought the babble about the typewriting would sink in. Only why lose your head and try to kill him? You could easily prove he'd had your machine. There was no real danger of it being pinned on you. Now we'd better get an ambulance and have you patched up."

"Never mind that. With a little help I can navigate. We'll grab a cab. But tell me one thing: How long have you suspected I was due to get it next?"

"You ask that because you think I took undue chances?" Fenner's eyebrows raised. "Perhaps so, but I think not. I have suspected that Parker was at the bottom of this since yesterday, but as for you, I only smelled a rat when I found this morning that Parker had returned your portable typewriter and had asked you to come so secretly to his office later in the morning. I feared then that your number was up, but you've been well taken care of since. You noticed that we were not five seconds behind you when you came in here. You'd better trot along now. The explanations can wait. Besides, you've got a valuable little hunk of evidence in your shoulder. Quade, you attend to that."

"Right, Sir." They went out.

Fenner turned his attention to Parker. Strong, Behrmann and Spar stood a little to one side watching the as yet unsuccessful efforts to revive him. Each of their faces registered the same mingled horror and incredulity. Johnny Bartlett was jabbing pot-hooks and other shorthand hieroglyphics into his notebook as fast as his excited hand would travel.

Fenner asked:

"You search him yet, Inspector?"

Bryce stopped fanning and went through Parker's pockets, placing their contents on the desk top. There was a wallet, fountain pen, keyholder, and a number of papers and envelopes. One envelope, a little cleaner and newer than the rest, Fenner snatched. It was unsealed and addressed:

TO THE POLICE, THE GENTLEMEN OF THE
PRESS AND THE PUBLIC AT LARGE

Fenner drew out and unfolded one of the by now too familiar Romaine Hotel prospectuses. Strong and Behrmann and Spar gathered around, Bartlett pricked up his ears avidly, even the Inspector temporarily abandoned his resuscitation endeavors. Fenner glanced through the letter hastily and remarked:

"It looks as if you'd been on the calendar, too, Mr. Behrmann. Listen:" He read the letter slowly and with faintly mocking solemnness. "To the Police, the Gentlemen of the Press and the Public at Large: It's all too sickening. As a self-appointed avenging angel I'm a flop. The public regards me as demented. Perhaps the public is right. I regard myself as only ill-qualified by hands too dirtied peddling F. W. Strong Bonds to ever get them clean, even in the blood I've shed of my own associates. I'm tired, now, and the role doesn't fit. I could quit but I know there would be no peace. I shall make myself my own last victim. The work I've done has not been wasted. There has been some slight salutary effect. For a time, at least, a few of the scoundrels have been frightened away. Drink to the glory of the House of Strong. Shorn. P. S. I may find it convenient to take Behrmann and Parker along with me. You will know when you read this whether or not I have. That will give the papers something to print. There has been a dearth of news lately. Good-by."

Fenner folded the paper up and looked at them. Over Behrmann's shoulder his eyes met those of Maurice Parker, partly open. They fluttered closed and the banker's head rolled slightly to one side.

"What happened?" His query was scarcely audible.

Bryce quickly turned back to him. There was more cold water and more groaning but in a few moments Parker was upright in the chair and staring dazedly around. He started to raise one hand to his head and discovered the manacles. His eyes passed from Fenner's to Bryce's, a weary hunted look in them, then all around the group. He summoned his strength and asked:

"What's the idea?"

"We thought it better. Relax a while."

Parker's faculties seemed to return in an instant. He raised his handcuffed wrists more in anger than despair and tried to get up, but the Inspector thrust him gently but firmly back into the chair.

Parker snapped:

"Where's Hood? The damned lunatic started to shoot me. Did I get him first?" He looked again at his wrists. "But this is an outrage! I demand to know with what I am charged! I demand counsel! A. L., why don't you tell these fools something?"

"I'm afraid we know too much already, Mr. Parker." Fenner spoke up. "As for the charge, there will be three first-degree murders, an attempted murder, conspiracy to defraud, and nearly every form of larceny and embezzlement charge known to the law. I dare say it will make two or three dozen counts."

Behrmann said:

"I'm afraid it's no use, Maurice. You see, Mr. Fenner has just read us the last letter."

"Last letter?"

"Why prolong it, Parker? It's up! It's over! That's all there is; there isn't any more! Words to that effect." Fenner's query was almost irritably put. "You're all through. Why not give in?"

"I wish I knew what you were talking about. You all saw Hood draw a gun on me. I shot him and had every right to defend myself. The rest—"

"I'll tell you about the rest," Fenner cut in. "I'll tell you at considerable length and in minute detail. When you realize that you can't possibly squirm out maybe you'll come clean and save the State, your associates, and yourself a great deal of trouble. A week ago last Saturday you murdered Martin Hoyle. Either you met him here by appointment with the idea of dividing an accumulation of loot from certain artful property mismanagement, and double-crossed him, or you discovered that Hoyle was on the point of running out himself and followed him back here. Hoyle had gone to your bank just before noon and cleaned out a safe deposit box that was maintained in your joint names. The deposit vault record card shows him in at eleven-forty-five and out at eleven-fifty-five. You sat beside him here chatting pleasantly and shot him in the head. Then you got his own gun out of his desk, slipped your silencer on it and fired it out of the window into that earth pile, recovered the shell from your own gun, tucked Mr. Hoyle's little satchel under your arm and beat it out the back way. It was a lucky thing both you and Hoyle had thirty-eights, or did you plan that, too?"

Parker was glumly silent.

"Whatever possessed you to mail those letters of Hoyle's—and if you wanted to, why downtown? That was a bad slip."

"I don't know what you're talking about."

"Of course not. Let's refresh your memory further. After Hoyle was found you sat tight until it became evident on Tuesday that the suicide arrangement had not deceived the police. The actual murder of Hoyle had been surprisingly easy. Fearing detection it was not unnatural that you should hit upon the idea of also eliminating those individuals in the F. W. Strong Company who were aware of the way things had been going and who might jump to conclusions about you. Wheeler and Parness and Behrmann were the ones most dangerous to you. I don't know what suggested the 'crank' campaign and who composed those letters. I suppose you did them yourself, but their tone as well as their content is so entirely alien to your own makeup that it must have been almost abortive. Tell me, why did you pick Wheeler next?"

There was no answer. Parker stared dully ahead. Fenner answered his own question.

"I think you picked Wheeler next for two reasons: first, because if he was cognizant of what you and several others had been doing he was more likely than some of the rest to spill his guts out—if you'll pardon the expression—to the authorities; and second, because the physical difficulties were small. All you needed to do was to hang around Wheeler's house Wednesday morning and follow him in to town. Living in the next town you were familiar with his commuting habits. It meant only that you used the Erie that morning instead of the D. L. and W. Hardly a bit out of your way and you got to the bank only a few minutes after your usual time. But didn't you feel a little uneasy, walking around with that incriminating letter on your person? You didn't mail it until you got all the way up town. What if a taxi had run you down, or if you'd had a stroke?"

Parker looked at Fenner with a little more life in his eyes but persisted in his stolid silence. He switched his glance to Strong and Behrmann, who seemed unable quite to return it. They shrank from him almost visibly and kept their eyes on Fenner or the carpet. Spar alone was able to watch him without recoiling, and even his face showed horror mingled with a sort of laboratory curiosity. Fenner's voice, resuming impassively to Parker, broke the waiting silence.

"Wheeler's murder was apparently successful. Emboldened by its ease and by the way the police and public had seized the Shorn bait, you could hardly wait for your next chance. Parness, by his own actions, made your task easier. Instead of staying within the shelter of the protection that the State was taking great pains to provide, he, for reasons of his own which have no bearing on this case, deliberately fled it. You followed him to the West End Avenue apartment and—but why go further. I'll wager you sat up half the night, though, composing your second literary venture, the one you posted on your way in Saturday morning. It really wasn't half bad! But if you had been wise you'd have written 'Finis' on it, Parker. Up to that point you'd done fairly well. You should have quit right there.

"You couldn't quit and stay here, but you might have quit and dropped out of sight and gotten away with it. Less clever men than you have done it. It might not have been fun but—the alternative you've fallen upon won't be pleasant either. You should have observed that our watch was tightening up and that any further eliminations would be attended with more difficulty. Still a little drunk with the heady brew of the three successful murders to your credit, you thought you could crash through with the one or two more that would win you undisturbed use of your ill-got gains.

"You must have been fairly sure by then that the Shorn pretense had become quite transparent, as far as we were concerned, that the police and even some of your associates here suspected that these murders were inside jobs with a definite motive. Weren't you worried, Parker?"

There was no answer. The banker's eyes were cast down to his manacled wrists.

You may have been, but not enough so. You jumped a step ahead. You would capitalize our own astuteness. If it was our thought that one of your number was involved, you would provide us with a very plausible criminal in the person of Mr. Hood, dead so he couldn't deny it. That would let you out. At the same time you would eliminate Mr. Behrmann, he being the only survivor who possessed what you regarded as a dangerous amount of information about you. To do this the three of you must be together. Your own presence you would account for in Hood's suicide letter by having him suggest that he might try to kill you, too. It was all very nicely thought out. There was only one thing wrong, a thing you could hardly be aware of. It was that by a process of elimination I had about concluded on Saturday that either you or Mr. Behrmann must be putting on this Shorn act; consequently you were both watched with a thoroughness of which you had no idea. Your typing was heard during the wee hours of Sunday night in your attic. Today you brought the machine to town in that big bag of yours and returned it to Hood. I found him innocently pecking away on it this morning. I didn't have to ask where it came from. We've known since Saturday just what typewriters there were in these offices, and have compared samples from all of them with your letters. Hood had no personal machine until this morning.

"Hood told me you had asked him to come in on the quiet. I didn't know just exactly what you could have in mind but I suspected it was plenty. The rest is familiar to the Inspector but not to the rest of you. We covered Hood with extra protection, rushed a sample from his machine to Headquarters, and waited for the zero hour. If we had come here ten minutes later do you know what we would have found?" The question was purely rhetorical. "Correct me, Parker, if I'm wrong. We'd have found you, Mr. Behrmann, stretched out with a bullet in your heart. Pleasant thought, isn't it. Makes you homesick for the country, what? We'd have found Hood with a close-up shot, probably in the head like Hoyle's, and apparently self-inflicted. We would have found Parker with an actually self-inflicted minor wound in a pseudo faint. Hood's letter would have probably been propped up in a prominent place on the desk. The gun with the silencer attached would be near Hood's body.

"It might not have been quite that way. Perhaps Parker would have rushed out with a terrified tale of how Hood had shot Behrmann dead, had shot at him and missed, and had then shot himself. If you had selected that presentation, Mr. Parker, I suppose the letter would have been tucked away in Hood's coat pocket?"

Fenner paused more for breath than for Parker's answer. The pudgy banker raised his eyes and looked at Fenner for a long searching moment. He turned listless. The Inspector pressed him.

"Why not say something, Mr. Parker?"

"What's the use? Anything I'd say would be turned against me. I'll wait and do my talking with lawyers."

Fenner looked up incredulously.

"I guess you hit him harder than you thought, Inspector," he said. "The man's crazy!" During the long recital Fenner had gradually edged to an alert uprightness at the front of his chair. Now he slid back deep into it, hooked his leg over the arm again, and resumed his solid comfort. His voice, which had developed an intense crispness, returned to the easy drawl. "Parker, when the Ballistics Bureau fires that thirty-eight of yours and finds the bullets scored to match the balance of their collection, all the Philadelphia lawyers east of the Mississippi won't be able to do you any good. And the letter was taken out of your pocket in the presence of a half dozen witnesses. Why, that alone would send you up. There's one more thing. Where's the silencer, Parker?"

"Silencer?" But Parker's tone was feebler.

"Never mind; we'll find it. It must be in some readily accessible place, because you intended using it. Look in the top desk drawer, Inspector. That will make the picture complete."

Bryce pulled out the center desk drawer.

"Not there. The second drawer on the right, Inspector. Let's get out of here." Parker was matter-of-fact but his abrupt reversal of attitude was the culminating shock for the others in the room. The dejected prisoner added a little more cheerfully: "You're to be congratulated, Mr. Fenner. I think you're a remarkable man. No reflections, Inspector, but I know to whom I owe my Waterloo. Well, Sig, A. L., Judge—I suppose I've given all of you some bad moments. I'm sorry. By the way, Sig, will you see that my bag gets out to my wife? Again, Mr. Fenner, my compliments! You are a master at your trade. I almost like you."

Fenner, who had interrupted the lighting of a cigarette to stare quizzically at Parker during the astonishing tirade, replied with a cold smile:

"And you, my dear fellow, are a loathsome, double-tongued, moderately clever murderer. You are also a thief, and last but not least, an incredible bore. The chair will be much too good for you. As for the bag, the salvage of which I suppose is the object of your crafty, nauseating effusiveness, Mr. Strong will not see to it that your wife gets it. I'll see to it that, with proper formalities, Mr. Horton gets it. By all logical sequence it should contain at least some of the loot I referred to before. At the bank this morning you had it with you when you visited the safe deposit vault. I think that we may as well adjourn." He turned to Bryce. "I suppose you will get a detailed confession from Mr. Parker downtown. Will you let me have a transcript of it? I'm curious to see in what details I'm mistaken."

"Come along to Headquarters with us, Max."

"I'd prefer not to. Besides, I have some business to wind up with Horton. But leave one man with me until I've disposed of that grip."

Bryce herded the others out. Strong, Behrmann and Judge Spar were regarded as material witnesses and held pending bail arrangements.

Word had spread from the moment of Parker's single desperate shot that something sensational was afoot at F. W. Strong's, but the police kept the building clear and the heavy rain discouraged the accumulating curious in the street, so that only a small crowd witnessed the departure of the police and their prisoners in four squad cars. Johnny Bartlett slipped into Hood's deserted office, locked the door, sat down to the telephone and gave the *Globe* its last and best scoop of the Shorn affair.

25

MR. FENNER RECAPITULATES

A HALF HOUR LATER at Police Headquarters a near-finale to the amazing series of events was written. Inspector Bryce, completely oblivious of the enormous public curiosity and interest with which the incident must necessarily be vested, had proceeded methodically with the customary preparations for interrogating Parker and recording his confession. He had notified the Prosecutor and, together with one detective and a stenographer, he waited in his dingy office while Parker was being booked, photographed, finger-printed and put through the usual routine. To Bryce Parker was no glamorous public figure. He was prisoner number —, a problem rather than a person, an antisocial unit to be dealt with mechanically, in a prescribed way and in the ordinary course of events, and certainly not to be glorified with special attention or singled out in any way. Therefore when the Commissioner himself with several deputies, and the Prosecutor and several extra assistants descended upon him to share the hearing, necessitating its transference to more spacious chambers, Bryce made no effort to conceal his annoyance.

The lobbies and newsmen's rooms were jammed with reporters and photographers. In the streets, now that definite word had gotten around, crowds, braving the rain, milled and jostled. It was not an ill-tempered mob. Rather, for a gathering of its kind, it was surprisingly good-natured. Feeling for the prisoner, whose identity had passed from lip to lip, was more of curiosity than animosity.

434

Strong and Behrmann and Spar, detained in a separate room, looked out at the assemblage through the high barred windows. Each kept to himself the thoughts crowding through his mind, or they would have discovered a galling unanimity: the forbidding, thick stone walls and the heavy bars set solidly in the narrow windows formed not a prison but a refuge.

Bryce waited, relating unenthusiastically to the Commissioner the principal events of the morning. After what seemed an ample interval had elapsed he excused himself and called to the detective:

"Go out and shake 'em up, will you, Meehan. We haven't got all day."

Meehan started but the door was opened in his face and a police surgeon came in. He cast a worried look in the direction of the Commissioner. Through the open door they heard a distant confusion. Bryce sensed the impending announcement before the surgeon spoke.

"The prisoner poisoned himself, Inspector. Just now, on the way up. He's in pretty bad shape!"

When the general clamor, the imprecations of the Commissioner, and the blatantly righteous fury of the Prosecutor had lashed themselves out Bryce learned what had happened. Parker had submitted with disarming cheerfulness to all the details of finger-printing and registration. He had talked amiably and seemed reconciled to his fate.

As they started for Bryce's office he had in one unguarded movement smothered a yawn and swallowed the contents of a tiny vial which he had contrived to keep from his searchers' notice. It had taken effect with electric suddenness and he had dropped into a crumpled, livid heap upon the floor. The vial was discovered clutched between his fingers, almost empty of its load of hydrocyanide. Antidotes and emetics had been administered immediately but the condition of the prisoner was grave. In any case, the hearing was postponed.

Bryce listened disgustedly. He telephoned Fenner who received the news without surprise, and discoursed with exasperating airiness:

"When men of his type turn to crimes of violence they often prepare for eventualities in just that way. My own idea would be to provide them with every opportunity to go their merry way. It saves the State time and expense."

Later in the afternoon Bryce had himself driven for the last time to the F. W. Strong Building. He found Fenner in Hoyle's room packing a heavy portfolio.

"You done?"

"Practically," Fenner confessed.

"There are some loose ends. Let's jaw a while."

"Fire away!" Fenner snapped the straps home and flopped the bulky briefcase on the desk. "Oh! How's Hood?"

"He's all right. Flesh wound. He'll be out tomorrow with his arm in a sling. He'll be sore for a while, but in a few weeks he'll have nothing left but a scar and tender memories!"

"Did you recover the bullet?"

"Yes, but it wasn't necessary. We'd already taken some other samples from Parker's gun. They were unmistakable."

The Inspector sank into a chair and relit his cigar. Now that the case was definitely at an end he permitted an accumulating fatigue to show in his bearing.

"What was it all for, Max? You were vague this morning. If Parker had waited until he had talked a little I wouldn't give a damn if he drank all the poison in New York City."

"It is unfortunate, in that way. There are some things that Parker could have told you that we can only guess at unless he recovers; but perhaps our guess won't be too far from the truth. A set of books, when you can get at them and read between the entries, tell a fairly accurate story. It's astonishing how difficult it is—how impossible, I might say—to manipulate figures in an accounting system and conceal irregularities from eventual discovery if the books are subjected to a leisurely and thorough scrutiny."

"But just where did Parker come in?"

"I'll get to that," Fenner said patiently. "It's not a short story. This affair had its real beginnings almost two years ago when F. W. Strong began taking back properties. Parker was a member of almost every one of the so-called Protective Committees set up to operate the various recovered properties, presumably for the benefit of the bondholders. The other members usually consisted of Mr. Hoyle, Mr. Behrmann and Judge Spar. Mr. Hoyle and Mr. Parker handled the funds, Mr. Behrmann the legal details, and Judge Spar lent weight. I suspect that his name on the Protective Committees was calculated to lend some degree of reassurance to the quaking bond-holders, and possibly to discourage the few who were intelligent enough and articulate enough to object to some of the proposed reorganizations.

"Well, the boys got together and inaugurated a quiet program of intensive milking by methods ranging all the way from techni-cally legal if morally execrable fee levying, to temporarily concealed plain larceny. They looted individually; then for some reason, the real truth of which will never be known unless I overrate Mr. Behrmann, or Parker talks, they looted collectively. It is barely possible that of the four Judge Spar might not have been involved. Martin Hoyle was about to run out with their mutual swag when Parker hi-jacked him and took it himself."

"You speak very positively."

"I can. Part of the stuff converted to negotiable securities was in the bottom of Parker's bag. More securities and a hundred and twenty thousand in cash was located in his deposit box. Horton has attached it. Altogether it takes care of about half the discrep-ancies in the books. However, half a loaf—you know. Imagine Horton's surprise!"

"Yeah. What I *can't* imagine is a guy of Parker's makeup going in for that much violence."

"You see, Parker was in pretty bad shape financially. The clos-ing of the bank was a matter of days. The injunction that put Strong out of business would also put the bank on the rocks. They were thoroughly interconnected, what with a lot of flukey loans and fishy collateral passed back and forth both ways. Parker had much to gain and little to lose. I rather imagine even his affairs at the bank would hardly stand the bright light of an insolvency investigation."

"But what about the others—Wheeler and Parness?"

"Wheeler and Parness had formerly been closely associated with the management of many of the properties taken over. They were familiar enough with their financing and earnings to have suspected such wholesale diversion. At least Parker probably figured that way, and I think he was right. I believe Parker was afraid of exposure. He feared that he or Behrmann might be suspected by Wheeler or Parness of murdering Hoyle, once it became evident that the police suspected someone associated with Hoyle. He was sure that Behrmann would eventually suspect him. Behrmann could not very well talk without revealing his own participation, but either of the others upon the slightest confirmation might voice their suspicions. Parker probably reasoned that he would never be quite secure while Parness or Wheeler or Behrmann lived.

"Parker had risen via the wholesale clothing route to a position of considerable eminence in the banking field—at least, there was a pseudo-prestige that extended well throughout the ranks of the pre-1930 cloak and suit bankers—and he was loathe to abandon it. The actual murder of Hoyle had been easy enough, but when it became apparent that the suicide representation was not going to be swallowed by the police Parker hit upon the crank idea. It was well suited to his purpose; it would divert suspicion in the case of the Hoyle murder already committed and it would provide a plausible explanation for the other murders which he had decided upon. What Parker did not take into account was that a terrorization campaign of that kind would make the police and also his prospective victims so careful that the balance of his program would be impossibly difficult. So when it came Parness' turn Parker abandoned the role of Shorn. He must have familiarized himself earlier with Parness' habits and must have known of his little foible with Mrs. Strong. By purest chance I came into Parness' office on Friday morning while he was talking on the telephone. It was obvious that he was ill at ease and was restricted in his speaking because he was not alone. I was only there for the end of it but Parker was there all through it. Parness ended up by giving a vague consent to do something or be somewhere about the middle of the afternoon. Parker must have taken it all in and leaped at the chance to catch Parness unprotected."

Bryce shook the ash from his cigar and leaned back.

"When you told me before we went in this morning to stay close to Parker I thought you'd gone nuts," he said. "What brought you to him finally? I gathered a certain amount this morning but it's still pretty foggy."

"Two tracks—" Fenner paused, searching for words. "There were two parallel approaches which I did my best to follow, each independent of the other. One was physical opportunity, the alibi angle, so to speak; the other was motivation. Consider the alibi line-up first." He drew from his pocket the piece of foolscap which Bryce remembered. "Here is the alibi schedule we started the other morning. I amended it with some additional data I obtained Saturday from your esteemed friend with the nose for news. He'd spotted Hood and Strong at the County Consolidated Bank on Wednesday morning. You see the two items I've added cuts the list right down to Parker and Behrmann."

The table now looked like this:

	Saturday P.M.	Wednesday A.M.	
Parness	East 44th St. 2:00 PM Central Pk. W. 2:30 PM	?	Dead
Hood	Drunk ? ? ?	Office (presumably)	County Consol. Bank
Strong	Club with Behrmann	In and out of office?	County Consol. Bank
Behrmann	Club with Strong	With Spar ? ?	
Parker	Bank, then home, D L & W ? ?	Bank (Maybe) ?	
Judge Spar	Football Game ? ?	Here with us	

"You see," Fenner explained, "Saturday's alibis really eliminate one man, Mr. Parness. He might conceivably have had time to pop in here between the time he left the garage and the time he met Mrs. Strong, but he couldn't possibly have mailed Hoyle's letters downtown. Wheeler could have or Parker could have. Strong or Behrmann might have, though not so easily, for it would have required that much longer an absence from the club.

"Wednesday morning's alibis were valueless until I learned that Bartlett had seen Strong and Hood at the County Consolidated Bank at or near the time that Wheeler was being shot. That let them out. Furthermore, I remembered that Bartlett had mentioned having had to wait a long time to see Mr. Parker at the bank Wednesday morning.

"Thus we're down to Behrmann and Parker. Now when Behrmann was brought back by the collar on Sunday he seemed to me a man genuinely frightened. If he had figured things out and suspected Parker of having killed Hoyle and Wheeler and Parness— and having gotten away with it, mind you—Behrmann would realize that his turn would inevitably arrive and that his life wasn't worth a plugged nickel while Parker was loose. And the worst of it was that he couldn't turn Parker in without also incriminating himself. I don't blame him for running away. If I had been in his shoes I'd have done the same thing—that or turned the tables and bumped off Parker before he could get a crack at me. Anyway, I figured that the incident Sunday threw the weight of probability from the two of them even, over toward Parker, and that Behrmann was about out of it.

"So much for the 'alibi' approach. Now considering motive, which, of course, unfolded concurrently: The first fact from the books was that, of the funds earned by the F. W. Strong managed properties, very large sums consistently dropped by the wayside. The second was that, from the set-up of the Committee, this continual drain was sure to be known by at least three of the committee, Hoyle, Behrmann and Parker, and I later learned that it was strongly suspected by Parness and Wheeler. Well, if Hoyle, Behrmann, Parker and Spar were acting in concert as they must have been, then what more natural than that one of them should have been involved in the killing?—or possibly Parness because he may have been suspicious of if not actually aware of their activities. I had reasoned just about that far on Wednesday when Wheeler was killed on the boat. That temporarily upset all of my calculations. I don't mind admitting that the 'crank' idea fooled me for a while. After all, it didn't seem unnatural that of all the

unfortunates whom F. W. Strong Company had swindled, one at
least might go haywire and rise up in his wrath with a cracked notion of righting his wrongs. When I thought much about that angle
I marveled that it hadn't happened sooner. But when I thought over
the details of the messages I saw that the theory wouldn't hold
water. Whoever wrote the notes was obviously conversant with the
F. W. Strong affairs. Anyone conversant with F. W. Strong affairs
would have known that Anthony Wheeler, victim number two, was
the most honest, or perhaps I should say least actively dishonest,
of the lot. I think the most vicious thing in his life was an occasional pinochle party in his neighbor's cellar barroom. Shorn by
picking him right off the bat made the swindled investor pretense
a farce.

"So I leaned back to our inside job theory. Next, Parness was
eliminated, leaving only Behrmann and Parker so far as that general motive was concerned. The direct motive could be the same in
either case—to silence witnesses whose testimony would be con-
victing when the inevitable showdown came. There was one additional factor throwing the weight of suspicion toward Parker: Hoyle
visited the safe deposit box just before noon on the Saturday of his
death. Of them all the banker was most likely to be cognizant of
that fact.

"At any rate, I eventually reached Mr. Parker as far as my own
suspicions were concerned; as far as actual proof went, I hadn't a
shred of it. One thing I did find, not proof but lending plausibility
to the whole idea: a magazine article several years old in the back of
one of Parker's desk drawers. It was one of those 'Success Stories,'
you know, and among other things it mentioned Mr. Parker's rather
unusual Spanish American War record. He was a sharpshooter!

"On Sunday Mr. Behrmann 'took it on the lam,' as your colleagues would phrase it. That, too, dropped right into place in the
picture. When we saw him he had all the earmarks of a man frightened half to death. I believe he reasoned somewhat as I did and
also arrived at Mr. Parker's doorstep. He couldn't squeal or beg
specific protection without getting himself into a jam, but he believed, and rightly, that he was next on the spot. With Parker's

amazing record in the form of Hoyle, Wheeler and Parness right before him, who can blame him for getting panicky?"

"He's the one you meant this morning when you said one other person beside yourself and Shorn suspected Shorn's identity?"

"Exactly."

"Whatever made Parker try to finish up the whole business this morning. Do you think he knew you were wising up?"

"I don't think he feared he was suspected by us. I think he was afraid Behrmann was about to break down. And there was the meeting scheduled for this afternoon. There would be most embarrassing questions. He knew Behrmann wouldn't shoulder the whole blame. With Behrmann out of the way Parker could just act dumb. The worst he could ever be convicted of would be that he'd been a 'director who didn't direct,' and Lord knows they're common enough!"

"Behrmann might spill his ideas about the money, too."

"Of course. So when I found Parker had brought the typewriter back to Hood and had asked him to come in, the light began to filter through. Not too soon, either. Do you see what a simple yet diabolically clever scheme he had? Two minutes alone with Hood and Behrmann was all he needed, that and his silenced thirty-eight. If Hood had been found dead, the farewell note and the other two all typed upon his machine, and Behrmann dead beside him, even you or I, suspecting what we might, could never make a charge stick to Parker. Why, even the letters! They're in the inimitable style and tone of a person of Hood's type, or at least of a person definitely *not* of Parker's type. He was an accomplished man! It's not until you look back that you realize his consummate histrionic ability. Throughout the past ten days he has sustained a pretense of fear, of ineffectual stupidity and uncertainty that would most certainly have completely deceived us if it had not been for the outside clues. And his fatness cloaked agility and speed—at least, speed in getting at that gun of his!"

"We could have pinched him right off, without taking a chance on Hood or Behrmann."

"Yes; and have taken a chance on a false arrest and defamation suit. Remember, I'm not a public officer. Anyway, there was still a great deal of conjecture. We knew Shorn wasn't any of the others but there was still a slim chance of an outsider. It was not until the last typing sample checked up that we were on absolutely sure ground. I was stalling in the room there this morning, waiting for that one bit of positive proof. If it hadn't checked up I'd have had to risk an accusation. Finding the gun and silencer would have been just as effective, and the letter on his person. But when you handed me that note I knew the case was in the bag. Now I think you know it all."

Bryce got to his feet.

"Yeah; and I also know that I'm going home and grab some shut-eye! See you later."

EPILOGUE

WITH THE HELP of the most skillful medication and care available to the civilized community Maurice Parker was painfully nursed back to comparative health; so that the civilized community might then, salving itself with resonant newspaper phrases to the effect that the "Extreme Penalty" had been exacted, steep itself for a short time in the entertaining spectacle, widely publicized, of Mr. Parker roasting in the chair.

Once under way, the trial and conviction of Parker was speedily accomplished, but the poison had incapacitated him for thinking or speech for a sufficient period to enable Messrs. Strong and Behrmann to make a quiet exodus across the border to Montreal, and thence wend their way by inconspicuous freight steamer to the Mediterranean for an extended vacation. Judge Spar took his in South America.

Shirley Strong did not accompany her husband. Parness dead was still Parness in Sigurd's mind and he could not bring himself quite to the point of overlooking him. Nothing was said. The Strongs mutually studiously avoided the subject. It was simply that Mr. Strong went and Shirley Strong stayed behind.

Nor had she wanted to go. The strain of keeping locked up within her certain horrible doubts and suspicions made Sigurd's company for her quite intolerable. It was not until an afternoon some ten days after Sigurd's departure that a brief but illuminating conversation with Maxwell Fenner had altered her viewpoint of a number of things.

Fenner had come to the town house on the day after sentence was pronounced upon Maurice Parker. The servants had all been dismissed with the exception of one maid, and most of the house was closed up. Shirley remembered Fenner's face, but little else about him. He had come without prearrangement or announcement, had rung the bell and she had let him in. With the barest of apologies for the intrusion he had come to the point of his call.

"The record," he said gravely, "is closed. What is not in it now Mr. Parker is going to take with him to his grave. He refuses to discuss these matters at all and I'm confident he won't be budged during the few weeks he will remain with us. But there are one or two things which you and I ought to clear up between ourselves. Why did you turn the gas on at the apartment that Friday afternoon?"

"I—I—" Shirley was taken quite by surprise. "How do you know—why do you say that?"

"I simply want to know. You must have had a reason. Was Mr. Parness on the divan, or did you have to lift him up there, too?"

"I—" Shirley fell into a frightened silence.

"Parker really *did* kill him, you know. You feared it had been someone else. I want to know who and why. Forget the first part; you feared it had been your husband. You may forget your fears. I assure you that your husband was nowhere near the apartment. In return please tell me why you assumed that."

"I found his cane there."

It was Fenner's turn to be surprised, but not for long. He thought back quickly, half aloud.

"The cane!—of course. Parker mentioned rather broadly that Sigurd didn't have it in the elevator that night. I didn't get the point. Stupid of me!" He looked up at Shirley. "You fixed things up in the apartment and brought the cane away? You haven't discussed the thing with Mr. Strong at all?"

Shirley shook her head mutely.

"Reticence is not always a virtue, my dear. I shall have a talk with him when he returns."

Shirley looked away.

"It isn't important," she said in a tired voice.

"Ah, but it is!" Fenner had a sudden flash of insight into Shirley's exact mental and psychical stage. The death of Parness had definitely marked the termination of a period, due to end anyway. From this time forward a certain racial serenity would make itself increasingly felt. Certainly there were salvable years for her and Sigurd. He suddenly saw them both, wrinkled, bickering amiably. By all means he would see Sigurd.

He would have to see the Inspector, too. Bryce had at the time remarked that Shirley seemed unnaturally (it could be suspiciously) unsurprised the evening they had called upon the Strongs with word of Parness' death. And sooner or later it would occur to Bryce, as it had to himself, that with the four gas burners turned on full blast as they had been found, the rickety building would have been filled from cellar to attic in spite of a rug or two across the door cracks, in a great deal less time than the four hours which had elapsed between Parness' death and their discovery of him. Very definitely Fenner would have also to see the Inspector.

Three days after this Mr. Hood's roadster, San Francisco bound, engine humming with a new-found merriness, raced between sear Indiana cornfields along a broad highway that headed directly into the dying sun. Hood squinted against its glare.

"Make Indianapolis by dark, Peggy."

Mrs. Robert Alanson Hood, 3rd, stirred lazily against his shoulder.

"What's your hurry?"

Hood threw the car out of gear and let it roll to a stop at the edge of the road. He gathered her to him, awkwardly, for one arm was sore and lame.

She said presently, "You won't make Indianapolis by next week at that rate."

"What's *your* hurry?"

Margaret looked out without answering. A farmhouse and a low group of red outbuildings, hovering in the shelter of a half dozen miraculously spared tall oaks, alone broke the sweep of rolling seas of fields. She felt the enormous evening peace.

"I feel as if I'm just coming awake. Did all of that really happen? Murders? Police? It seems ages back and so unreal. And Mr. Parker waiting! It makes me shudder to think of him."

"It happened. But we've left it all behind, Peggy. We'll never get away from it unless we pretend that it didn't. Let's push on."

Johnny Bartlett recovered with astonishing celerity from a fondly nursed sense of bereavement at the sudden marriage of Margaret and Hood. He recovered so rapidly that even he himself was not surprised when, upon the occasion of his next visit to his home town, he acquired, for better or for worse but with dizzying abruptness, a bride in the person of the baker's blonde daughter with whom he had played as a child. Johnny wasn't sure how it all happened but he took it with good grace.

A month slipped by, bringing one gray morning the first snowfall of an early winter. Johnny walked out of the *Globe* Building, cast a morose glance in either direction and headed for Gallagher's and consolation. There was no news! He'd have to write up the old one about the first snowfall.

The Shorn sensation had died as quickly as it had risen. Two days after the private but thoroughly photographed and completely written up interment of Maurice Parker, scarcely a paper carried a line regarding any aspect of the Strong–Shorn affair. Unobtrusively real estate bankers and mortgage loan directors had cut short hastily arranged vacations and filtered back into the city.

Over his third beer Johnny had an inspiration. (It wasn't very good beer.) He went back to his desk and sat down before the typewriter. That evening the public was regaled with a rehash of the F. W. Strong murders, justified in the preliminaries of the article by the tremendously important fact that an exact month had elapsed since its sordid termination at Sing Sing. The article concluded with a beautiful word picture, based upon what scanty information Johnny could obtain, but largely suppositious:

".... and so today while Maurice Parker, murderer,
and Martin Hoyle, Anthony Wheeler and Winthrop

Parness, his victims, share the common sod; Sigurd
Strong, financier and ex-master of borrowed mil-
lions, and Abraham Behrmann, his crafty counselor
and fellow fugitive, idle away long afternoons in the
tiny Grecian coast village of Manolada, sipping cool
drinks and casting nostalgic glances over the Gulf
of Patras, past Cephalonia and in the general direction of the unhospitable American shore."

Johnny's romantic imaginings were somewhat less than accurate. Some days later—as many, in fact, as it required for Strong's
New York newspapers to get from the Metropolitan presses to their
Grecian refuge—Sigurd Strong read the article and handed the
paper to Behrmann. They were not on a cool balcony by the shore;
they were seated at a very inferior sidewalk café in a hot and smelly,
narrow street which twisted a tortuous way from the fish markets
at the water's edge, through a scattering group of one-story shops,
and died away among the olive farms up beyond the town. They
were not sipping cool drinks; they were making the best of a luke-
warm, insipid local Greek wine. It was all they could afford. And
they were not casting nostalgic glances toward American shores;
they were casting weary, mildly venomous glances at each other,
weighted with that peculiar negative malevolence which can be
attained only by marooned expatriates totally dependent upon each
other for company.

"I thought it was over with. Why can they never let a thing die?"
Strong complained when Behrmann had finished reading the article
and had laid the paper down.

"Some things never die. We ourselves will long be dead before
this thing is let die."

In the face of Behrmann's malicious cold comfort Strong sought
refuge in counter irony and a change of subject.

"The heat and dirt of this place have a distinct originality. I
believe that even the smells are unique. We're at least fortunate in
the surroundings for our sojourn."

"If you call staying in this God-forsaken hole the rest of our lives a sojourn," Behrmann amended. His eyes met Sigurd's over his raised glass and he added hearteningly, "We may not be permitted, however, to enjoy this delightful environment indefinitely. An extradition treaty is almost certain to result from the public pressure that is being brought to bear. I suggest, then, that we make the most of our uncertain tenure on these hospitable shores by getting, if this vile slop will lend itself to that lofty purpose, comfortably anesthetized!"

They drained their glasses.

COACHWHIP PUBLICATIONS

COACHWHIPBOOKS.COM

THE LAST
TRUMPET
A HUGH RENNERT MYSTERY

TODD DOWNING

ISBN 978-1-61646-152-2

Coachwhip Publications

CoachwhipBooks.com

ISBN 978-1-61646-275-8

COACHWHIP PUBLICATIONS

COACHWHIPBOOKS.COM

THE
DARTMOUTH
MURDERS

THE
WAILING ROCK
MURDERS

CLIFFORD
ORR

ISBN 978-1-61646-323-6

THE MUMMY
CASE MYSTERY

DERMOT
MORRAH

ISBN 978-1-61646-250-5

COACHWHIP PUBLICATIONS

COACHWHIPBOOKS.COM

THE
$WEEPSTAKE
MURDERS

J. J. CONNINGTON

ISBN 978-1-61646-321-2

COACHWHIP PUBLICATIONS

ALSO AVAILABLE

MYSTERY AT
LYNDEN SANDS

J. J. CONNINGTON

ISBN 978-1-61646-320-5

COACHWHIP PUBLICATIONS

COACHWHIPBOOKS.COM

THE
DEATH
OF A
CELEBRITY

HULBERT
FOOTNER

AN AMOS LEE MAPPIN MYSTERY

ISBN 978-1-61646-263-5

THE QUINNY HITE
MYSTERIES

CHINESE RED · HERE LIES THE BODY

RICHARD BURKE

ISBN 978-1-61646-247-5

www.ingramcontent.com/pod-product-compliance
Lightning Source LLC
Chambersburg PA
CBHW030850030726
47495CB00005B/1452